SELMA LAGERLÖF (1858-1940) was born on a farm in Värmland, trained as a teacher and became, in her life-time, Sweden's most widely translated author ever. Novels such as *Gösta Berlings saga* (1891; *Gösta Berling's Saga*) and *Jerusalem* (1901-02) helped regenerate Swedish literature, and the school reader about Nils Holgersson who traverses Sweden on the back of a goose has become familiar the world over. Two very different trilogies, the Löwensköld trilogy (1925-28) and the Mårbacka trilogy (1922-32), the latter often taken to be autobiographical, give some idea of the range and power of Lagerlöf's writing. Several of her texts inspired innovative films, among them *Herr Arnes pengar* (*Sir Arne's Treasure*), directed by Mauritz Stiller (1919) and based on *Herr Arnes penningar* (1903; *Lord Arne's Silver*), and *Körkarlen* (*The Phantom Carriage*), directed by Victor Sjöström (1921) and based on Lagerlöf's *Körkarlen* (1912). She was awarded the Nobel Prize for Literature, as the first woman ever, in 1909, and elected to the Swedish Academy, again as the first woman, in 1914. Having been able to buy back the farm of Mårbacka, which her family had lost as the result of bankruptcy, Lagerlöf spent the last three decades of her life combining her writing with the responsibilities for running a sizeable estate. Her work has been translated into close to 50 languages.

LINDA SCHENCK grew up in the United States, and has lived in Sweden since she was a young adult. Her professional life has been devoted to translation and interpreting. She has translated five novels by Kerstin Ekman and is translating a tetralogy for young people by Annika Thor, the first volume of which, *A Faraway Island*, received the Mildred L. Batchelder Award for the most outstanding children's book originally published in a foreign language in 2010. She has also translated the first volume of the Löwensköld trilogy, *The Löwensköld Ring* (1991/2011).

Some other books from Norvik Press

Kjell Askildsen: *A Sudden Liberating Thought* (translated by Sverre Lyngstad)

Victoria Benedictsson: *Money* (translated by Sarah Death)

Hjalmar Bergman: *Memoirs of a Dead Man* (translated by Neil Smith)

Jens Bjørneboe: *Moment of Freedom* (translated by Esther Greenleaf Mürer)

Jens Bjørneboe: *Powderhouse* (translated by Esther Greenleaf Mürer)

Jens Bjørneboe: *The Silence* (translated by Esther Greenleaf Mürer)

Kerstin Ekman: *Witches' Rings* (translated by Linda Schenck)

Kerstin Ekman: *The Spring* (translated by Linda Schenck)

Kerstin Ekman: *The Angel House* (translated by Sarah Death)

Kerstin Ekman: *City of Light* (translated by Linda Schenck)

Arne Garborg: *The Making of Daniel Braut* (translated by Marie Wells)

P. C. Jersild: *A Living Soul* (translated by Rika Lesser)

Selma Lagerlöf: *Lord Arne's Silver* (translated by Sarah Death)

Selma Lagerlöf: *The Löwensköld Ring* (translated by Linda Schenck)

Selma Lagerlöf: *Nils Holgersson's Wonderful Journey through Sweden* (translated by Peter Graves)

Selma Lagerlöf: *The Phantom Carriage* (translated by Peter Graves)

Viivi Luik: *The Beauty of History* (translated by Hildi Hawkins)

Henry Parland: *To Pieces* (translated by Dinah Cannell)

Amalie Skram: *Lucie* (translated by Katherine Hanson and Judith Messick)

Amalie and Erik Skram: *Caught in the Enchanter's Net: Selected Letters* (edited and translated by Janet Garton)

August Strindberg: *Tschandala* (translated by Peter Graves)

August Strindberg: *The Red Room* (translated by Peter Graves)

Hanne Marie Svendsen: *Under the Sun* (translated by Marina Allemano)

Hjalmar Söderberg: *Martin Birck's Youth* (translated by Tom Ellett)

Hjalmar Söderberg: *Selected Stories* (translated by Carl Lofmark)

Anton Tammsaare: *The Misadventures of the New Satan* (translated by Olga Shartze and Christopher Moseley)

Elin Wägner: *Penwoman* (translated by Sarah Death)

CHARLOTTE LÖWENSKÖLD

by

Selma Lagerlöf

Translated from the Swedish
and with an Afterword
by Linda Schenck

Series Preface by Helena Forsås-Scott

Norvik Press
2014

Originally published in Swedish by Bonniers Förlag under the title of
Charlotte Löwensköld (1925)

This translation and afterword © Linda Schenck 2014
This preface © Helena Forsås-Scott 2014

A catalogue record for this book is available from the British Library.

ISBN: 978-1-909408-06-7

Norvik Press gratefully acknowledges the generous support of the
Anglo-Swedish Literary Foundation towards the publication of this
translation.

Norvik Press
Department of Scandinavian Studies
University College London
Gower Street
London WC1E 6BT
United Kingdom

Website: www.norvikpress.com
E-mail address: norvik.press@ucl.ac.uk

Managing editors: Sarah Death, Helena Forsås-Scott, Janet Garton, C.
Claire Thomson.

Cover illustration: based on *Photograph of writer Selma Lagerlöf*, taken
in 1906 by A. Blomberg, Stockholm.

Layout: Elettra Carbone
Cover design: Sture Pallarp (winner in 2011 of a competition run in
cooperation with Beckmans designhögskola in Stockholm and the
Embassy of Sweden in London).

Printed in the UK by Lightning Source UK Ltd.

Contents

SERIES PREFACE

In the first comprehensive biography of the Swedish author Selma Lagerlöf (1858-1940), Elin Wägner has provided a snapshot of her at the age of 75 that gives some idea of the range of her achievements and duties. Sitting at her desk in the library at Mårbacka with its collection of classics from Homer to Ibsen, Lagerlöf is also able to view several shelves of translations of her books. Behind her she has not only her own works and studies of herself but also a number of wooden trays into which her mail is sorted. And the trays have labels like 'Baltic Countries, Belgium, Holland, Denmark, Norway, England, France, Italy, Finland, Germany, Sweden, Switzerland, the Slavic Countries, Austria-Hungary, Bonnier [her Swedish publisher], Langen [her German publisher], Swedish Academy, the Press, Relatives and Friends, Treasures, Mårbacka Oatmeal, Miscellaneous Duties'. Lagerlöf's statement, made to her biographer Elin Wägner a few years previously, that she had at least contributed to attracting tourists to her native province of Värmland, was clearly made tongue in cheek.

How could Selma Lagerlöf, a woman born into a middle-class family in provincial Sweden around the middle of the nineteenth century, produce such an *œuvre* (sixteen novels, seven volumes of short stories) and achieve such status and fame in her lifetime?

Growing up on Mårbacka, a farm in the province of Värmland, at a time when the Swedish economy was predominantly agricultural, Selma Lagerlöf and her sisters learnt about the tasks necessary to keep the self-sufficient household ticking over, but their opportunities of getting an education beyond that which could be provided by their governess were close to non-existent. Selma Lagerlöf succeeded in borrowing money to spend three years in Stockholm training to become a teacher, one of the few professions open to women at the time, and after qualifying in 1885 she spent ten years teaching at an elementary school for girls in Landskrona, in the south of Sweden. Mårbacka had to be sold at auction in 1888, and Lagerlöf only resigned from her teaching post four years after the publication of her first novel, establishing herself as a writer in a Sweden quite different from the one in which she had grown up. Industrialisation in Sweden was late but swift, and Lagerlöf's texts found new readers among the urban working class.

Lagerlöf remained a prolific author well into the 1930s, publishing chiefly novels and short stories as well as a reader for school children, and she soon also gained recognition in the form of honours and prizes: an Honorary Doctorate at the University of Uppsala in 1907, the Nobel Prize for Literature, as the first woman, in 1909, and election to the Swedish Academy, again as the first woman, in 1914. Suffrage for women was only introduced in Sweden in 1919, and Lagerlöf became a considerable asset to the campaign. She was also able to repurchase Mårbacka, including the farm land, and from 1910 onwards she combined her work as a writer with responsibility for a sizeable estate with a considerable number of employees.

To quote Lagerlöf's most recent biographer, Vivi Edström, she 'knew how to tell a story without ruining it'; but her innovative literary language with its close affinity with spoken language required hard work and much experimentation. 'We authors', Lagerlöf wrote in a letter in 1908, 'regard a book as close to completion once we have found the style in which it allows itself to be written'.

Her first novel, *Gösta Berlings saga* (1891; *Gösta Berling's Saga*), was indeed a long time in the making as Lagerlöf experimented with genres and styles before settling for an exuberant and innovative form of prose fiction that is richly intertextual and frequently addresses the reader. Set in

Värmland in the 1820s with the young and talented Gösta Berling as the hero, the narrative celebrates the parties, balls and romantic adventures throughout 'the year of the cavaliers' at the iron foundry of Ekeby. But it does so against the backdrop of the expulsion of the Major's Wife who has been benefactress of the cavaliers; and following her year-long pilgrimage and what has effectively been a year of misrule by the cavaliers, it is hard work and communal responsibility that emerge as the foundations of the future.

In *Drottningar i Kungahälla* (1899; *The Queens of Kungahälla*) Lagerlöf brought together a series of short stories and an epic poem set in Viking-age Kungälv, some distance north of Gothenburg, her aim being to explore some of the material covered by the medieval Icelandic author Snorri Sturluson in *Heimskringla*, but from the perspectives of the female characters. The terse narrative of *Herr Arnes penningar* (1903; *Lord Arne's Silver*), set in the sixteenth century in a context that reinforces boundary crossings and ambivalences, has a plot revolving around murder and robbery, ghosts, love and eventual punishment. The slightly earlier short novel *En herrgårdssägen* (1899; *The Tale of a Manor*) similarly transcends boundaries as it explores music and dreams, madness and sanity, death and life in the context of the emerging relationship between a young woman and man.

A few lines in a newspaper inspired Lagerlöf to her biggest literary project since *Gösta Berling's Saga*, the two-volume novel *Jerusalem* (1901-02), which also helped pave the way for her Nobel Prize later in the decade. The plot launches straight into the topic of emigration, prominent in Sweden since the 1860s, by exploring a farming community in the province of Dalarna and the emigration of part of the community to Jerusalem. The style was inspired by the medieval Icelandic sagas, but although the focus on emigration also established a thematic link with the sagas, the inversions of saga patterns such as bloody confrontations and family feuds become more prominent as the plot foregrounds peaceful achievements and international understanding. Yet this is first and foremost a narrative in which traditional structures of stability are torn apart, in which family relationships and relations between lovers are tried and often found wanting, and in which the eventual reconciliation between old and new comes at a considerable price.

Lagerlöf had been commissioned to write a school reader in 1901, but it was several years before she hit on the idea of presenting the geography, economy, history and culture of the provinces of Sweden through the narrative about a young boy criss-crossing the country on the back of a goose. While working on *Nils Holgerssons underbara resa genom Sverige* (1906-07; *Nils Holgersson's Wonderful Journey through Sweden*), Lagerlöf doubted that the text would find readers outside Sweden; paradoxically, however, *Nils Holgersson* was to become her greatest international success. Once perceived as an obstacle to the ambitions to award Lagerlöf the Nobel Prize for Literature, *Nils Holgersson* is nowadays read as a complex and innovative novel.

Körkarlen (1912; *The Phantom Carriage*) grew out of a request from The National Tuberculosis Society, and what was intended as a short story soon turned into a novel. The narrative about a victim of TB, whose death on New Year's Eve destines him to drive the death cart throughout the following year and who only gains the respite to atone for his failures and omissions thanks to the affection and love of others, became the basis in 1921 for one of the best-known Swedish films of the silent era, with Victor Sjöström as the director (Sjöström also played the central character) and with ground-breaking cinematography by J. Julius (Julius Jaenzon).

The First World War was a difficult time for Lagerlöf: while many of her readers, in Sweden and abroad, were expecting powerful statements against the war, she felt that the political events were draining her creative powers. *Kejsarn av Portugallien* (1914; *The Emperor of Portugallia*) is not just a novel about the miracle of a newborn child and a father's love of his daughter; it is also a text about a fantasy world emerging in response to extreme external pressures, and about the insights

10

and support this seemingly mad world can generate. Jan, the central character, develops for himself an outsider position similar to that occupied by Sven Elversson in Lagerlöf's more emphatically pacifist novel *Bannlyst* (1918; *Banished*), a position that allows for both critical and innovative perspectives on society.

Quite different from Lagerlöf's war-time texts, the trilogy consisting of *Löwensköldska ringen* (1925; *The Löwensköld Ring*), *Charlotte Löwensköld* (1925) and *Anna Svärd* (1928) is at once lighthearted and serious, a narrative *tour de force* playing on ambivalences and multiple interpretations to an extent that has the potential to destabilise, in retrospect, any hard and fast readings of Lagerlöf's *œuvre*. As the trilogy calls into question the ghost of the old warrior General Löwensköld and then traces the demise of Karl-Artur Ekenstedt, a promising young minister in the State Lutheran Church, while giving prominence to a series of strong and independent female characters, the texts explore and celebrate the capacity and power of narrative.

Lagerlöf wrote another trilogy late in her career, and one that has commonly been regarded as autobiographical: *Mårbacka* (1922), *Ett barns memoarer* (1930; *Memories of My Childhood*), and *Dagbok för Selma Ottilia Lovisa Lagerlöf* (1932; *The Diary of Selma Lagerlöf*). All three are told in the first person; and with their tales about the Lagerlöfs, relatives, friends, local characters and the activities that structured life at Mårbacka in the 1860s and 70s, the first two volumes can certainly be read as evoking storytelling in the family circle by the fire in the evening. The third volume, *Diary*, was initially taken to be the authentic diary of a fourteen-year-old Selma Lagerlöf. Birgitta Holm's psychoanalytical study of Lagerlöf's work (1984) read the Mårbacka trilogy in innovative terms and singled out *Diary* as providing the keys to Lagerlöf's *œuvre*. Ulla-Britta Lagerroth has interpreted the trilogy as a gradual unmasking of patriarchy; but with 'Selma Lagerlöf' at its centre, this work can also be read as a wide-ranging and playful exploration of gender, writing and fame.

With the publication over the past couple of decades of three volumes of letters by Lagerlöf, to her friend Sophie Elkan (1994), to her mother (1998), and to her friend and assistant Valborg Olander (2006), our understanding of Lagerlöf has undoubtedly become more complex. While the focus of much of the early research on Lagerlöf's work was biographical, several Swedish studies centring on the texts were published in connection with the centenary of her birth in 1958. A new wave of Lagerlöf scholarship began to emerge in Sweden in the late 1990s, exploring areas such narrative, gender, genre, and aesthetics; and in the 1990s the translation, reception and impact of Lagerlöf's texts abroad became an increasingly important field, investigated by scholars in for example the US, the UK and Japan, as well as in Sweden. Current research is expanding into the interrelations between media in Lagerlöf, performance studies, and archival studies. As yet there is no scholarly edition of Lagerlöf, but thanks to the newly established Selma Lagerlöf Archive (Selma Lagerlöf-arkivet, SLA) a scholarly edition in digitised form is underway.

By the time Lagerlöf turned 80, in 1938, she was the most widely translated Swedish writer ever, and the total number of languages into which her work has been translated is now close to 50. However, most of the translations into English were made soon after the appearance of the original Swedish texts, and unlike the original texts, translations soon become dated. Moreover, as Peter Graves has concluded in a study of Lagerlöf in Britain, Lagerlöf 'was not well-served by her translators [into English]'. In other words, the publication of high-quality new translations into English of the major works of this Swedish author of world renown is long overdue.

Helena Forsås-Scott

THE COLONEL'S WIFE

I.

Once upon a time in Karlstad there was a colonel's wife whose name was Beate Ekenstedt.

Being a Löwensköld from Hedeby, she was born into the nobility. She was a distinguished and amiable woman, and so cultivated that her poems were as entertaining as those of Anna Maria Lenngren.

She was short of stature but, like all the Löwenskölds, she had stately bearing and an interesting face. She spoke charmingly and elegantly to everyone she met. There was something romantic about her, and no one who had met her ever forgot her.

She wore exquisite clothing, and her hair was always meticulously arranged; she was also always the one with the loveliest brooch and the most tasteful bracelet and the most brightly gleaming gems. She also had the smallest feet any person could possibly have, and always wore little gold-brocade high-heeled shoes, whether or not they were in fashion.

She lived in the finest home in Karlstad, which was located not amongst the cramped dwellings in the narrow streets, but by the shore of the Klarälv River, which meant that from the window in her little letter-writing room, the colonel's wife looked down over the water. She often recounted how one

15

night, when the moon shone bright over the river, she had seen Näcken the river sprite sitting playing his golden lyre right below her window. Not a soul doubted that she had truly seen him. Would Näcken not wish to serenade Beate Ekenstedt, the colonel's wife, as so many others had?

Every prominent visitor who came to Karlstad paid his respects to the colonel's wife. They were always instantly charmed by her, and came away feeling it was a shame that she was confined to such a small town. Bishop Tegnér was said to have written a poem in her honor, and the Crown Prince to have declared her a charmeuse. Even General von Essen and others who remembered the days of King Gustav III avowed that dinner parties of the kind Beate Ekenstedt gave were incomparable in all respects – the food, the service and the conversation.

The colonel's wife had two daughters, Eva and Jaquette. They were enchanting, well-disposed girls who would have been admired and esteemed wherever in the world they had happened to live, but in Karlstad no one even looked their way. They were completely outshone by their mother. At balls, the young gentlemen rivaled each other to dance with the colonel's wife, while Eva and Jaquette sat like wallflowers. And, as mentioned, Näcken wasn't the only one who had serenaded Beate Ekenstedt, but never did a soul sing under the windows of her daughters. Young poets would compose verses to B.E., but not a single one ever scribbled down any couplets to E.E. or J.E. There were even spiteful people who spread the rumor that the one time a non-commissioned officer had proposed to little Eva Ekenstedt, he had been refused because her mother maintained he had no taste.

The colonel's wife also had a colonel, a good and decent man who would have been greatly appreciated wherever he was, excepting in Karlstad. In Karlstad people compared Colonel Ekenstedt with his wife, and when they saw him beside that woman, so stunning and so exceptional, imaginative, playful and lively, they said he looked the part of a well-to-do farm owner. People who visited his home barely heard a word he said; in fact it was as if they didn't see him at all. There was never the least risk that the colonel's wife would have allowed any of the men who swarmed around her to approach her in any unseemly way, there was never the slightest hint about her respectability, it was just that the thought of shifting her husband out of the shadows never so much as crossed her mind. She seemed to think he was best suited to being in the wings.

But this charming colonel's wife, this celebrated colonel's wife, not only had a husband and two daughters; she had a son as well. A son she loved, admired and put in the limelight whenever she could. It was impossible for anyone who visited the Ekenstedt home to neglect or disregard him, at least if they harbored the slightest hope of being invited back. Still, it cannot be denied that the colonel's wife had every reason to be proud of her son. He was gifted and had pleasant manners and an attractive appearance. He was neither rude nor forward like other spoiled children. He never played truant from school, and he never played tricks on the teachers. He was of a more romantic bent than his sisters. By the age of eight he could pen a very sweet verse. He sometimes told his mother that he had heard Näcken play or seen the fairies dancing in the meadows at Voxnäs. He was fine-featured with big, dark eyes, and he was, in every respect, the apple of his mother's eye.

Although he took up all the space in his mother's heart, one couldn't exactly say she was an undemanding mother. Karl-Artur Ekenstedt certainly learned to work. She held him higher than every other being in creation, but for that very reason she could not accept his coming home from the upper forms with any but the highest marks. And everyone was aware that as long as Karl-Artur was in a certain class the colonel's wife never invited any of the teachers to her home. No, she would not have it said that Karl-Artur did well at school because he was the son of Beate Ekenstedt, who had such grand dinner parties. Oh no, Beate Ekenstedt was a woman with style.

According to Karl-Artur's diploma from Karlstad he left the upper forms with great distinction, as had the poet Erik Gustav

Geijer in his day. And it was just as self-evident to him as it had been for Geijer that he would continue his education in Uppsala. The colonel's wife had seen stocky little Professor Geijer many a time, and had sat at his right-hand side at dinner tables. There was no question that he was gifted and remarkable, but she still couldn't help thinking that Karl-Artur had just as good a head on his shoulders and was likely to end up a renowned professor with so widespread a reputation that Crown Prince Oskar and County Governor Järta and Malla Silfverstolpe the author and all the other famous figures in Uppsala would flock to his lectures.

Karl-Artur began his studies in Uppsala in the autumn of 1826. That entire first semester, and then for all the years he spent at the university, he wrote home once a week. And not a single one of those letters was ever thrown away. The colonel's wife saved them. She read them over and over again, and at the Sunday dinners at which the whole family gathered regularly she would read out his most recent epistle. It's understandable that she read them aloud; they were letters she had every reason to be proud of.

The colonel's wife harbored a slight suspicion that the rest of the family expected Karl-Artur to be less exemplary once he left home. Thus it was a triumph for her to read to them about the inexpensive, furnished rooms Karl-Artur rented, and about how he went to the market for butter and cheese in order not to have to go out for his meals, and how he got up at five every morning and worked for twelve hours a day. Not to mention all the respectful turns of phrase he used in his letters, and all the expressions of admiration he devoted to his mother. Beate Ekenstedt did not charge anything to sit and read them to Sjöborg, the cathedral dean who was married to an Ekenstedt, or to Judge Ekenstedt, her husband's uncle, or to her cousins, the Stakes, who lived in the mansion on the corner by the market square, to read to them that Karl-Artur, who had now flown the nest, was still of the opinion that his mother might have become a poet of rank, had she not considered it her duty to live only for her husband and children. No, she didn't charge a penny; she was happy to do it for nothing. And in spite of the fact that she was so accustomed to compliments of all kinds, she was unable to read those words without tears coming to her eyes.

But the colonel's wife celebrated her greatest victory of all as Christmas approached and Karl-Artur wrote that he had not used up the entire allowance his father had sent with him when he left for Uppsala, that he would be bringing nearly half the sum back with him. This astonished both the dean and the justice, and the taller of the Stake cousins swore that nothing of the kind had ever happened before and would surely never happen again. The entire extended family agreed that Karl-Artur was a marvel.

Yes, the colonel's wife did find it lonely with Karl-Artur away at the university for most of the year, but she had his letters, which gave her so much pleasure that she could hardly wish for things to be different. When he had attended a lecture held by the great neo-romantic poet Atterbom, he sent along such interesting comments on philosophy and poetry. Upon receiving that kind of letter the colonel's wife could sit and dream about how great Karl-Artur was sure to become. She couldn't imagine his not surpassing Professor Geijer in reputation. Perhaps he would become as renowned as Carolus Linnaeus. Why shouldn't he achieve world fame? Why shouldn't he become a great poet? Why shouldn't he become the new Tegnér? Ah, there is no banquet so enjoyable in reality as in anticipation.

Each Christmas and summer vacation, Karl-Artur came home to Karlstad, and every time she saw him again the colonel's wife found him more manly and more handsome. But in all other respects he was unchanged. He treated her as adoringly as ever, was as respectful toward his father, as amusing and playful as ever with his sisters.

Occasionally the colonel's wife grew a little impatient with his staying on year after year in Uppsala without making any tangible progress. Everyone told her that because Karl-Artur was enrolled to complete the most demanding course of studies, he needed time to finish. They told her she should consider how difficult it was to complete a degree, to finish all those subjects, ranging from astronomy to Hebrew and geometry. He was required to complete them all, and pass the exams. The colonel's wife called the program grueling, and no one disagreed, but there was no changing it just for Karl-Artur's sake.

Late in the autumn of 1829, when Karl-Artur was in his seventh semester in Uppsala, he wrote a letter home, to the delight of his mother, saying that he had put his name down for the written examination in Latin. It wouldn't be a particularly difficult test, he wrote, but it was an important one, because you had to pass written Latin to be eligible for the final examination.

Karl-Artur made no fuss at all about the examination, but simply wrote that he was looking forward to having it over and done with. He had never had any quarrel with Latin, as some people do, so he felt it was safe to anticipate doing well.

In the same letter he mentioned that it was the last time this semester he was sitting down to write to his loving parents. As soon as he had his examination results in hand he intended to begin the journey home, so he fully expected to be able to embrace his parents and sisters by the last day of November.

No, Karl-Artur had made no fuss at all about the Latin examination, and he was glad about that afterwards, because he actually did fail. The professors in Uppsala allowed themselves to fail him in spite of his having passed every course in Karlstad with great distinction before coming to the university.

He was actually more taken aback and startled than humiliated. He personally thought his way of writing Latin was perfectly defensible. And although it was annoying to come home a defeated man, he believed that his parents, or at least his mother, would understand that the explanation must have to do with some kind of small-mindedness. Perhaps the Uppsala professors wanted to prove that their demands were higher than those of the upper form teachers in Karlstad, or perhaps they took the fact that he hadn't attended a single tutorial as a sign of excessive self-esteem.

It was a journey of several days from Uppsala to Karlstad, and one might say that he had forgotten the entire mishap by the time the coach entered Karlstad by the eastern gates at dusk on the thirtieth of November. He was pleased with himself for arriving on exactly the day he had mentioned in his letter. He sat thinking about how his mother was probably standing at the drawing-room window watching for the coach, and his sisters were undoubtedly laying the table for coffee and cakes.

The coach crossed the town, and he remained in the same bright mood as they passed through the narrow, crowded streets until he saw the western branch of the river with the Ekenstedt mansion standing on its bank. What in the entire world was going on? Every lamp in the house was lit; it looked like a church on Christmas morning. Sleighs filled with people in furs shot past him time after time; they all appeared to be on the way to his home.

'There must be a huge party,' he thought to himself, and that thought made him feel not a little uncomfortable. He was tired after the journey, and now he wouldn't have a restful evening. Instead, he would have to change his clothes and be sociable until midnight.

He suddenly felt alarmed.

'I do hope Mama hasn't gone and arranged a big party to celebrate my having passed the Latin exam!'

He requested the driver to drop him at the tradesmen's entrance, and entered that way so as not to have to encounter the guests.

A few minutes later, the lady of the house was sent for. She was requested to make her way to the housekeeper's quarters for a word with Karl-Artur, who had just returned home.

The colonel's wife had been very concerned that Karl-Artur would not arrive home in time for dinner. She was overjoyed when she heard that he had arrived, and hurried out to see him.

But Karl-Artur received her with a stern countenance. He did not notice her extending her arms to embrace him. In fact, he made no move to greet her at all.

'Mama, what on earth have you done?' he asked. 'Why have you invited the whole town here today of all days?'

Not a word this time about dearest parents. He didn't indicate that he was the least bit pleased to see her.

'Well, I thought a celebration was in order,' said the colonel's wife, 'now that you've been through that horrid examination.'

'And it never occurred to you, Mother, that I might not pass it,' Karl-Artur said. 'But that's precisely what happened.'

The colonel's wife was nonplussed.

You see, the possibility would never, ever have so much as entered her mind that Karl-Artur could allow himself to fail.

'Actually, it makes no difference whatsoever,' said Karl-Artur, 'except that the whole town will find out about it now. I suppose, Mama, that you invited them all here to celebrate my triumphs?' The colonel's wife just stood there, as much at a loss as before.

She knew, you see, what the people of Karlstad were like. They surely thought that diligence and thrift were fine things in a student, but to them those qualities did not suffice in themselves. They anticipated prizes from the Swedish Academy, and thesis defenses so brilliant that all the old professors blanched under their beards. They expected clever improvisations at student parties and invitations to the literary salons of Professor Geijer, County Governor von Kræmer or Malla Silfverstolpe.

Those were the kind of successes they understood, but so far in Karl-Artur's career there had been none of these distinctions and honors to indicate his outstanding promise. The colonel's wife knew they were waiting for all this, and so she thought it would be a good idea to make a bit of fuss about his now having completed an examination.

The idea that Karl-Artur would not pass was not one she had ever so much as entertained.

'No one who's here knows anything for certain,' she said pensively. 'No one but the servants. I've only told the others there would be a pleasant surprise.'

'In that case, Mama, you'll just have to invent some pleasant surprise for them,' said Karl-Artur. 'I intend to go up to my room, and I won't be coming down to dinner. Not that I think the people of Karlstad will take it so hard that I didn't pass, but I don't want their sympathy.'

'What on earth shall I invent?' moaned the colonel's wife.

'Mama, I leave it to you to come up with something,' Karl-Artur told her. 'I'm going upstairs now. There is no need for your company even to know I have come home.'

But this was far too painful and impossible. Was the colonel's wife to sit there being witty and thinking, all the time, of him up there in his room, miserable and angry? Was she not to have the pleasure of seeing him at dinner? It was too much for her.

'Dearest Karl-Artur, you must come down to dinner. I shall hit upon something.'

'What could you possibly come up with, Mama?'

'Goodness, I don't know. Oh, now I have it! You'll be perfectly satisfied. No one will find out that the dinner party was arranged for your sake. Just promise me you will change and come down to dinner.'

The party was a great success. Of all the many successful, brilliant parties at the Ekenstedts, it was among the most memorable.

When the meat course had been served and the champagne poured, there was a true surprise. The colonel rose and asked his guests to join him in a toast to Lieutenant Sven Arcker and his daughter Eva, whose engagement he wished to announce.

There was general jubilation.

Lieutenant Arcker was a man of no means and with no indication that he could expect to make a particularly outstanding military career. Everyone knew he had long cared for Eva Ekenstedt, and because the Ekenstedt girls seldom had admirers the whole town had taken an interest in the matter. However, they all expected the colonel's wife to reject him.

In due time the news leaked out of the real reason behind the engagement announcement. The people of Karlstad learned that the colonel's wife had allowed Eva and Arcker to become engaged only so no one would suspect that things had gone awry with the surprise she had originally intended for her guests.

But in fact no one admired the colonel's wife any less than before. On the contrary, people simply said that there was no one better at coping with difficult, nerve-racking situations than Beate Ekenstedt, the colonel's wife.

II.

Beate Ekenstedt, the colonel's wife, was the kind of person who, when someone had offended her, expected that person to come and apologize. Once that ritual had been performed, she was more than happy to forgive and forget, and she returned to being as affable and as intimate as she had been prior to their quarrel.

Throughout the Christmas holidays, she waited for Karl-Artur to ask her forgiveness for having spoken so harshly to her the evening of her dinner party on his return from Uppsala. To be sure, she found it perfectly understandable that he had lost his head in the initial argument, but she could not comprehend why he continued to say nothing about it, to pretend he had never offended her, even after he had had some time to reflect.

Karl-Artur, however, let the holiday season pass without a word of regret or apology. He enjoyed himself as usual at parties and on sleigh rides and was attentive and pleasant at home, but he never uttered those few words for which his mother was waiting. She and he may have been the only two to notice, but an invisible wall arose between them, preventing any real closeness. It was not for want of love; each spoke as tenderly as usual to the other, but the thing that had separated them and that was keeping them apart was never eliminated.

When Karl-Artur returned to Uppsala, he was fully occupied

with the need to repair his defeat. If the colonel's wife had anticipated a written apology, she was disappointed. He wrote about nothing but his Latin studies. He was now attending Latin lectures daily and had two different tutors as well. In addition, he had joined a society the sole purpose of which was to practice debating and oration in Latin. He was doing all that was in his power to pass the examination at the next opportunity.

His letters home exuded optimism, and the colonel's wife responded in kind. But she was worried about him. He had been rude to his own mother without asking forgiveness, and for that he might very well be punished.

Not that she wished a punishment upon her son. She prayed to God not to pay any heed to his little offense, and to allow all to be forgotten. She did her best to explain to Our Lord that the entire matter had been her fault.

'I was foolish and vain and desiring to bask in his success,' she said. 'I, not he, am the one who deserves to be punished.'

But she continued to seek those words she had been waiting for in every letter that arrived. And when she did not find them, her concern was amplified. She sensed that Karl-Artur could not possibly pass the examination without first asking her forgiveness.

And so one day, toward the end of the semester, the colonel's wife announced that she was going to make a trip to Uppsala to visit her dear friend Malla Silfverstople. They had met the previous summer at Kavlås, the Gyllenhaal's estate, and had become so close that Malla had kindly invited her to come to Uppsala sometime during the winter to make the acquaintance of her literary friends.

All of Karlstad was astonished that the colonel's wife would undertake such a journey at that time of year, during the snowmelt, when the roads were quite impassable. Although they said Colonel Ekenstedt ought to prohibit her from going, he acquiesced as always, and so his wife departed. The roads were awful and the trip was terrible, just as the people of Karlstad had predicted. Her carriage became mired down in mud time after time, and had to be hoisted out on crossbars. A spring also broke at one point, and at another a shaft split in two. But Colonel Ekenstedt's wife was plucky. She was small and delicate, but she was also high-spirited and had a sense of humor, so innkeepers and stable grooms, blacksmiths and farmers and all the people she met on the road to Uppsala were soon prepared to risk their lives for her. It was as if they knew how important it was for Colonel Ekenstedt's wife to get to Uppsala.

She had, of course, notified Malla Silfverstople of her impending arrival, but she had not told Karl-Artur, and she had also requested that Malla keep it from him. She was so looking forward to surprising him.

When Colonel Ekenstedt's wife had finally reached Enköping, the journey was interrupted anew. They were not terribly far from Uppsala, but one of the wheel rings had come loose, and she would not be able to continue until it was repaired. She was terribly worried. She had been on her way for so long, and the Latin examination might be any time now. She was going to Uppsala for one reason only, so Karl-Artur would be able to apologize to her before the test. She knew that if it did not happen, neither tutorials nor lectures would help him. He would inevitably fail, absolutely inevitably.

She could not sit still in the room at the inn that had been put at her disposal. She found herself going downstairs time and again, and out into the courtyard to find out whether the carriage wheel had been returned from the smithy.

On one of these occasions she saw a cart turn in to the yard, with a student on the seat next to the young coachman, and the student who hopped down from the cart was – no, she could not believe her eyes – it really was Karl-Artur!

He came over to where she was standing. He did not embrace her, but seized her hand, pressed it to his chest, and with his beautiful, dreamy childish eyes he looked straight into hers.

'Mama,' he said, 'forgive me for behaving so badly last winter, when you had planned a party to celebrate my passing the

Latin exam!'

Her happiness was almost too great to be true.

The colonel's wife snatched back her hand, threw her arms around Karl-Artur, and kissed him over and over again. She could hardly believe what was happening, but at the same time she knew that she now had her son back, and she felt it was the happiest moment of her life.

She pulled him inside the inn, and he began to tell his tale.

No, the test had not yet taken place. It was scheduled for the very next day. But in spite of that fact, he had decided to make the journey to Karlstad to see her.

'What a madcap you are!' she said. 'Did you think you could go there and back by tomorrow?'

'No,' he replied. 'I had given the whole thing up, because I knew I had to do that first. There was no point in trying. I couldn't possibly pass until I had obtained your forgiveness.'

'But my dear boy, it would have required no more than just a word by letter.'

'It has been hanging over me in some vague, muddled way the entire semester,' he said. 'I've been anxious, I've had no confidence, but I didn't realize why. Last night, though, it struck me. I had deeply offended your heart, which beats with such love for me. I knew I would never be able to work successfully until I had humbly begged my mother's apology.'

The colonel's wife was sitting at a table. She covered her tear-filled eyes with one hand, and extended the other to her son.

'This is wonderful, Karl-Artur. Go on!'

'Well,' he said, 'on the same floor where I have my rooms, there lives another student from Karlstad, by the name of Pontus Friman. He is a Pietist and does not socialize with other students, nor have I had any contact with him myself. But early this morning I went into his room and told him what I was going through. "I have the most loving mother one could possibly have," I said, "but I have wounded her and I have not apologized. What shall I do?"'

'And his answer?'

'He simply said: "Go to her at once!"

I explained that there was nothing I would rather do, but that I had to take the *pro exercitio* tomorrow. My parents would certainly not be pleased if I missed the test. Friman, however, wouldn't hear of it. "Go at once!" he said. "Think of nothing else but being reconciled with your mother! God will help you."'

'And so you left?'

'Yes, Mama, I left to throw myself at your feet. But once I was sitting in the cart I deemed myself unforgivably idiotic. I fought the strongest possible urge to turn back. I knew then that even if I stayed for a few more days in Uppsala your love would enable you to forgive me everything, and still I continued my journey. And God helped me, I found you here. I have no idea what brought you to this place, but it must have been His doing.'

Tears were pouring down the cheeks of both mother and son. Had not a miracle taken place, for their sakes?

They both felt that gracious Providence had been watching over them. And also, more clearly than ever, they both felt the strength of the love that bound them.

They sat together at the inn for an hour, after which Colonel Ekenstedt's wife sent Karl-Artur back to Uppsala, asking him to let her dear friend Malla Silfverstolpe know that his mother would not be coming to visit right now.

The colonel's wife, you see, could not be bothered to travel on to Uppsala. The goal of her journey had already been achieved. Now she knew that Karl-Artur would pass his examination and she returned to her home with an easy mind.

III.

All of Karlstad knew that Colonel Ekenstedt's wife was religious. She attended every church service as dependably as the clergyman, and on weekday mornings and evenings she held a few moments of devotion with her entire household.

She was a benefactor of the poor, whom she visited bearing gifts not only at Christmas but all the year round. She supplied various needy schoolboys with dinner and once a year, on her name day, she held a huge coffee party for all the women at the poorhouse.

But it never entered the mind of a single soul in Karlstad, Colonel Ekenstedt's wife least of all, that it would be displeasing to God when she and the dean and the justice and the older of the Stake cousins played a friendly round of Boston whist after their family dinners on Sundays. Nor did anyone imagine that it might be sinful for the young ladies and gentlemen who often stopped in at Colonel Ekenstedt's on Sunday evenings to take a little turn on the floor of the large drawing room.

Neither Colonel Ekenstedt's wife nor any of the other people of Karlstad had ever heard that it was reprehensible to serve a glass of fine wine at a dinner party or to raise one's voice in song at the table, often to a text written by the hostess herself, before imbibing that wine. And they had no idea whatsoever that Our Lord could not tolerate novel reading or theater-going. The colonel's wife enjoyed arranging parlor performances and taking part in them herself. It would have been a great sacrifice for her to give up that pleasure. She was cut out for the stage, and the people of Karlstad used to say that if Sara Fredrika Torsslow was only half as good an actress as Beate Ekenstedt they could understand why the Stockholmers were so taken with her.

But Karl-Artur Ekenstedt stayed on for a whole month in Uppsala after successfully passing his troublesome Latin exam, and during that month he spent a great deal of time with Pontus Friman. Friman was a zealous, orthodox and eloquent adherent of the Pietist movement, and there was no denying that he had influenced Karl-Artur.

Not that he had been redeemed or converted, but Karl-Artur had begun to be uneasy about all the worldly pleasures and entertainments that took place in his parental home.

Understandably, at that point in time the relationship

between mother and son was indescribably devoted, and Karl-Artur spoke quite openly with his mother about the things he found objectionable. His mother acceded in every possible way to his requests. Because it pained him that she played cards, she pleaded a headache at the next family dinner and let the colonel take her place at the Boston table. To deny the dean and the justice their usual game of cards was out of the question.

And because Karl-Artur did not approve of her dancing, she renounced that as well. When the young people stopped in as usual of a Sunday evening, she explained that now that she had turned fifty she felt too old to go on dancing. But when she saw the disappointment on their faces, she was touched. So she sat down at the grand piano and played dance melodies for them until midnight.

Karl-Artur gave her books to read and she accepted them gratefully and found them quite beautiful and uplifting.

But those solemn, Pietistic books were not enough to satisfy the colonel's wife. She was a cultivated lady and kept up with the latest world literature, and so it happened that one day Karl-Artur came across her with Byron's Don Juan on her lap under her devotional. He turned his back on her without a word and this, the fact that he had not reproached her, she found touching. The next day she packed all her books up in a crate and had them carried to the attic.

There is no denying that the colonel's wife tried to be as accommodating as she possibly could. Clearly she was an intelligent and gifted woman, and she knew that all this piety was nothing but a passing enthusiasm on the part of Karl-Artur. It would vanish with time, and the less resistance he encountered, the faster it would disappear. Fortunately, it was summer. Nearly all the wealthy families in Karlstad were out of town, so there were no big dinner parties. People took their amusement in the form of walks in the countryside, long rowboat outings on the Klarälv River, berry-picking and outdoor games.

Toward the end of the summer, though, Eva Ekenstedt was to

marry her lieutenant, and the colonel's wife could not help but be a bit worried about how it would come off. She felt more or less obliged to give her daughter a large, extravagant wedding. If Eva were married without due pomp and circumstance, the people of Karlstad would once again be gossiping about her and about how she had no heart for her girls.

Luckily, though, it already seemed that her concessions had had a placating effect on Karl-Artur. He raised no objections to the planned twelve-course dinner, the croquembouche pastry or the sweets. In fact he did not even protest about the wine and other alcoholic beverages that had been ordered from Göteborg. He said not a word about the fact that the marriage ceremony was to take place in the cathedral, or about the garlands decorating the streets along which the bridal procession would pass; nor did he object to the candles, the torches, the barrels of burning tar, or the fireworks along the riverbank. On the contrary, he participated in the preparations and toiled in the sweat of his brow making garlands and nailing up flags, working as hard as everyone else.

There was only one conviction he upheld firmly, that there should be no dancing at the wedding. So the colonel's wife promised. She found it a pleasure to acquiesce to him on that one point, since he was being so accepting of all the other arrangements.

The colonel and his daughters did try to protest a bit. They asked what all the officers and all the young ladies of Karlstad who were invited and who, naturally, expected to dance the night away were supposed to do instead. The colonel's wife replied that if God was on their side it would be a lovely evening, and the officers and young ladies would be able to walk in the garden listening to the military band and watching the fireworks rising skyward and the reflections of the torches in the river. She said she thought it would be such a fine sight that no one could possibly wish for any other entertainment. And surely this would be a more dignified and auspicious beginning of the new marriage than romping about on the dance floor.

The colonel and his daughters let her have her way, as ever, and family tranquility remained undisturbed.

When the wedding day arrived, everything was arranged and in order. Things went off without a hitch. Luck was on their side as regarded the weather, and the church ceremony and the many speeches and toasts proceeded smoothly. The colonel's wife had written a lovely wedding song that was sung at the dinner, and the Värmland military band stood in the scullery playing a different march as every course was carried in and served. The guests found everything plentiful and generous, and everyone was in as merry and festive a mood as could be throughout the meal.

But when they had left the tables and coffee had been served, they were all accosted by the most strange and powerful urge to dance.

Imagine it. The dinner had begun at four o'clock, and since it had all been as well arranged as everything else, with waiters and waitresses aplenty, it was all over by seven. It was astonishing that the twelve courses and the many speeches and fanfares and drinking songs had all been accomplished in the space of three hours. The colonel's wife had hoped that the guests would remain at the tables until eight o'clock, but her hopes were dashed.

And so it was only seven, and there was no way anyone could consider leaving before midnight. The guests were displeased with the idea of all the idle hours that lay ahead.

'If only we could dance!' they sighed to themselves, the colonel's wife having been so prudent as to forewarn them that this would be a wedding without dancing. 'How shall we amuse ourselves? It's going to be dreadfully dull sitting here trying to pass the hours with small talk and with no opportunity to shake a leg.'

The young women looked down at their thin, summery dresses and white silk shoes, simply made for dancing. When a person was dressed in such finery, the desire to dance came completely naturally. It was impossible to get it out of one's head.

The young officers of the Värmland regiment were precisely the kind of men one wanted to dance with. During the winters they were invited to so many balls they nearly tired of them and it was sometimes difficult to get them onto the dance floor. But there hadn't been a single big dance all summer. Their desire to dance was rekindled and they could have danced for a day and a night. They said they had hardly ever seen so many beautiful young women in one place. What kind of a celebration was this? How could anyone invite so many young men and beauties and keep them from dancing with each other?

Nor was it only the young people who were longing for dancing. Even the older ladies and gentlemen thought it a pity that the younger ones weren't able to dance and provide them with something to look at. The best musicians anyone could ask for in all of Värmland were at hand. There was a perfect ballroom. Why in the world should they not be allowed to take a spin around the floor?

In spite of all her charm, Beate Ekenstedt certainly had always been on the selfish side. She very likely felt that she was too old to take part in the dancing herself now that she was over fifty, and for that reason alone all the young people who were her guests that night had to sit around like wallflowers.

The colonel's wife saw and heard and felt and realized that everyone was dissatisfied with her, and for such a good hostess who was accustomed to seeing everyone enjoy themselves at her parties, there was something indescribably trying and vexing about the situation.

She knew that the next day and for days and days to come, people would be talking about the Ekenstedt wedding and holding it up as an example of the dullest event they had ever attended in their lives.

She made a great effort with the older guests, being as charming as only she knew how. She told her best anecdotes, she made her wittiest remarks, but nothing won their approval. They could hardly even be bothered to listen to her. There was no matron at the entire wedding so dull that she didn't sit there thinking to herself that if she ever had the good fortune to be marrying off her daughter, all the young people would most definitely be allowed to dance, and the older ones too, for that matter.

The colonel's wife extended herself for the young people. She suggested games on the lawn. But they just stared at her. Games at a wedding! And had she not been the woman she was, they would have laughed right in her face.

When the fireworks display was announced, the gentlemen offered the ladies their arms and walked with them down by the riverbank. The young couples absolutely had to drag themselves. They could hardly be bothered to look up long enough to watch the fireworks rise. They baulked at accepting anything as a substitute for the entertainment for which they were yearning.

The full moon rose too, as if to enhance the brilliant display. It did not resemble a flat disc that night but rolled into the sky, as round as a ball, and one witty guest maintained that it had expanded in astonishment at seeing so many handsome officers and so many beautiful young ladies standing there staring glumly down into the river, as if contemplating suicide.

Half the people of Karlstad had gathered along the garden fence to see the display. As they watched the young people drifting around on the other side, listless and indifferent, they commented that this was the dreariest wedding they had ever seen.

The musicians of the Värmland regiment were doing their best. But since the colonel's wife had banned dance music, saying that otherwise she feared she would not be able to keep the young people in check, there were not so very many pieces on the program, and they had to keep playing the same ones over and over again.

It wouldn't be fair to say that the hours dragged on. No, time stood still. The minute hands of all the watches moved at the same slow pace as the hour hands.

A couple of big barges were moored in the river by the Ekenstedt manor, and on the deck of one there sat a music-

34

loving mariner playing a peasant *polska* on a squeaky, home-made fiddle.

All the poor people who were walking around the Ekenstedt garden in misery brightened up. This was dance music at any rate, and they made haste to sneak out through the back gate, and a few moments later they could be seen dancing to the folk *polska* tune on the tarred deck of the river barge.

The colonel's wife soon noted the mass exodus and the dancing and realized, of course, that it wouldn't do to have the finest young women from Karlstad dancing on a dirty freight barge. She instantly sent someone to tell the young people to come back. But never mind that she was the wife of a colonel; not even the youngest of the non-commissioned officers made the least move to obey her orders.

At that point the colonel's wife gave the game up for lost. She had done as much as anyone could possibly have asked of her to give Karl-Artur his way. Now the time had come to rescue the reputation of the Ekenstedts. She had the band ordered up into the ballroom, and instructed them to play an *anglaise*.

It only took a few moments for all the eager dancers to come rushing up the stairs, and dance they did. The ball that followed was one of the most incredible ever. Every single person who had spent the early part of the evening waiting and longing was anxious to make up for lost time. They spun and floated, kicked and pirouetted. No one was tired or out of sorts. And there wasn't a single girl so unattractive as to be left without a partner.

The older folks were equally unable to sit still, and the most amazing thing was that the colonel's wife – can you imagine, the colonel's wife who had given up dancing and card playing and who had had all her secular literature carted up to the attic – was unable to sit still herself. She was light on her feet, spinning round and looking every bit as young as, no even younger than, her daughter who had stood at the altar that very day. The people of Karlstad were delighted to see their cheerful, charming, beloved colonel's wife back again.

Happiness abounded, the night was now both fair and delightful and the river sparkled in the moonlight; all was right with the world.

The strongest proof of the contagious effects of the joy spreading around the room was that Karl-Artur, too, was caught up in it. He was suddenly unable to imagine what could possibly be sinful or evil about moving to the beat of the music in the company of other young, carefree people. It was merely natural for youth, health and happiness to take that expression. If, as otherwise, he had considered it a sin, he would not have danced. But that evening everything about it seemed to him nothing but an innocent, childlike pleasure.

However, just as Karl-Artur was dancing an *anglaise*, he began to sense that he was being observed from over by the open ballroom door. Looking toward the doorway he saw a pallid face, surrounded by a head of black hair and a beard, with a pair of wide, gentle eyes staring at him in pained amazement.

He stopped abruptly in the middle of the dance. To begin with he wondered whether he was seeing things, but it did not take long for him to recognize his friend Pontus Friman, who had promised to come visit him when he was passing through Karlstad, and who had just happened to arrive that particular evening.

Karl-Artur took not another single step in the dance, but rushed right over to the new arrival who, without a word, drew him along down the stairs and out into the evening air.

THE PROPOSAL

Schagerström proposed! Wealthy Schagerström from Stora Sjötorp.

You don't say! Really? Schagerström?

Oh yes indeed, I assure you Schagerström proposed.

But what in the world possessed Schagerström to propose?

Well, what happened was that there was a young girl at the parsonage in Korskyrka by the name of Charlotte Löwensköld. She was distantly related to the pastor and provided companionship for his wife, and she was engaged to be married to the pastor's assistant, the curate.

So why ever did she have anything to do with Schagerström in that case?

Well, Charlotte Löwensköld was sprightly and light on her feet and free-spoken, and from the very first moment she set foot in the parsonage it was as if a brisk wind blew through the place. The pastor and his wife were elderly, and had been living there as shadows of their former selves until she breathed new life into them. The curate was thin as a rail and so pious that he dared neither eat nor drink. He had official duties to perform from dawn to dusk, and he spent the nights on bended knee at his bedside, weeping over his sins. He was very close to being lost to the world, but Charlotte came along and prevented him from destroying himself entirely.

But what on earth does all this have to do…

You must understand that five years ago, when the curate first arrived at the parsonage at Korskyrka, he had only just been ordained and was entirely unfamiliar with what the profession demanded of him, and it was Charlotte Löwensköld who helped him learn the ropes. She had spent her whole life at parsonages, and she was well acquainted with all that was required, and taught him everything from baptizing babies to addressing parish meetings. In the course of all this they fell in love, and now they've been betrothed for a full five years.

But surely this is getting us completely off the track of Schagerström...

The special thing about Charlotte Löwensköld was that she had this remarkable ability to work things out and arrange matters for others. And no sooner had she become engaged to the curate than she had worked out that his parents were displeased that he had become a clergyman. They had wanted him to finish his doctorate and then stay at the university as a lecturer with the title of professor. And he had indeed been enrolled at Uppsala University for five years and been working on his first degree, and at the end of the sixth year he would have had his master's, except that just then he changed his mind and decided to enter the clergy. His parents were well-to-do and had their ambitions. They did not approve of their son having chosen such a modest path. Even once he was ordained they continued to beg and plead with him to stay on at Uppsala, but he refused. Now Charlotte Löwensköld could see that if he only had a higher degree he would have better prospects for promotion, and so she sent him back to Uppsala. And as he was the most diligent student anyone could have wished, she had him finished with the entire project and with a doctorate conferred upon him in the space of four years.

But what in the world does Schagerström have to do...

You see, Charlotte had it figured out, that once her fiancé had received his degree, he would be eligible to apply for a teaching position in the upper forms with a salary sufficiently high that they would be able to marry. If he absolutely insisted on being a clergyman, in a few years he would be able to get a promotion to one of the large parishes, as was common. It was the path the pastor from Korskyrka and many before him had taken. But in this respect things did not develop as she had planned, because her fiancé immediately refused to be anything but a man of the cloth and follow the path of the ministry, which was how it happened that he returned to Korskyrka again in the capacity of pastor's assistant. And so in spite of being a doctor of philosophy, he had a salary that could barely compete with that of a stable boy.

So what about Schagerström?

You can imagine that Charlotte Löwensköld, who had already spent five years waiting, couldn't possibly be satisfied. She was, of course, glad that her fiancé had been posted to Korskyrka. He was living at the parsonage, so she saw him daily, and she probably thought that she would be able to cajole him into taking a teaching position, just as she had managed to get him to complete his doctoral studies.

But you're not telling us anything about Schagerström!

Well, I can tell you that neither Charlotte Löwensköld nor her fiancé had anything at all to do with Schagerström. He was from a completely different set. He was the son of a prominent government official from Stockholm, so he was of wealthy stock, and had married the daughter of a foundry owner from Värmland who stood to inherit so many foundries and mines that her dowry probably came to several million. Initially, Schagerström continued to live in Stockholm and only spent a couple of summer months on one of the Värmland estates, but after a year or two his wife died in childbirth, and he settled down at Stora Sjötorp in Korskyrka parish. He was so grief-stricken and in such deep mourning he couldn't stand being anywhere where his wife had lived. Schagerström almost never accepted invitations to dinners, but to distract himself he began supervising the administration of the many foundries and renovating the manor house at Stora Sjötorp, making it so beautiful it was soon reputed to be the most elegant home in Korskyrka. In his solitude, he surrounded himself with a large staff, and lived like a *grand seigneur*. And Charlotte Löwensköld knew that it was about as likely that she would pick the seven sisters out of their constellation to decorate her bridal tiara as that she would become the wife of Schagerström.

You know, Charlotte Löwensköld was the kind of person

who always said whatever she was thinking. And once, at a party at the parsonage with many guests, Schagerström happened to pass by in his landau, pulled by a handsome team of four, and with a servant in livery on the box alongside the coachman. So of course everyone rushed to the windows to watch Schagerström pass, keeping their eyes on him until he was completely out of sight. Once he was gone, Charlotte Löwensköld turned to her fiancé and said so loudly that everyone heard her:

'I want you to know, Karl-Artur, that although I do care for you, I can only say that if Schagerström proposes to me, I shall say yes.'

All the guests knew, of course, that she would never catch Schagerström, and they burst out laughing. Charlotte's fiancé laughed as well, since he realized the only reason she had said it was for the amusement of their visitors. The look on her face made it clear that she was dismayed at having let those words cross her lips, but at the same time there was no being sure that she didn't have something of an ulterior motive. Perhaps she hoped to intimidate her dear Karl-Artur just enough that he would begin to consider that teaching position.

Well, Schagerström himself was still fully absorbed by his loss and had not a thought of marriage. But the more involved he became in business life the more friends and acquaintances he made, and soon enough they began urging him to remarry. He claimed he was far too melancholy and dull for any woman to want him, and turned a deaf ear to all assurances to the contrary. One time, though, the subject came up at a large business dinner Schagerström had felt obliged to attend, and when he made his usual excuses one of his neighbors from Korskyrka told him that there was a young woman who had said that she would send her fiancé packing if only Schagerström would propose to her. It was quite a lively dinner party, and people had a laugh at this story as if it had been nothing but a good joke, just as they had at the parsonage.

Truth be told, Schagerström had often found it difficult to cope without a wife, although he was still so much in love with the one who had died that the very idea of replacing her filled him with abhorrence.

Until that time he had always imagined an alliance with someone of his own class, but after hearing about Charlotte Löwensköld he began to see the idea differently. Perhaps he ought to enter into a marriage of convenience, perhaps he ought to marry a simple woman who would make claims on neither his late wife's place in his heart nor on the high social standing she had held by virtue of her wealth and lineage. In that case a new marriage suddenly seemed much more feasible to him; it would no longer be an offense to his beloved departed wife.

The following Sunday Schagerström went to church to have a look at the young woman, who was sitting beside the pastor's wife in the family pew. She was simply and modestly dressed, and appeared unpretentious. But this was no impediment. On the contrary, if she had been a striking beauty he would never have considered marrying her. He would not have wanted his deceased wife to believe that his new spouse could possibly replace her.

While Schagerström was sitting contemplating Charlotte Löwensköld, he began thinking about what she would do if he really went to the parsonage and invited her to become mistress of Stora Sjötorp. Of course she would never possibly have imagined that he might really propose to her, and for that very reason he was amused by the idea of seeing the look on her face if he were really to do it.

On his way home from church he was wondering what it would do for Charlotte Löwensköld's appearance to be elegantly and expensively dressed. All of a sudden he found himself enticed by the idea of this marriage. The thought of so unexpectedly bringing great happiness to a poor girl who had no prospects in life had something of a romantic shimmer to it that pleased him. However, at the very moment Schagerström caught himself thinking like that, he put the matter out of his mind. He rejected it as a temptation. He had been living with the notion that his wife had only left him briefly. He had planned to be faithful to her until they were reunited.

That night Schagerström saw his deceased wife in a dream and awakened with a powerful sense of his love for her. The misgivings that had come over him on his way home from church felt superfluous. His love was alive and well, and there was no risk at all that the simple young woman he intended to wed would eradicate the image of his wife from his heart. He needed a wise and worthy woman to keep him company and to keep his home in order. There was no one among his relations who was suited to the task, and he had no desire to engage a woman to manage the house. He saw no alternative but to marry.

The very same day, and dressed to the nines, he made his way to the parsonage. He had lived in such solitude for the past few years that he had not even stopped by to introduce himself, so there was quite a commotion when the great landau with its four elegant black horses drew up inside the gate. He was invited inside, and into the upstairs drawing room, where he sat for some time conversing with the elderly couple.

Charlotte Löwensköld had withdrawn to her room, but after some time the pastor's wife came personally to fetch her, requesting that she join them. They had received a visit from Schagerström the foundry owner, and it was dull for him to only have two old people to talk to.

The pastor's wife was excited and solemn at once. Charlotte Löwensköld looked at her wide-eyed, but asked no questions. She untied her apron, dipped her fingers in the washbowl, straightened her hair and put on a clean collar. She began to walk behind the pastor's wife, but just as she was about to leave the room she turned and put her long apron back on.

Barely had she entered the drawing room and been introduced to Schagerström when she was invited to have a seat, after which the pastor held a little speech to her. He was voluble in his praise of all the joy and the pleasant sense of comfort she had brought to the parsonage. She had been like a dear daughter to both him and to his wife, and they would be terribly sad to lose her. But now that such a fine man as foundry owner Gustav Schagerström had come asking for her hand, they must not think of themselves, and so they were advising her to accept his offer, which was a far better one than any she might have anticipated.

The pastor did not say a single word to remind her that she was already betrothed to the curate. Both he and his wife had long been opposed to that alliance, and wished with all their hearts that it might be broken off. A poor girl like Charlotte Löwensköld certainly could not insist on staying with a man who refused point blank to make a decent living.

Charlotte Löwensköld listened without moving a muscle, and as the pastor wanted to give her enough time to compose an appropriate answer he added a lengthy harangue about Schagerström, his impressive estates, his competence, how seriously he took life, how well he treated his employees.

The pastor had heard so many good things about him that although it was the first time Schagerström the foundry owner had shown his face at the parsonage, he already considered the man a friend and was delighted to be able to place the destiny of his young relation in his hands.

Schagerström sat the entire time observing Charlotte Löwensköld to see what effect his proposal was having on her. He noted that her posture was now more erect, and that she had thrown back her head. Her cheeks had also taken on a bright red blush, while her eyes had darkened, turning a very deep blue. Then her upper lip curled into an impudent little grin.

Schagerström was dismayed. The Charlotte Löwensköld he now saw was a beauty, and not only that, a beauty who seemed neither humble nor modest.

His offer had obviously made a deep impression on her, but he was utterly unable to decide whether or not she was pleased.

He was not kept in suspense for long. The moment the pastor finished, Charlotte Löwensköld took the floor.

'I'm wondering, Mr. Schagerström, whether you have not heard that I am engaged?' she asked.

'Yes, of course,' he replied, which was all there was time for him to say before Charlotte Löwensköld continued:

'Then how can you have the temerity, Sir, to come here and request my hand?'

Those were her very words. She used phrases like 'have the temerity' in spite of the fact that she was addressing the wealthiest man in Korskyrka. She had completely forgotten that she was a lady's companion with no means of her own, and was feeling like a proud Miss Löwensköld from the finest of stock.

The pastor and his wife looked as if they might fall off their chairs with the shock, and Schagerström, too, appeared somewhat taken aback, but being a man of the world, he knew how to behave in awkward situations.

He went to Charlotte Löwensköld and, taking one of her hands in both of his, clasped it warmly.

'My dear Miss Löwensköld,' he said. 'Your reaction merely serves to increase the admiration I feel for you.'

Bowing to the pastor and his wife, he gestured to them neither to speak nor to accompany him out to his carriage. Both they and Charlotte Löwensköld were amazed at the dignified bearing of this rejected suitor as he left the room.

WISHES

It can't make any difference, can it, for a person to sit and wish?

If she doesn't go an inch out of her way to approach the person she's pining for, but just sits still, wishing, that can't matter, can it?

When the wisher is very well aware that she is insignificant and unattractive and poor, and knows that the person whose heart she'd like to win never spares her a thought, then it must surely be all right for her to pass the time with her wishes, as much as she likes.

If, moreover, she is married and is a faithful wife with a slightly Pietist bent and if there is nothing in the world that could possibly entice her to commit a sin, then it can't possibly have the slightest influence on anything if she sits there wishing.

When she is old, on top of it all, an ancient thirty-two years, and the man, the one she thinks about, is only twenty-nine, and when she is awkward and timid and utterly unable to assert herself in social life, and when she is the organist's wife, then surely she can go on wishing from morning to night. There can be nothing sinful about it, and nothing can possibly come of it.

Even if she thinks that other people's wishes are like light spring breezes while hers are heavy, powerful hurricanes that can move mountains and jolt the earth out of its orbit, she knows that those thoughts are nothing but her imagination. In reality her wishes cannot influence anything either in the present or in the future.

She'll have to be satisfied with living in one of the little houses nestled around the church, right by the main street in the village, that she is able to see him pass by her window almost every day, that she is able to hear him preach every Sunday and that she is sometimes invited to the parsonage and is able to be in the same room with him, in spite of the fact that she is so shy she cannot possibly address a single word to him.

Strangely enough, there is one little link between herself and him. He may not even know about it, and she hasn't had the opportunity to tell him, but it's there, nonetheless.

You see, her mother was the Malvina Spaak who had been Baron Löwensköld and his wife's housekeeper at Hedeby – his maternal grandparents. When her mother was around thirty-five, she had married a penniless peasant farmer, after which she had devoted herself to the weaving and housekeeping in her own home, as she had previously done in the homes of others. But she had always kept contact with the Löwenskölds, they had paid her visits and she had spent long periods at Hedeby, helping with the autumn baking and the spring cleaning, times that had brightened her life. She had often and gladly spoken to her little daughter about the years she had served at Hedeby, about the old General whose spirit had haunted the place, and about young Baron Adrian, who had wanted to help his old ancestor find peace in his grave.

The daughter understood that her mother had been in love with young Baron Adrian. It was clear from the way she talked about him – he had been such a kind man, and so handsome! He had the dreamiest look in his eyes, and his every movement was so graceful!

When Malvina described him, her daughter Thea always said to herself that she was exaggerating. There could be no such young man on earth.

Ultimately, however, she saw one. Not long after she had married the organist and moved to Korskyrka, she saw him step up to the pulpit one Sunday. He wasn't a baron, merely a Pastor Ekenstedt, but he was the nephew of Baron Adrian for whom Malvina Spaak had cared, and he was just as handsome and boyishly gentle, and just as slim and elegant. She recognized his large, dreamy eyes and his soft smile from her mother's descriptions.

When she saw him she wondered if she had wished him into being. She had always wanted to see a man who corresponded to her mother's tales, and there he was. She knew, of course, that wishes had no power, but it still seemed remarkable to her that he had arrived.

He paid her no attention, and toward the end of the summer he became engaged to that saucy Charlotte Löwensköld. When autumn arrived he went back to his studies in Uppsala. Her only thought was that he had vanished from her life forever. No matter how hard she wished, he would never return.

But when five years had passed she saw him step up to the pulpit again. And once again she imagined it was her wishing that had brought him there. He gave her no reason to think so, of course. He still paid her no attention, and he was still engaged to be married to Charlotte Löwensköld.

She had never wished any evil on Charlotte. No, she was prepared to swear on the Bible that she never had, but sometimes she did hope Charlotte would fall in love with someone else or be invited on a long trip abroad by some wealthy relation, so that, in some agreeable, pleasant way, she would be separated from young Ekenstedt.

Because she was married to the organist and was invited to the parsonage from time to time, she happened to be there when Schagerström drove by and Charlotte said that she would say yes if he proposed. Ever since that day she had been wishing Schagerström might propose to Charlotte, and there could of course be nothing wrong in that. In any case, it certainly made no difference.

Because if wishes had any power things would surely look different here on earth than they do now. Just imagine all the things people have wished! Just imagine how many good things they have wished for! Just imagine how many people have wished to be free from sin and illness! Just imagine all the people who have wished they wouldn't die! No, she knew wishing was something you could do with impunity. Wishes have no power.

And still, one lovely summer Sunday she saw Schagerström come into the church, and she noticed how he chose his seat so as to be able to see Charlotte, who sat in the pastor's family pew, and she wished that he would find her lovely and captivating. She wished it with all her soul. She believed she was doing Charlotte no wrong by wishing her a wealthy husband.

The whole rest of the day, after she saw Schagerström at church, she had the feeling something was happening. That night she lay in bed, feverish with agitation, just waiting for something to happen. The feeling continued the next morning. She sat at the window unable to work, hands in her lap, waiting.

She expected to see Schagerström drive by, but something even more remarkable happened. In the middle of the morning, some time between eleven and noon, Karl-Artur came to see her.

You can understand how astonished and pleased she was, and at the same time how overwhelmingly bashful she felt.

She could not recall, afterwards, how she had managed to welcome him or invite him inside. But somehow before she knew it he was sitting in her very best armchair in her little parlor, and she was seated opposite him, simply staring.

She hadn't really realized how very young he looked, until she had him so close. Because she knew every detail about his family, she knew he was born in 1806, so he must be twenty-nine. But you couldn't tell by looking at him.

He explained in his charmingly simple, grave manner that he had only just recently learned in a letter from his mother, that she was the daughter of the Malvina Spaak who had been a close friend and guardian angel of the Löwenskölds. He apologized for not having known before. He wondered why she hadn't made herself known to him.

She was overjoyed to know the reason for his never having paid any attention to her. But she couldn't say a thing, couldn't explain. She merely mumbled some silly, incoherent words he probably didn't even understand.

He looked at her with some bewilderment. Surely there was no way he could know that an old woman could be so timid as to lose the ability to formulate words.

As if to give her time to pull herself together, he began talking about Malvina Spaak and Hedeby. He mentioned the story of the haunting and of the dreadful ring.

He said he found the details somewhat incredible, but that to him there was a deeper meaning concealed there. He regarded the ring as a symbol of the craving for earthly possessions, which keeps the soul captive and prevents it from entering the kingdom of heaven.

Imagine that he was sitting there right in front of her looking at her with his captivating smile and speaking confidentially and naturally as if to an old friend! It was too much – the happiness threatened to suffocate her.

Perhaps he was accustomed to not being replied to when he visited the poor and destitute to bring them consolation and encouragement. He went on talking tirelessly.

He told her that Jesus' words to a wealthy youth often came into his mind. He was convinced that the primary reason for most human misery was that mankind had more love for the things God had created than for God as Creator.

Although she said nothing, she must have reacted to his words in a way that enticed him to go on confiding in her. He admitted that he had no desire to be promoted to parish priest or dean. He had no desire for a large congregation, a stately residence, huge fields, thick parish ledgers or a great deal of responsibility. No, his only wish was for a little parish where he could devote himself to curing the souls of his parishioners. His parsonage would be no more than a little unpainted cottage, but it would be beautifully situated in a birch grove by a lake. And he wished for no larger a salary than would just be enough to make ends meet.

She understood this was how he intended to show people the right way to true happiness. She felt devotion deep down in her soul. Never before had she encountered anything so young and pure as he was. Ah, how people were going to love him!

Then, suddenly, she realized that what he had just been saying was contradictory to something she had heard not long before, and she wanted to clarify the matter.

She asked him whether she could have misheard, because the last time she had been at the parsonage, his fiancée had mentioned that he was going to apply for a teaching post in the upper forms.

He jumped up from his chair and began pacing back and forth in the little parlor.

Had Charlotte said that? Was she certain that was what Charlotte had said? He asked her so urgently it frightened her, but she answered very humbly that as far as she could recall, that was precisely what Charlotte had said.

The blood rushed to his head. He looked more and more vexed.

She was so shocked she nearly fell to her knees to beg his forgiveness. She had certainly never thought her words about Charlotte would wound him so deeply. What could she say to make him agreeable again? What could she do to pacify him?

In the midst of his agitation she heard horses' hooves and the rolling of carriage wheels, and she turned to the window by force of habit. It was Schagerström, but she was so preoccupied with Karl-Artur that she didn't have time to wonder where he was going. Karl-Artur hadn't even noticed him passing. He just continued to pace back and forth, a look of rage on his face.

Now he approached her, hand extended, to say farewell, and it was a terrible disappointment to her that he was leaving so soon. She would have liked to bite off her tongue for having let it say that little thing, those couple of words that had provoked his wrath.

But there was nothing to be done. She had no choice but to extend her own hand and accept his. She had no choice but to be silent and let him go.

At that very moment, in her deepest misery and despair, she bent down and kissed his hand.

He withdrew it in haste. After that, he just stood there,

staring at her.

'I only meant to beg your forgiveness,' she stammered.

He saw the tears in her eyes, and was moved to give her some kind of explanation.

'Just imagine, Mrs. Sundler, that for one reason or another you had tied a blindfold over your eyes and were unable to see, and had put yourself in the hands of another person so that she could lead you – what would you say if the blindfold had suddenly come loose and you found that the other person, your friend, your companion, whom you had trusted more than you trusted yourself, had led you right up to the edge of an abyss, and that the next step would have thrown you over that edge and into the depths? Would that not cause you hellish torment?'

He spoke vehemently and passionately, after which he walked out of the room and into the hall without waiting for an answer.

Thea Sundler thought she heard him halt once he was out on the front steps. She could not know why. Perhaps because he had begun to remember how pleased and carefree he had felt just a little while ago when he walked into her home, though he was the same man who was now departing it, furious and despondent. In any case, she hurried out to see if he really was still standing there.

He began to speak the moment he saw her. Emotion had caused him to be thinking very fast. He was pleased to have an audience.

'I am standing here looking at the roses you have planted along the path to your house, dear Mrs. Sundler, and asking myself whether this summer is not the loveliest I have ever experienced. It is now late July, and wouldn't you agree that the part of the summer that is already past has been perfect? Have not all the days been long and light, longer and lighter than ever before? The weather, well, it has certainly been quite hot, but the heat has never been oppressive, because there has almost always been a refreshing breeze. Neither has the land had to suffer from drought as in other nice summers, since there have been a couple hours of rain almost every night. And everything has grown amazingly. Have you ever seen the trees so heavy with leaves, or the flowerbeds so full of gorgeous blossoms? Ah, I dare to assert that the wild strawberries have never been so sweet, the birdsong so melodious or the people so happy and eager for entertainment as this year.'

He stopped speaking for a moment to catch his breath, but Thea Sundler was very careful not to disturb his thoughts by interjecting anything. She remembered her mother, and understood how she had felt when the young baron had come to find her in the kitchen or the dairy to confide.

The youthful pastor went on:

'In the mornings, around five o'clock, when I pull up my shade, I can hardly see anything but haze and clouds. I hear pattering against the windowpane, and rain rushing down the drainpipes; I see flowers and grass bend under the heavy shower. The skies are full of clouds, heavy with rain, so heavy that they are nearly dragging along the ground. "From today we shall have no more nice weather," I say to myself, "and that may be for the best."

'And although I am nearly certain that the rain will continue all day, I stay at the window for a little while to see what happens. And at five minutes past five, the drops cease to clatter against the window. The water continues to run down the drainpipes for a while, but soon it, too, ceases to gush. In the middle of the spot in the sky where the sun ought to be, a crack appears in the clouds, and an enormous beam of light is cast down into the earthly mist. Soon the gray haze of rain rising up from the hills in the distance is transformed to pale blue fog. The drops on the blades of grass slowly run down into the soil, and the flowers raise their anxiously lowered heads. Our little pond, which I can just glimpse from my window and which just a moment ago looked quite miserable, begins to glisten, as if large shoals of goldfish were swimming just below the surface. And in rapture over all that beauty I often open my window and inhale the air, which is also full of perfume of a never previously known sweetness, and cry out: "Ah, my God, you made your world far too beautiful.'"

The young pastor stopped himself with a gentle smile, shrugging his shoulders. He appeared to be thinking that the last thing he said had taken Thea Sundler by surprise, and hastened to explain.

'You know,' he said, 'I meant what I said. I had been afraid that this beautiful summer would mislead me into loving the things of this world. How many times have I not wished that the lovely weather would come to an end, that this summer would turn into a time of thunder and lightning, drought and oppressive heat, rainy days and frosty nights, the kind of summers we often have?'

Thea Sundler was soaking up his every word. What was he getting at? Where was he taking all this? She had no idea but she hoped, almost desperately, that he would continue, so that she could go on enjoying his sonorous voice for a long time yet, his beautiful words, and his expressive face.

'Do you understand me?' he cried. 'No, perhaps nature has no power over you. Perhaps nature does not speak to you in her secretive language, with her powerful words. Perhaps nature never asks you why you fail to enjoy her good gifts gratefully, why you fail to seize happiness when it is within easy reach, why you fail to arrange for a home of your own and to marry the love of your life, as every other creature in creation is doing this blissful summer.'

He raised his hat and wiped his brow.

'This glorious summer,' he continued, 'arrived as an ally for Charlotte. You see, this luxuriance, this softness, this general pleasure has intoxicated me. I have been wandering like a blind man. Charlotte has seen my love grow, and my longing, my eagerness to possess her.

'Oh, you cannot know ... each morning at about six o'clock I leave the small building where I have my rooms, and walk to the manor house to have my morning coffee. Charlotte comes toward me, in the large, bright dining room, with the gentle breeze wafting in through the open windows. She is cheerful and chirping like a bird, and we have our coffee, the two of us, alone. Neither the pastor nor his wife is present.

'Perhaps you imagine that Charlotte takes the opportunity on those occasions to speak with me about our plans for the future. Certainly not. She talks to me of my parishioners who are ill, who are destitute, she talks about ideas from my sermons that appealed particularly to her. She shows herself to be, in every way, exactly the kind of wife a pastor would want. Only very occasionally, only in jest, does she ever, in passing, mention the teaching position. And with every day I have come to love her more. When I get back to my desk again, I find it difficult to concentrate. I sit dreaming of Charlotte. A little while ago I described to you the life I would like to live. At these times I dream that my way of life will release Charlotte from her earthly fetters and that she will accompany me to my little unpainted cottage.'

When he has made this admission, Thea Sundler cannot help but utter a cry.

'Of course,' he said, 'you are right. I have been blind. Charlotte has walked me to the edge of the abyss. She has been waiting for a moment of weakness to entice me into promising to apply for that teaching position. She could see how the summer was aiding her in making me carefree. She believed she was close to her goal, and wanted to prepare you and everyone else for my change of course. But God has preserved me.'

Suddenly he stepped very close to Thea Sundler. Perhaps he was reading her facial expression, saw what pleasure she derived from his words, saw how delighted and carried away she was feeling. But it seemed to have aggravated him that she took pleasure in the eloquence his suffering had evoked. A look of resentment came into his eyes.

'But do not dare to imagine that I thank you for the words you said to me!' he burst out.

Thea Sundler was horrified. He had raised his fists and was shaking them at her face.

'I do not thank you for having removed the blindfold from my eyes. You must not take pleasure in what you have done. I despise you for not having allowed me to plunge into the abyss. I never want to see you again.'

He turned away from her, rushing down the narrow path between Mrs. Sundler's lovely roses and running out into the street. Thea Sundler went back into the drawing room and threw herself prostrate to the floor, weeping harder than she had ever wept before.

IN THE PARSONAGE GARDEN

The stretch of road connecting the area around the church and the parsonage was a short one, only five minutes' walk for someone as quick as Karl-Artur. But in those five minutes he had a large number of firm and proud thoughts, thoughts he intended to repeat to his fiancée the minute he saw her.

'At last,' he said to himself, 'the time has come! Nothing can stop me. Today we must settle the matter. She must understand that however much I love her, nothing will ever persuade me to strive for the secular advantages on which she has her heart set. I must serve God, I have no choice. If I have to, I shall tear her out of my heart.'

He felt the self-assurance of a proud man. He could tell that the words that would make her contrite, that would move and convince her, were at his disposal today in a new way. He was shaken by the powerful emotional experience he had just had; it had opened a door to a room in his soul to which he had never before had access. In this room the walls were hung with enormous clusters of flowers and beautiful, blossoming climbers. But these clusters and climbers were words, grand, lovely, perfectly shaped. All he needed to do was to approach and take possession of them. All this was there for him to use. An abundance, an overwhelming abundance.

He laughed at himself. Until that time, every sermon had been a labor; he sat for hours composing them, torturing the ideas up from his mind. Little had he known that all this abundance was somewhere inside him!

When it came to Charlotte, everything would have to change. In fact, until that day she had been the one doing her utmost to govern him. From now on things were going to be different. He would speak, she would listen. He would lead and she would follow. Henceforth she would be glued to his every word in the same way that poor organist's wife had been just now.

A confrontation was imminent and nothing would persuade him to abandon his cause.

'If I have to, I shall tear her out of my heart,' he repeated to himself. 'If I have to, I shall tear her out of my heart.'

Just as he reached the parsonage, the gate opened and an elegant coach drawn by four black horses drove out.

He realized this was Schagerström, the foundry owner, who had come to pay his respects at the parsonage. And that made him remember what Charlotte had said at the coffee party earlier in the summer. Like a bolt of lightning, the thought struck him that Schagerström had come to the parsonage to propose to his fiancée.

It was an absurd thought, and yet it clutched at his heart.

Had the wealthy man not given him an extremely peculiar look as his carriage turned onto the road? Was it not a look that contained curiosity, scorn and, at the same time, compassion?

There was absolutely no doubt. His guess was correct. But this was far too terrible a blow. His heart stopped. The world went black before his eyes. He could only just drag himself over to the gatepost.

Charlotte had accepted. He was going to lose her. He would die of despair.

In the midst of this overwhelming grief he saw Charlotte coming out of the parsonage and towards him at a quick pace. He saw how red her cheeks were, how moist her eyes, how victorious her lips. She was coming to tell him that she was going to marry the wealthiest man in Korskyrka parish.

Oh, what shamelessness! He stamped his feet and clenched his fists.

'Don't come near me,' he cried.

She stopped. Was she dissembling, or was her astonishment real?

'What's got into you?' she asked, perfectly at ease.

He gathered all his force and was able to exclaim:

'You know that better than anyone. What was Schagerström doing here?'

When Charlotte realized he had guessed the purpose of Schagerström's visit, she moved very close to him. She raised her hand. She was close to striking him.

'Oh, so you believe, too, that I would break my pledge for a handful of chattels and gold.'

At that, she gave him a look full of disdain, turned her back and left.

At least her words had calmed his worst fears. His heart began beating again, his strength returned. He was able to follow her.

'So he did propose, then?' he asked.

She did not deign to answer his question. She held herself erect and continued walking straight ahead, but instead of going into the parsonage, she turned onto a narrow path leading into the garden through a hedge.

Karl-Artur understood that she had a right to feel offended. If she had said no to Schagerström, she had done a great deed. He tried to excuse himself.

'You should have seen the look he gave me when he passed. He certainly didn't look like a man who had been turned down.'

Her back merely became even straighter, her neck more arrogant, and her pace quickened. There was no need to speak. Her posture spoke for itself: 'Do not come near me! I am walking this way because I want to be alone.'

But he, becoming more and more certain of how loyal, how self-sacrificing her action had been, followed behind.

'Charlotte,' he said, 'my dearest Charlotte!'

She was unmoved. Unrelenting, she continued along the path.

Ah, that parsonage garden, that parsonage garden! Charlotte could not have steered her steps anywhere more full of precious, shared memories.

The garden had been laid out in the traditional French

style, with crossing paths galore, all bordered by lilac bushes, planted close together and now very tall. Here and there were little openings in the hedges, through which you could enter to find intimate arbors with simple benches made of blocks of turf, or open lawns with a single rosebush in the middle. It was not a particularly large garden and it might not even have been beautiful, but what a wonderful refuge it was for a couple wishing to meet alone!

As Karl-Artur rushed along in Charlotte's footsteps and she refused to so much as look his way, she awakened in him the memory of all the times he had walked here with her as his sweet beloved, times he might never experience again.

'Charlotte,' he burst out once again, in a voice suffused with passion.

There must have been something about the way he said it that caught her attention. She did not turn around, but the stiffness in her posture relaxed. Without moving, she leaned so close that he could nearly see her face.

In no time he was close behind her, took her in his arms and kissed her.

Then he pulled her along into one of the arbors with a turf bench, where he knelt before her and poured out his admiration for her loyalty, her love, her heroism.

She seemed surprised by his passion, by his rapture. She listened to him with something approaching suspicion. He knew why. His usual attitude toward her was a more negative one. To him, she had represented the world and its temptations, against which he had to be on guard.

But at this glorious moment, when he knew that she had resisted the temptation of vast wealth for his sake, he had no need to restrain himself. She wanted to tell him about the proposal, but he could hardly listen, so eager was he to interrupt her with kisses.

When she had finished her tale, he had to kiss her again any number of times, but eventually they were locked in an embrace, still as statues.

Where had his proud, severe words gone, the ones he had

intended to say to her? Gone from his mind, eradicated from his memory. They were no longer needed. He now knew that this dear girl could never represent danger to him. She was not the thrall of Mammon he had feared. Just look at the great riches she had sacrificed today to remain faithful to him!

As she sat there in his embrace, a little smile played at her lips. She looked happy, happier than ever before. What was she thinking about? Perhaps at that moment she was saying to herself that the only thing she cared about was his love, perhaps she was resigning herself to no longer considering the teaching post that had been so close to tearing them apart.

She said nothing, but he listened to her thoughts. 'Let us soon be united. I put no conditions upon it, I want nothing more than your love.'

Ah, but would he allow her to surpass him so completely in noble-mindedness? No, he wanted to give her the greatest pleasure. He wanted to whisper to her that now that he knew her mind, now he would be bold. Now he would do his best to arrange a decent income for them.

How glorious this silence was! Perhaps she could hear what he was saying to himself? Could she hear the promises he was making to her?

He made an effort to put his thoughts into words:

'Dear Charlotte,' he began, 'how will I ever be able to reciprocate all that you have sacrificed for my sake today?'

She was sitting with her head on his shoulder, so at that moment he was unable to see her face.

'My love,' he heard her answer, 'I'm not the least bit concerned. I know very well that you will make full compensation to me.'

Compensation – what did she mean? Did she mean that she wished for no other compensation than his love? Or something else? Why was she holding her head down? Why was she not looking him in the eye? Did she think of him as such a poor catch that she wanted to be compensated for having remained loyal to him? He was a man of the cloth and a doctor of philosophy, the son of eminent parents, had always tried to do his duty, had begun to gain a reputation for his preaching, had lived a life of exemplary moral conduct. Did she really mean that it had been such a huge sacrifice to refrain from marrying Schagerström?

No, of course she meant nothing of the kind. He must stay calm; he must scrutinize her thoughts kindly and gently.

'What do you mean by compensation? As you know I have nothing to offer you.'

She moved closer, so she could whisper right into his ear.

'You have far too humble a picture of yourself, my dear. You could become both dean and bishop.'

He moved away from her so fiercely that she was about to fall over.

'Ah, so that's the reason you said no to Schagerström! Because you expect me to become both dean and bishop!'

She looked up at him, bewildered, like one who has just awoken from a dream. Yes, of course she had been dreaming, she had been talking in her sleep, and in her sleep she had revealed her most covert thoughts. She did not reply to him. Did she think that his question required no answer?

'I asked whether you said no to Schagerström because you think I am going to become dean and bishop.'

Now the color rose in her cheeks. Ah, her Löwensköld blood was boiling. And still she did not deign to answer his question.

But he required a reply. He must have one.

'Did you not hear me asking you whether it was because you expect me to become dean and bishop that you said no to Schagerström?'

She tossed her head, eyes aflame. In a tone of the deepest disdain she burst out:

'Of course.'

He stood up. He no longer wanted to sit beside her. The pain he felt at her response was enormous, but he was not about to acknowledge it in front of a creature like Charlotte. At the same time, he did not want to have anything to reproach himself for. He made one more effort to speak in a kind, friendly tone to this lost child of the world.

'Dearest Charlotte, I could not be more grateful to you for

your forthrightness. I know now that, to you, earthly status is everything. Impeccable moral conduct, constant striving to walk in the footsteps of Christ, my master, means nothing to you.'

Well-chosen, peaceable words. He awaited her answer eagerly.

'My dear Karl-Artur, I do believe that I am aware of your worth although I do not fawn or bow down to you as much as the ladies who live by the village church.'

This response struck him as truly offensive. She was angry at having been exposed, and was venting that anger.

Charlotte rose to go, but he seized her by the arm, holding her back. They had to conclude this discussion.

What Charlotte had said about the ladies by the church had made him think of Mrs. Sundler. He remembered what she had told him. That memory made his ire rise. He felt his emotions boil.

Those strong feelings opened the door in his soul that led into the room where his powerful, eloquent words hung from vines. He began to speak to her in a loud, admonishing tone. He reproached her for her love of earthly possessions, her arrogance and her vanity.

But Charlotte was no longer paying attention.

'Although I may be a very bad woman,' she suggested to him gently, 'I did refuse Schagerström today.'

This shameless statement horrified him.

'Good God, what kind of a woman are you?' he burst out. Hadn't she just admitted to him that she imagined it finer to be married to a bishop than to a foundry owner?

All the while, though, a soft little voice was speaking from his soul, placating him. It told him to think twice. Had he not noted that Charlotte Löwensköld was the kind of woman who would never deign to defend herself? If anyone believed anything bad about her, she never made the least effort to persuade them otherwise.

But he ignored this placating little voice. He refused to believe it. Charlotte was revealing new depths of baseness with her every word. Just hear what she was saying now!

'My dear Karl-Artur, pay no mind to what I said about your rising in the ranks. I said it merely in jest. I do not really believe that you could become either dean or bishop.'

He was already deeply offended. This new assault made him silence that placating voice. His blood was roaring in his ears. His hands were trembling. This wretched woman had stripped him of his self-control. She was driving him mad.

He knew he was jumping up and down in front of her. He knew he had raised his voice to a scream. He knew his arms were waving, his chin quivering. But he made no attempt to rein himself in. The loathing he felt for her was indescribable. It could not be put into words. It had to be expressed in movements.

'All your vileness is now entirely apparent to me,' he shouted. 'I see you as you really are. Never, never, never will I marry a woman like you. That would be my demise.'

'Well, I have actually done you some good,' she answered. 'Am I not the one you have to thank for your doctoral degree?'

Once she had uttered these words, it was no longer he who was replying to her. It was not that he did not know what he was saying, or that he did not agree with it, but his words were still a surprise to himself, and unexpected. Someone other than himself put them into his mouth.

'Ah yes, I see,' he cried. 'Now you are trying to remind me how you have been waiting for me for five years and that for that reason I must marry you. But it is no use. I will never marry anyone but the woman God chooses for me.'

'Do not bring God into this,' she said.

He raised his head and leaned backwards, seeking divine guidance.

'Yes, yes, yes, I shall allow God to choose for me. The first unmarried woman who crosses my path will be my wife.'

Charlotte cried out. She hurried to his side.

'Oh, no, Karl-Artur, Karl-Artur!' she said, trying to force down one of his arms.

'Do not come near me!' he screamed.

But she could not understand the depth of his rage. She threw her arms around him.

He heard a shout of disgust rise in his throat. His hands seized her arms in an iron grip and he pushed her back onto the turf bench.

After that, he vanished from her sight.

THE PEDDLER GIRL
FROM DALARNA

The very first time Karl-Artur Ekenstedt saw the parsonage at Korskyrka, standing by the road with the tall lindens, the green fence and the venerable gateposts and the white gate through the slats of which you could see the yard with its circular flower bed and gravel drive sweeping round it, the large, red, two-story building straight ahead and the two identical side buildings to the left and right, one for the curate and the other for the tenant farmer, he had said to himself that this was precisely how a Swedish parsonage ought to look, pleasantly homey, inviting and peaceful, and yet imposing.

And even later, when he had had time to notice the well-kept lawns, the well-tended flower-beds planned so everything grew to the same height and was evenly spaced, the neatly-raked gravel drive, the nicely-pruned creepers growing up the front porch, and the long curtains covering each window and hanging in lovely, even folds, all this had filled him with the same sense of delight and deference. He had a very clear feeling that anyone who lived in this parsonage must feel obligated to maintain decorous, tranquil behavior.

Never could he have imagined that he, Karl-Artur Ekenstedt, would one day rush toward the white gate, arms flailing, hat askew, with little howls bursting from his lips.

He laughed wildly as he closed the gate behind him. He seemed to feel the parsonage and the flower-beds staring at him in astonishment.

'We have never seen the like! What kind of a person could that be?' the flowers were whispering to each other.

Indeed the trees were wondering, the lawns were

wondering, the whole estate was wondering. He could hear their amazement.

Could that possibly be the son of the charming Beate Ekenstedt, the colonel's wife and the most cultivated woman in all of Värmland, who wrote poetry that was more entertaining than Mrs. Lenngren's – could that be him, the man who was rushing through the parsonage garden as if fleeing from a den of iniquity?

Could that be the quiet, modest, boyish curate who held such lovely, ornamented sermons, running with a bright red face, his features distorted in agitation?

Could a clergyman from Korskyrka parsonage, which had housed so many worthy, considerate servants of our Lord, be the man who was standing at the gate, intending to go out onto the country road to act on his firm decision to propose to the first unmarried woman he met?

Could it be young Ekenstedt, who had been brought up with such refinement, and who had always lived among people of a better sort, wanting to subject himself to the necessity of taking as his wife and comrade for his entire life the first woman who crossed his path? Did he not know that he might run into a gossip or a lazybones, a silly goose or a haranguing harpy, a Slatternly Sarah or a Shrewish Sophie?

Did he not know that he was about to embark upon the most hazardous journey of his entire life?

Karl-Artur stood by the gate for a moment, listening to all these questions as they blew from tree to tree, from blossom to blossom.

Oh, yes, he did know that this was a perilous journey, and an important one. But he also knew that during the course of that summer in Korskyrka he had loved the world more than God. He knew that Charlotte Löwensköld had been a danger to his soul, and that he wanted to raise a bulkhead between himself and her, through which she would never be able to break.

And he knew that from the moment he tore the love of Charlotte out of his heart it was open to Christ once more. He wanted to show his savior that he loved Him above all else, and that he trusted Him implicitly. That was why he was now having Christ choose him a wife, to demonstrate his huge, awesome trust in Him.

He was not afraid as he stood there by the parsonage gate looking out onto the country road. He was not afraid, but he did feel that he was now displaying the greatest courage a person can possess by placing his fate entirely and completely in the hands of God.

The last thing he did before walking out through the gate was to recite the Lord's Prayer. And as he prayed his inner calm came back. Even his outer tranquility returned. The excited blush vanished from his cheeks, and his chin stopped trembling.

However, as he began walking toward the village church, the direction in which he had to go if he wanted to meet anyone at all, he was not entirely without qualms.

He got no further than to the end of the parsonage fence when he came to a sudden halt. It was the poor, frightened being that inhabited his body who stopped him. He remembered how just an hour ago, when he came from the village, he had encountered at this very spot the deaf beggar woman, Karin Johansdotter, in her threadbare shawl, with her patched skirt and her big beggar's rucksack. True, she had once been married, but now she had been a widow for many years, and was free to marry again.

The sudden thought that she might be the one who crossed his path halted him.

But he reproached the poor, frightened sinner in his breast for believing that he now had the power to stop him from pursuing his conviction, and he walked on.

Only a few seconds later he heard a carriage approaching from behind. Soon he was overtaken by a cart drawn by a handsome steed.

In the conveyance was one of the most powerful, proud mine owners for miles around, an old man who owned so many mines and foundries he was thought to be as wealthy as Schagerström. His daughter was at his side, and had he come from the other direction the young clergyman would have had to follow through on his pledge and give the powerful man a sign to stop, so that he could propose to his daughter.

It was not easy to say what the results of such a venture might have been. A stroke of the whip across his face was not inconceivable. Mine owner Aron Månsson was accustomed to giving his daughters away to counts and barons, but not to curates.

Once again, that old sinner living in Karl-Artur's breast was frightened. He advised him to turn back; he said this was far too daring a journey.

But the bold new man of God who also abided within him raised a shout of joy. That man was pleased to have undertaken a perilous pilgrimage. He was glad to have the opportunity to demonstrate his faith and his trust.

On the right side of the road was a steep sandy ridge on which young pine trees, birches and bird cherry bushes were growing. Out of this dense undergrowth a voice was raised in song. Karl-Artur could not see who it was, but he knew that singing voice very well. It was the voice of the slatternly daughter of the innkeeper, a young woman who ran after every man in sight. She was very close. Any minute, she might choose to turn onto the road.

Unable to help himself, Karl-Artur slowed down, walking so quietly that the woman who was singing would not be able to hear that there was anyone there. He even looked about for a way to escape.

On the other side of the road there was a meadow, where a herd of cows was grazing. However, the cows were not alone, there was a woman milking them, and she was also someone he recognized. It was the dairymaid of the tenant farmer who leased the land belonging to the parsonage. She was tall as a man and had three children out of wedlock. His entire being constricted with horror, he whispered a prayer to God and walked on.

The innkeeper's daughter went on singing in the bushes and the very tall dairymaid finished her milking and prepared to go home, but neither of them went out onto the road. They never crossed his path, although he saw and heard them.

The poor old sinner inside him came up with a new idea. He told him that God might have been showing him these two loose-living women not so much to test his faith and his courage as to warn him. Perhaps he was trying to tell him he was behaving foolishly and excessively.

But Karl-Artur quieted the weak, faltering sinner in his breast and continued his pilgrimage. Was he to give it up for so little? Was he to believe more in his own fear than in the power of God?

At last a woman came walking toward him on the road. He could not avoid encountering her.

Although she was still a distance away, he could see that she was Elin, the daughter of Matts the crofter, a woman with a birthmark covering her entire face. For a moment he stood still. Not only was that poor girl awful to look at. She was probably the poorest person in the parish. Both her parents had passed on, and she had been left with ten brothers and sisters to support.

He had been inside her barren cottage, full of ragged, dirty children whom she, the eldest of the siblings, was trying in vain to clothe and feed.

Anxiety brought perspiration to his brow, but he clasped his hands and went on walking.

'It is for her sake, so that she gets the help she needs, that all this is happening,' he said to himself, as they moved closer and closer to their encounter.

He began to imagine his future as pure martyrdom, although he hesitated to give in to such a feeling. He felt no revulsion for that poor young woman, as he had felt for the innkeeper's daughter or the dairymaid. He had heard nothing about her that was not good.

And yet, when there were no more than two steps between them, she turned off the road. Someone had called her from in amongst the trees, and she vanished quickly into the undergrowth.

Now that Matts the crofter's Elin was out of the way, he felt an enormous burden lift from his heart. With a new sense of confidence he continued along the road, head held high, as proud as if he had had the opportunity to prove the strength of his faith by walking on water.

'God is with me,' he said to himself. 'Christ is accompanying me on my pilgrimage, holding His shield above me.'

This exalted him and filled him with intense happiness.

'Now the right woman will soon be coming,' he thought. 'Christ has put me to the test. He has seen that I am serious. I am not turning back. My chosen one is approaching.'

One minute later he had completed the short walk from the parsonage to the village, and was about to turn down the main street, when the door of a cottage opened and a young woman came out. She walked through the little garden, like the one all the village houses had in front of them, and stepped out onto the road right in front of Karl-Artur.

She had come so suddenly that they were only a step or two apart when he noticed her. He stopped in his tracks. His first thought was this:

'Ah, there she is! Wasn't I right? I knew she was about to cross my path.'

And he clasped his hands in gratitude to the Lord for His great and wonderful grace.

The woman who was coming toward him was not a woman from the village; he could see she was one of those peddler women from northerly Dalarna. As such women were, she was dressed in the traditional folk dress of her parish, red and green and black and white, and in Korskyrka, where such parish costumes had long been out of use, she shone like a wild rose. Moreover, the young woman was even more beautiful than her costume. Her hair curled around a lovely face, with a forehead that might have been thought too high without all that hair, and a face with noble features. Above all, though, it was her deep, sorrowful eyes and her thick, dark eyebrows that made all the difference. The moment one saw them, one had to admit that they were so lovely they would have made any face radiate with beauty. In addition to all this, she was tall, not slim but well proportioned, and had elegant bearing. There was no need to doubt that she was healthy and strong. On her back she had a large black leather rucksack of goods to trade, and yet she still walked fully erect and she moved with such lightness one would have thought she had nothing at all to carry.

Karl-Artur felt almost blinded. He said to himself that what he saw approaching was summer personified – the full, warm, flourishing summer they had had that year. If he had been able to paint it, she was exactly what he would have painted.

Still, if she was summer approaching, she was not a summer he had reason to fear. On the contrary, it was God's intention for him to take that summer to heart and celebrate its beauty. He need not feel any apprehension. This woman, his beautiful bride, came from the mountainous region afar, from poverty and a humble station. She knew nothing of the temptations of wealth or of the strange love of worldly things that makes people of the plains abandon their creator in favor of his creations. She, this daughter of destitution, would not hesitate to be joined in matrimony to a man who wished to remain poor for the rest of his life.

In truth, there is nothing greater than the wisdom of the Lord. He knew what Karl-Artur needed. With no more than a wave of His hand, God put the young woman in his path that suited him better than any other.

The young clergyman was so full of his own thoughts that he did not make a move to approach the beautiful girl from Dalarna. But she noticed how he was devouring her with his eyes, and could not help but giggle.

'You're staring at me as if you had met a bear!'

Karl-Artur laughed too. It was uncanny how his heart suddenly eased.

'No,' he said, 'I don't suppose I was seeing a bear.'

'In that case, it must have been the forest sprite. People do say that menfolk go so wild when they see 'er they gets turned to stone.'

71

She laughed, showing the loveliest, brightest teeth, and started to pass him by. He rushed to stop her.

'You mustn't go. I need to speak with you. Sit down here, by the side of the road!'

She looked surprised at his urging, but assumed that he wanted to buy something from her sack of goods.

'Sorry, I jes cain't open my sack right out on the road.'

A moment later the penny dropped: 'Golly, aren't you the minister hereabouts? Didn't I see you in the pulpit yesterday?'

Karl-Artur was overjoyed that she had heard him preach and recognized him.

'That's right, I was the one who gave the sermon, but I'm just the assistant pastor, you know.'

'But you must live at the parsonage? I was just heading over there. Come along to the kitchen and I'll sell you my whole sackful if you like.'

With that, she thought he would let her go, but the young man just went on blocking her way.

'I don't want to buy your goods,' he said. 'I want to ask you to be my wife.'

He pronounced these words in a strained voice. He was deeply moved. He thought the whole natural world – the birds, the whispering leaves on the trees, the grazing cattle – must know about his solemn statement, and that the world was standing still in anticipation of what the young woman would answer.

She turned quickly toward him, as if to see whether he was serious, but except for that she appeared quite indifferent.

'We can meet here on the road at ten tonight. For now, I've got my work to do.'

She went on walking in the direction of the parsonage, and he let her go. He knew she would be back, and that she would accept him. Was she not the bride God had decided on for him?

He himself was not at all in a state of mind to go home and work. He turned off onto the hill around which the road wound. When he had got far enough into the brush that no one could see him, he threw himself to the ground.

What joy, what wondrous joy! What perils he had escaped! How great were not the events of this day?

At once he was free from all his worries. Charlotte Löwensköld would never again entice him to become a thrall of Mammon. He would henceforth be able to live in accordance with his own leanings. This simple, poor wife would allow him to follow in Jesus' footsteps. He saw the little unpainted cottage before him. He saw the simple, pleasing way of life. He saw the total harmony between what he preached and what he practiced.

For a long while he lay staring up into the branches of the undergrowth, through which the rays of the sun were trying to penetrate. Karl-Artur felt, similarly, that a new love, bearing good fortune, was trying to break into his wounded, tattered heart.

MORNING COFFEE

I.

There was one person who could have made everything right again, if only she had wanted to. But perhaps that was asking too much of someone who had been sitting there, year after year, just filling her heart with wishes.

You know, it is difficult to prove that sitting and wishing can have any impact whatsoever on how the world turns. Still, there is no doubt that wishing can take you in its grip, weaken your willpower and muffle your conscience.

Mrs. Sundler had spent all Monday afternoon regretting that she had uttered those words about Charlotte that had made Karl-Artur rush off. She could hardly believe he had been there, in her home, and spoken with her of such intimate things, and been more charming than she could ever have dreamt, and that in her indiscretion she had offended him so deeply that he had told her he never wanted to see her again!

She had been furious with herself and the entire world, and when her husband, Sundler the organist, had suggested that they go across to the church and sing for a while, as they often did on summer evenings, she had rebuffed him so curtly that he had fled the house and taken refuge at the inn.

This made her even more miserable, because she always wanted to be faultless and irreproachable to both others and to herself, and she knew very well that Sundler had married her for the sole reason that he admired her singing voice so greatly that he wanted to be able to hear it daily. And she had repaid him this debt honorably, because she had him to thank for the fact that she now had a sweet little home and did not have to earn her keep as a pitiful governess, but that day it was just not within her power. Had she raised her voice that evening in the house of the Lord, no harmonious sounds or pious words would have crossed her lips, but rather laments and curses.

Then to her indescribably great joy, Karl-Artur had come to see her around half past eight that evening. He had entered cheerfully and at his ease, and asked whether she might provide him with supper. She had probably looked a bit surprised at this request, so he had gone on to explain that he had been lying in the woods asleep all afternoon. He must have been very tired, since he had slept through both dinner and supper, which was always served at eight on the dot at the parsonage. Did Mrs. Sundler just happen to have a bit of bread and butter in the house? If so, he would be very grateful if he could still his ravaging hunger.

Mrs. Sundler was not the daughter of such an excellent housekeeper as Malvina Spaak for nothing. No one could say of her that she did not keep her house in order, and she was quick to open the pantry and place on the table not only bread and butter but also eggs, ham and milk.

And with her delight that Karl-Artur had returned and requested her help, as if she was an old friend from their childhood days, some of her self-confidence also returned, and she was able to tell him how miserable she was over having said those offensive words about Charlotte earlier in the day. She hoped, she added, that he had not thought she had intended to cause any friction between him and his fiancée? Still, although she knew that it was a fine calling, too, to decide to devote oneself to education, she could not help but hope, in fact she prayed to God every day, that Doctor Ekenstedt would stay on as their rural clergyman, since there were so few good pastors in the countryside, and so few opportunities for the parishioners to hear the Gospel preached in such a lively manner.

Karl-Artur replied, of course, that if anyone owed anyone an apology, it was he. And there was absolutely no reason for her to regret what she had said. He now knew that it was destiny that had put those words into her mouth. Her words had aided and enlightened him.

That said, one thing led to another, and soon Karl-Artur had confided it all in her, everything that had happened to him since they saw each other last. He was so overjoyed and so full of amazement at the great grace God had shown him, that he was unable to keep it to himself, and just had to share it with someone. It was sheer serendipity that this woman, Thea Sundler, who already knew all about the family situation through her mother, had crossed his path.

Now when Mrs. Sundler heard about the broken engagement and about the one newly entered into, she should of course have realized that this boded ill. She should have realized that Charlotte had answered her fiancé's question as to whether she was looking forward to his becoming a bishop in the affirmative out of nothing but contrariness and provocation. She should have realized that his bond with the girl from Dalarna was not yet so firmly tied that it would be impossible to undo it.

But for someone who had been sitting and wishing, year after year, that she might somehow make contact with a charming young man and become his friend and confidante, and certainly nothing more, perhaps it is not possible to be strong enough to talk sense with him the very first time he bares his soul to her? Perhaps it was all one could ask of Thea Sundler that she fall at his feet in admiration and sympathy, and consider his pilgrimage to the village a true feat of heroism?

But what about exonerating Charlotte, was that too much to ask of her? Might she, for instance, have reminded Karl-Artur that although Charlotte was so very capable when it came to arranging things for others, she seldom had any wisdom left to apply to herself? No, it was impossible to expect that of Thea Sundler.

It is possible, of course, that Karl-Artur was not as sure

of himself as he was pretending to be. In that case a small objection might have raised doubts in his mind. A frank reaction of horror might have made him able to refrain from his new engagement. But Mrs. Sundler did nothing to frighten or warn him. She found the entire situation absolutely marvelous. Just imagine putting one's fate in God's hands! Just imagine tearing one's beloved out of one's heart in order to walk in the footsteps of Jesus! She certainly did not try to frighten Karl-Artur. On the contrary, she encouraged him to pursue his chosen course.

And who knows? Perhaps Mrs. Sundler was being entirely honest? She had books by both Almqvist and Stagnelius on the table in her drawing room, and was a romantic from head to toe. Here, at last, was real adventure. Here was something to be rapturous about.

In Karl-Artur's entire story, there was only one thing that worried Mrs. Sundler. How did it all fit in with Schagerström's proposal? If Charlotte were so eager to achieve worldly advantage as Karl-Artur maintained, and Mrs. Sundler had no reason to doubt that it was so, why had she said no to Schagerström? What good had she expected to derive from saying no to Schagerström?

But as Mrs. Sundler sat puzzling over the matter, the answer came to her. She understood everything. She understood Charlotte. She had played for high stakes, but Thea Sundler understood her.

Charlotte had instantly regretted saying no to Schagerström, and wanted to be released from her obligations in order to give the wealthy foundry owner a different answer.

That was why she had made a scene, and aggravated Karl-Artur so much that he had broken off with her. That was the reason. That was it; that was the explanation.

Mrs. Sundler shared this discovery of hers with Karl-Artur, but he refused to believe her. She explained and put forward evidence, but he still refused to believe her. But she did not give up, either. In this respect she dared to contradict him.

When the clock struck ten and he was due to depart for his

rendezvous with the girl from Dalarna, they were still at odds on that point. The only progress Mrs. Sundler had made was, perhaps, to have sown a little seed of doubt in Karl-Artur's mind. She, in contrast, was still entirely convinced. She swore that the very next day, or at least within a few days, Charlotte was sure to become engaged to Schagerström.

That was how they had spent the evening. Thea Sundler had not made things right. On the contrary she had cast a new flaming brand of anger into Karl-Artur's heart, which was probably all that could be expected of her.

But there was another person who would have liked to be of help and make things right, and that was Charlotte. Indeed, indeed, but what could she do just then? Karl-Artur had torn her from his heart as if she were a weed. She had stood between him and his God. She no longer existed for him.

And even if he had been prepared to listen to her, would it have been possible for Charlotte to find the right words? Was it possible to imagine that she, young, hot-blooded creature that she was, would be wise enough to put her pride aside and say the good, kind words of reconciliation that would have saved her beloved?

II.

The next morning when Karl-Artur, as usual, made his way to the main house for his morning coffee, he stopped over and over again to admire the freshness of the air, the silkiness of the dewy lawns, the brightness of the stocks, and the pleasant buzzing of the nectar-drinking bees. Deeply satisfied, he felt that only today, only now had he liberated himself from the temptations of the world, and become able to take in the wonders of nature with total relish.

When he entered the dining room, to his surprise he saw Charlotte standing there to greet him quite as usual. His pleasant cast of mind turned to mild irritation. For his part, he had thought that he was free, that the battle had come to an end. Charlotte, though, did not seem to have realized that the rupture between them was conclusive and beyond repair.

He said good morning casually, not wanting to be directly rude, but ignored her outstretched hand, going straight over to the table and sitting down.

He thought that would suffice to show her that she ought not to trouble him further with her presence, but Charlotte was obviously not interested in understanding, and remained in his company.

Although he was careful to keep his eyes lowered so as not to meet her gaze, the one glimpse of her he had was enough to reveal that her skin appeared quite grey and her eyes were red-rimmed. Her whole appearance bore witness to a sleepless night of anguish and, perhaps, remorse.

Well, so what? He had not slept, either. From ten to two he had been sitting in a hillside grove conversing with the bride God had chosen for him. Of course the usual morning rain shower had caused them to part and driven him to the parsonage, but the next few hours, as the joy of new love filled his soul, had been too wonderful to waste in sleep. Instead, he had sat down at his desk to write to his parents about the new events in his life, so to re-experience the joy of the past few hours. And yet he was certain that no one would be able to tell from his appearance that he had not slept a wink. He had never felt healthier, never felt such *joie de vivre*.

It embarrassed him to see Charlotte serving him as if nothing had happened. She pushed the creamer and the basket of rusks in his direction, and went over to the scullery hatch to get the hot coffee.

While Charlotte was pouring it for him, she asked him calmly and casually, quite as if she were asking about something totally ordinary and everyday:

'How did you get on?'

It was entirely repugnant to him to answer. There was still a glow of grace over the summer night he had just spent in the company of the young woman from Dalarna. He had passed the time not assuring her of his affection, but describing to her his plan to model his life on that of Christ. Her quiet listening, her hesitant, gentle replies, her timid agreement had given him the certainty he required. But how would Charlotte be able to understand the peace, the blessedness, all this had brought to him?

'God helped me,' was the only thing he was eventually able to reply.

Charlotte had been pouring coffee into her own cup when his answer came. It seemed to have frightened her. Perhaps she had thought his reluctance indicated that he had been unable to bring his plan to fulfillment. She sat down abruptly, as if her legs had given way under her.

'Good Lord, Karl-Artur, don't tell me you've gone and done something foolish?'

'Charlotte, did you not hear what I said I was going to do when we parted yesterday?'

'Of course I heard you, but my dear, I could hardly believe it was more than an empty threat.'

'You may be sure, Charlotte, that if I said I intended to place my fate in the hands of God, I was indeed going to do so.'

Charlotte said nothing for a few minutes. She helped herself to sugar, poured herself some cream, and crumbled one of the hard rye rusks. He assumed she was trying to gain time to compose herself.

For his part, he was surprised to find Charlotte so anxious. He recalled what Mrs. Sundler had said about Charlotte wanting to break off their engagement, and therefore provoking a scene. In that respect his new friend appeared to have been wrong. Charlotte clearly had no intention of becoming engaged to Schagerström.

'And so you rushed off and proposed to the first woman you met?' Charlotte asked, in the same casual tone in which she had begun the conversation.

'Yes, Charlotte, I let God make my choice.'

'And of course things went utterly and completely wrong,'

she exclaimed.

He recognized the old Charlotte in these irreverent words of hers, and could not deny himself the pleasure of giving her a suitable reprimand.

'Certainly', he said. 'Putting one's faith in God has always been quite foolish in your eyes, Charlotte, hasn't it?'

Her hand trembled slightly. The spoon clinked against the cup, but she did not allow herself to be distracted and fly into a rage.

'No,' she said, 'we must not go at each other as we did yesterday!'

'I couldn't agree more, Charlotte. Particularly as I have never been so happy in my life.'

Perhaps it was cruel to say that, but he felt an irresistible urge to let her know that he was reconciled with his God, that his soul had found peace.

'Aha, you're happy,' Charlotte said.

It wasn't easy to know what she was putting into that statement. Was it bitter pain or nothing but scornful astonishment?

'I see my path clearly before me. Every impediment to living a life in the spirit of Jesus has been removed. God put the right woman on my path.'

He put more emphasis on his present happiness than he needed to. But there was something about her calmness that upset him. She still did not seem to understand that he was perfectly serious, that the matter was settled forevermore.

'It looks as though things might have worked out better for you than I had imagined,' Charlotte went on in a perfectly everyday tone of voice. 'I shall say nothing, until you tell me to whom you are now betrothed.'

'Her name is Anna Svärd,' he said. 'Anna Svärd.'

He couldn't resist repeating her name. The enchantment of the summer night, the charm of new love, came back to him with the sound of it, doing away with all the unpleasantness of the present moment.

'Anna Svärd,' Charlotte repeated, but oh, in what a different tone of voice! 'Do I know her?'

'I certainly think you must have seen her, Charlotte. She's from Dalarna.'

Charlotte's facial expression remained helplessly bewildered.

'She is a simple woman, Charlotte, from simple circumstances. I suggest you stop thinking in terms of your fine acquaintances.'

'You can't possibly mean…!' she cried with such vehemence he had to look at her. Her face, which always gave her away, truly reflected the greatest horror.

'That Dalarna peddler who came by the kitchen yesterday … God in heaven, Karl-Artur! I do believe I heard someone say her name was Anna Svärd.'

Her dismay was honest, he had no reason to doubt it, but that didn't make it any pleasanter. How overprotective of him Charlotte was! And how unsympathetic she was being! She should have heard Thea Sundler the evening before.

He hastened to soak another rye rusk in his coffee, realizing that he ought to fill up quickly so as to escape all the recriminations that were sure to follow.

But strangely, there were none. Charlotte simply turned on her chair so he could not see her face. Although she was sitting perfectly still, something told him she was crying.

He rose to leave the room, in spite of the fact that he was anything but full. Oh, so she was going to take it like that. It was surely impossible, then, to confirm Mrs. Sundler's hypothesis that Charlotte had been the one who wanted to break things off. He had to believe in her overwhelming grief about their broken engagement. And as this grief made him a touch conscience-stricken, he preferred not to witness it.

'No, please don't go!' Charlotte begged without turning around. 'Don't go! We have to continue talking about this. It's so awful. It simply must not be.'

'I'm sorry to see you taking it so hard, Charlotte. But I assure you that you and I were not made for each other.'

At these words, Charlotte rose hastily from her chair. There she stood, right in front of him, stamping her foot on the floor with her head proudly erect.

'Were you imagining that I was crying for my own sake?' she asked, tossing her head so indignantly that a tear flew from the corner of her eye. 'Do you imagine that I am worrying about being unhappy myself? Can't you see that I am crying over you? You were meant for great things, but it will all run down the privy if you take a wife like her.'

'Charlotte, what a way to speak!'

'I say what I mean. And I counsel you most firmly, my friend, that if you have suddenly decided to marry a peasant wench, the least you can do is to marry one from hereabouts, from stock you know. But don't go marrying a peddler woman who's been traveling up and down the country roads all alone and unprotected! You aren't a child, after all. You must know what happens to people like that.'

He tried to bring to a halt this offensive flow of words from that narrow-minded woman who just refused to see what it was all about.

'She is the bride God has chosen for me,' he reminded her.

'Oh no she's not.'

She may have wanted to tell him that the bride God had decided on for him was herself. Perhaps it was that thought that made the tears run down her cheeks. Fists clenched, she struggled to regain control of her voice.

'Think of your parents!'

He interrupted her.

'I do not fear my parents. They are deeply Christian people, and they will understand me.'

'Beate Ekenstedt, the colonel's wife, do you really imagine she'll understand you? God, Karl-Artur, how poorly you know your mother, if you can imagine that she will ever accept a peddler from Dalarna as her daughter-in-law! Your father will disown you, he will never want to see you again.'

Anger was beginning to take possession of him, though until then he had been able to remain calm throughout.

'Let us not speak of my parents, Charlotte.'

Charlotte appeared to realize that she had gone too far.

'No, let us not speak of your parents. Let us speak instead of the pastor here in Korskyrka and his wife, and about the bishop in Karlstad and the entire cathedral chapter! What do you think they are going to say when they hear about one of their men of the cloth rushing out onto the country road to propose to the first woman he met? And here in Korskyrka of all places, where they put such store by clergymen setting a good example, what will people say? You might not even be able to stay here. You may have to move away. And what do you think the other clergymen in the diocese will think about your proposal? You can be certain that they, and everyone else in all of Värmland, will be horrified! You'll see that people will lose all respect for you. No one will come to church when you are preaching. You will be sent off to the impoverished parishes way up north. You'll never be promoted. You'll end your days as a curate.'

She was so moved by her own words she could have gone on for much longer, but she must suddenly have noticed that she was not making the slightest impression on him with her outpouring of vehement words, and she stopped abruptly.

He was truly surprised at himself. He had really changed. As recently as yesterday, her every word would have been important to him. Now he was almost indifferent to how she felt about his behavior.

'Is what I have been saying not true?' she asked. 'Can you deny the truth of it?'

'I cannot discuss these matters with you, Charlotte,' he said with some arrogance, feeling that since yesterday he had somehow become her superior. 'You speak of nothing, Charlotte, but promotions and high standing in the minds of people with power, but it is my view that those are the very things that are harmful to a man of the cloth. Instead, I maintain that a life in poverty with a simple wife who bakes his bread and scrubs his floors herself, that and nothing else, is what makes a clergyman able to take his distance from the things of the world, which is what raises and liberates him.'

Charlotte did not answer at once. When he looked at her, he saw her standing, eyes lowered, moving the tips of her shoes back and forth like an embarrassed child.

'I do not want to be the kind of clergyman who merely points out the way to others,' Karl-Artur went on, 'I want to walk that path myself.'

Charlotte remained silent. A slight blush spread across her cheeks and an unusually kind smile played at her lips. After some time she said something astonishing:

'Do you not believe that I, too, can both bake and scrub?'

Was she jesting, or what was she getting at? She had the same innocent look on her face as a young person in confirmation class.

'I have no desire to stand in your way, Karl-Artur. You will, of course, serve Christ, and I shall serve you. I came into this room this morning to tell you that everything will be precisely as you want it. I would do everything for you if only you did not turn me away.'

He was so amazed that he took a few steps toward her, but then he stopped, as if he feared falling into some kind of trap.

'Dearest,' she went on in a voice that was almost inaudible but that quivered with tenderness, 'you have no idea what I went through last night. I realized that I had to be this close to losing you to know how great my love for you is.'

He came one step closer. His searching look appeared to be trying to scan her soul.

'Do you no longer love me, Karl-Artur?' she asked, raising to him a face deathly pale with anxiety.

He intended to say that he had torn her from his heart. But at once he realized it was not true. Her words touched him. They rekindled a dying flame in his soul.

'Can I be certain you are not playing with me?' he asked.

'Karl-Artur, you must see how serious I am.'

A resurrection occurred in his soul at these words. Like a fire given new fuel, his old love flared up. The night in the forest grove, his new love, receded like a mist and were destroyed. He forgot them as one forgets a dream.

'I have already asked Anna Svärd to be my wife,' he mumbled uncertainly.

'Ah, Karl-Artur, I'm sure you could make matters right on that point if you wished. You have only been engaged to her for one night.'

She put forward that suggestion with such trepidation and trembling that he was inevitably drawn closer to her. The love she radiated was powerful and irresistible.

All at once she threw her arms around him.

'I ask for nothing, nothing. Just do not turn me away.'

He continued to hold back. He could hardly believe that she was giving in to him so totally and unconditionally.

'But you must allow me to go my own way.'

'You will be a true, living pathfinder, Karl-Artur. You will teach people to walk in the footsteps of Jesus, and I will assist you in your work.'

She spoke with the warmest, fullest conviction. At last he believed her. He knew that the long battle they had been fighting for five years was finally over. And there he stood, victorious. He could set all his qualms aside.

He was leaning toward her to conclude the new treaty between them with a kiss, when the door from the hallway opened.

Charlotte stood facing the open door. Her face took on a look of absolute terror. Karl-Artur turned around quickly and saw the housemaid standing at the open door with a bouquet of flowers in her hand.

'These are from Schagerström, the foundry owner at Stora Sjötorp,' she said. 'His gardener just brought them. He's still in the kitchen, if you want to thank him yourself, ma'am.'

'There must be some mistake,' said Charlotte. 'Why would I be getting flowers from Stora Sjötorp? Alma, go back at once and return the flowers to the gardener!'

Karl-Artur followed this exchange with the greatest attention. This was a test. It would give him proof.

'The gardener was perfectly clear about the flowers being for you ma'am,' the housemaid insisted, unable to imagine why anyone would refuse a few flowers.

'All right, put them over there, then!' said Charlotte, indicating a table.

Karl-Artur inhaled deeply. So she was going to accept the flowers. That was knowledge enough for him.

When the girl had left the room and Charlotte turned back toward him, he had no thought of kissing her. No, fortunately, the warning had arrived in time.

'I'm sure, Charlotte, you'd like to go out and ask the gardener to pass along your thanks,' he said. And with a bow with which he displayed as much scornful civility as he could put into it, he left the room.

III.

Charlotte did not go after him. A sense of dejection came over her. Had she not humbled herself sufficiently in her efforts to save the man she loved?

Why did those flowers have to appear at such a crucial moment? Did not God want him to be saved?

She went over to the bouquet, lying there freshly picked and bright, and with tears in her eyes, hardly knowing what she was doing, she began to pull the petals off the blossoms.

She was still doing so when the housemaid came in again, with another message for her. It was a small envelope with Karl-Artur's handwriting on it.

When she tore it open, a gold ring slipped through her trembling hands and fell to the floor. She let it lie there while she read the few lines Karl-Artur had scribbled on the enclosed sheet of paper.

'Someone I met yesterday evening and spoke openly with about everything that was on my mind hinted, Charlotte, that you had probably regretted your refusal to marry Schagerström, and that you had therefore been intentionally provocative so that I would break off our engagement. That way you would be able to open your arms to Schagerström at the next opportunity. I was not prepared to believe that could have been the case, but now I see that it is true and for that reason, Charlotte, I hereby return your ring.

'I presume that you had communicated to Schagerström yesterday that our engagement was broken; I also assume that because he was slow in responding, you became uneasy and tried to make matters good between us. Furthermore, I assume that the bouquet of flowers was the sign upon which you had agreed. Had that not been so, then you would never have accepted it under the circumstances at hand.'

Charlotte Löwensköld read and reread the letter. 'Someone I met yesterday evening – – –'

'I just don't understand,' she wondered to herself, and began to read again. 'Someone I met yesterday evening – – –' 'Someone I met – – –'

All at once she felt as if something clammy and slippery, something like a huge serpent, was winding its way up her body to strangle her.

It was the serpent of vicious slander ensnaring her, and it would hold her captive for a very long time to come.

THE SUGAR BOWL

Five years earlier, when Karl-Artur came to Korskyrka for the first time, he was a terribly strict Pietist. He regarded Charlotte Löwensköld as a lost child in the world, and was loath to so much as exchange words with her.

This had, of course, piqued her. She set her mind to making him atone for his error of judgment as soon as possible.

She was quick to note how inexperienced he was at all the practical things a man of the cloth needs to be able to do, and she began to assist him. To begin with he was embarrassed and did not encourage her, but after some time he began to be grateful, and to request her assistance more frequently than she really wished.

He often walked long distances to visit the elderly poor, who lived in little forest huts, and he always asked her to accompany him. He assured her she was far better than he at being sociable with older people, at cheering them up and comforting them for their little woes.

During these walks when the two of them were alone together, Charlotte found herself falling in love with Karl-Artur. In the past she had always dreamt of marrying some tall, handsome officer, but here she was, hopelessly infatuated with this delicate, upper-class young clergyman who wouldn't hurt a fly and who had never allowed a curse to cross his lips.

Ah well, for some time they continued their walks and conversations in peace, until in early July Jaquette Ekenstedt, Karl-Artur's sister, came to visit. There was nothing remarkable about that. Mrs. Forsius, the wife of the pastor in Korskyrka, was an old, close friend of Beate Ekenstedt, the colonel's wife, and it was perfectly natural, of course, for her to invite Karl-Artur's sister to spend a few weeks at the parsonage.

Jaquette Ekenstedt shared Charlotte's room with her, and the two young women soon became very close. Jaquette became particularly fond of Charlotte, and soon one might have thought she had come to Korskyrka to visit Charlotte instead of her own brother.

When Jaquette returned home, a letter arrived from the colonel's wife to the wife of the pastor, who shared it with Charlotte. It contained an invitation for Charlotte to come to Karlstad and visit Jaquette. The colonel's wife wrote that Jaquette could hardly talk about anyone but the charming young woman whose acquaintance she had made at the parsonage. She was literally pining for her company, and had described her with such enthusiasm that her dear mother was also eager to meet her.

Beate Ekenstedt also wrote that she, personally, was particularly interested in Charlotte because she was a Löwensköld. Although she was a member of the younger branch of the family that did not belong to the nobility she was, after all, of the lineage of the old General from Hedeby, so they were distantly related.

The moment she had read the letter Charlotte said in no uncertain terms that she did not want to make the journey. She was no idiot, and had realized that first the pastor's wife, and then Jaquette, had reported to the colonel's wife about her and Karl-Artur, and that she was now being sent to Karlstad so the colonel's wife could form her own impression and decide whether she would make a suitable daughter-in-law.

But the pastor's wife and, not least, Karl-Artur had persuaded her to go. By that time she and Karl-Artur were secretly betrothed, and he put it to her that he would be infinitely grateful if she fulfilled his mother's wishes. He had, as she knew, become a clergyman against his parents' will, and although he was certainly not going to break off his engagement with her whatever they thought, he really did not want to cause them any further grief. And he knew that they would be fond of her from the minute they met her. He had never seen a young woman as good as Charlotte at being sociable with older people. It was this very gift, when he had noticed how good she was with the elderly pastor and his wife and with all the elderly parishioners, which had originally attracted him to her. So he was certain that if she would just make the trip to Karlstad it would all work out for the best.

He urged and pleaded with her and in the end he persuaded her to accept the invitation.

It took a full day to travel to Karlstad, and since it was not suitable for Charlotte to travel unaccompanied, the pastor's wife had arranged for her to go along in the carriage with the Mobergers, a foundry owner and his wife who were traveling to the city for a wedding. After incessant admonishments and words of wisdom, she sent her off and Charlotte, of course, promised to be prudent.

However, sitting in a covered carriage for an entire day on a little back-facing seat staring at the Mobergers, who were asleep in the two corners, may not have been the best preparation for her sojourn in Karlstad.

Mrs. Moberger found it drafty, and was firmly opposed having the window open on more than one side of the carriage, and sometimes even that was too much. And the hotter and sultrier it was in the conveyance, the better she slept. To begin with, Charlotte had tried to initiate a conversation with her travel companions, but the Mobergers had been very busy preparing for their journey and needed to rest.

Charlotte's little feet hammered away at the carriage floor, although she was completely unaware of it until Mrs. Moberger woke up and asked if she would please be so kind as to sit still.

At the inns along the way the Mobergers took out their provisions and ate, and of course they remembered very politely to offer food to Charlotte. They were very friendly toward her throughout the journey, yet it was probably a miracle that she was still in the carriage with them when they arrived.

The longer she sat suffering in the heat, the more

downhearted she became. She was, she knew, making the trip for Karl-Artur's sake, but now and then she felt her love for him dissipate, and was unable to imagine why on earth she had agreed to go to Karlstad and put herself on display. Time after time she considered opening the carriage door, jumping out and running back home. The only reason she just sat there was that she was so lethargic and unhappy she couldn't budge.

When she arrived at the Ekenstedt residence she wasn't exactly in the mood to be on her best behavior. She felt more like screaming or thrashing about or breaking things. That would have brought her back into a better frame of mind. Jaquette Ekenstedt greeted her, friendly and cheerful, but the moment Charlotte saw her she was overwhelmed by a feeling of being very badly dressed, simply and out of fashion and, above all, that there was something wrong with her shoes. She had ordered them for the trip, and the parish cobbler had done his very best, but they clattered with every step and smelt of new leather.

Jaquette guided her through a number of lovely rooms and into her mother's boudoir for an introduction to the colonel's wife. As Charlotte walked through the house, noticing the parquet floors, the large mirrors and the lovely paintings above the doorways, she gave it all up for lost. She would never be accepted as a daughter-in-law in this home, she knew that. It had been terribly foolish of her to come.

Charlotte's first encounter with Beate Ekenstedt did nothing at all to lessen her feeling that she had made a terrible mistake, of course. The colonel's wife was sitting by the window in an Empire chair, reading a book in French. When she noticed Charlotte's presence she said a few words in French. She must have been so preoccupied with her reading she did not even realize it herself. Although Charlotte understood what she was saying, it disturbed her that this fine lady would try to weasel out of her what languages she could speak, so she answered in her coarsest Värmland dialect instead of the dialect used by finer folk from the province, which is quite easy to understand. This coarse dialect, the language of servants and peasant farmers, is something else altogether.

The colonel's wife raised her eyebrows slightly and looked quite amused, so Charlotte went on displaying her amazing mastery of the Värmland vernacular. Since she could not possibly scream, thrash about or start breaking things, it was a comfort to speak her local language. The game was up in any case, so she thought she might as well show these gentlefolk that she had no desire to try to appear finer than she was, just to make a good impression.

Since Charlotte had arrived so late that the others had already had their evening meal, the colonel's wife soon asked Jaquette to take her friend down to the dining room and see to it that she was given a bite to eat.

And that was the end of that day.

The next day was a Sunday, and as soon as breakfast was over it was time to go to church and listen to Dean Sjöborg's sermon. The service took the usual two and a half hours, and when it was over Colonel Ekenstedt, his wife, Jaquette and Charlotte spent quite a long time circulating around the main town square. They met a large number of the family's acquaintances, and several of the gentlemen began walking with them. Or rather with the colonel's wife, as they walked alongside her and spoke with no one but her, giving neither Jaquette nor Charlotte so much as the time of day or a passing glance.

After their walk, Charlotte went along back to the Ekenstedt home for a family dinner, for which the dean and his wife, the judge and his wife, the Stake brothers, and Eva Ekenstedt with her lieutenant joined them.

During dinner, the colonel's wife engaged in cultivated conversation with the dean and the judge. Neither Eva nor Jaquette said a word, and Charlotte held her tongue as well, having understood that in that household the young people were expected to stay silent. But she spent the whole mealtime sitting wishing she were far away. She was on the alert, you might say, for an opportunity to show Karl-Artur's parents that she knew very well she was not a suitable prospective daughter-in-law. She had noted that her use of the Värmland dialect had not sufficed, and knew she would have to seize on something more forceful and conclusive.

After such a journey and such a sermon and such a walk and such a dinner, it was essential that she make them see that she had no desire to play along any further.

One of the robust, well-mannered girls who was looking after things at the table was serving a bowl of raspberries, and Charlotte helped herself, like everyone else. Having done so, she reached for a nearby sugar bowl and began to sugar her berries.

Charlotte had no idea that she was taking more sugar than might be necessary until Jaquette turned to her and whispered very fast:

'You mustn't take so much sugar. Mother doesn't approve.'

Charlotte knew very well that many older people considered it sinfully excessive to sweeten one's food. At home in Korskyrka she could barely touch the spoon in a sugar bowl before the pastor was there scolding her, so she wasn't at all surprised. But at the same time she realized this was the perfect outlet for the rebellious spirit that had been brewing in her ever since she left home. She dug deep into the sugar bowl with the spoon and covered her bowl of berries with so much sugar that it resembled a snowdrift.

A peculiar silence descended upon the table. Everyone knew the scene could not possibly end well. And in fact it did not take long for a little remark to cross the lips of the colonel's wife:

'What sour raspberries you must have in Korskyrka. Ours aren't at all bad. I hardly think you need any more sugar.'

But Charlotte just went on, as she said to herself: 'If I put on more and more sugar I shall lose Karl-Artur and be miserable for eternity, and yet I have no choice but to continue.'

The colonel's wife gave her shoulders a little shrug, turned to the dean and continued conversing. It was clear that she did not wish to take the strong line.

The colonel, however, decided to try to assist his wife.

'You're completely spoiling the taste of the berries, my dear Miss Charlotte.'

Hardly had these words escaped him before Charlotte set the sugaring spoon aside and, grasping the sugar bowl in both hands, inverted it over her dessert bowl, emptying the entire contents into it.

Having done so, she placed the sugar bowl back on the table and put the spoon back. She sat up straight in her chair and glared at the assembled guests, prepared for the onslaught.

'Jaquette,' said Colonel Ekenstedt, 'perhaps you could take your friend up to your room?'

His wife, however, held up a hand to halt all activity.

'No, no, no, by no means,' she said. 'We'll have nothing of the kind.'

She sat silent for a moment or two, as if considering how to formulate her words. Soon there was a little twinkle in her lovely eyes, and she spoke, turning not to Charlotte, but to the cathedral dean.

'Have you heard, good sir, how it happened that my Aunt Clementine married Count Cronfelt? Their fathers had met in Stockholm, as members of Parliament, and agreed on the match, but when their decision was announced, the young count objected that at the very least he wanted to see his future wife before he committed himself. But Aunt Clementine was back at Hedeby, and as people would have talked if she had suddenly been called to Stockholm, it was decided that he would travel to the parish of Bro in order to see her in church. Well, my aunt had nothing against marrying a handsome young count, but when she found out that he was coming to church to have a look at her, she did not like the idea of being put on display. Given the choice, she would have preferred not to attend church at all that Sunday, but in those days it was unthinkable for a child to take a stand against a decision of her parents. So she had to make herself as attractive as she could and go and sit in the Löwensköld pew so that Count Cronfelt and a friend of his would be able to scrutinize her. But do you know what she did, good sir? Well, when the precentor raised his voice in the first hymn, she began singing very loudly and completely out of tune. And she continued to do so, hymn after hymn, until the service was over. Afterwards, when she came outside, Count Cronfelt was standing there, and he bowed to her. "Mademoiselle, I owe you my most humble apologies. I realize now that a Miss Löwensköld could never allow herself to be examined like a horse at a market." At that he departed, but he returned on other occasions to become properly acquainted with the young woman in her home at Hedeby, and after some time they were married, and they were happy as well, I believe. Perhaps you had heard that story before, good sir?'

'Indeed, but never told so well,' said the cathedral dean, thoroughly baffled.

However, there was one person who knew perfectly well what was going on, and that was Charlotte. She sat there filled with the greatest amazement, simply soaking up the storyteller with her eyes. The colonel's wife looked at her, gave a little smile, and turned once again to the cathedral dean.

'You will have noticed, good sir, that there is a young woman at the table with us today. And she arrived here so that my husband and I would be able to scrutinize her and see whether she would do as a wife for Karl-Artur. But this young woman, my friend, is a Löwensköld of the right sort, and she does not appreciate being put on display or exhibit. I assure you that ever since she arrived yesterday evening she has done her very best to sing as out of tune as my Aunt Clementine. So now I shall do as Count Cronfelt did, good sir, and offer her my most humble apologies, and say that I realize now that a Miss Löwensköld could never allow herself to be examined like a horse at a market.'

She stood right up and opened her arms, and Charlotte flew into her embrace and kissed her and wept with joy, admiration and gratitude.

And from that day forth she had loved her presumptive mother-in-law almost more than she loved Karl-Artur. For her sake, and so that her dreams would come true, she persuaded

Karl-Artur to return to Uppsala and complete his studies, for her sake she had spent the summer doing her utmost to get him to apply for that teaching position so that he would have some status in the world and be more than a penniless rural clergyman.

For her sake she had restrained herself and humbled herself that morning.

THE LETTER

Charlotte Löwensköld sat in her room writing to her mother-in-law or, more correctly, to the woman who until that very day she had regarded as her mother-in-law, Beate Ekenstedt, the colonel's wife.

She wrote a long letter, filling page after page. She wrote to the only person in all the world who had always understood her, to explain what she was about to do.

To begin with she described Schagerström's proposal of marriage and everything that had happened since. She wrote about the conversation in the garden, and she did not paint a flattering picture of herself. She admitted that she had been angry with Karl-Artur and that she had provoked him, but she swore that she had never intended to break off their engagement.

She went on to describe that morning's conversation, and Karl-Artur's remarkable admission that he was now betrothed to a peddler woman from Dalarna. She wrote about how she had tried to win him back, that she had been close to succeeding, but that all had been lost owing to the arrival of that confounded bouquet.

Furthermore, she wrote about the deranged note from Karl-Artur, and of the decision it had triggered in her, and her hopes that her fiancé's mother would understand her, just as she had understood her from the very first time they had met.

She had no other choice. Someone, she knew not who, although she believed it was one of the women who lived in the village, close to the church, had accused her of acting under false pretenses, of being underhanded and covetous.

She was not about to let that kind of talk pass unnoticed.

Because she was a woman of little means who ate at the table of others, and because she had neither a father nor a brother to defend her honor, she would have to see to it herself that justice was done.

She was, however, perfectly capable of handling the matter. She wasn't one of those run-of-the-mill obliging women who were good for nothing but sweeping and mending. She knew both how to load a shotgun and how to use it, and last autumn during the elk-hunting season it was she who had felled the largest bull elk.

Neither did she want for courage. One time at the fair she gave a vagrant a slap across the face for mistreating his horse. She had expected him to pull a knife and use it on her, but that had not kept her from smacking him.

Perhaps the colonel's wife recalled the time she had risked her entire position on Boxing Day by taking the pastor's beloved team of horses out of the stable without asking, to race against the stable boys. Not many people would have been inclined to take such a risk.

She was also the one who had made a deadly enemy of the vicious Captain Hammarberg by refusing to sit next to him at a dinner party. She couldn't bear the thought of spending a whole long meal sitting talking to a man who, not long ago, had caused a friend's bankruptcy after which the man took his life. So when she had been so bold about a cause that was not her own, she could hardly hesitate to look out for her own interests, could she?

She had a feeling that the creature who had accused her to Karl-Artur's face must be such an uncharitable being that she poisoned the very air she breathed, she must spread misfortune wherever she went, hearing her speak must be like being bitten by a venomous snake. There was no greater service one could do for one's fellow human beings than to deliver them from such a monster.

As soon as she had read his note and absorbed its implications, she had known what she had to do. She had an urge to go straight to her room and take her shotgun. It was loaded. All she would have had to do was to remove it from the wall and hang it over her shoulder.

No one in the parsonage would have stopped her. She would have called her dog and taken off in the direction of the lake, as if going to check whether the ducklings were fully-grown. Once she was out of sight of the parsonage, she would have turned off toward the village, where the person who had dripped poison into Karl-Artur's ear would be, of course.

She imagined that she would have stopped outside the house where 'that person' lived and called her out into the street. And the minute she had come into Charlotte's field of vision she would have aimed straight for her heart and brought her down.

If only she had known who it was, of all those women who lived over by the church, she would already have meted out that punishment, but she realized that she would have to wait until she was completely certain. For one moment she considered doing as Karl-Artur had done and just heading off with the shotgun in confidence that God would lead the guilty woman to cross her path, but she had abandoned that idea. The real criminal might have gone free, and she didn't want to allow that.

There was no use going down to his rooms to ask Karl-Artur who it was he had been confiding in the evening before. Oh no, he was intelligent enough not to answer that question.

Instead, she had decided to use her wiles. She wanted to give the impression of being calm. Calm and composed. That was the best way to weasel the secret out of him, and she would do it soon enough.

She had tried to bring herself back under control. She had torn Schagerström's bouquet to pieces in the first moments of confusion; now she gathered up all the petals and threw them in the rubbish bin. She had forced herself to find the engagement ring Karl-Artur had sent her, which had rolled out onto the floor. Then she had gone up to her room and, discovering that it was only half past seven, and there was plenty of time before breakfast, when she would next see Karl-Artur, she had sat down to write to the beloved mother of her fiancé.

By the time that letter reached Karlstad it would all be over. Her decision was as firm as it had been initially. But she was glad of a short reprieve. It had also given her the opportunity to explain the whole thing to the only person by whose judgment she really set store, and to tell her that her heart, at all times, was with this mother, whom she admired so greatly and loved above all others.

— — —

That was as far as she had got. She had finished the letter and begun rereading it. Yes, she found it clear and explicit. She hoped that the colonel's wife would understand that she was blameless, that she was being unjustly accused, and that she had the right to exact her revenge.

But after Charlotte had read through the letter, something else began to preoccupy her. She could see that in her desire to profess her own innocence, she had portrayed Karl-Artur unfairly.

She read and reread, and became so agitated it made her feel dizzy. What if she had written in a way that made the colonel and his wife angry with Karl-Artur?

Just a short time ago she had warned him against making his parents angry, and here she was stirring them up against Karl-Artur!

She had sat there promoting herself at his expense. She had been noble-minded and sensible, but she had written about him as if he were utterly out of his senses.

And she had intended to send what she had written to his mother, his mother who loved him! She must have been out of her senses, too.

Had she meant to cause her fiancé's beloved mother so much sorrow? Did she not remember how indulgent the colonel's wife had been toward her, Charlotte, from their very first meeting and ever since? Had she lost all sense of charity?

She tore the long letter in two, and sat down to write a different one. Now she wanted to shoulder the burden of guilt herself. She wanted to exonerate Karl-Artur.

Of course that was the right thing to do. Karl-Artur was destined for greatness; she ought to be pleased if she could keep all evil far from him.

He had divorced himself from her, but she held him just as dear as ever, and she wished to protect and help him as much now as ever before.

She began her letter to the colonel's wife: 'My esteemed lady, may you not think all too ill of me – – –'

After having written that, she lost her train of thought. What could she say? She had never been much of a liar, and the truth was not easy to mitigate.

Moreover, before she had time to deliberate on what it was she wanted to say, the breakfast chimes rang. There was no more time to think.

So she simply signed her name to that single line she had written, folded the letter and sealed it. She carried it downstairs with her, put it into the bag the postman collected, and went into the dining room.

At that moment it struck her that there was no longer any need for her to do any detective work concerning who the 'person' was. If she wanted the colonel's wife to believe her, and if she really wanted to take the blame herself, the logical consequence was that she could not punish anyone else.

IN THE CLOUDS

I.

Breakfast at the parsonage, with fresh eggs, bread and butter, soft oatmeal with cream, and finally a little cup of coffee with the most delicious cinnamon twists, the like of which no other kitchen in the parish could produce, was usually the pleasantest meal of the day. The two elderly people, the pastor and his wife, had just woken up and were as chipper as seventeen-year-olds. Their night's sleep had refreshed them. The fatigue of old age they often felt later in the day was nowhere to be found, and they often jested with the young people and with each other.

But of course there could be no bantering on a morning like this one. Both the young people were out of favor. Charlotte had upset them terribly by the way she had responded to Schagerström the previous day, and the curate had offended them the same day by failing to appear for meals without so much as notifying them.

When Charlotte hurried into the room to take her place at the table where the others were already seated, she was met with a firm reprimand from the pastor's wife:

'Were you thinking of sitting down with fingers like that?'

Looking down at her hands, which were certainly filthy with ink after her energetic letter writing, she laughed:

'Good gracious no. You are quite right, madam. Excuse me, excuse me!'

She rushed back out, returning with clean hands and without the slightest sign of crossness over having been reproached, in spite of the criticism having been received in the presence of her betrothed.

The pastor's wife looked at her in some astonishment. 'What could be going on now?' the old woman wondered to herself. 'One day she was hissing like a snake, the next she is cooing like a dove. There's certainly no understanding young people today.'

Karl-Artur hastened to apologize for his negligence the previous day. He had been out walking when he found he was so tired he had to lie down to rest on a hillside in the woods. He had fallen asleep and upon waking discovered to his surprise that he had slept through both dinner and supper.

The pastor's wife was pleased that the young man was willing to explain himself.

'Karl-Artur, you needn't be bashful with us. I'm sure we could have found you a little something to eat, even after our own meal.'

'Ah, Regina, you are far too generous.'

'Well, you'll just have to eat double now, to make up for what you missed.'

'I must admit, madam, that I did not want for anything. I stopped by the organist's on my way back, and Mrs. Sundler provided me with an evening meal.'

There was an almost inaudible little cry from Charlotte's direction. Karl-Artur turned his gaze quickly toward Charlotte, blushing furiously. He ought not to have mentioned Mrs. Sundler by name. Now Charlotte might jump up and say she realized it was Mrs. Sundler who had accused her, and make a scene.

But Charlotte did not move. And her face gave the impression of total tranquility. Had Karl-Artur not known what wiles were concealed behind that peaceful visage, he would have said it was radiating with some inner light.

It was hardly surprising that Charlotte was making the other people at the table feel bewildered. Inside her something really very remarkable was happening.

Or perhaps that is not the correct way to describe it, since it was nothing more than what all of us have experienced at one time or another, when we were doing our best to fulfill some demanding obligation or pledged to undergo some privation. We were, more than likely, in a bad humor while we submitted to it. No enthusiasm aided us, we had no confidence that we were doing the right and wise thing, and all we expected from our good deed was even more lamentation and misery. But then suddenly and unexpectedly we felt how our heart leapt with joy, felt it moving as lightly as a dancer, and we were filled with a sense of complete satisfaction. Miraculously, we felt raised above our ordinary, everyday selves, felt absolute indifference to anything unpleasant, in fact we were convinced that from that moment on nothing in the world would ever touch us, nothing could disturb the calm, solemn happiness that filled us.

Something like that had overwhelmed Charlotte while she was having her breakfast. All her feelings of misery, her rage, her desire for revenge, her injured pride and rejected love, all those feelings gave way to the great jubilation she felt in her soul at having sacrificed herself for her beloved.

At that moment there was nothing inside her but gentle affection and tender understanding. She found every human being admirable. She could not love mankind sufficiently.

She sat looking at pastor Forsius, a dry little man with a bald head, a shaven chin, a huge forehead and small, bright eyes. He looked more like a university professor than a clergyman and, in fact, he had studied the natural sciences. He was born in the eighteenth century, when the world was still in the grip of Linnaeus, and he had devoted himself to studies of nature and had just been appointed to a chair in botany at Lund when he was called to serve the ministry in Korskyrka, the reason being that the parishioners there had been shepherded for many years by pastors with the surname of Forsius. The parish had been handed down from father to son as if it were a hundred-year leasehold, and as Petrus Forsius, professor of botany, was the last bearer of that name, he had been begged and pleaded with to take over the curing of their souls, leaving the flowers to their fates.

Charlotte had known all of that for a long time, but never before had she really understood what a sacrifice it must have been for this older man to abandon the studies he loved so deeply. There was no question but that he had become a very good clergyman. He had the blood of so many fine men of the cloth in his veins, and had carried out his duties as if he had always known how, and as if it were the easiest thing in the world. But from many little indications, Charlotte believed she had seen that he was still grieving over not having been allowed to continue with the occupation that was rightfully his, and not being able to devote himself to his intended life's work.

Now that he had a curate, the seventy-five-year-old man could be seen resuming his studies in botany and taking long walks to collect plants, which he pasted onto sheets of paper and arranged as part of his herbarium. Still, he didn't leave his parishioners to look after themselves entirely. Above all it was very important to him to keep the peace, not to allow discord to sneak in and make people bitter, so he always tried to get at the root of every problem. That was why he was so upset about the brusque answer she had given Schagerström yesterday. But yesterday Charlotte had been a different person. One who had found the old man merely and unnecessarily anxious. Now she understood him in quite a different way.

And the pastor's wife …

Charlotte turned her gaze on the elderly woman, who was tall and bony, without the least trace of anything attractive to her appearance. She wore her hair, which just wouldn't turn gray although she was nearly as old as her husband, parted in the middle and combed down over her ears, where it was concealed under a black tulle cap. It hid much of her face, and Charlotte more or less assumed that was intentional, since the pastor's wife did not have much beauty to display. Perhaps she thought it was enough for people to see her eyes, which

resembled two black peppercorns, her snub nose with its wide
nostrils, her eyebrows, which were short and bushy, her wide
mouth and her prominent cheekbones.

She looked stern, but if she was demanding of the other
people in her household, she was hardest on herself. She never
allowed herself any rest. The parishioners often said it couldn't
be easy to be the body of Pastor Forsius' wife. She was never
content to sit on the couch with embroidery or crocheting, oh
no, she had to do the really heavy work if she was going to be
satisfied. In her entire life she had never undertaken anything
as futile as reading a novel or tinkling at the piano.

That morning Charlotte, who may at times have found her
quite unnecessarily zealous about her work, could not admire
her enough. Was it not commendable never to hold back, but
to be untiringly active even at her quite advanced age? Was
it not estimable to want to have everything, into the tiniest
corner, neat and tidy, and never to ask anything more of life
than to be allowed to toil?

Moreover, she was far from dull. She had such a sense of
humor and such an ability to say amusing things that she
would double people over with laughter!

The pastor's wife went on talking with Karl-Artur about Mrs.
Sundler. He told her that he'd gone to see her because she was
the daughter of an old friend of his family, Malvina Spaak.

'Of course, of course,' said the pastor's wife, being a woman
who knew all of Värmland, and particularly anyone who had
been a decent housekeeper, 'Malvina Spaak was a capable and
responsible person.'

Karl-Artur asked whether she didn't find the daughter
absolutely as excellent as her mother.

'I can say nothing but that she keeps her house in order,' said
the pastor's wife, 'though I'm afraid she's not quite all there.'

'Not all there?' Karl-Artur repeated in an inquiring tone.

'That's it, not all there. Since no one likes her, I have tried to
talk with her now and then, Karl-Artur, and do you know what
she once said to me when she was leaving? "You know," she
said, looking up at the sky: "When you see a silver cloud with

a golden lining, Mrs. Forsius, think of me!" Yes, that's what she said. What do you think she meant by it?'

As the pastor's wife was telling this story, the corners of her mouth began to twitch. It was so irresistibly comical to imagine that any sensible person would ask her, Regina Forsius, to go looking for clouds with golden linings.

She did her very best to restrain her laugh. She had made up her mind to be strict and serious throughout breakfast. Charlotte could see her struggling. She fought hard, but all of a sudden her whole face began to tremble. Her eyes crinkled, her nostrils widened, her mouth opened and, finally, she burst out laughing. Her whole face was contorted, and her entire body was pulsating.

So everyone else just had to join in, there was no alternative. Really, Charlotte thought, you only had to see Regina Forsius laugh, to be fond of her.

You no longer noticed that she was homely. You had to appreciate anyone who had such a wonderful sense of humor.

II.

Just after breakfast, as soon as Karl-Artur had left the dining room, the pastor's wife told Charlotte that the pastor had decided to pay a visit to Stora Sjötorp that morning. Although the young woman was still in the same state of exultation, this information gave her a slight sense of apprehension. Would this not confirm Karl-Artur's suspicions? But she immediately calmed down. She was living up in the clouds, wasn't she? So what happened down here on earth didn't really matter very much.

It was only half past ten when the large, covered carriage drew up to the door. Of course Pastor Forsius could not afford a whole team, but he had every reason to be proud of his little gray-white fjord horses with their black manes and tails, and his handsome coachman who looked extremely dignified in his black livery. Truth be told, there was not a fault to be found with the parsonage horses and carriage except that the horses were a bit pudgy. The pastor looked after them far too well. He had even found it difficult to decide to use them that day. He would have far preferred to head over in a gig, if that had been possible.

That morning the pastor's wife and Charlotte had been invited for an eleven o'clock coffee at the home of Mrs. Gråberg, the apothecary's wife, to celebrate her name day. As the pastor had to pass the village to get to Stora Sjötorp, they went along in the carriage for that part of the ride. As they were passing through the yard-gate, Charlotte turned to the pastor as if she had just had an idea.

'Mr. Schagerström sent me a bouquet of lovely roses this morning, before the two of you were even awake. Dear Sir, if you are so inclined, you might mention my gratitude to him.'

You can imagine the pleasure the elderly couple felt, and their astonishment. What a great relief to them this was. There would be no discord in the parish. Schagerström was not offended, in spite of having every good reason to be.

'And you've waited until now to mention it,' the pastor's wife exclaimed. 'You certainly are a most curious young woman.'

In any case, she was delighted, asked how the bouquet had been delivered to the parsonage, whether it had been artfully composed, whether there might even have been a note inserted among the flowers, and all kinds of questions like that.

The pastor merely nodded to Charlotte and promised to pass her thanks along. But she saw him straighten up, truly looking as though an enormous weight had fallen from his shoulders.

Charlotte wondered whether she had just done something rash again. But on that morning she was unable to be at peace until she knew everyone was as pleased with her as she could make them. She felt an enormous need to sacrifice herself to the happiness of others.

The carriage stopped where the village street turned off the country road, and the women disembarked. It was actually just about the very spot at which Karl-Artur had met the lovely peddler girl from Dalarna the day before.

Whenever Charlotte went to the village she always stopped here for a moment to admire the vista. The little lake that formed the center of the landscape was more visible here than from the parsonage, which was undeniably quite low-lying. From here one could see the whole lake, the shores of which presented quite a varied sight. On the west side, where they were standing, smooth fields of crops opened out, and it was clear that this was very fertile arable land from the many groups of farms dotting the landscape. To the north was the parsonage, also surrounded by even, well-tended fields, while to the northeast there was an area covered with leafy forest land. There was also a rushing river with frothy rapids, and between the trees one could glimpse black roofs and tall chimneys. Down there were two sizeable iron foundries, which contributed even more to the wealth of the community than the farmland and woods. Looking again to the south, one saw nothing but rocky bareness, and some low hills with dense vegetation. The eastern shore looked much the same, and it would have been a dull, heavy sight had not the fine idea of building a manor house up on a high hill in the woods come to the foundry owner. The sight of that white building sticking up in the dark forest was a fine one. Clever garden planning also gave rise to a peculiar optical illusion in the park surrounding the manor. It looked as if there were a proper walled castle with side towers. It was the crowning glory of the entire area, and no one would have wanted the place to look any other way.

Charlotte, whose mind was completely preoccupied, did not so much as glance at either the lake or the handsome manor house. In contrast, the elderly pastor's wife, who didn't normally pay much attention to a lovely view, simply stood there, staring at the landscape.

'Oh, do stop a moment!' she said. 'Just take a look at the Berghamra estate. And people say that Stora Sjötorp is bigger and even more beautiful! Do you know what? If I knew someone about whom I cared was living at a big place like that, it would make me truly happy.'

That was all she said, but she stood there nodding her head and clasping her old, wrinkled hands almost as if in prayer.

Charlotte, who understood perfectly well what she was getting at, answered promptly: 'Oh, yes, it must be grand living in those deep dark woods, where no one ever comes to visit. Quite a fine thing compared with living along the country road, as we do at the parsonage.'

At that, the pastor's wife, who very much enjoyed watching people pass by along the road, shook a finger at her in warning: 'All right, all right, then.'

She took Charlotte by the arm and began to walk down the pleasant village street, lined from one end to the other with large properties resembling miniature manor houses. Only at the very beginning were there some little cottages. Otherwise, the smaller places were crowded away further back toward the edge of the woods, not visible from the main street. The old stave church with its tall steeple, extending up like an awl, the courthouse, the parish hall, the big, lively tavern, the doctor's residence, the judge's home, set back slightly from the street, a couple of large farmhouses, and the apothecary, a building at the far end of the street which sort of closed it off, all this bore witness not only to the fact that Korskyrka was a wealthy area, but also to how up-to-date it was, not just some lazy old backwater.

Still, as the pastor's wife and Charlotte walked the length of the village in perfect accord, they thanked God that they did not have to live here, with neighbors so close by, and where one couldn't stick one's nose out the door without everyone knowing all about it and wondering where one was going. Whenever they came to the village they were quickly filled with longing for the parsonage, where there were no other houses close by, and where one was one's own mistress. They said they would not be fully at ease again until they were on their way back home, and could see the sturdy trunks of the parsonage linden trees in the distance.

At last they entered the apothecary shop. They seemed to be a bit late. As they walked up the stairs from the shop to the residence, they could hear lots of voices. It sounded like a buzzing beehive.

'Listen to them today! They are carrying on worse than usual. Something must be going on.'

Charlotte stopped in her tracks on the stairs. It had never crossed her mind that Schagerström's proposal, the broken engagement and Karl-Artur's betrothal to the girl from Dalarna might already be a topic of general discussion, but now she was beginning to fear that these were precisely the subjects being gossiped about so eagerly and in such loud voices.

'It must be that confounded woman, the organist's wife, who's been leaking like a sieve,' she thought to herself. 'What a fine confidante Karl-Artur picked for himself.'

But not for an instant did she consider turning back. There would never have been any question, even under ordinary circumstances, of giving in to a gaggle of gossiping women, and all the more reason not to do so today, when she was totally indifferent to anything even vaguely resembling censure.

The roomful of women gathered to celebrate the name day of the lady of the house fell totally silent when the new guests entered. Only one old woman who was excitedly telling her neighbor something and wagging her index finger in the air, could be heard exclaiming: 'And can you guess what, my dear? You'll never believe what happened the other day!'

Everyone looked embarrassed. No one seemed to have expected the ladies from the parsonage to turn up that day.

The wife of the apothecary, however, hastened to greet them, and Mrs. Forsius, who knew nothing of all the fuss Charlotte and Karl-Artur were already causing, was entirely at her ease, although she did notice that something was in the air. Old as she was, her joints were as limber as a dancer's, and she began by curtseying deeply to everyone in the room. Then she walked all around saying hello, with another little curtsey for each person in turn. Charlotte, who felt that the air was full of poorly-concealed distaste for her, followed behind. Her curtseys were nowhere near as deep as those of the pastor's wife, but there was never any competing with her in any case.

The young girl was quick to notice how everyone avoided her. When she had been given a cup of coffee and was sitting down at a table by the window, no one joined her on the free chair opposite. Even when everyone had had their coffee and took out their crocheting and embroidering from their capacious needlework and net bags, she was still sitting there all alone, feeling utterly invisible.

All around her were groups of ladies, their heads so close together that the lace and ruffles on their large tulle caps became entangled. They were all whispering to keep Charlotte from hearing and still, time after time she was able to discern their earnest: 'Can you guess what, my dear? You'll never believe what happened the other day!'

There they were, telling each other how she had first refused Schagerström, then changed her mind and intentionally sparked a quarrel with her fiancé to provoke him into breaking off their engagement. She was a sly one! All the blame would fall on him. No one would be able to say of her that she had turned down a poor man in order to marry the master of Stora Sjötorp and become a fine lady. And her whole plan would have succeeded, she would have escaped all censure, had not the wife of the organist intuited her evil intent.

Charlotte sat silent, listening to the buzz. Not for an instant did she consider standing up to defend herself. The state of exaltation she had been in all day had peaked. She felt no pain, and found herself in the clouds high above all worldly things.

The entire toxic buzz would have been turned on Karl-Artur, had she not been protecting him. If that had happened, every corner of the room would have been humming with: 'Can you guess what, my dear? Have you heard? Young Ekenstedt broke with his fiancée. And do you know what, do you know what? He ran out onto the country road to propose to the first woman he met. What do you think, what do you think? Can a man like that stay on as a curate in Korskyrka parish? What else? What else? What will the bishop say?'

She was pleased to be the one about whom they were gossiping.

While Charlotte sat there, her soul enraptured because she was protecting Karl-Artur, a pale, thin little woman came over to her.

It was her sister, Marie-Louise Löwensköld, the wife of Doctor Romelius. She had six children and a drunkard of a husband. She was ten years older than Charlotte, and there had never been any love lost between them.

She asked no questions, just sat down opposite Charlotte and went on knitting a child's sock. But she had a very resolute look on her face. You could tell she knew what she was doing when she chose to sit down by the window.

The sisters just sat there. Each of them kept hearing that: 'Can you guess what, my dear?'

In a little while they noticed that Mrs. Sundler was sitting whispering to Mrs. Forsius, the pastor's wife.

'Now Regina's finding out,' Charlotte's sister said.

Charlotte made a move to stand up, but had second thoughts immediately and sat back down.

'I wonder, Marie-Louise,' she asked a few minutes later, 'what you remember of that woman Malvina Spaak? Wasn't there some kind of prophecy or prediction?'

'I do believe you're right,' her sister replied, 'but I cannot recall the details either. Something about a curse that would fall upon the Löwenskölds.'

'Do you think you could find out?' Charlotte asked.

'Certainly. I think I have something about it on paper somewhere. But it didn't apply to us, anyway. Only to the Löwenskölds from Hedeby.'

'Thank you,' said Charlotte, after which silence again prevailed between them.

A few minutes later, though, Mrs. Romelius seemed to lose patience with all the slander that was buzzing around the room. She leaned over to Charlotte.

'I know what's going on,' she whispered. 'You're keeping

silent for Karl-Artur's sake. I imagine I could tell them all what really happened.'

'No, for goodness sake don't say anything,' Charlotte responded in alarm. 'What difference does it make how things go for me? Karl-Artur is a man of such great gifts.'

Her sister understood her at once. She loved her husband in spite of the fact that for their entire married life he had made her miserable with his drinking. She never gave up hope that he would turn himself around and become a medical genius.

When the name-day party finally ended and the ladies were leaving, the stout organist's wife was the one who helped Mrs. Forsius on with her shawl and tied her hat ribbons for her in the vestibule.

Charlotte, who always reserved the right to help her old friend, stood there very pale, watching but not saying a word. When they went out onto the village street it was, once again, the organist's wife who hastened to offer the pastor's wife her arm. Charlotte had to accept just walking alongside.

Mrs. Sundler tried her patience more than anyone else, but she knew they would be going their separate ways once they reached her cottage at the other end of the street.

However, when they got there Mrs. Sundler asked whether it would be all right if she accompanied them back to the parsonage, since it was ever so good for her to stretch her legs a bit after sitting still for so long.

The pastor's wife made no objection, and they walked on as before. Nor did Charlotte say anything. She merely extended her stride so as to walk a little ahead of the others and not have to go on listening to the ingratiating voice of the organist's wife.

SCHAGERSTRÖM

Throughout the ride home from his failure of a proposal at the parsonage, Schagerström just sat with a little smile on his lips. Had it not been for the coachman and the servant, he might have burst out laughing – that was how absurd it seemed to him that he, who had made his journey in order to do a greatly charitable deed for an impoverished lady's companion, had been so duly rebuffed and cut down to size.

'But everything she said was absolutely right,' he mumbled to himself. 'By God she was right. In fact I find it difficult to understand how I did not think about it myself, before I went off courting.'

'What's more,' he thought, 'flaring up like that was strikingly becoming to her. Seeing her like that was a reward for my trouble. It gave me great pleasure to see her so beautiful.'

When the carriage had been on the road for a while, he said to himself that even if he had behaved foolishly he was still glad about the whole affair, because it had given him the opportunity to make the acquaintance of someone who couldn't care less that he was the wealthiest man in Korskyrka. The young woman certainly hadn't made the slightest effort to flatter him. It had not seemed to matter to her that she was talking to a millionaire. No, she had treated him as if he were just any old vagabond.

'That young woman certainly has character!' he thought. 'I should really like her not think terribly ill of me. God save me from proposing to her ever again, but at the same time I would like to prove to her that I am not such a dunce as to be angry about the lesson she taught me.'

He spent the whole afternoon ruminating over how to atone for his forwardness, and in the end he thought he had truly found a suitable way of doing so. This time, though, he would not rush blindly into anything. He wanted to prepare his deed, and make the necessary inquiries so as not to get himself into trouble again.

On toward evening it occurred to him that it could do no harm to show Charlotte a bit of consideration even at this early stage. He would be pleased to send her some flowers. If she accepted them, that would make it easier to get on good terms with her later. He hurried right out into the garden.

He said to his gardener: 'Now my good man, I will be wanting a really pretty bouquet. Show me what you have in bloom.'

'I'd say the nicest thing I have just now would be these red carnations. We could put them in the middle, with some stocks around them and bit of mignonette here and there for good measure.'

But Schagerström wrinkled his nose. 'Carnations and stocks and mignonette!' he snorted. 'Every manor house in the province has them. You might as well have offered me ox-eye daisies and harebells, my good gardener.'

The foundry owner reacted similarly to snapdragons, larkspur and forget-me-nots. He rejected them all.

Finally, Schagerström found himself standing in front of a little rose bush covered in flowers and buds. The buds were particularly appealing: with a hint of pink petals peeking up through such a prickly casing it looked like sticky moss.

'Now this is my idea of beauty,' he said.

'Well master, that's my moss rose! This is the first year I've gotten it to bloom. They don't really thrive this far north. There's nothing to compare with this bush in all of Värmland.'

'That's precisely the kind of thing I was looking for. The bouquet's to go to Korskyrka parsonage where, as you know, good gardener, they already have all the other flowers themselves.'

'Ah, to the parsonage!' the gardener exclaimed, in a much happier tone of voice. 'That's a different matter altogether. I'm delighted to know the pastor will get to see my moss roses. He's quite the expert.'

And so the roses were cut and sent to the parsonage, where an adverse fate awaited them.

Someone, however, was most kindly received when his carriage arrived at Stora Sjötorp the next morning, and that was the pastor from Korskyrka.

The little clergyman was probably quite solemn and ceremonious at first, but basically both he and Schagerström were straightforward, unpretentious men. They soon realized that there was no need for courtesies and compliments, and were talking frankly and openly, like old friends.

Schagerström took the opportunity to ask some questions about Charlotte. He wanted to know about her parentage and her means, but above all he asked about her fiancé and his prospects for the future. Wasn't a curate's salary too little for him to marry on? Did the pastor know whether young Ekenstedt had any hope of a promotion soon?

The pastor was highly astonished, but as none of the things Schagerström was asking about was anything but public knowledge, he answered clearly and straightforwardly.

'This is what businessmen are like,' the clergyman thought to himself. 'They get right to the heart of the matter. All right, all right, I suppose that's the way people behave nowadays.'

After some time Schagerström informed the pastor that he was the chairman of the board of directors of a foundry in Uppland, and that he had been assigned to appoint a man of the cloth to serve in the parish. The post had been vacated a couple of weeks earlier. The salary was nothing to boast about, but the parsonage was a pleasant one, and the previous pastor had been happy with the position. So he wondered whether Pastor Forsius thought it might suit young Ekenstedt?

Forsius had seldom found a suggestion more surprising, but he was a clever man and took the matter in stride.

After pulling out his snuffbox, filling his large nose with snuff and polishing the box with a silk handkerchief, he began to speak:

'Sir, I find it difficult to imagine a young man more worthy of your aid.'

'Fine, that settles it,' said Schagerström.

The pastor put his snuffbox away. He was absolutely overjoyed. Wasn't this a wonderful piece of news to bring home with him? He had often been concerned for Charlotte and about her future, and although he had the greatest respect for his curate, it displeased him that he did not seem intent on ensuring himself of a post that would make it possible for him to marry.

Suddenly the kind, elderly gentleman turned to Schagerström:

'Sir, I know you enjoy making people happy. Do not content yourself with a half measure! Accompany me to the parsonage and inform the young couple of your fine intentions personally! Come and witness their joy! It is a pleasure of which I would not want to deprive you.'

This proposal brought a smile to Schagerström's lips. Clearly it pleased him.

'But what if I arrived at a bad moment?'

'Not a chance! A bad moment indeed! No question about it. There can be no bad moment for such good news!'

Schagerström looked ready to accept the pastor's offer, and then suddenly he struck his brow.

'I cannot come after all. I'm leaving today on a long journey. I've ordered my traveling carriage for two o'clock.'

'Oh, what a shame, Sir. But I understand. We all have our commitments.'

'And I've had notice sent to all the inns along the way, reserving meals and accommodation,' said Schagerström, looking glum.

'But couldn't you come with me in my carriage, which is ready and waiting? We could leave at once. Your conveyance could collect you at the parsonage at whatever time you say.'

And so the matter was settled. The pastor and Schagerström left for Korskyrka, having ordered the foundry owner's coachman to collect him there as soon as all the packing and preparations had been completed.

The two gentlemen spent the journey as merry as farmers on their way to market.

'If you ask me,' said the pastor, 'Charlotte doesn't really deserve this kindness, considering her behavior toward you yesterday, Mr. Schagerström.'

Schagerström burst out laughing.

'Now she'll be in a real spot,' the pastor went on. 'I look forward to seeing how she works it out. I imagine you'll find, Sir, that she comes up with something entirely unexpected, something no one else would ever do. Ha, ha, ha, this is sure to be great fun!'

It was a huge disappointment to the travelers when they arrived at the parsonage only to hear from the housemaid that the pastor's wife and her companion had not yet returned from the name-day party in the village. But the pastor, who knew they wouldn't be much longer, invited Schagerström to join him in his own rooms on the ground floor. Today it never occurred to him to invite him into the upstairs drawing room.

The pastor had two rooms at his disposal. The first was his official office, large and formal. An enormous desk, two desk chairs, a long leather couch and a built-in bookshelf for the voluminous parish ledgers was all there was in the way of furnishings, if you didn't count a few large cactus plants in one window, blossoming as if on fire. The pastor's wife had furnished the second room very comfortably for her beloved husband. The entire floor was covered with a rug she had woven herself; the furniture was attractive and practical. There were upholstered couches and armchairs, a desk with lots of drawers, and long bookshelves. There was also his large pipe collection, not to mention the stacks of pressed flowers in pressing paper on every available surface.

This was the room to which the pastor was leading Schagerström, but when they walked through the office they found Karl-Artur sitting at the big desk registering births and deaths in an enormous ledger. He rose when they came in, and was introduced to Schagerström.

'Well, Sir,' he said, shaking the foundry owner's hand. 'Today there will be no need for you to leave here without having accomplished your errand,' he said in a spiteful voice.

It is not surprising, is it, that he was extremely agitated by Schagerström's arrival at the parsonage? How could he think anything other than that all of them – the pastor, his wife and Charlotte – were conspiring to assure themselves that Charlotte's hasty refusal could be reversed? Surely if he had still had the slightest doubt as to Charlotte's dishonesty, it must have been utterly counteracted by the fact that her suitor had not only returned the next day, but had been brought back by the pastor himself? It was, of course, no longer of any concern to him who Charlotte married, but he did find something a bit improper about the haste they were making. It seemed inconsiderate. It was quite simply disgusting to see the clergyman and his wife so extraordinarily eager to help their relation make a wealthy marriage.

The elderly pastor, who had no idea that the engagement between Karl-Artur and Charlotte had been broken, gave his curate a quizzical look. He was unable to take in the full impact of his words, but from the tone he realized the man's hostility toward Schagerström and felt it would be wise to let him know that this time the foundry owner was not there with courtship in mind.

'Actually, what brings Mr. Schagerström here is an errand having to do with you,' he said. 'I don't know that I have the right to give his plan away before Charlotte returns, but you will be pleased, my young friend, you will be pleased indeed.'

His kind voice had no effect on Karl-Artur, who just stood there, rigid and cheerless, without a smile.

'Mr. Schagerström, Sir, if you have something to say to me there is no need to await Charlotte's return. She and I have nothing more to do with each other.'

Having said that, he extended his left hand so that the pastor and Schagerström could see the absence of the engagement ring on his ring finger.

The old pastor spun almost all the way around in

astonishment.

'What in the world, young man, have you two been up to in my absence?'

'Not in your absence, Pastor. The matter was settled yesterday. Mr. Schagerström proposed to Charlotte around midday. An hour later our engagement was broken.'

'Your engagement? But Charlotte never said a word.'

'Forgive me, Pastor, forgive me!' said Karl-Artur, whose patience with the old man's attempts to play innocent was running thin, 'but it is most evident to me that you have been playing *postillion d'amour.*'

The elderly pastor straightened right up, becoming stiff and formal.

'Come in to my room at once,' he said. 'We must get to the bottom of this.'

A moment later, when they were seated, with the pastor at his desk, Schagerström at the far end of a sofa toward the back of the room and Karl-Artur in a rocking chair near the door, the pastor turned to his curate.

'You are quite right, young man. Yesterday I advised my sister's granddaughter to accept Mr. Schagerström's proposal. She has spent five years waiting for you. I did ask you once this summer if you were not prepared to take a single step that would enable your union, and you responded in the negative. You may recall my telling you at that juncture that I was planning to do everything in my power to persuade Charlotte to terminate your relationship. Charlotte has not a penny to her name, and the day I die she will have neither protector nor provider. You know my attitude, and I feel no qualms about having counseled her to that effect. But, in any case, she followed her own inclinations and refused Mr. Schagerström, and that was that. She and I never discussed the matter further, young man.'

From his seat at the far end of the sofa, Schagerström was watching young Ekenstedt closely. There was something about his behavior that upset him. He was tipping his chair and rocking it on its back legs, as if to show that the old man's words were beneath his attention. He tried several times to interrupt, but the pastor pursued his subject.

'You will have an opportunity to speak, young man, you will have the floor for as long as you wish, but it is my turn now. When I decided to go to Stora Sjötorp today I had no idea that your engagement had been broken, and I had no intention of offering Charlotte to Mr. Schagerström. I went to Stora Sjötorp because I want no strife in my parish, and I personally felt that Mr. Schagerström had every right to be displeased with Charlotte's way of answering him. However, when I arrived at Stora Sjötorp it transpired that Mr. Schagerström disagreed with me. He found my views outdated, and felt that Charlotte had responded appropriately. He was so satisfied with the entire course of events that the only thing he had in mind was your happiness as a couple, and for that reason he wanted to offer you the post of pastor at the church for the Örtofta foundry and mines, of which he is the patron. It was to speak with the two of you to that end that he came here today. I presume that you can see from all this that neither Mr. Schagerström nor I had the slightest idea that your engagement was off. Now that you have heard what I had to say, you are free to apologize to both of us for your base accusations, young man.'

'It would never occur to me to be skeptical about what you have said,' Ekenstedt the curate began, standing up in the pose of an orator, arms crossed over his chest, back to the bookshelves. 'You are a most honest and straightforward gentleman, and having heard your words I realize that Charlotte would never have considered confiding her unscrupulous plans in you. I also agree with what you, honored sir, have said about my not being a suitable match for Charlotte. Had Charlotte been as frank and forthright as you, Sir, in admitting that, I would naturally have been deeply pained, but in the end I would have understood and forgiven her. Charlotte, however, chose a different course. Perhaps out of fear of losing face with people, she begins by refusing you, Mr. Schagerström, proudly and unselfishly. However, it is not her intention to frighten you off for good. Instead, she gets me to be the one to break off our engagement. She knows that my disposition is of the highly vulnerable sort, and she takes advantage of me. She says things she knows are certain to make me fly into a rage. And she succeeds. I break with her, at which point she considers herself to have won the game. She intends to cast all the guilt upon me. She intends to turn your wrath, Sir, and everyone else's on me. I break with her, a woman who had just refused a gallant offer for my sake. I break with her after she had waited five years for me. Who can fail to understand her turning around and accepting Mr. Schagerström's proposal after I have behaved like that toward her? Who can blame her?'

He threw his arms wide. The pastor sat up in his chair with a jolt, looking away.

The old man had five little lines in his high forehead. As Karl-Artur spoke, these lines grew redder and redder, until they were bright as a bleeding wound. This was a sign that the peaceful pastor was as furious as could be.

'Well, young man…'

'Excuse me, Pastor, but I was not quite finished. At the very moment when I felt compelled to break with Charlotte to save my own soul, God brought another woman into my life, a simple, unprepossessing woman of the people, and last night she and I exchanged vows of eternal fidelity. Thus I have found a perfectly satisfactory replacement. I am quite happy and am not standing here to lament my situation. But I do not feel it necessary to bear the detestable burden of general contempt which Charlotte wishes the world to turn on me.'

Suddenly Schagerström looked up. During the very last sentences young Ekenstedt had uttered, he had become aware, one might say, of a change in the ambiance in the room. He saw that Charlotte Löwensköld was standing in the doorway, just behind her fiancé.

She had approached so quietly that no one had heard her. Karl-Artur was entirely unaware of her presence, and went on speaking. And as he was haranguing the men about her underhandedness and wiles, there she stood, gracious as a guardian angel, looking at him with the purest compassion, the most devoted affection. Schagerström had seen that expression on his own wife's face often enough to know what it meant, and that it was genuine.

Schagerström did not think for a moment about whether she was beautiful. He thought she looked as she ought to look if she had been through a trial by fire and come out neither soot-covered nor scorched, but instead found herself with every bit of dross and imperfection removed, so she stood there now whole and transfigured. He could hardly imagine how young Ekenstedt could fail to sense the warmth of her gaze, could fail to be aware of her love encompassing him.

He, personally, felt as if it were filling the entire room. He felt the force of its radiance all the way over in the corner where he sat. It made his heart throb.

It disquieted him terribly to know that she was standing there listening to all that slander, which seemed to him utterly senseless and unfounded. He made a move, as if to rise.

Charlotte turned her gaze in his direction, and she discovered his presence in that dark corner. She must have realized how impatient he was, and gave him a little smile of collusion, putting a finger to her lips as a sign to him not to expose her.

A moment later she was gone just as silently as she had come. Neither the pastor nor her fiancé knew that she had been in the room. From that moment on, Schagerström was overcome with worry. Until then he had not paid Karl-Artur's tirades much mind. He assumed the whole thing was all a lovers' tiff, and would be all right once Charlotte's fiancé calmed down. But as soon as he saw Charlotte he knew that what he had witnessed in the parsonage was a true tragedy.

And since he seemed to be the one who, owing to his ill-advised proposal, had given rise to this misfortune, he began to seek a way to reconcile the disputing parties. Charlotte's innocence would have to be proven. But that ought not to be too difficult.

Being a man of great property and the chairman of many boards of directors, he had had plenty of opportunities to practice his skill at mediating between contending parties. He was quite sure it would not take him long to see precisely how the matter should be handled.

Just as Karl-Artur was winding up his harangue, the heavy footsteps of an elderly person could be heard in the next room, and Regina Forsius, the pastor's wife, appeared in the doorway. She saw Schagerström at once.

'Good grief, Sir, are you here again?'

The question came quite naturally to her, so totally taken aback was she. She simply blurted it out, before she had time to pull herself together and ask in a more formal, more suitable way.

'Yes, but luck is no more on my side than it was yesterday,' he replied. 'Yesterday I came with an offer of Stora Sjötorp, and today with one concerning a post and a parsonage, but I find myself refused today as well.'

The pastor seemed to gather new courage when his wife entered. He rose, and with his five little lines still bright red, he made a commanding gesture and quite simply showed Karl-Artur the door.

'You'd better go down to your rooms and reconsider. Charlotte has her faults, the usual Löwensköld faults. She is hotheaded and proud, but neither underhanded nor cunning, nor for that matter covetous of money. No, those things she has never been. And had you not been the son of my respected friend Colonel Ekenstedt…'

But there his wife interrupted him.

'Naturally,' she said, 'Pastor Forsius and I prefer to take Charlotte's side, but I do not know if we can do so this time. There are too many things I cannot understand. First and foremost, I cannot see why she failed to say anything to us yesterday or today. Nor do I understand why she seemed so pleased that my husband was going to Stora Sjötorp, or why she sent a word of thanks to Mr. Schagerström for the roses, when she knew what Karl-Artur thought she was up to. Still, I wouldn't judge her on those grounds, if it weren't for one other thing.'

'What other thing?' the pastor asked impatiently.

'Why does she not speak out?' his wife replied. 'Over at the name-day party in the village everyone already knew about both the proposal and the break-up. And some people avoided her, while others actively provoked her, but she let it all wash over her without a word in her own defense. If she had thrown her coffee cup in the face of one of them I would have thanked my Lord and Creator, but she sat there, submissive as someone sentenced to crucifixion, and just let them go on being as cruel as they could possibly be.'

'You can't possibly mean that you believe she committed such an evil deed, simply because she has not defended herself?' the pastor asked.

'As we walked home,' his wife continued, 'I decided to really put her to the test. The person who was most eager to accuse her was that woman who is married to the organist, for whom Charlotte has never cared. So I took Mrs. Sundler's arm and let her walk me all the way to the parsonage gate. And she let that go, as well. Now, would Charlotte Löwensköld have allowed anyone else to walk me home if she had a clear conscience? I ask you that.'

None of the three men answered her with so much as a word. Finally the pastor spoke, and his voice sounded fatigued: 'For the moment, we do not appear to be getting any closer to clarity. Time will tell, I suppose.'

'Pardon me, Pastor,' said Karl-Artur, 'but I require immediate clarity. My conduct must appear extremely unsuitable for a man of the cloth, extremely reprehensible, to anyone who does not understand that Charlotte herself was the one who brought about the rupture.'

'We must ask her ourselves, then,' suggested the pastor.

'I need a more reliable witness,' said Karl-Artur.

'If you'll permit me to involve myself in the matter,' Schagerström now interjected, 'I might propose a way of achieving clarity. The matter at hand is determination of whether or not Miss Löwensköld deliberately deceived her fiancé into breaking off their engagement in order to be able to say yes to my proposal of marriage. Is that not so?'

Indeed, it was so.

'I consider the whole issue a misunderstanding,' said Schagerström, 'and I now suggest that I repeat my proposal once more. I believe and know that she will say no.'

'But, Sir, are you prepared to take the consequences? Imagine if she says yes.'

'She will say no,' Schagerström said. 'And as it is clearly my fault that this misunderstanding arose between the learned Mr. Ekenstedt and his fiancée, I would very much like to do whatever I can to ensure that the good relations between them can be restored.'

Karl-Artur gave a skeptical sneer.

'She'll accept,' he said, 'unless someone warns her in advance about what we are after.'

'It is not my intention to ask her in person,' said Schagerström, 'but rather to write.'

He went over to the pastor's desk, helped himself to pen and paper, and scribbled a couple of lines.

'Forgive me, Miss Löwensköld, for making a nuisance of myself again, but having heard from your fiancé that your engagement has been broken off, I wish to repeat the offer I made yesterday.'

He showed Karl-Artur what he had written. He nodded approvingly.

'May I be so bold as to ask that one of the servants be the one to take the letter to Miss Löwensköld?' asked Schagerström.

The pastor rang the beaded bell pull on the wall. The housemaid appeared.

'Alma, do you know where Miss Charlotte is?'

'Yes, in her room.'

'Please deliver this to her immediately, from Mr. Schagerström, and tell her that he awaits her reply.'

When the housemaid left, the room went completely quiet. The gentle tinkling of an old-fashioned spinet penetrated the silence.

'Her room is right above us,' said the pastor's wife. 'That's her, playing.'

Not daring to look at one another, they simply listened. They heard the housemaid's footsteps on the stairs; they heard a door open. The music stopped. 'Charlotte's reading the note,' each one thought.

The pastor's elderly wife sat there, all atremble. The pastor's hands were clasped in prayer. Karl-Artur had sat roughly back down in the rocker, an incredulous little smile on his lips. Schagerström sat there looking unperturbed, as he always did when major business transactions were being concluded.

Now they heard someone's light footsteps crossing the floor up there. 'Charlotte's sitting down at her desk,' they thought. 'What will she write?'

A couple of minutes later the light footsteps crossed the floor again and went over to the door, which was opened and then shut. That was the housemaid, leaving.

Although they were all doing their utmost to appear calm to the others, they were unable to sit still. All four were standing in the pastor's outer office when the housemaid returned.

She handed a little note to Schagerström, which he opened and read.

'She has accepted,' said Schagerström, and the disappointment in his voice was clearly audible.

He read Charlotte's note to the others:

'Sir, if you wish to marry me in spite of all the unkind things people are saying about me now, I cannot but accept your proposal.'

'My congratulations to you, Sir,' said Karl-Artur in his most jeering tone.

'But it was all just a test,' said the pastor's wife, 'by which you are in no way bound, Sir.'

'Of course not,' the pastor agreed. 'Charlotte would be the first to…'

Schagerström truly looked as if he had no idea which foot to stand on.

At that very moment the sound of carriage wheels was heard, and they all looked out the window. It was Schagerström's traveling carriage, stopping at the door.

'May I request of you, good Pastor and of your wife, that you send my thanks to Miss Löwensköld for the answer she has given me. A long-planned journey compels me to be absent for the coming weeks. The moment I return, I hope that she will allow me to make the arrangements for the reading of the banns and for our marriage.'

THE STERN SERMON

'Gina my dear,' the old pastor said, 'I cannot understand Charlotte. I must ask her for an explanation.'

'You're quite right, of course, to do so,' his wife hastened to reply. 'Would you like me to call her in at once?'

Schagerström had left, and Karl-Artur had gone out to his own rooms. The older couple were alone in the pastor's inner room. If they wanted to hold a little interrogation of Charlotte, it was a very appropriate opportunity.

'One day she refuses Schagerström, the next she gratefully accepts his proposal,' the pastor said. 'Have you ever heard such inconstancy? I must really give her a good dressing-down.'

'She never has paid any attention to what people said about her,' his wife replied, 'but this time she's gone much too far.'

She was about to pull the beaded bell pull, but stopped herself suddenly. As she passed her husband she noticed his face. While those five little lines in his forehead were still bright as burning coal, the rest of his face was ashen.

'You know,' she said to him, 'you may not be quite well enough prepared to talk with Charlotte at once. She isn't the easiest person to bring to reason. What about waiting until this afternoon, to give yourself time to think out some really striking comments?'

There was no question but that the elderly woman felt that her lady's companion deserved to be taken down a peg or two, but her husband was clearly fatigued after his long journey and all the commotion. It would not be good for him to have another upsetting conversation right away.

Just then the maid came in and announced that dinner was

served. This gave them another reason to postpone taking Charlotte to task.

Dinner was eaten in oppressive silence. None of the four people around the table had much appetite, or any desire to converse. The platters and serving bowls were carried out almost as full as they had been carried in. The foursome was simply sitting at the table because that was the way it had to be.

When the meal was over and Charlotte and Karl-Artur had gone their separate ways, the pastor's wife insisted that her husband should not miss his afternoon nap because of Charlotte. There was certainly no hurry about giving Charlotte her comeuppance. She was at home. He would be able to talk with her whenever he chose.

Presumably the pastor was not particularly difficult to persuade. Still, it might have been better if he had gone to battle at once, because the moment he awoke from his afternoon nap there was a couple to marry, who insisted that the ceremony be conducted by the pastor himself. Thus passed the time before afternoon coffee, and the moment they finished their coffee the bailiff stopped in for a game of backgammon. The two elderly men sat all evening, thumping their checkers until bedtime, and thus the day came to an end.

But postponement is not neglect. On Wednesday the pastor was looking very chipper. Now there was no reason for him not to take Charlotte to task.

Alas, though, at mid-morning the pastor's wife discovered her husband weeding one of the vegetable patches, where the thistles were getting the upper hand. She hurried out to him.

'Yes, I know you think I ought to have a word with Charlotte,' he said the moment she came into sight. 'It's uppermost in my mind. I'm going to give her a lecture she'll never forget. I just came out into the garden to get my thoughts in order.'

The pastor's wife went back to the kitchen with a little sigh. She had her hands full. It was late July, time to salt down the spinach, dry the peas, and make jam or cordial from the raspberries.

'Oh my,' she thought, 'he's taking too much trouble over the matter. He's putting together a proper sermon. But that's the way they are, men of the cloth. They waste far too much eloquence on us poor sinners.'

It is understandable that, in spite of all her work, she was also keeping an eye on Charlotte, so that she would not undertake anything unseemly. But really there was no need to monitor her. On the Monday, long before Schagerström had come to the parsonage and caused all the commotion, Charlotte had started cutting rags into strips with which to weave a rug. She and the pastor's wife had gone up to the attic to find clothes no one wore any more that could be cut up, and they carried them down to the scullery, along with various other disused garments. The scullery was the place where they always did messy work that couldn't be done in the finer, more frequently dusted rooms. So Charlotte spent all Tuesday afternoon and the whole of Wednesday just sitting there, cutting and cutting. She took no breaks, and never left the room. One might even say she had sentenced herself to voluntary house arrest.

'I'll just leave her be,' thought the pastor's wife to herself. 'It's no better than she deserves.'

She also continued keeping an eye on her husband. He did not leave the vegetable patch, and he certainly did not send for Charlotte to come out. 'Forsius must be thinking out a sermon that's going to last for a couple of hours,' she thought. 'And though Charlotte certainly has behaved badly, I'm starting to think there will be good reason to feel sorry for her.'

In any case, nothing came of the matter before the midday meal. The meal was served, and the afternoon nap was followed by the usual afternoon coffee and backgammon. The pastor's wife decided not to fuss about the matter any more. She was just sorry not to have given her husband his way the previous day, when he was still angry and could have been straightforward about it.

But that night, when they were lying side by side in their big, wide bed, the pastor tried to explain why he was taking so long.

'You know, giving Charlotte a stern lecture isn't an easy matter,' he said. 'So many things come to mind.'

'Don't bother about the old errors of her ways!' his wife advised him. 'I imagine you're remembering the time she convinced the stable hand to agree that they ought to take your horses out for nocturnal rides, because she was worried about their getting too fat. But forget all those things! Just see to it that we find out for certain whether she was the one who enticed Karl-Artur to break off their engagement! That's the crux of the matter. You must know that people have already started speculating as to why we still have Charlotte under our roof.'

The pastor smiled gently.

'Indeed, she was only trying to do me a pure act of friendship that time, with those nightly rides. Which reminds me of the time she wanted to give me the pleasure of seeing that my horses could run just as fast as anyone else's, so she arranged a horserace.'

'Truly, we've had our trials and tribulations with that young woman,' his wife sighed. 'But all those old transgressions are forgotten and forgiven.'

'Indeed, indeed,' the pastor allowed, 'but there are a couple of other things I cannot get out of my mind. Do you remember what it was like here seven years ago when Charlotte had lost both her parents and we had no choice but to take her in? Gina, my love, in those days you didn't look like you look now. You might have been eighty already. You were so weak you couldn't walk without shuffling your feet. Every single day, I feared I might lose you.'

His wife knew right away what he was referring to. The day she turned sixty-five she had said to herself that she had been doing the household drudgery for long enough, and she hired a housekeeper. She got hold of an excellent woman, and no longer had to do any chores at all, in fact the housekeeper preferred her not to even come into her kitchen. But what happened was that the health of the pastor's wife had quickly begun to decline, she began to feel tired and weak and peculiarly downhearted and unhappy. People really began to fear that her days were numbered.

'It's true,' she said, 'I wasn't very well when Charlotte came to us, in spite of the fact that I had never had as easy a time of it as then. But Charlotte and my housekeeper never saw eye to eye. Charlotte told her off, just at the time of year when all the Christmas preparations have to be made, in fact on the very day of Saint Lucia, and the housekeeper up and left and I, sick and miserable, had to go out to the washhouse and soak the stock fish for our Christmas dinner. You're right, I shall never forget it.'

'No, I certainly hope not,' the pastor laughed. 'Gina, my love, you're nothing but an old workhorse. Your health was restored the moment you were able to get back to soaking fish and brewing holiday beer. Charlotte has always been forward and difficult, I admit it freely, but that telling off saved your life.'

'Well, and what about you then?' the old woman interjected, not wanting to hear any more about how much she supposedly enjoyed heavy chores and couldn't live without them. 'Yes, what about you? I think you'd also be dead and buried by now if Charlotte hadn't fallen out of the church pew.'

Her husband knew right away what she was referring to. When Charlotte came to the parsonage he was still doing all the church administration and curing of souls, as well as preaching every Sunday. His wife had been nagging at him to take on a curate to assist him in his duties. She had seen how he was wearing himself out, and how at the same time he was never really content, because there was no time for him to devote to his beloved botany. But he had said he intended to go on doing his duties for as long as there was a spark of life left in him. Charlotte did not nag, but she saw to it to fall asleep one Sunday right in the middle of the sermon. In fact, she slept so deeply that she fell out of the pew, which made a great stir in the congregation. Of course the pastor had been furious, but the unpleasant experience had made him realize he was too old to go on preaching. He had arranged for a curate, after which he was spared many of the tasks he had found dull, and became a new man.

'You're right,' he said. 'That mischief of hers added a number of good years to my life. That's precisely the thing that keeps coming back to me now that I need to give her a dressing down, and it's keeping me from getting anywhere with this stern lecture of mine.'

His wife said nothing, but covertly wiped a tear from the corner of her eye.

At the same time, she knew that it was not possible to allow Charlotte to get away without a reprimand this time, so she brought the subject up again.

'Yes, you may be absolutely right about all that, but you can't possibly mean that you do not intend to find out whether it was Charlotte who terminated the engagement?'

'When one does not see the way forward clearly, the best thing is to stand still and wait,' her husband answered. 'I think that's what we ought to do this time, both of us.'

'You cannot bear responsibility for letting Schagerström marry Charlotte if she is the kind of woman people are saying she is.'

'If Schagerström were to come and ask me,' said the pastor, 'I know what I would tell him.'

'And what would that be?'

'I'd tell him that if I were only fifty years younger and a bachelor...'

'What?' his wife exclaimed, sitting right up in bed.

'Yes, I'd tell him,' the pastor went on calmly, 'that if I were fifty years younger and a bachelor and caught sight of a girl like Charlotte, so vivacious and sprightly and with something special about her, something no one else has, well, then I would propose to her myself.'

'Aha!' his old wife cried out, 'you and Charlotte! Oh, she'd be a fine match for you, she would.'

She gesticulated, made a face, and leaned back on the pillow, laughing heartily.

The old man gave her a slightly indignant look, but she just went on laughing. And soon he was laughing too. They fell to such paroxysms it was long past midnight before they were able to get to sleep.

THE CUT TRESSES

Quite late on Thursday evening Beate Ekenstedt, the colonel's wife, arrived at the parsonage in her large traveling carriage. She had the coachman stop at the front steps, but she did not disembark. Instead, she told the housemaid, who had rushed out to assist her, that she should ask her mistress to take the trouble of coming out. She only had a few words to say to her.

Regina Forsius, the pastor's wife, came immediately, curtseying and smiling from ear to ear. What a great pleasure, what a lovely surprise. Would not dear Beate step down from her carriage and come inside and rest up in their humble abode after her long journey?

Yes, of course, the colonel's wife would be delighted, but not until she could be sure that that horrible woman was no longer in the house.

The pastor's wife looked extremely bewildered.

'If you mean that inferior kitchen maid I had the last time you were here, she moved out ages ago. This time you'll find the food more to your liking.'

But the colonel's wife just continued to sit in her carriage.

'I'll not have you dissembling to me, Gina! You know perfectly well I am talking about that nasty piece of work to whom Karl-Artur was so long engaged. I want to know if she is still under your roof.'

No room for ambiguity remained. But whatever the pastor's wife might have been feeling about Charlotte deep down, she was certainly prepared to defend any member of her household against the rest of humanity.

'I beg your pardon, Beate, but we cannot cast out the young

woman who has been like a daughter to Pastor Forsius and me for seven long years just like that. Not to mention the fact that no one knows how the whole story fits together.'

'I have received letters from my son, from Thea Sundler and from the young woman herself,' said the colonel's wife. 'To my mind the matter is perfectly clear.'

'If you have received a letter from her personally admitting to her guilt, you had blasted well not think I would let you leave here without showing it to me,' said the pastor's wife with such amazement and eagerness that she allowed an expletive to cross her lips.

She approached the petite, unyielding colonel's wife, who pulled back into the carriage. The pastor's wife looked ready to lift her out of her conveyance by brute force.

'Drive on, won't you? Drive on!' the colonel's wife shouted to her coachman.

At that very moment, Karl-Artur came out of the side building where his rooms were. He had recognized his mother's voice and hurried right over to the main parsonage building.

What followed was the most loving reunion. The colonel's wife threw her arms around her son, kissing him with such intensity and emotion one would have thought he had recently escaped mortal danger.

'Dear Mama, do step out of the carriage,' he said, somewhat embarrassed about all the kissing witnessed by the coachman, the local driver, the housemaid and the pastor's wife.

'I shan't,' she replied. 'For this whole journey I have been telling myself that I cannot possibly sleep under the same roof as that woman who has betrayed you so shamelessly. You get in with me, instead, and we shall go to the inn.'

'Come now, Beate, don't be childish!' said the pastor's wife, who had had a few minutes to pull herself together. 'If only you'll stay I promise you'll not have to so much as catch a glimpse of Charlotte.'

'That doesn't matter. I shall sense her presence.'

'People have quite enough to gossip about already,' said the pastor's wife. 'Do you really want to give them more grist for their mill, letting them say you refused to stay with us?'

'Mama, of course you must stay here,' determined Karl-Artur. 'I see Charlotte every day, and it doesn't bother me in the least.'

Hearing Karl-Artur sound so sure of himself, the colonel's wife looked around, as if seeking a way out. At last she pointed to the side building where her son had his rooms.

'Might I stay down there, at Karl-Artur's?' she asked. 'If I knew he was in the next room, I might not think about that horrid woman. Regina dear, if you really want me to stay here,' she said, turning to the pastor's wife, 'let me stay in the same building as my son! You need make no special arrangements. All I require is a bed, nothing more.'

'Well, I really can't see why you won't stay in the ordinary guest room,' complained the pastor's wife, 'but anything at all would be better than to see you go off!'

In truth, she was quite annoyed. While the traveling carriage drove across to the side building, she mumbled to herself that Beate Ekenstedt, however fine she made herself out to be, honestly lacked for good breeding.

Going back into the dining room she found Charlotte standing at an open window. Clearly, she had heard the entire altercation.

'Well, then, I suppose you heard that she doesn't want to see you,' said the pastor's wife. 'She even refused to sleep under the same roof as you.'

But Charlotte, who had never been so happy as just now, witnessing the loving reunion of mother and son, stood there content, with a little smile on her lips. Now she was certain her sacrifice had not been for naught.

'I'll just have to stay out of sight, then,' she said as calmly as could be, slipping out of the room.

The pastor's wife felt as if she were going to choke. She had to find her husband.

'What do you say about this? It must mean that Karl-Artur and the organist's wife were right after all. She hears Beate Ekenstedt say she refused to sleep under the same roof as her, and just gives me a little smile, looking as pleased as if she had been crowned Queen of Spain.'

'Now, now my love,' the pastor said, 'be calm for a little while still! The mist begins to disperse. I am certain the colonel's wife will help bring our uncertainty to an end.'

Mrs. Forsius feared that her dear husband the pastor was entering his second childhood; until now he had remained, by the grace of God, of sound mind. That madwoman Beate Ekenstedt? How could she help them?

Her husband's comment had merely served to feed her disgruntlement. She went out to the kitchen and instructed them to make up a bed for the colonel's wife in the side building. She also had a tray of food sent over, after which she went up to her bedroom.

'I suppose it's best to have her meals sent across,' she thought. 'Just let her sit there cuddling up with her son to her heart's content. I thought she'd come here to give him a dressing-down about his new engagement, but she just kisses and spoils him. If she imagines anything will ever become of him that way….'

The next morning the colonel's wife and Karl-Artur both appeared at the breakfast table. The former was in fine fettle, and entertained her hosts most politely. But still, when Mrs. Forsius saw Beate Ekenstedt in broad daylight, she could see that she was nothing but a pale shadow of her former self. In spite of being many years her senior, the pastor's wife felt full of vigor and strength in comparison with her friend. 'I suppose she is having a difficult time,' she thought to herself, 'and is not nearly as happy as she pretends to be.'

When breakfast was over, the colonel's wife sent Karl-Artur to the village to collect Thea Sundler, with whom she wished to speak. The pastor went into his rooms to work, as usual, and the two women were left alone.

The colonel's wife immediately began talking about her son.

'Ah, my dear Gina,' she said, 'I am happier than I can say. I left home the moment I received Karl-Artur's letter. I thought I would find him desperate, even contemplating suicide, but I have found him perfectly contented. Isn't that admirable? After such a shock…'

'Well, he did arrange immediate comfort for himself,' said the pastor's wife in her wryest tone.

'Oh, I know. That peddler girl from Dalarna. An insignificant little caprice. A sweet to put in your mouth to counteract a bad taste. How could a man of Karl-Artur's background ever put up with a person like that in the long run?'

'I've seen her,' said the pastor's wife, 'and I want you to know, Beate, that she is lovely, a really splendid specimen of the female race.'

The colonel's wife blanched, but only momentarily.

'The colonel and I are in agreement, and shall treat the entire matter *en bagatelle*. We will not refuse him our blessing. He has been cruelly deceived and was surely beside himself with grief. If we do not incite him further by resisting, he will soon forget that little plaything.'

That morning, for once, the pastor's wife knitted with such vigor that her knitting needles clattered. It was her only way of staying calm in the face of all this insanity. 'My dear friend,' she thought to herself, 'aren't you the woman everyone considers so wise and so gifted? And yet you cannot see that this whole scheme is totally doomed to fail.'

Her nostrils flared, the lines in her face began to live a life of their own, but at the same time she felt incomprehensibly compassionate with the colonel's wife, and that helped her to refrain from laughing aloud.

'Oh yes, I've understood that children nowadays cannot bear to be contradicted by their parents.'

'We've made mistakes about Karl-Artur in the past,' the colonel's wife went on. 'We objected to his becoming a man of the cloth. To no avail. The only thing that did was to make him a stranger to us. This time we do not intend to object to his betrothal to the peddler girl from Dalarna. We have no desire to lose him altogether.'

The pastor's wife raised her eyebrows so high they nearly touched her hairline.

'I do declare. That is very loving, indescribably loving.'

The colonel's wife confided to her that it was to consult with Thea Sundler on these matters that she had sent for her. She seemed to be a wise person, and extremely devoted to Karl-Artur. He had the greatest respect for her judgment.

Mrs. Forsius could barely contain herself. Thea Sundler, the organist's wife! That trifling little fool, and Madame Ekenstedt, the colonel's wife, a very prominent woman despite all her peculiarities! She didn't dare speak a word of sense to her own son. She intended to leave it to someone else, to the organist's wife!

'Well, no one bothered about the finer points like that in my day,' she replied.

'Thea Sundler wrote me such an excellent and reassuring letter after the engagement was broken off,' the colonel's wife explained.

At the mention of the word letter, the pastor's wife flew up, one hand to her brow.

'How lucky I remembered. Would you be so kind as to tell me what Charlotte wrote to you about that unfortunate development?'

'You shall read the entire letter,' said the colonel's wife. 'I have it right here in my needlework bag.'

She passed a folded letter to the pastor's wife, who proceeded to unfold it. It contained these words, and these words alone: 'My esteemed lady, may you not think all too ill of me.'

The pastor's wife returned the letter, looking crestfallen.

'Well, that didn't make me any the wiser.'

'It had a completely convincing effect on me,' the colonel's wife said emphatically.

It struck the pastor's wife that her visitor had been speaking unusually loudly the entire time. That was unlike her, but perhaps it had to do with her being upset, and somewhat out of kilter. At the same time, though, it occurred to her that if Charlotte was still sitting out in the scullery cutting those rags into strips, she must have heard every word. The scullery hatch was far from soundproof. Many were the times she had

143

complained that every sound the staff made out there could be heard in the dining room.

'What does Charlotte herself have to say?' asked the colonel's wife.

'She has said nothing at all. Pastor Forsius had decided to interrogate her, but now he maintains that there is no need. I don't understand.'

'How extraordinary!' exclaimed the colonel's wife. 'How extraordinary!'

The pastor's wife took the opportunity to suggest that they retire upstairs, apologizing for not having thought of it earlier. Such a distinguished visitor should surely not be sitting in the dining room as if she were just anyone.

The colonel's wife, however, had no desire at all to be cooped up in the upstairs rooms, which were admittedly far less pleasant than the ones they used on an everyday basis. She preferred to go on sitting in the dining room, and she continued to speak of Charlotte in the same loud voice. What was she doing to keep busy, she wondered. Where was she doing her work? Did she look happy at the prospect of marrying Schagerström?

Suddenly the colonel's wife had tears in her voice.

'I did really love her dearly,' she said. 'This was the last thing I would ever have expected of her. The very last thing.'

The pastor's wife heard a pair of scissors clank to the scullery floor. 'She can't possibly go on sitting there listening to all this any longer,' she thought, 'without rushing in here to defend herself.'

But there were no further sounds. Charlotte did not come in.

This awkward situation was finally resolved by the return of Karl-Artur from the village, accompanied by Thea Sundler. Right away, the colonel's wife went out into the garden with her son and Mrs. Sundler, and the pastor's wife hurried out into the kitchen to cut some sugar from the block, arrange a plate of cookies and grind some coffee beans. There was no need for her to do any of that herself, but it calmed her nerves.

In the kitchen she puzzled over the short note Charlotte had sent to her presumptive mother-in-law. Why had she been so brief? She recalled Charlotte's having come down to breakfast one day with ink on her fingers. Surely she had not needed to get herself so inky just to write that single line to the colonel's wife? She must have written another letter as well. And hadn't that been Tuesday? The day after the first time Schagerström had proposed to her. This was a matter she would have to look into.

In the meantime she sent the housemaid to lay the table in the large lilac bower for coffee. They would serve mid-morning coffee today since they had such an eminent visitor.

'Charlotte must have written a long letter,' the pastor's wife thought. 'What did she do with it? Did she post it? Or tear it up?'

She went on mulling this over while they had their coffee and, in contrast to her usual behaviour, she did not speak at all. Mrs. Sundler was there, though, and was anything but silent, jabbering the entire time. To the pastor's wife she resembled the toad in the fable, the one who puffed himself up to the bursting point. That was how self-important and arrogant she had become, now that finer folk were wanting her help. In the past the elderly woman had simply found her ridiculous, but now she began to actively dislike her. 'She's swaggering and feeling so pleased, while all the rest of us are worried and miserable,' she said to herself. 'She's no good, that woman.'

But naturally she poured coffee for her and offered her more, curtseyed and fussed and insisted she taste all her best baking. The laws of hospitality had to be obeyed, even in relation to one's worst enemy if that person happened to be visiting one's home.

After coffee the pastor's wife excused herself and went back out to the kitchen. The colonel's wife was supposed to leave around two, and before that she planned to serve her a midday dinner. This was an important occasion, and she wanted to supervise the kitchen herself.

When one o'clock arrived, Mrs. Sundler came into the kitchen to say goodbye. The others were still out in the arbor, but she needed to go home to prepare her husband's dinner.

The pastor's wife, leaning over the stockpot, put down the slotted spoon with which she was skimming and accompanied her out to the vestibule, where she curtseyed, apologized and sent her greetings to the organist.

She thought Thea Sundler ought to realize that she was in a rush, but there she stood for an eternity, holding her hand and talking about how sorry she felt for the colonel's wife about this new betrothal.

Yes, the pastor's wife had to agree.

The organist's wife pressed her hand even harder, saying that she did not want to leave without asking how Charlotte was.

'Well,' said the pastor's wife. 'She's sitting right in there cutting rags to weave a rug. You can go in and ask her yourself!'

They were just outside the scullery, and with sudden determination the pastor's wife opened the door and pushed Mrs. Sundler over the doorsill.

'I imagine this was what she was hoping for,' she thought. 'Charlotte has never cared much for her, and now Thea wants to see her in her humiliation. What a toad! I hope Charlotte will give her the reception she deserves.'

'Ha ha ha,' she laughed to herself. 'I'd like to see their encounter.'

As quietly as she could, she tiptoed over to a different door, the one to the dining room. She opened it silently and an instant later was standing by the scullery hatch.

Opening it a crack gave her quite a good view of the little room where Charlotte sat, surrounded by dresses from the pasts of both Mrs. Forsius and a number of other pastors' wives. She was cutting all the green fabric into one pile, all the blue into another, and all that was bright or patterned into a third. The floor was full of piles of narrow strips, and there was also a crate full of strips she had already sewn together and rolled into balls. Clearly Charlotte had not been twiddling her thumbs.

She was sitting with her back to Thea Sundler, who stood in the doorway looking quite hesitant.

'Ah, that's as far as she's come,' thought the pastor's wife.

'This is off to a fine start. She's sure to have a grand time.'

She watched Thea Sundler compose a face both regretful and encouraging, and heard her say in the mild, pitying tone of voice one would use when speaking to the sick, or to prisoners or workhouse inmates:

'Good day, Charlotte.'

Charlotte did not reply. She sat there, scissors in hand, but not cutting anything.

A little sneer passed over Thea Sundler's face. She bared her sharp teeth. It only lasted a moment but that was quite sufficient. Now the pastor's wife knew where she had her.

An instant later Thea Sundler was mild and pitying once more. She took one step into the room and said, in the kind, cheerful tone of voice one would use when talking to ignorant servants or mischievous children:

'Good day, Charlotte.'

Still Charlotte did not move.

So Thea Sundler leaned over her to see her face. Perhaps she thought Charlotte was sitting there weeping because Karl-Artur's mother did not want to see her. As she did so, a few locks of Mrs. Sundler's hair brushed Charlotte's shoulder, which was bare because the shawl she usually wore had slid down while she was working.

At the very second those locks brushed her shoulder, Charlotte came to life. Quick as a bird of prey, she grabbed a whole handful of those well-groomed tresses, raised the scissors that were open in her hand, and cut them off.

It was not a premeditated act. When it was done she stood up, looking a bit baffled. The other woman was screaming at the top of her lungs with horror and outrage. It was the worst thing that could have happened to her. Her hair was her pride and joy. Those tresses were the only things of beauty she possessed. She would not be able to show herself in public until they grew out again. She gave another wail of sorrow and wrath.

In the kitchen, although it was right alongside, there was such a commotion of boiling pots, crackling wood and banging pestles that no one heard a thing. The colonel's wife and her son were still out in the yard and must not have heard either. No one came to her aid.

'Well, gracious me, what on earth did you come in here for?' Charlotte asked. 'I'm not saying anything, for Karl-Artur's sake, but you can hardly believe that I am such a fool as not to know that you are the one who has brought all this upon us.'

With those words she walked over to the door and threw it open.

'Go now,' she said.

At once she chopped at the air with the scissors, which was all that was needed to make Thea Sundler dash right out.

The pastor's wife shut the hatch carefully. Then she clapped her hands and laughed.

'Good Lord above,' she said, 'that was a sight for sore eyes! Now my dear husband will also have something to laugh about.'

Suddenly she grew serious.

'Bless that child,' she mumbled. 'She has just been sitting there letting all of us think the worst of her. We're going to have to bring this to a close once and for all now.'

Moments later the pastor's wife was tiptoeing up the stairs. Quiet as a thief, she made her way along the hall to Charlotte's room at the eastern end under the gable.

Barely taking the time to look around the room, she went straight over to the tiled stove, inside which she found some torn and crumpled sheets of paper.

'May God forgive me this!' she said. 'He knows this is the first time in my life I am reading anyone else's letter without permission.'

She took the closely written pages along to her bedroom, located her spectacles, and read.

'I see, I see,' she said when she had finished. 'This was the real letter, just as I thought.'

Letter in hand, she went back down the stairs, intending to present it to the colonel's wife. But once out in the yard, she saw her guest sitting with her son on a bench outside the building where his rooms were. How gently she laid her head on his shoulder! What devotion and adoration there was in the way she looked up to him!

The pastor's wife held back. 'How in the world could I possibly read this to her?' she asked herself.

Changing course, she went in to see Pastor Forsius instead.

'I've brought you some pleasant reading, my dear,' she said, spreading the letter out before him. 'I found it in Charlotte's tiled stove. She had put it there to burn, but neglected to light it. Just read! You won't regret it.'

The pastor could see that his wife's face now wore a completely different expression from the one she had had for these last few dreadful days. He assumed she meant that reading the letter might cheer him up as well.

'Yes,' he said when he'd finished reading. 'Of course that's what happened. But why didn't she post this letter?'

'I wish I knew the answer myself!' his wife replied. 'All I can say is that I brought it down to show Beate but, you know, when I came out onto the front steps and saw her sitting there giving her son such a worshipping look, I thought I'd show it to you first.'

The pastor stood up and looked out the window, over to where the colonel's wife sat.

'That's it,' he said, nodding. 'Gina, my love, Charlotte found it impossible to send that letter to such a mother. That's why she threw it into the stove. She just couldn't defend herself. Nor can we intervene in their affairs.'

They sighed with the hopelessness of their inability to immediately clear Charlotte's good name in the eyes of the world, and yet deep down they felt a powerful sense of relief. When they sat down to dine with their guest, they were in the best possible mood.

Strangely, the colonel's wife, too, seemed to have undergone some kind of catharsis. There was no longer any strain to her gaiety, as there had been at breakfast time. She looked like a woman who had been given a new lease on life.

The pastor's wife wondered if it was Thea Sundler who had

brought about the change. And indeed it was, though not quite in the way she imagined.

The colonel's wife had been sitting with Karl-Artur on the bench outside the building where he had his rooms when Mrs. Sundler came rushing out of the main house, flying like a dove that had been in the claws of a hawk.

'What on earth can be wrong with your friend Thea?' the colonel's wife asked her son. 'Look at her running with one hand to her cheek. Goodness, Karl-Artur, do run and intercept her at the gate. Could there be a swarm of bees chasing her? You must see if she needs some help!'

Karl-Artur hurried to fulfill his mother's request, and although Mrs. Sundler signaled desperately to him to keep his distance, he caught up with her at the gate.

When he returned to his mother, he had a most indignant look on his face.

'Charlotte's been at it again. She's really terribly inconsiderate. Imagine, Mrs. Sundler went to see her to ask how she was, and Charlotte took the opportunity to chop off several locks of her hair all the way up at the ear.'

'You don't say?' his mother cried, an impish grin crossing her face. 'Mrs. Sundler's lovely tresses! She must look a fright.'

'It was revenge, Mama,' said Karl-Artur. 'Mrs. Sundler knows what Charlotte has been up to. She was the one who opened my eyes.'

'I see,' said the colonel's wife.

She sat still for a moment, musing thoughtfully. Then she turned to her son.

'Let us speak no more of Thea or Charlotte, Karl-Artur. We have so few minutes before my departure. Let us talk about you and your plans to help us poor sinners!' – – –

And thus, a little while later at the table, the colonel's wife was cheerful and amusing, the way she was known to be. She and the pastor's wife rivaled each other in wittiness and in jests.

Every now and then the colonel's wife glanced toward the hatch. She must have been wondering how Charlotte was feeling, all alone in the scullery. She must have been wondering whether that young woman, who had always been so devoted and loving toward her, was longing to see her.

After the meal, when the traveling carriage was already waiting at the door, the colonel's wife found herself, by chance, alone in the dining room. It did not take her a moment to walk over to the hatch and open it wide. Before her stood Charlotte, who had been sick with longing all day; she was standing there in the hope of at least seeing the beautiful eyes of the woman about whom she cared so deeply.

Quick as lightning, the colonel's wife took Charlotte's face between her gentle hands, pulled it to her, and kissed it over and over. Between kisses she whispered a few short sentences.

'My darling, can you manage to stay silent for a few more days, or even a few more weeks? It will all work out. Have I caused you great pain? But I wasn't sure what to think until you chopped off her locks. Colonel Ekenstedt and I will take the matter in hand. Can you keep it up, for Karl-Artur's and my sake? He will be yours again, my child. He will be yours.'

Someone was opening the door. The hatch flew closed, and a few moments later Beate Ekenstedt was sitting in her traveling carriage.

CHILD OF GOOD FORTUNE

Wealthy Schagerström knew perfectly well that he would never have become anything but a boor and a scoundrel had he not been accompanied, throughout his youth, by extraordinary good fortune.

He, the son of well-to-do and distinguished parents, could have grown up very comfortably in the lap of luxury. He could have slept every night in a soft bed, been given fine clothing and fed plentiful, well-prepared meals, just as his siblings had. But he would never have been able to stand it. Not with his inborn inclinations. And he knew that better than anyone.

He had had the very good fortune to be plain and ungainly. His parents, particularly his mother, found it impossible to take to him. They could not imagine how they had come to be saddled with this child, who had such a big head, short neck and stocky body. The two of them were handsome, elegant people, and all their other children were lovely as angels. It seemed to them that this Gustav of theirs must be a changeling, and they treated him accordingly.

It could not have been much fun to be the one who always got the blame. Schagerström was the first to admit that he had been bitter many a time, but as soon as he reached maturity, he began to see the whole situation as a real blessing. If he had heard his mother say, every single day, how much she loved him, and if, like his brothers, he had had pockets full of money, he would have been lost. Not that he considered his siblings anything but kind, decent people. Perhaps they had been made of stronger stuff from the very outset, and been able to cope with good fortune. But he would never have found it to his liking.

The fact that he had so much trouble with Latin and failed year after year was also, needless to say, something for which he thanked Lady Luck. Well, perhaps not while it was happening, but afterwards. It was the thing that caused his father to take him out of school and send him to Värmland as an apprentice at an iron foundry.

Once he was there, his good fortune again served him well, and saw to it that he found himself in the hands of a tough, mean supervisor, who was able to give him the upbringing he needed, far better than his own parents. Under that man's tutelage he certainly didn't sleep on a feather bed. He was lucky if there was a thin straw mattress on top of the wooden slats. Under that man's tutelage he learned to eat gruel even if it was burnt, and herring even if it was rancid. Under that man's tutelage he learned to work from morning to night without pay, but secure in the knowledge that he had to be prepared for a couple of sharp strokes of the rod if he neglected the slightest duty. None of this, of course, was much fun while it was happening, but wealthy Schagerström knew that he could never be sufficiently grateful to the fate that had taught him to sleep on straw and live on poor man's fare.

When he had been apprenticed at the foundry for quite a few years, he was transferred to another foundry, Kronbäcken near Filipstad, where he became an accountant. This foundry was owned by an ironmaster named Fröberg. In him, Schagerström found a kind master, and at Kronbäcken he was able to eat his fill of good food at the table with the gentry. He also received some wages, with which he was soon able to buy himself some proper clothing. Suddenly things were fine and life was pleasant. That might not have been very good for him in the long run, but he never had the opportunity to feel spoilt, because his old, good fortune was still with him.

He had not been a month at Kronbäcken before he fell in love with a young woman who was the ward and foster daughter of ironmaster Fröberg. This was the worst thing that could have happened, since the young woman was not only extraordinarily beautiful and talented and well-liked; she also stood to inherit foundries and mines worth millions. It would have been presumptuous for any accountant to so much as look her way, and it was all the more so for one whose appearance was unpleasing and ungainly, who had been the object of abomination of his family and never had any help, but who had had to make his way all on his own. Schagerström realized from the very outset that he had no choice but to stay in the background and give no one any reason to guess he was in love with her. All he could do was sit watching when the young lieutenants and university students flocked to Kronbäcken each Christmas and each summer to court her. It was a matter of gritting his teeth and sitting on his hands as he listened to their bragging about dancing with her this and that many times in one and the same evening, about her giving them this and that many ball favors or this and that many kind gazes and smiles.

He did not get a great deal of pleasure out of his excellent position since it had brought unrequited love in its wake, a love that accompanied him to work during the week and to the hunt on Sundays. The only times he was more or less free from his emotional torment was when he sat reading about mines and the mining industry in the two huge volumes on the shelf in his office, which clearly no one had ever considered opening before him.

Ah well, although he realized later in life that his unrequited love had also been educative, he never really came to terms with it. It had been far too heavy a burden.

The young girl with whom he was enamored was neither kind nor unkind to him. Since he did not dance and never attempted to approach her in any other way, she never really had the opportunity to speak to him. But one summer evening there had been dancing in the large upstairs drawing room at Kronbäcken, and Schagerström had, as always, stood over by the door watching the woman he loved so dearly. Never would he forget how it had dismayed him when, in an interlude between dances, she walked over to him.

'Mr. Schagerström, I really think you ought to go to bed,' she informed him curtly. 'It's midnight, and you have to be at work at four o'clock. The rest of us can sleep until noon if we please.'

He slouched right off to the office, understanding perfectly well that she was tired of seeing him hang about by the door. She had spoken kindly and looked pleasant enough, but it would still never have crossed his mind that her comment could be interpreted as concern for him, or that she felt sorry for him tiring himself out for no good reason.

Another time they had been out fishing, she and a couple of her typically flirtatious suitors, with Schagerström as their oarsman. It was a hot day, and the boat was quite heavy, but he had nevertheless been happy, with her in the stern, facing him; he was able to gaze at her throughout.

When they returned home and had pulled up to the jetty and he was helping her out of the boat, she had thanked him for rowing in a very kind voice, but then added, as if she were afraid he might misunderstand her kindness:

'Mr. Schagerström, I find it difficult to understand why you do not enroll at the mining academy at Falun. The son of a director cannot possibly content himself with being no more than an accountant at a foundry.'

Of course she had noticed how he had been devouring her with his eyes as he rowed. She had realized how devoted he was to her, felt annoyed by it and wanted to be rid of him. To see her encouragement as proof that she took an interest in his future, that she had heard her guardian say that Schagerström had the potential to become a true expert in foundries and mining with the right schooling, and that she might actually have come up with her suggestion as a way of reducing the gap between herself and him, between the accountant and the foundry owner's daughter, no, that was far beyond his wildest imagination.

But because she wanted it, he wrote to his parents and asked for their help to enable him to attend the mining academy, and they acquiesced. He might have been happier to accept their money if his father had not written that he hoped his son would do better at this school than he had done at Klara, his upper form school in Stockholm, or if the letter had not made it so eminently clear that his parents did not really believe he could make anything more of himself than an accountant, even if he attended fifteen mining academies. But afterwards he had understood that it was really thanks to his old Lady Luck. She was still doing her best to make a man of him.

In any event, he could not deny that he got a great deal out of his time at the mining academy, that his teachers had been pleased with him, and that he had thrown himself into his studies with a kind of hunger. He might have been perfectly happy with his fate, if every free moment had not made him think about her, the woman back in Värmland, and all the men swarming around her.

When he finally completed the two-year course of studies, undeniably with highest honors, her guardian wrote to him and offered him the position of manager at the mine known as Gammalhyttan, which not only belonged to her but which was her largest and loveliest estate. It was a fine position, and far better than anything a young man of twenty-three could expect. Schagerström would have been thrilled, had he not realized that she was the person behind the offer. He was careful not to imagine that she had confidence in him and wanted to give him the opportunity to prove himself. No, the offer could only mean that she was tactfully trying to prevent his returning to Kronbäcken. It wasn't that she had anything against him, no, she did want to help him, but she couldn't bear the idea of his being nearby.

He would also have liked to satisfy her wishes and never show his face in her presence again, but before he took up his new post he had to stop in at Kronbäcken to receive his instructions. And upon his arrival he was told by Mr. Fröberg to go into the main house and ask for the ladies, as his ward had some instructions for him as well.

Thus he made his way to the little drawing room, to the right of the entrance hall, where the women of Kronbäcken usually sat with their needlework, and she approached him directly, with open arms, just as a woman goes to meet a man for whom she has been longing. And to his horror he saw that she was alone in the room. This was the first time in their lives the two of them had been alone together.

That made his heart throb in itself, and then the situation was exacerbated when, in her usual cheerful and straightforward way, she told him that Gammalhyttan, the foundry he was now going to manage, had a handsome manor house, so there was no reason for him not to begin considering marriage.

He was incapable of replying, because this caused him such great pain. It had not been enough for her to get rid of him from Kronbäcken, now she wanted him married off in the bargain. He did not feel he deserved this treatment. He had never been forward with her.

And she continued, as frankly as before:

'Gammalhyttan is the loveliest of my estates. I have always thought I would want to live there when I married.'

This would have been explicit enough for anyone else, but Schagerström had been sternly raised from earliest childhood, so he turned to leave the room.

She got to the door before him, and put her hand on the lock.

'I have refused many a suitor in my day,' she said, 'so perhaps it is only fair that I should be refused the one time I do the proposing.'

At that he put a hard hand on hers, to open the door.

'Do not tease me,' he said. 'I take your words seriously.'

'So do I,' she answered, looking him firmly in the eye.

And that was the moment at which Schagerström knew how much good fortune Lady Luck had always had in store for him. All the loneliness, all the cruel treatment, all the losses life had inflicted upon him until that time, had only been preparing him to take this superhuman bliss to heart, to penetrate his soul and expand there so that bliss and only bliss would fill that space.

THE LEGACY

When Schagerström lost his beloved wife after three years of marriage, it transpired that she had bequeathed everything she owned to her husband, should she die childless before him. When the estate inventory had been completed and a number of bequests to elderly servants and distant relatives had been paid, Schagerström inherited an enormous legacy.

At all the Schagerström mines and foundries, the employees heaved a collective sigh of relief when the process was complete. They were pleased that the estate was not being divided up, and it was truly a blessing to have a real expert in foundries and mining in charge of it all.

But shortly after Schagerström had come into his legacy the foundry managers, inspectors, leaseholders, forest rangers, yes everyone who had anything to say about the management of his properties, began to suspect that the new regime was not likely to be as satisfactory as they had anticipated. Schagerström stayed on in Stockholm, which was bad enough, but might have been all right if he had answered their letters. However, he almost consistently failed to do so. There was pig iron to be bought, iron ingots to be sold. There were contracts to be entered into concerning deliveries of coal and wood. Vacancies needed filling, buildings needed repairing, invoices needed paying. But from Schagerström came neither letters nor funds. Sometimes he acknowledged receipt of a letter and wrote that he would be in touch, but he never was.

After just a few weeks, chaos reigned. Some managers merely sat twiddling their thumbs, others took the liberty of making decisions on their own, which was almost worse.

Everyone was of the opinion that Schagerström was not the right man to keep the huge fortune under control.

The person who was most dissatisfied of all was probably Mr. Fröberg, the ironmaster at Kronbäcken. Schagerström had always held a special place in his estimation, and he expected great things of him. In his deep grief over the fact that the kind, radiant young woman who had grown up in the Fröberg home was no longer among the living, he had taken some comfort in the fact that her property, which had so long been under his management, all those munificent mines and the rapids that provided power for the mills, those lovely manor houses and enormous forests, those wealth-producing forges and foundries, had ended up in good hands.

He knew that Schagerström had been well prepared for his position as the owner of such a vast estate. For the first year of their marriage, Schagerström and his wife had made an extensive study tour abroad at the urging of his wife's guardian. From their letters he knew they had not frittered their time away at museums or historical sites. No, those two sensible souls had studied mining in Germany, factories in England and cattle breeding in Holland. They had been indefatigable. Schagerström had sometimes expressed regrets: 'We pass by the most beautiful spots,' he had written, 'without taking the time to visit them. We only think about gathering useful knowledge. Disa is the real driving force. I, poor soul, would be content just to live for our love.'

The last few years they had lived in Stockholm, where they had purchased a large house, furnished it splendidly, and been endlessly hospitable. This, again, was at the advice of her guardian. Schagerström was now a man of affairs and would be mixing with the highest-ranking individuals in the country, so he needed to gain experience of society, meet influential people, win the confidence of the powers that be.

It is easy to see how the Kronbäcken ironmaster, although he no longer had anything to do with Schagerström's business, would still have been extremely upset. He wanted very badly to speak with Schagerström, hear what was plaguing him, prevail upon him to take up his work again.

And so one day he summoned one of his accountants, a young man who had come to Kronbäcken around the same time as Schagerström, and who had been closer to him than anyone else. Everyone referred to him as 'good-natured Nyman.'

'I've been thinking, Nyman,' he said, 'that there must be something very wrong with Schagerström. And this explains, good-natured Nyman, why I have decided to send you to Stockholm forthwith, to bring him back. You may take my traveling carriage. And, Nyman, if you come back without him, you will find yourself without a job.'

Good-natured Nyman stood there perplexed. He would not have jeopardized his position at Kronbäcken for all the tea in China. He was basically a clever fellow but quite lazy, and he had managed to make himself indispensable to the ladies of the estate, so he almost never had to do any office work. The mistress's mother needed him for a game of whist, the young ladies wanted him to read aloud to them, draw patterns for them, accompany them out riding, and be their generally faithful escort. Good-natured Nyman was needed everywhere the minute any kind of entertainment was in the offing. He was indeed completely content with this existence, and had no desire for any of it to change.

Nyman the foundry accountant thus headed for Stockholm, to save both his own skin and Schagerström's. He travelled night and day, arriving around eight o'clock one morning. He took a room at an inn and, before doing anything else, arranged a team of horses for the return journey, after which he had a bite to eat and made his way to the Schagerström residence.

He rang the bell and informed the servant who opened that he needed a word with Schagerström. The servant answered immediately that he could not see Schagerström, because he was out.

The accountant left his name and asked him to tell his master that he had come on an important mission on behalf of ironmaster Fröberg. He would be back in an hour.

An hour later he returned to the Schagerström residence,

this time in Fröberg's traveling carriage drawn by a fresh team of horses, with the necessary provisions aboard, ready to depart for Värmland.

But in the vestibule the servant gave him a message from Schagerström, requesting the accountant to return later in the day. He had an important meeting to attend.

Nyman thought he heard a forced awkwardness in the man's voice. He began to fear he was prevaricating, and asked where that meeting was being held.

'The gentlemen have gathered here, in the main drawing room,' said the servant, and Nyman could see that there were indeed a number of hats and overcoats hanging in Schagerström's vestibule.

He immediately removed his own coat and hat, handing them to the servant.

'I suppose there's a room where I can sit and wait,' he said. 'I have no desire to wander the streets aimlessly. I travelled all night to arrive early.'

The servant did not look particularly inclined to let him in. Mr. Nyman, however, did not give up until he had been shown into a small study just beside the main drawing room.

A little while later, two gentlemen apparently on their way to the meeting passed through the study, accompanied by the servant, who opened the drawing room doors for them. Nyman the accountant took the opportunity to peek into the meeting room. He saw a large number of elderly gentlemen sitting around a large table covered with documents. He was also quite sure the documents were written on paper with official seals.

'What on earth can be going on?' he asked himself. 'Those certainly looked like purchase deeds and titles to property. Schagerström must be in the middle of some major transaction.'

A moment later he realized he had not seen Schagerström himself amongst the people around the table.

What could that mean? If Schagerström were not participating in the meeting, then he ought to be free to speak with him, Nyman.

Another gentleman passed through the office on his way to the meeting. Nyman recognized him as a young official he had met at Kronbäcken in the past, when that young man and others like him had come courting. He hurried to say a few words to him.

'Well if it's not good-n… I mean Mr. Nyman!' exclaimed the young official. How nice to see you here in Stockholm. How are things at Kronbäcken?'

'Ah, Sir, I would so appreciate if you could urge Mr. Schagerström to give me a moment of his time. I've travelled night and day on urgent business, and now he won't even see me.'

The official consulted his watch.

'I'm afraid, Nyman, that you'll have to have patience for a couple of hours, until we're finished in there.'

'Whatever are they doing?'

'I'm not sure I am at liberty to talk about it yet.'

The accountant thought about the very pleasant way of life he had made for himself at Kronbäcken as the jack-of-all-trades for the mistress of the house and her daughters, and he braved a wild guess.

'I know,' he said, 'that Schagerström intends to divest himself of all his property.'

'Aha, so the rumor has already reached the foundries,' said the official.

'Yes, but that's all we've heard. We don't know who the purchaser is.'

'Purchaser?' the young official exclaimed. 'There's no question of any purchaser. He's donating it all to religious foundations, to the Freemasons' orphanage and the Widows' Provident Fund and the like. But I must take my leave! I have been appointed to draw up the deeds of donation once the gentlemen in there have reached agreement on the terms and conditions.'

The accountant swallowed, and swallowed, like a fish tossed up on dry land. If he returned home with news to that effect, old Fröberg would be so furious that he, Nyman, would not be retained in his comfortable position even for a day. What was he to do? What could he come up with?

Just as the official was about to vanish through the open door, Nyman scurried over to him and tugged at his coat sleeve.

'Please, my good Sir, won't you be so kind as to tell Schagerström that I must have a word with him? Tell him it's urgent! Tell him Gammalhyttan's burned down.'

'Yes, of course. What a tragedy!'

A few seconds later there stood in the doorway a pale little man, highly emaciated and with bloodshot eyes.

'What is it?' Abrupt and gruff, he turned to accountant Nyman like a person who detests being disturbed.

The foundry accountant stood there swallowing again, unable to get his words out. Good heavens, so this was what Schagerström had come to. He had never been an elegant or handsome man, but there had always been something indescribably kind about him, as he went about his business at Kronbäcken, lovesick. Now Nyman felt almost intimidated by the man who had once been his friend.

'Did I hear correctly?' Schagerström continued. 'Has there been a fire at Gammalhyttan?'

The accountant had only intended to utilize that little white lie in order to gain access to Schagerström. Suddenly, though, he decided not to put his cards on the table for some time yet.

'Yes,' he replied, 'there's been a fire at Gammalhyttan.'

'What burned down? Was it the main house?'

The accountant looked sharply at Schagerström. His eyes were glazed, and his hair had begun to thin out at the temples.

'The main house won't do,' he thought to himself, 'the man needs a real shaking up.'

'Ah, no, if only it had been the main house,' he sighed.

'The forge?'

'No not the forge. It was that awful big building you had twenty families living in. Two of the women were trapped inside and died, and some hundred people have no roof over their heads. The people who were rescued came out stark naked, and have neither clothing nor shoes. Everything down there is in utter chaos they say. I haven't been down myself, having been sent here to fetch you.'

'The manager didn't write to me about it,' said Schagerström.

'There's no use writing to you. Börjesson let old man Fröberg know, so he could come and help, but the old man found the whole thing too much for him. You're going to have to straighten it out yourself.'

Schagerström went to the door and rang for the servant.

'I need to go to Värmland immediately,' he said. 'Tell Lundgren to ready my carriage.'

'If you'll allow me' said Mr. Nyman, 'I have ironmaster Fröberg's traveling carriage and a fresh team of horses outside the door. As soon as you are dressed for the journey, we can leave.'

Schagerström seemed about to do as he said, until suddenly he put his hand to his brow.

'My meeting!' he exclaimed. 'It's extremely important. I can't get away for another half hour.'

But Nyman did not intend to give him time enough to donate his property.

'Well, I suppose half an hour is neither here nor there,' he said, 'but for the people who have to sleep out of doors on the cold ground now, what with the autumn chill, it probably seems quite a long time.'

'Why are they sleeping out of doors on the cold ground?' Schagerström asked. 'The main house is still standing.'

'Börjesson didn't dare put them up in there without your permission.'

Schagerström was still hesitant.

'I can't help but wonder whether Disa Landberg would have stayed around to finish a meeting if she had received such news.'

Schagerström gave him an impatient look. He went into the drawing room and soon reemerged.

'I told them the meeting would have to be postponed for a week,' he said.

'Let us depart!'

It would be wrong to say that Nyman the accountant had a very pleasant journey back to Värmland in the company of Schagerström. What particularly disturbed him was that he had lied about the fire, and he would very much have preferred to admit this white lie to Schagerström if he had only dared.

'If I admit there was no fire, and no one burned to death or left homeless,' he thought to himself, 'he'll turn right around and go back to Stockholm. It's the only hold I've got on him.'

He wondered if there might not be a way of distracting Schagerström, and so he began to chatter, telling him all kinds of anecdotes about what had been going on at the foundries. He talked about the funny, apt comments the old workers had made, about the wily charcoal drivers who had deceived the inexperienced inspectors, about the rumors that huge ore finds had been made near Gammalhyttan, about an auction he'd attended where enormous parcels of forest land had gone under the gavel for a song.

He talked to save his life, as it were, but Schagerström, who must have found Nyman's efforts to awaken his interest in the foundries he owned a bit overt, interrupted him:

'I cannot retain my property. I am giving it all away. Disa would never believe I was mourning for her if I accepted that huge legacy.'

'You ought not accept it as a source of pleasure,' said Nyman, 'but as your cross to bear.'

'I do not have the strength for it,' Schagerström replied, with such desperation in his voice that the other man did not dare to continue.

The second day of the journey was the same. The foundry accountant had expected Schagerström to liven up once they had left the city behind and he was surrounded by farmland and forests, but no improvement was discernible. He was growing very worried about the man who had once been his friend.

'He won't be able to carry on like this for long,' he thought. 'As soon as he has divested himself of his legacy, he will lie down and die. He is quite beside himself with grief.' So it was really not just to rescue his own position but also to help his old friend that he once again tried to change his mind about the legacy.

'Just think of all the people whose efforts have gone into making that fortune!' he said. 'Do you think they did it just for their own sake? No, their intention, when it came to gathering so much power in one place, was to be able to accomplish great things, things that would benefit the entire province. And now you wish to divide it up and give it away. I call that unconscionable. I don't think you have the right to do it. I think you ought to shoulder your burden and manage what is yours.'

He was unable to see that his words had any effect at all, and still he pursued it bravely:

'Come join us in Värmland, and work. You are too good a man to spend your days amusing yourself in Stockholm in the winter and just coming down to the estates during the summer to idle about. No, come and manage your property! I assure you, it needs managing.'

He really admired his own eloquence, but once more Schagerström interrupted him:

'My my, listen to good-natured Nyman!' he said a bit mockingly.

The accountant felt his face go bright red.

'Well, I know I have no right to preach,' he said, 'but I don't have either a penny to my name or any prospects. I believe I have the right to make life as pleasant as I can for myself. But if I owned so much as an inch of land … I'd protect it to my last breath.'

They arrived on the morning of the third day, approaching the manor house at Gammalhyttan around six in the morning. The sun shone brightly on the bright yellow and red crowns of the trees. The sky was clear blue. The little lake at the foot of the estate was gleaming, shiny as a steel plate, under a light shroud of mist.

Not a soul came to greet them. While the coach driver headed behind the manor house to find the farmhand, the accountant took the opportunity to confess.

'There's no use talking to Börjesson about the fire!' he said. 'There was none. I just had to find a way of getting you to come along with me. Fröberg threatened to sack me if I came back without you.'

'But what about the people who died in the fire, and the ones who lost their homes?' asked Schagerström, who found it difficult to change the picture he had in his mind so rapidly.

'There never were any,' the foundry accountant allowed miserably. 'What was I to do? I had to lie so you wouldn't have the time to give away your property.'

Schagerström looked at him coldly and disinterestedly.

'I realize you meant well,' he said, 'but it was all quite useless. I shall travel back to Stockholm the moment a fresh team of horses can be readied.'

The foundry accountant sighed, but stayed silent. There was nothing to do. The game was up.

Just then, however, the coach driver returned.

'There's not a man on the entire estate,' he said. 'I met an old crone who claims the manager and all the foundry workers are out hunting elk. The beaters have been out since four this morning, and they got going so fast the stable boy didn't even have a chance to give the horses their morning fodder ration. I suppose you can hear them stamping, gentlemen.'

Indeed, a terrible noise could be heard from the stable, where the hungry animals were kicking up a real ruckus.

A very slight tinge of red came to Schagerström's cheeks.

'Would you be so kind as to feed them, please,' he instructed, giving the coachman a coin for his trouble.

He looked about the estate with newly awakened interest.

'There's no smoke coming from the foundry chimney,' he noted.

'That's right. The foundry's closed down for the first time in thirty years,' Mr. Nyman said. 'They ran out of ore. What was to be done? Börjesson goes off hunting, as you see, and all the staff with him. I sympathize.'

Schagerström's blush deepened a bit.

'Is the forge closed, too?'

'Surely. The smiths are the drivers on the hunt. But none of it has anything to do with you, does it? You're giving it all away.'

'You're right,' Schagerström yielded. 'It's got nothing to do with me.'

'No, it will be up to the fine gentlemen on the board of directors of the Freemasons' orphanage to deal with all this, not you,' the accountant confirmed.

'Right,' Schagerström replied again.

'Do you care to go inside?' Mr. Nyman asked, walking toward the manor house. 'Breakfast was served early today, to the hunters you know, so the mistress of the house and the serving maids will have gone back to bed after their early morning work.'

'There's no need to wake them,' said Schagerström. 'I'll be leaving directly.'

'I say,' Nyman suddenly shouted. 'Look! Look that way!'

A shot rang out. From over in the park an elk came running. It had been hit but not downed and was still trying to get away. One of its front legs hung lame, and the elk was dragging it, making awkward progress on the other three.

A moment later one of the hunters appeared through the park at full tilt. He aimed and felled the creature with a well-aimed shot. The bull elk dropped to the ground, moaning, right at Schagerström's feet.

The marksman approached slowly and somewhat hesitantly. He was a tall man with very erect posture.

'This is Captain Hammarberg,' Nyman told Schagerström.

Schagerström raised his eyes and looked sharply at the tall hunter. He recognized him at once as that fair-haired, reddish-complexioned officer who had such a remarkable way with the women. They were all attracted to him in spite of knowing that he was a scoundrel and a blackguard, one might say. He would never forget how that man had tried to win the affections of Disa Landberg when she was still a young girl, how he had more or less bewitched her, how she had allowed him to walk out with her, to go riding with her, to dance with her.

'The wretch, how does he have the temerity to turn up

here?' he muttered.

'Well, I don't think you can do much to prevent it,' replied Mr. Nyman in an anything but good-natured tone of voice.

Memories stormed in over Schagerström. That captain, who had probably intuited how he felt about the heiress, had tortured and ridiculed him, boasting about his feats in front of him, as if to make Schagerström feel doubly bitter that Disa Landberg was likely to have a husband like Hammarberg. He gritted his teeth and looked more and more grim.

'Get over here, damn you, and put the poor beast out of its misery!' he called to the captain, turning his back on him to walk to the manor house and pound at the door.

Börjesson, the estate manager, and the other hunters had now come through the park as well. Recognizing Schagerström, Börjesson hurried toward the front steps to greet him.

Schagerström gave him a withering look.

'I shall not even mention the other things,' said Schagerström. 'Not a word about the foundry being down, or even the forge, not a word about the horses in the stable not being fed. Those things may be just as much my fault as yours, Sir. But allowing Hammarberg, that villain, to hunt on my land, was not my decision. And you, Sir, may consider yourself sacked.'

With those words, Schagerström once again took charge of his estates, and it was a very long time before he ever again considered letting them go.

THE MAIL COACH

I.

When Schagerström left Korskyrka parsonage after proposing for the second time, he had no desire at all to burst out laughing. The previous day he had left elated, believing he had met a proud, unselfish person. Now that Charlotte Löwensköld had proven to be low and calculating, however, he felt deeply dejected.

His downheartedness was so grave he began to realize the young woman had made a greater impression on him than he had imagined.

'Well I'll be damned,' he thought to himself. 'If she had passed the test I'm afraid I might really have fallen in love with her.'

There was no question of that, though, now that she had exposed her real character. True, he would have to marry her, but he knew himself. A woman who was scheming, unreliable and money-grubbing he could never love.

That day Schagerström was traveling in the little covered carriage he always used for long journeys. At once he drew down the leather shades over the carriage windows. It plagued him to see the eternal sunshine and the fields with their swelling crops.

But when he had nothing else to look at, in the dimness of the carriage, a charming sight came back to him time after time. He saw Charlotte as she looked when she gazed in through the doorway at young Ekenstedt. If love had ever radiated from a face, it was from hers.

As this image continued to haunt him, the young foundry owner felt his ire rise.

'You can go to hell! There you stood, with that angelic expression on your face, and then just ten minutes later you still went and accepted wealthy Schagerström's proposal.'

As one can well imagine, his downheartedness grew, the longer his journey lasted. He was seized by the most horrible contempt for himself, thinking about how badly he had bungled the whole affair. What he'd done was to stand up and vouch for a fellow human being for the sake of nothing but her lovely eyes. How foolish he had been, how gullible! The whole business of the proposal was almost unforgivably ill advised. Had he lost his mind? Would his parents be proven right after all? In this respect at least he had shown himself quite sufficiently oafish and unintelligent to confirm their impression of him.

It didn't take long for him to conclude that his failure was a punishment for having been unfaithful to the memory of his late wife, for wanting to remarry. His punishment lay in the fact that he was now to be united with a woman he could neither respect nor love.

This awakened his old burden of grief. He felt this state of mourning was his rightful place. Life, with its obligations and complications, was distasteful to him.

The purpose of the journey Schagerström had now embarked upon was to inspect his mines and ironworks. He would go through the managers' books, check whether the black forges with their gaping furnaces and iron-clad hammers were in serviceable condition, and determine how much coal and pig iron needed to be purchased in anticipation of the coming winter.

In other words, he really did have to be away on business. He made a similar journey every summer; it was a necessity.

After a few hours he arrived at Gammalhyttan, where his good friend Henrik Nyman was now in charge. Of course

Nyman and his wife – he was now married to one of the sweet Fröberg sisters from Kronbäcken – would show him the greatest possible hospitality. At Gammalhyttan, rather than being perceived as an intimidating owner, he was welcomed as an old friend.

Schagerström could not have found himself in better hands, but the melancholy that had come over him as he traveled just would not subside. In fact, Gammalhyttan was the last place he ought to have gone as a newly engaged man. Every path in the park, every tree in the lane, every bench in the yard seemed to have retained the memory of words of love and tenderness exchanged between himself and his wife. Here, she was still alive, beautiful, young and radiant. He would see her, hear her voice. How could he possibly have been unfaithful to her? Was there any woman on earth worthy of her place in his heart?

Of course his hosts saw how dejected he was. They wondered what had made him so gloomy and low-spirited, but as he did not seem inclined to confide in them, they chose not to be forward and inquisitive.

However, Gammalhyttan being as close as it was to Korskyrka, it was almost inevitable that the news of Schagerström's proposal and all the relevant details of the story would make their way there before he had completed his inspection. The foundry manager and his wife thus soon knew the cause of his melancholy.

'He's having second thoughts,' they said to each other. 'Now isn't that a shame? Charlotte Löwensköld would make him a fine wife. She would pull him up out of his eternal sadness and brooding.'

'I'd really like to talk to him about all this,' Mrs. Nyman said. 'I've known Charlotte for so long. All the gossip about her now, about her playing false and being sly cannot possibly be true. She is honesty personified.'

'I'd stay out of it if I were you,' her husband advised. 'Schagerström's eyes are glazed over just the way they were six years ago when I lured him out of Stockholm. You know, there might be serious consequences.'

172

His wife took her husband's counsel to heart, and managed to restrain herself until almost the end of Schagerström's stay. But on the Friday evening when he had completed his scrutiny of the books, and was due to leave the next morning, she could no longer control her good, helpful heart.

'It would be unkind to let him leave feeling so distressed and regretful,' she said to herself. 'Why should he go around being miserable for no good reason?'

And in the most tactful way, as if by complete coincidence, she brought the conversation that evening around to Charlotte Löwensköld. She told various familiar anecdotes about her. She talked about the time she told off the housekeeper at Korskyrka, and about that astonishing day she fell out of the pew at church. She talked about the sugar bowl, about taking the pastor's horses out racing, and lots of other stories. Her intention was to give Schagerström the overall impression of a proud, cheerful, rash and yet extraordinarily wise and loyal human being. She feigned total ignorance of his proposal to her.

But right in the middle of Mrs. Britta Nyman's description, just as she was reaching the peak of her eloquence in defense of her friend, Schagerström stood up and threw the chair he had been sitting on right across the room.

'You do mean well, Britta,' he said. 'I realize you are only trying to comfort me, take the edge off my misery. But I for one want to face the truth. Having been so heartless as to consider remarrying, it is only right for me to be landed with a wife who is an intriguer and who plays false – those being the vilest traits I know.'

With those words, Schagerström rushed out of the room. His horrified hosts heard him open the front door and head out into the open.

Schagerström wandered through the ancient forest that surrounded Gammalhyttan. He walked for a couple of hours with very little idea of where he was.

As he walked, old ideas he had abandoned six years earlier were reawakened in him. All that wealth with which he was burdened and which was a source of nothing but misery and trouble to him, why did he not rid himself of it?

He thought to himself that in some ways Britta Nyman might have been right. Charlotte was no worse than anyone else, but she had fallen prey to a temptation that had overpowered her.

Why should he go around tempting people? Why not give his property away? He had been accompanied by enormous good fortune since receiving his legacy, and it had nearly doubled in value. That was another good reason to divest himself of his heavy burden.

There he had it! It might also spare him his second marriage. Miss Charlotte Löwensköld would probably refuse matrimony with a pauper.

He stumbled around in the dark, sometimes falling, sometimes pausing in reverie, having as much trouble making his way through the tangled wilds as through his own thoughts.

In the end he found a wide graveled road, and then he knew where he was. This was the main road to Stockholm, which ran east of Gammalhyttan.

He set off along it. Was this not a sign from above? Was there not a concealed meaning in his ending up on the road to Stockholm at the very moment when he had made up his mind to give away his property?

He picked up speed, with no intention of returning to Gammalhyttan. He had no desire to become embroiled in explanations. He had money in his pockets and could arrange for horses and a carriage at the first inn to which he came.

Toiling up a steep incline, he heard a conveyance approaching from behind. Turning around, he saw a large stagecoach, pulled by a team of three horses.

The Stockholm mail coach! A second sign. This would be the fastest means of transport to Stockholm. Before anyone hereabout suspected a thing, the meeting that had been interrupted six years earlier would be reconvened, and the donation deeds issued.

He stood waiting for the coach. As it passed, he shouted:

'Hallo there! Stop! Is there a seat?'

'Indeed there is,' answered the postilion, 'but we don't take tramps.'

The coach rolled on, but at the top of the hill it stopped. When Schagerström came up to it, the postilion tipped his cap:

'My local driver claims he recognized you by your voice, Mr. Schagerström.'

'So he did.'

'Please get right in! The only other passengers are two women.'

II.

Any reasonable person would have to admit that it is difficult for older people, who set store by respect, to acknowledge that they have been peeping through hatches and raking through tiled stoves for discarded letters. Thus there is no reason to be surprised that the pastor and his wife in Korskyrka said nothing to Charlotte about their discoveries.

On the other hand, although they did not wish to reveal what they had been up to, they could not bear to leave the young woman out there in the scullery at such a dull task. Moments after Beate Ekenstedt's carriage had disappeared through the yard-gate, the pastor's wife looked in on Charlotte.

'Do you know what, my little ace of hearts?' she asked, her visage radiating kindness. 'Watching the colonel's wife depart, I had an idea. Isn't it lovely weather for a journey? You know, I haven't seen my older sister in Örebro for ages. I think she'd be delighted if we came for a visit.'

Charlotte's first reaction was astonishment, but it was only moments ago that she had felt the soft little hands of the colonel's wife stroking her cheeks and heard her gentle whispering. It is easy to understand that her whole world had brightened up. An outing, to almost anywhere, was just what she needed.

Being back in the good graces of the pastor and his wife was another uplifting factor. All afternoon she was happy as a lark, chattering and chirping. She seemed not to be thinking at all about unrequited love or dreadful slander.

The necessary preparations were made in haste, and at ten that evening the two women were standing in the corner of the garden waiting for the mail coach to Stockholm, which they knew would pass. When the heavy yellow coach came into view, pulled by a fresh team of three, harnessed in the village a few moments earlier, and they heard the cheery creak of the wheels, the clattering of the harnesses, the cracking of the whip and the bright sound of the postilion's horn, they naturally began to look forward to their journey. Charlotte was rapt with the thrill of it.

'Ah, the pleasure of an outing!' she cried. 'An outing! I could travel day and night, travel around the world!'

'My dear girl, I imagine you'd tire of it,' said the pastor's wife, 'though who knows? Your wish may be granted sooner than you can imagine.'

They had sent word to the village inn to book their seats, and the coach stopped to collect the new passengers. The driver, who didn't dare let go of the reins, remained seated, shouting a friendly greeting:

'Good evening Mrs. Forsius and Miss Löwensköld! Please take your seats. There's plenty of room; in fact you are my only passengers.'

'What a shame,' the merry old woman replied. 'Do you mean to say we ought to be pleased about that? We would certainly have preferred to have the company of a couple of handsome young men to flirt with.'

This made everyone burst out laughing, from the postilion to the local driver and all the people of the parsonage who, with the exception of Karl-Artur, had turned out to witness the ladies' departure. The pastor's wife, delighted, settled into the right-hand corner. Charlotte sat beside her, and with another toot of the postilion's horn they were off.

For some time, the pastor's wife and Charlotte went on with

their chat and banter, but then something awful happened. Her older companion fell asleep. Charlotte, who was in a talkative mood, tried to awaken her, but in vain.

'Oh, well, she's had a long day,' the young woman mused. 'I'm not surprised she's tired. But I am disappointed. I thought we'd have such a lovely time. Personally, I could have gone on talking all night.'

Actually, being left alone with her thoughts made her a bit anxious. It was getting dark. The road ran through deep forests. Dejection and doubts were crouching there, ready to attack.

When they had been on the road for a couple of hours, she heard someone on foot shout out to the postilion. A few minutes later the stagecoach stopped and the new traveler opened the door and took the seat opposite Charlotte, facing backwards.

For a short time the only noise in the coach was the steady breathing of a couple of sleeping passengers. Charlotte's first impulse had been to pretend to be asleep so as not to have to talk to Schagerström. But once the first shock passed, the mischievous child in her came to life. What a golden opportunity! She couldn't let it pass. She might even find some cunning way to induce Schagerström to refrain from his marriage plans. And if she managed to make fun of him a little in the bargain, well that wouldn't do any harm.

Schagerström, still as miserable as could be, was startled to hear himself addressed by a voice from across the way. He could see nothing of the person sitting there. It was night, and he could just barely make out the oval shape of a face.

'Excuse me, but I thought I heard the coach driver call you Schagerström. Do I have the honor of finding myself opposite foundry owner Schagerström from Stora Sjötorp, about whom I have heard so much?'

Although more than a little annoyed at having been recognized, Schagerström could hardly do anything but admit the truth. He raised his hat, mumbling a few innocuous words.

The voice from the darkness made itself heard again.

'I cannot help but wonder what it is like to be so wealthy,' the voice said. 'I've never been in the company of anyone who possessed an entire million. I don't think it's right for me to keep the forward-facing seat while you, Sir, travel backwards. I'd be happy to change places.'

The voice in the coach was modest and ingratiating, with a little lisp. If Schagerström had socialized with the villagers of Korskyrka, he would instantly have recognized it as belonging to Thea Sundler, the organist's wife. However, things being as they were, all he could think was that he had seldom heard a more irritating voice, or one he instinctively trusted less.

'It doesn't matter in the least! Please, keep your seat!'

'Well, you see,' said the voice, 'I am accustomed to drudge and toil, I am. It's second nature to me to sit where no one else wants to. Whereas you, Sir, I suppose, are used to sitting on a gilt chair, and eating from a golden plate with a golden fork.'

'I can tell you, Madame,' said Schagerström, who had begun to feel provoked, 'that for a good bit of my life I have slept on straw and eaten from tin bowls with a wooden spoon. I had one master who pulled so much of the hair out of my head when he lost his temper with me that I collected it all and stuffed a pillow with it. That pillow was the only soft piece of bedding I had.'

'Oh, how romantic, how romantic,' said the modest voice. 'How grand and romantic!'

'Pardon me, Madame, but it wasn't the least bit romantic. However, it was educational. It prevented me from becoming the kind of fool you seem to take me for.'

'Good heavens, Sir, how can you say such a thing? A fool? Could any person of my status ever consider a millionaire a fool? Though I do find it fascinating to learn how a person of such rank thinks, and what he feels. Could I possibly inquire as to how you felt when your luck finally turned? Was it not ... how shall I put it? Was it not like seventh heaven?'

'Seventh heaven?' Schagerström repeated. 'I would have given it all away if only I could have.'

In Schagerström's opinion, the person sitting over in the corner ought to have understood by that point that he was in a terrible state of mind and that she had offended him, and so stopped conversing with him, but her meek, unctuous voice just went on, untiringly.

'It's fine to hear of wealth granted to someone not unworthy of it! It's fine to know that virtue is its own reward!'

Schagerström said nothing. It was the only way he could think of to get her to stop talking about him and his wealth.

The lady in the corner of the stagecoach may have realized she had been a bit overly intimate. This did not stop her from talking, but she did change the subject.

'And they say, Sir, that you'll be marrying that uppity Charlotte Löwensköld.'

'I beg your pardon?' Schagerström burst out.

'Forgive me,' said the voice, if anything meeker and more ingratiating than ever. 'I come from humble circumstances and am not accustomed to spending time with finer folk. I'm sure I'm not expressing myself as I ought and would like to, and I can't help but find the word uppity on the tip of my tongue whenever Charlotte comes to mind. I shall cease and desist from using it if it displeases you, Sir.'

Schagerström groaned. Let the woman in the corner take that as an answer, if she pleased.

'Of course, Sir, you must have made a considered choice,' the voice went on. 'I have heard that everything you do, Sir, is very well planned and thought through, so I assume that your proposal was, too. And yet I'd like to know if you are really aware, Sir, of what she is like, the uppi… – oh no oh no, forgive me, forgive me! – the lovely, charming Charlotte Löwensköld. They do say, Sir, that you had not exchanged so much as a word with her when you proposed, but, Sir, I am certain that you had your ways of finding out whether she was well suited to be mistress of Stora Sjötorp.'

'Madame, you are well informed,' said Schagerström. 'Perhaps you are a very close friend of Miss Löwensköld?'

'I have the privilege of being the confidante of Karl-Artur Ekenstedt, Sir.'

'Ah,' said Schagerström.

'But getting back to Charlotte! Excuse me for saying it, Sir, but you do not appear to be happy. I hear you sighing and groaning. Might it be the case, Sir, that you are having second thoughts about having promised to have the banns read and to marry that … what shall I call her? … capricious young woman? I hope the word does not bother you too much. Capricious can mean any number of things. Of course I know that no Schagerström would ever take back a promise, once given, but the pastor and his wife are fair-minded souls. They know very well what Charlotte has put them through over the years.'

'The pastor and his wife are extremely fond of their ward.'

'Say, rather, that they have the patience of saints. That's the truth, Sir. Imagine this: the pastor's wife, once upon a time, had an excellent housekeeper, but she was not to Charlotte's liking. One day, right in the midst of all the Christmas preparations, Charlotte told her off. The poor offended woman upped and left, after which dear Gina, ill as she was, had to take over all the holiday preparations herself.'

Schagerström had recently heard the story told from a different angle, but he didn't bother to register a protest.

'And just imagine, Sir, the pastor's horses, of which he is so fond…'

'I know she took them out galloping,' said Schagerström.

'And do you not, Sir, find that horrifying?'

'I've heard that the horses were likely to have died for want of exercise otherwise.'

'And have you heard, Sir, perchance, how she treated the mother of her fiancé?'

'The time she emptied the sugar bowl?' Schagerström asked.

'Yes, the time she emptied the sugar bowl. Surely the woman who becomes mistress of Stora Sjötorp ought to have decent table manners.'

'Indeed, Madame.'

'And, Sir, I don't suppose you would want a wife who refused to receive your visitors?'

'Certainly not.'

'Well, that is precisely the risk you would be taking, Sir, by marrying Charlotte. Just think of how she behaved at Chamberlain Dunker's. There was a big dinner party, and she was supposed to sit beside Captain Hammarberg, but she declared she would refuse to go to the table in that case. She would rather go home, she said. Well, as you know Sir, Captain Hammarberg does not have the best of reputations, but he does have his redeeming sides as well, and I, Sir, sure as I am talking to you now, I have spoken with the Captain in confidence, and I know how miserable he is, in heart and soul, at not finding a woman who understands and believes in him. And in any case, Charlotte surely has no right to set herself up to judge him. If the Chamberlain invited him, there was no reason for her to mark her disapproval.'

'Well, that shouldn't be a problem,' said Schagerström, 'since I have no intention of inviting Captain Hammarberg to my home.'

'Ah well, ah well, that may be so,' said the voice. 'That's another matter entirely. I note, Sir, that you have more feelings for Charlotte than I had presumed. It's a fine and noble thing. I'm sure, Sir, that you are quick to defend anyone who might be the subject of slander. But deep down, Sir, I believe that you agree with me. You know full well, Sir, that marriage between a person of your situation and a capricious soul like Charlotte is utterly unthinkable.'

'You appear to be implying, Madame, that with the aid of the pastor and his wife … but no, it cannot be.'

'What cannot be, Sir,' said the oily, unctuous voice in its very meekest tone, 'is a marriage between yourself and a woman so disgraced.'

'Disgraced?'

'Forgive me, Sir, but you have no idea. You are such a good-hearted gentleman. Karl-Artur Ekenstedt has told me, Sir, how you stood up and were prepared to defend Charlotte. And even now that you know the accusation against her was true, you still defend her. Other people, however, are not like you, Sir. Beate Ekenstedt, the colonel's wife, visited the parsonage yesterday, leaving today. She refused to see Charlotte. She even refused to sleep under the same roof.'

'Is that so?' asked Schagerström.

'It is,' said the voice. 'It is absolutely true. And Sir, do you know that quite a few of the gentlemen from the village were so upset about Charlotte's behavior they decided to have a whistle serenade outside her window, like the students in Uppsala do when they are dissatisfied with one of the professors.'

'Oh?'

'The young men came to the parsonage and began their whistling, but were prevented from continuing. Karl-Artur put a stop to it. You see, his mother was spending the night in one of the parsonage side buildings, and she would never have tolerated such a racket.'

'Had she not been there Ekenstedt would, I imagine, have let things run their course?' Schagerström asked.

'I couldn't tell you. But in the name of fairness, Sir, I do hope the young men will come back another night. And I also hope Blind Karl will wander the roads singing his ballad about her for a long time yet. Captain Hammarberg wrote the text, and it's terribly amusing. It goes to the tune of "When I was a young maid". When you've heard it, Mr. Schagerström, I'm quite sure you will realize you cannot possibly marry Charlotte Löwensköld.'

The speaker stopped suddenly. Schagerström was knocking on the stagecoach wall, probably signaling to the driver to stop.

'What on earth's the trouble, Sir? Are you wanting to disembark, Mr. Schagerström?'

'Yes, Madame,' he replied in just as angry a tone of voice as he had used earlier in the evening when Britta Nyman had tried to sing Charlotte's praises. I see no other way to be spared more defamation of the woman I admire and intend to make my wife.'

'Good heavens! I had no such intention.'

The stagecoach stopped at once. Schagerström wrested open the door and got out.

'No, I'm sure it was not your intention,' he said in his firmest voice, slamming the door hard and fast.

He walked over to the postilion to pay for his passage.

'Leaving us already, Sir?' the postilion said. 'I don't suppose the ladies will be pleased. The pastor's wife berated me when she came on board, for not having any gentleman passengers.'

'The pastor's wife? What pastor?'

'From Korskyrka. Who else? Do you mean to say, Mr. Schagerström, that you have spoken so little to your fellow passengers that you do not even know that she and Miss Löwensköld were the other two?'

He tipped his cap and snapped his whip. The stagecoach continued on its way. Schagerström stood staring for a long time.

'Charlotte Löwensköld!' he repeated. 'Was that Charlotte Löwensköld?' – – –

It was long past midnight by the time Schagerström was back at Gammalhyttan. Foundry manager Nyman and his wife had not gone to bed. They had been anxiously awaiting his return, wondering whether they ought not send out a search party to find him. The two of them were pacing up and down the tree-lined lane leading up to the house when they caught sight of him at last.

They saw the large, somewhat thickset shape in the darkness and recognized Schagerström, but they could hardly believe their eyes and ears. The man who was approaching was humming an old popular tune.

When the three met, Schagerström burst out laughing.

'Come along, then, it's past your bedtime,' he said, 'and tomorrow I will tell all. Oh, incidentally, Nyman, I'm afraid you'll have to get your things in order and make the annual inspection tour in my place. I have urgent business and must personally return to Korskyrka tomorrow.'

THE BANNS

I.

On Saturday morning Schagerström reappeared at the parsonage in Korskyrka. He wanted to speak with the pastor about the persecution of Charlotte that was taking place, and consult him as to the best way to bring it to an end.

As it transpired, he could not have turned up at a more fitting moment. The elderly pastor, poor man, was beside himself with anxiety. The five little lines on his forehead were once again bright red.

That very morning three gentlemen from the village – the apothecary, the organist and the bailiff – had come to see him. They had come with a shared mission: to express a request on their own part, and on the part of the parish as a whole, that he turn Charlotte out of his home.

The apothecary and the bailiff had been perfectly civil. It was very obvious that they found the whole situation more than a little awkward. The organist, on the other hand, had been in quite a rage. He spoke very loudly and precipitously and entirely neglected the respect owed to his elder.

He informed the pastor in no uncertain terms that he was jeopardizing his reputation in the parish by allowing Charlotte to remain at the parsonage. Not only had she shamefully deceived her fiancé, and behaved inappropriately on any number of occasions: the previous day she had done violence to his wife, who had certainly not anticipated that anything terrible might befall her when she was a guest in his home, a home she held in high esteem.

The pastor had explained briefly and simply that his relation, Miss Löwensköld, was going to remain at his home as long as his old head sat where it belonged, on his shoulders, and with those words his visitors had no reason to tarry. There is no question, however, that the whole matter was terribly distressing to a peace-loving elderly man like the pastor.

'It's a never-ending bother, this,' he said to Schagerström. 'I've spent the whole week at it. And you can rest assured, Sir, that the organist will not give up after only one try. He's quite a gentle man himself, but his wife eggs him on.'

Schagerström, who was in an excellent mood that day, did his best to placate him, but to no avail.

'I promise you, Sir, that Charlotte is as innocent in this business as a child born yesterday, and it would never occur to me to make her move away. But the sense of peace in my parish, Sir, the peace I have spent thirty-five years safeguarding, will be lost.'

Schagerström could see that the pastor now felt that all the more creditable things he had accomplished during his years as the parish priest were at risk. He truly began to doubt whether the old man would have the courage and strength to resist the continual persuasions of his parishioners.

'To be honest I, too, have heard about the way people have begun to persecute Miss Löwensköld. The reason I came here today was to consult you, Pastor, as to how best to combat them.'

'I am certain, Sir, that you are a man of many talents,' said the pastor, 'but I doubt that your skills extend to curbing vicious slander. No, I think we must keep our counsel and prepare for the worst.'

Schagerström was about to protest, but the old man went on, just as despondently as before:

'Yes, we must prepare for the worst. Ah, Sir, if only you were already married! … If only the banns had at least been read!'

At those words, Schagerström jumped up out of his chair.

'What are you saying, Pastor? Do you really think it would help if we had the banns read?'

'Naturally it would help,' said the pastor. 'If my parishioners knew that Charlotte was definitely going to become your wife, I think they would let her be. At least she would be able to stay here at the parsonage until your wedding day with no further ado. That's the way people are, Sir. They tend not to offend anyone who has a prospect of becoming rich and powerful.'

'In that case I suggest we have the banns read for us immediately on the morrow,' said Schagerström.

'Very kind of you indeed, Sir, but unfortunately impossible. Charlotte is away, and I presume you do not happen to have the necessary documents in your breast pocket.'

'The papers are at Stora Sjötorp and can be fetched. And Pastor, you witnessed my definite acceptance from Charlotte. And surely you are her legal guardian?'

'Now, now, Sir! Let us not be over-hasty.'

The pastor changed the subject. He showed Schagerström some of his rarest botanical finds, and described their sites. While he was talking about plants he grew lively and eloquent. One might have thought he had forgotten all his woes. But a few minutes later he returned to the suggestion of having the banns read.

'Well, reading the banns isn't the same as a marriage ceremony,' he allowed. 'If Charlotte should disapprove, they can always be revoked.'

'It is a mere contingency measure,' said Schagerström, 'to restore the equilibrium of the parish and to bring the defamation and slander to a halt. I assure you I have no intention of dragging Miss Löwensköld to the altar against her will.'

'Indeed. Who knows?' said the pastor, who may have been remembering a certain letter he had read without permission. 'Charlotte is quite hotheaded, Sir, I must admit. I think it would be best for her sake as well if the matter could be concluded. In the longer term she might not content herself with just chopping off a few locks of hair.'

They went on discussing the matter for quite some time. The more they talked about having the banns read, the more convinced they became that it was the best possible expedient under the circumstances.

'I'm sure my wife would agree,' said the pastor, who was beginning to feel quite optimistic.

Schagerström was thinking about the fact that from the very moment the banns were read for Charlotte and himself, he would have the right to defend her in public. Whistle serenades and satirical ballads would be out of the question.

It must also be borne in mind that since the conversation in the mail coach, which had convinced him of Charlotte's unselfishness, he had had the tenderest possible feelings for her. The step he was now proposing to take was extremely attractive to him.

Of course he was not prepared to admit as much, even to himself. He was persuaded that he was behaving out of a pure sense of the urgency of the situation. That's how it always is with people who are in love, and that is the reason we must overlook their foolishness.

And thus it was really determined that the banns would be read in church the next day. Schagerström departed and returned with the necessary documentation, and the pastor wrote out the announcement of the banns in his own hand.

When it was all arranged, Schagerström was left with a great sense of satisfaction. He was not at all averse to the idea of his name being read out from the pulpit in conjunction with that of Charlotte Löwensköld.

'Foundry owner Gustav Henrik Schagerström and the esteemed Miss Charlotte Löwensköld.' He thought that had an excellent ring to it.

Eager to hear how it sounded, he decided to be present at the church service in Korskyrka the next day.

II.

Now on that first Sunday the banns were read, Karl-Artur Ekenstedt gave a very peculiar sermon. Or perhaps it was no more than was to be expected after the many upsetting events he had experienced during the past week. Perhaps it was also the case that these events, both the broken engagement and the one newly entered into, increased the impact of his words.

The Bible passage for that Sunday had to do with false prophets, against whom our Redeemer warned His disciples. He had not found the subject at all relevant as a point of departure for his sermon, considering his state of mind. He would have preferred to speak about the vanity of earthly possessions, the perils of wealth and the delights of poverty. Above all he felt the need, more than ever before, to come close to his listeners in a familiar, simple manner, and make them understand that he cared about them, and to win their confidence.

Miserable as he was with doubt and uncertainty, he had failed during the week to formulate a sermon that satisfied him. The whole of the past night he had gone on working, but to no avail. His sermon was still unfinished when it was time to go to church. So as not to find himself utterly wordless, he had pulled a few pages containing a discourse on the text for the day out of an old book of sermons, and folded them into his pocket.

But standing at the pulpit reading the Bible text, an idea began to take shape in his mind. It was unusual and enticing. He thought it must have come from the Lord.

'My beloved listeners!' he began. 'I am standing here in order, in the name of Jesus, to warn you against false prophets, but perhaps in your hearts you are wondering: "That man who is speaking to us, is he a right-thinking instructor? What do we know about him? How can we be certain that not even he is a briar bush on which no grapes can grow, or a thistle, from which no figs can be picked?"

'For that reason, listeners, let me tell you something of the ways God has appointed for me to wander, having chosen me to preach his word.'

Deeply moved himself, the young curate then began to tell the simple story of his life and destiny to the parishioners. He explained to them how, during his early years at the university, he had invested all his energy in the dream of becoming a great and renowned scholar. He related the to-do after the Latin exam he had failed, his return home and losing his temper with his mother, their reconciliation, and finally how all this had led to his becoming acquainted with Pontus Friman, the Pietist.

He spoke quite softly and modestly; no one could doubt the truth of every word he uttered. What captured the interest of his listeners most must have been the exaltation in his voice. From his very first sentences they sat stock still, craning their necks, eyes glued to the preacher.

And as always when a person speaks freely and frankly to others, they were drawn to him, and from that moment he won a place in their hearts. The poor people who lived in cottages in the forest and the wealthy people with authority from manor houses alike, all of them could see that he was confiding all this in them to win their trust and confidence. They hung on his every word as they seldom did during a sermon; they found themselves moved and enthralled.

He went on telling them about his first tentative attempts to follow in Jesus' footsteps, and he described the wedding party at his parents' home, when earthly pleasures had bewitched and transported him, so that he had taken part in the dancing.

'After that night,' he said, 'my soul was in gloom for many weeks. I felt as if I had betrayed my Redeemer. I failed to take up the combat or keep a vigil with Him. I was a slave to the world. Its temptations had vanquished me. Heaven would never be my lot.'

Some of the people in church were so moved by the anguish

he portrayed that they began to weep. The man in the pulpit had them completely under his spell. They felt and suffered and struggled with him.

'My friend Friman,' he went on, 'tried to comfort and help me. He told me that in the love of Christ there was redemption, but I was unable to lift up my soul and love my Redeemer. I worshipped all the things of creation more than their Creator.

'Then one night, in my hour of greatest need, Christ appeared to me. I could not sleep. Throughout those nights and days there was no sleep to be had. But pictures, like those we see in our dreams, often came to me. I knew, though, that it was my terrible exhaustion that was calling them forth, so I paid them no heed.

'But suddenly there was a picture that was so distinct and clear and that did not vanish in a moment, but remained. I saw a lake with bright blue water and a huge crowd of people gathered on its shore. In the midst of the great crowd a man with long wavy hair and heavy, sad eyes was sitting, and he seemed to be talking to them. As soon as I saw him, I knew he was Jesus.

'And to my astonishment a young man stepped up to Jesus, bowed deeply before him, and asked him a question.

'Although I was unable to hear the words, I knew that the young man was the wealthy youth of whom we read in the Bible, and that he was asking the master what he ought to do to attain eternal life.

'I watched as Jesus exchanged a few words with him, and I knew he had told him to observe the Ten Commandments.

'The young man bowed once again to the master and smiled smugly. And I knew he had answered that he had observed them all since he was very young.

'But Jesus gave him a long, searching gaze and spoke to him again. This time, too, I knew what he was saying.

'"If you would be perfect, go away and sell all you own and give to the poor, and you will be rewarded in heaven. Then come follow me!"

'At those words, the young man turned away from Jesus and

walked off, and I knew it grieved him, because he had many possessions.

'But when the wealthy youth was leaving, Jesus watched him go with a penetrating gaze.

'And in that gaze I read such compassion and such love. Ah, my listeners, I read something so heavenly in it that my heart began to throb with joy, and the light returned to my gloom-filled soul. I jumped up, I felt like rushing over to Him myself and telling Him that I now loved Him more than anything on earth. Now everything worldly was indifferent to me. I asked nothing more than to be allowed to follow Him.

'The vision passed when I awoke, but the memory of it remains, my friends and listeners, the memory remains.

'The next day I went to see my friend Pontus Friman and asked him what he thought Christ was asking of me, since I had no possessions to give up. My friend said then that Jesus most surely wished for me to sacrifice to him all the honor and recognition I would have won through my learning, and instead be his insignificant, destitute servant.

'And so I threw it all aside and became a man of the cloth in order to speak to the people of Christ and His love.

'But you, my listeners, pray for me, because I have to live in this world as do all of you, and the world goes on tempting me, and I live in fear and trembling that it will turn my inclination from Christ and make me one of the false prophets.'

At this he clasped his hands and appeared to be seeing before him all the temptations and anguish that awaited him, and the thought of his weakness made him burst into tears. Emotion overwhelmed him so that he was unable to continue. He merely said Amen and fell to his knees in prayer.

Throughout the church, the congregation burst out in noisy sobbing. With a single short sermon Karl-Artur had aroused the love of each and every one of them. They would have carried him on their bare hands; they would have been willing to sacrifice themselves for him as he had sacrificed himself for his Savior.

But no matter how powerful his words had been, they

would not have made such a deep impact had they not been succeeded directly by the reading of the banns.

The young clergyman began by reading a few names to which he was indifferent, and about which no one thought much. But then they saw him blanche slightly, and bend over his papers to make sure he had not misread them. He went on and read the banns in a soft voice, as if he had wanted people not to hear.

'A holy union in Christ is hereby announced for the first time in this parish between foundry owner Gustav Henrik Schagerström from Stora Sjötorp and the esteemed Miss Charlotta Adriana Löwensköld from the parsonage, both residing in this parish.

And in the significant union that is marriage, we wish them all good fortune and the blessing of God, at whose behest the institution of holy matrimony was established.'

It did not help that the young clergyman had lowered his voice. Every syllable was audible to the very back of the church, silent as it was.

It was dreadful.

Schagerström, too, was aware of how dreadful it was. There stood a man who was willing to deny himself all that was worldly in order to imitate Christ in poverty, reading that the woman he had loved was going to marry one of the wealthiest men in the country.

It was absolutely dreadful. There stood the man who had been Charlotte's fiancé for five whole years, the man who as recently as last Sunday had worn her ring on his finger, reading out a statement that she had already accepted a different proposal of marriage.

The people were ashamed; they dared not look at one another. Leaving the church, they seemed very disquieted.

Schagerström felt it more than anyone else. He retained his apparent calm, but inside he was thinking that it would not have surprised him if people had spat at him or thrown stones.

And this was what he had thought of as a way of obtaining redress for Charlotte!

He had often felt incompetent and foolish, but never as much so as that Sunday, walking up the aisle after church.

III.

Schagerström's first thought was to write to Charlotte to explain and apologize. But he soon realized it was far too difficult a matter to put in writing. Instead, he ordered a coach and horses, and headed for Örebro.

He had heard Pastor Forsius mention the name of the elderly woman his travelling womenfolk were visiting. On the Monday morning he went to her home, announced himself, and asked Charlotte for a word.

Immediately, he admitted the inappropriate and shameless thing he had done. He was hardly making excuses, merely explaining to her how it had all happened.

It is no exaggeration to say that Charlotte collapsed, almost as if she had been fatally wounded. So as not to fall, she sat down in a low little armchair, from which she barely moved. She did not burst out in reproaches. Her pain was far too great and too real.

Until that very moment she had been able to tell herself that once Karl-Artur, with the aid of the colonel's wife, had come around, once he had reestablished his engagement with her, her honor would be restored, and the people who were now her detractors would realize that the entire matter had been nothing but a lovers' spat. Now that the banns had been read in church for herself and Schagerström, however, everyone must believe that it was truly her intention to marry the wealthy foundry owner.

There was no more help to be had. No explanations were possible. She was disgraced forever. People would always believe she was a false, greedy woman.

She had a terrible sense of being walked in a given direction like a prisoner, toward a goal of which she was not aware. Everything she wanted to avoid she had done, everything she wanted to prevent, she had promoted.

It was as if an evil spell had been cast. Nothing was happening as it was meant to. Ever since the day Schagerström proposed for the first time, her free will had been lost to her.

'But, Sir, who are you? Why are you constantly impeding me? Why am I unable to break free from you, Sir?'

'Who am I?' asked Schagerström. 'Well, I shall tell you, Miss Löwensköld. I am the greatest imbecile on God's green earth.'

He said this with such firm conviction that the shadow of a smile crossed Charlotte's lips.

'From the very first time I saw you in the parsonage pew at church, Miss Löwensköld, I have wanted to help you and make you happy, but I have brought you nothing but grief and suffering.'

The little smile was already gone. Charlotte sat there, pale and still, arms hanging at her sides. Her glazed eyes appeared to see nothing but the terrible misfortune he had brought upon her.

'Now I grant you my explicit permission, Miss Löwensköld, to revoke the banns next Sunday,' Schagerström said. 'As I am sure you are aware, the banns have no legal force until they have been read three Sundays in a row from the same pulpit.'

Charlotte waved one hand just slightly, as if to indicate that the permission she had just been granted was now entirely insignificant. Her reputation had been destroyed beyond repair.

'And I promise, Miss Löwensköld, not to encroach upon you again until you call for me yourself.'

He moved toward the door. There was one more thing he wanted to tell her. It actually required more of an internal struggle with himself than all the rest.

'I wish to add,' he said, 'that I am beginning to understand you, Miss Löwensköld. I have been somewhat bewildered about how you could love young Ekenstedt so deeply that for his sake you endured all the slander and all the persecution, because I do know that you have been thinking of him and him alone. But today, having heard him preach, I understand that he requires protection. He is destined for greatness.'

He was duly rewarded. She gave him a glance. Her cheeks brightened a little.

'Thank you,' she said. 'Thank you, Sir, for understanding!'

Then she sank back into despair. There was nothing more he could do. He bowed deeply and left the room.

THE PAUPERS' AUCTION

They say misfortune seldom comes alone, but always brings a little good luck in its wake, and as regards Charlotte Löwensköld, her grief and indignation endowed her with the very attributes she needed to be truly captivating.

Her deep gloom banished from her manner forever her tendency to be overly boyish, overly high-spirited. It gave her voice, movements and features a kind of tranquil dignity. It gave her eyes that gleam of longing, that touching, uncertain glow that speaks of happiness thrown away. That sorrowful, charming young woman readily aroused the interest, compassion and tenderness of all she met.

Charlotte and Mrs. Forsius had returned from Örebro on the Tuesday morning, and that very afternoon young people from the nearby foundry at Holma had come on foot to the parsonage. Among those kind people were some friends of Charlotte's who, like Mrs. Nyman at Gammalhyttan, refused to believe she had been playing false. Now all they needed was to see her to know she had been afflicted by a great sorrow. They asked no questions, made no oblique references to her forthcoming marriage, but only extended themselves to show her as much friendship as they possibly could.

Although they had not really come to congratulate Charlotte upon having heard the banns read, when they saw how despondent she was, they hardly dared ask their favor.

Gradually, though, it all came out. They had come to tell her about Matts the crofter's Elin, the woman with the birthmark and the ten younger brothers and sisters. She had turned up at Holma earlier that day, just after breakfast, lamenting to the

196

lady of the house the fact that her younger siblings were going to be auctioned off to the highest bidder.

Matts the crofter's Elin and her brothers and sisters had been living as beggars. How else could those poor destitute souls have survived? But now people had begun to tire of the large number of mouths to be fed, of their wandering from homestead to homestead, and so the powers-that-be in the parish had decided that the children ought to be farmed out to board. An auction had been announced, and anyone who was interested in taking on one or more of the children was invited to place a bid.

'I'm sure you know, Ma'am, how it is done. The authorities just want to find out who'll take on the youngsters at the least possible expense to the parish. No one, though, considers the fact that they need to be raised and cared for.'

The poor young woman who had hitherto borne the brunt of caring for her sisters and brothers all on her own was horrified. She said anyone who would bid for a child at an auction had to be a poor crofter himself, in want of a low-price herder for his sheep and goats, or cheap household help because his wife was overworked. Her little sisters and brothers would be expected to carry and toil like properly paid domestic help – no one cared what happened to kids who were auctioned off. They had to earn their keep. One of her little sisters, the youngest, was only just three, and couldn't possibly herd animals or be a serving maid. She would surely starve to death, unable as she was to earn her living.

The thing that upset Elin most, however, was that the family would be scattered to the winds. They were so closely knit now, but in a few years' time the little ones would have forgotten both her and each other. And who would teach them to be honest and love the truth, as she had tried to do until now?

The mistress at Holma had been very touched by the poor young woman's lament, but had not seen how she could help her. There were already far too many runny-nosed children living around Holma in need of her care. All she could do was to send a couple of her own daughters to attend the paupers' auction later that morning at the parish hall, so she would at least know who bought the poor little ones.

The two young women from Holma arrived just as the auction was beginning. The poor children were seated on a bench at the front of the room, the eldest sister in the middle with the three-year-old on her lap, the others on either side. They had not sobbed aloud, but soft, unremitting weeping could be heard. One might have thought, seeing how ragged and hungry they already were, they could hardly be worse off. Still, it was evident that what they were anticipating must have thrown them into the depths of misery.

On the benches that lined the walls of the parish hall, as one might have expected at such a gathering, sat a number of poor crofters. Up near the auctioneer's stand were a few of the local bigwigs, a couple of homesteaders and a few mine owners. They had been appointed to ensure that the auction was carried out in an orderly fashion, and that the children were put in the hands of decent folk, locally known.

The oldest child, a tall, lanky lad, was standing on display on the auction table. The auctioneer was praising his shepherding skills and his wood-chopping, and one woman, extremely poor to judge by her attire, had stepped up close to better be able to inspect what he was fit for.

That was as far as things had proceeded when the door opened and Karl-Artur Ekenstedt came in. He stood in the doorway looking around the room, then raised his arms heavenward shouting:

'My God, turn Thy gaze from us! Do not see what is taking place here!'

After this he walked over to the officials at the podium and said:

'I beg you as fellow Christians not to commit this great sin! Let us not sell other human beings into thralldom.'

Everyone in the room was dismayed at his conduct. The impoverished woman moved away quickly from the table and back toward the door. The farmers serving as officials shifted uncomfortably on their bench. They looked, however, as if what was making them uncomfortable was more the inappropriate intervention of the clergyman in the business of the parish than their own activities. After some time, one of them stood up.

'This auction is being carried out on the basis of a decision taken by the parish council.'

The young clergyman just stood there, handsome as a god, head raised, eyes gleaming. He certainly did not look as if he intended to yield to any decision of the parish council.

'I request that mine owner Aron Månsson cancel this auction.'

'As you have been informed, Doctor Ekenstedt, the auction is being held on the basis of a decision adopted by the parish council.'

Karl-Artur turned his back on the man, shrugging his shoulders. He placed a hand on the shoulder of the boy who was up for bidding.

'I am buying him,' he said. 'My bid is so low no one will be able to go lower. I am offering to care for him with no remuneration from the parish.'

Aron Månsson, the mine owner, stood up, but Karl-Artur did not look his way.

'No more bidding will be necessary,' said Karl-Artur to the auctioneer. 'I am bidding for all the children at once, and at the same price.'

Now they were all on their feet. Only Matts the crofter's Elin and her sisters and brothers sat still, unmoving, unable to absorb what was happening.

Aron Månsson, the mine owner, voiced objections.

'There will be no end to the bother. We have arranged this auction in order not to have to be subjected to their eternal begging.'

'These children will never beg again.'

'Who will guarantee that?'

'Jesus Christ, who said "Let the little children come unto me." He will be the guarantor of all these little ones.'

There was such commanding power and solemnity about the young clergyman's person when he said this, that the mine owner, an important local official, was unable to find words to reply.

Now Karl-Artur approached the children.

'Be off with you!' he said. 'Run back home. I've bought you.'

They still did not dare to move, at which Karl-Artur picked up the youngest one, and with the three-year-old in his arms and the other ten following close behind, he left the parish hall.

No one stood in their way. Many of the bidders, ashamed and diffident, had already taken their leave.

When the two sisters were back at Holma and had told their mother all this, she exclaimed that something would have to be done to help the young clergyman with all his young wards. Her idea was that a collection be taken up for an orphanage, which was why they had now come to the parsonage.

The moment they had finished telling their tale, Charlotte stood up and left the room in tears. She rushed right up to her room to be alone and kneel down to thank the Lord.

The thing about which she had been dreaming for so long had finally come to pass. Karl-Artur had stood up as a leader of the people, as a model to them all, showing his fellow human beings the way of God.

THE TRIUMPH

A couple of days later Mrs. Forsius went in to see her husband in the morning when he was sitting at his desk.

'My dear, if you would like to see a lovely sight, find a reason to go into the dining room!'

Her husband stood right up. He went to the dining room, where he found Charlotte, sitting at one of the little tables over by the window with an embroidery frame in her lap.

She was not working, just sitting with her hands in her lap staring out in the direction of the side building where Karl-Artur had his rooms. That day a steady stream of visitors passed through the yard-gate and went directly to the side building, which was what she was looking at.

The pastor spent a few minutes ostensibly looking for his glasses, which he knew perfectly well were in his office. What he was really doing was watching Charlotte observe the scene being played out over by the side building with a gentle smile on her lips. Her cheeks were rosy and her eyes gleamed softly with rapture. She was truly a beautiful sight.

When she noticed the pastor, she said a few words:

'People have been going in and out of Karl-Artur's all day.'

'Yes,' responded the pastor dryly. 'They don't give him a moment's peace. I'll soon have to start doing the registers myself again.'

'The woman who went in there just now is Aron Månsson's daughter. She was carrying a crock of butter.'

'A contribution to the upkeep of the children, I presume.'

'Everyone adores him,' said Charlotte. 'I knew it would be so one day.'

'Ah, well, when a person is young and handsome,' said the pastor, 'it's not difficult to make old ladies weep buckets.'

Charlotte did not allow her admiration to be disturbed.

'A little while ago I saw one of the smiths from the forge at Holma go in to see him. You know, uncle, one of those Pietists who never attend church and are unwilling to hear any of the ordinary pastors preach.'

'Good grief!' the old man exclaimed, showing a real interest. 'Don't tell me he's softened up one of those men? They're like blocks of ore! Verily, my dear, in that case I do believe he may make something of himself after all.'

'I'm thinking of the colonel's wife,' Charlotte went on, 'and what pleasure it would give her to see all this!'

'Personally, I wouldn't have thought it was this particular type of success she imagined for her son.'

'He's improving people. Some of them leave his rooms in tears, wiping their eyes. Marie-Louise's husband has been in, too. Just think if Karl-Artur could help him! Wouldn't that be wonderful?'

'Well, certainly, my dear. And the best thing of all is that you take pleasure in sitting here watching all the people.'

'I'm actually sitting here wondering about all the things they want to discuss with him, and I can imagine what he's telling them.'

'That's a fine thing. Ah, I just realized my glasses must be in my office.'

'Had this not happened, it would all have been incomprehensible to me,' said Charlotte. 'I would not have been rewarded for my efforts to protect him. But now I see the point.'

The pastor hurried out of the room. That girl was about to reduce him to tears.

'What in the name of God are we to do with her?' he mumbled. 'I do hope there is no risk of her losing her mind.'

And if Charlotte was taking pleasure in Karl-Artur's triumph now, during the week, how much more reason she had to rejoice when Sunday came around!

The road was packed with people, as if the King were

arriving. On foot and by carriage they streamed along. There was no question that the rumors about the new preaching method of the young clergyman, his piety and power, had spread to the farthest reaches of the parish.

'The church cannot hold so many people,' said the pastor's wife. 'Everyone's turned out, from every hut and cottage as they say. Let us just hope no fires start anywhere, now that there is no one at home to notice!'

The pastor was not at ease. He sensed an impending religious revival, and he would not have had anything against it if only he had been convinced that Karl-Artur was the right man to keep the kindled fire burning. But he did not mention these concerns out of consideration to Charlotte, who was in utter ecstasy.

The elderly couple left for church, but there was no question of Charlotte's accompanying them. On Friday, Charlotte had received a short note from the colonel's wife appealing to her to hold out for a few more days, and for that reason she had not taken advantage of Schagerström's offer for her to revoke the banns. The pastor and his wife were truly worried that all the people who worshipped Karl-Artur might insult Charlotte, so it had been agreed that she would stay at home.

However, the moment their carriage was out of sight of the garden, Charlotte put on a hat and shawl and headed for the church. She could not resist the urge to hear Karl-Artur preach in the new, forceful way that had won him a place in the heart of every member of the congregation. Neither could she deny herself the gratification of witnessing all the devotion that now surrounded him.

She managed to squeeze into a seat in one of the back pews, where she sat, breathless with excitement and anticipation, as she watched him approach the pulpit.

She was surprised to hear how naturally he spoke to the people. He sounded as if he were merely conversing with a group of friends. He did not use a single word these simple people would be unable to understand, and he confided in them his struggles and tribulations, as if they might be able to offer him solace and guidance.

The Bible passage that Sunday was Jesus' parable of the unjust steward, and when Charlotte realized what a difficult text it was, she grew worried. She had heard many a man of the cloth complain about how abstruse it was, and how difficult to interpret. The beginning and the end did not really mesh. The powerfully abridged form in which the parable was recounted probably made it almost incomprehensible for readers of the day. She had never heard it explained satisfactorily. She had heard clergymen talk about the beginning, she had heard clergymen talk about the last part of the parable, but never anyone who had been able to elucidate it or give it coherence.

It is easy to imagine that everyone in church was thinking similar thoughts. 'Surely he will deviate from the text,' they thought. 'It will be too awkward for him. He will do as he did last Sunday.'

But the young pastor approached his difficult subject with great courage and confidence, endowing it with sense and significance. Under the guidance of divine inspiration, he recounted the parable in its original beauty and mystical depth. It was like watching century-old dust being removed from an ancient painting, and finding oneself before a masterpiece.

The longer she listened, the more amazed Charlotte felt. 'Where is he getting it from?' she asked herself. 'He is not speaking as himself. God has lent him His voice and is speaking through him.'

She could see the pastor sitting listening intently, hand cupped behind one ear, so as not to miss a single word. She saw that the people who were most attentive of all seemed to be the elders of the congregation, the ones who preferred profundity and solemnity. She knew that from that day on, no one would dare to claim that Karl-Artur preached for the women, or that his handsome appearance helped him along.

It was all perfect. She was thrilled. She wondered whether life could ever again be as wonderful and rich as it was at this very moment.

The most remarkable thing about Karl-Artur's sermon may

have been that as he was speaking, people were at peace and forgot all their troubles. It was as if they were under the guidance of a good and wise spirit. They were not afraid; they felt uplifted. Many made silent vows they then tried faithfully to live up to.

And yet, however great and good his sermon was, it was not what made the deepest impression on the congregation that Sunday. Nor was it the reading of the banns. The reading of the part where Charlotte's name was mentioned was followed closely and disapprovingly, but everyone had known in advance that it was coming. No, what made the deepest impression was something that happened after the service.

Charlotte had tried to leave the church directly after the sermon, but full as it was, she had been unable to make her way out, and had had to stay for the rest of the service as well. As people began to move toward the exit, she hoped to hurry out before the crowd, but that, too, failed. No one made way for her. No one spoke to her either, and no consideration was shown her.

She felt surrounded by hostility. Many of her acquaintances turned away when they saw her coming. One single person came up to her. It was her valiant sister, Marie-Louise Romelius, the doctor's wife.

When the two of them were finally able to get out through the church door, they stood for a moment in the churchyard.

They saw a number of parishioners, young men, gathered on the gravel path. In their hands they had bouquets of thistles, yellow leaves and dry grass, which they had just hurried to pick outside the churchyard wall. They were clearly preparing to give them to Charlotte to congratulate her on her engagement. Tall Captain Hammarberg was at the head of the group. He was considered the wittiest and nastiest man in the parish, and now he was clearing his throat to deliver a suitable congratulatory speech.

The rest of the congregation had formed a tight circle around the young gentlemen. They were looking forward to hearing the young woman who had left her beloved for goods and gold reviled and ridiculed. They were smiling to themselves in anticipation. Hammarberg could be counted on not to spare her.

The doctor's wife had begun to be anxious. She tried to draw her sister back into the church, but Charlotte refused.

'It doesn't matter,' she said. 'Nothing matters any more.'

They therefore slowly approached the group of gentlemen, who were waiting for them with their faces settled in amicable smiles.

Suddenly Karl-Artur was beside the two sisters. He had been passing, observed their plight and came to their rescue. He offered the elder sister his arm, tipped his hat to the congratulatory gentlemen, implying with a flick of the hand that they had better refrain from doing what they had been about to do, and accompanied the ladies safely out to the main road.

There was something beautiful about him, as the injured party, taking Charlotte under his wing; it wasn't the kind of thing you saw every day. It was what made the deepest impression on people that day.

A STERN LECTURE TO THE GOD OF LOVE

On Monday morning Charlotte walked to the village to speak with her sister, Marie-Louise Romelius, the doctor's wife. Like most Löwenskölds, Marie-Louise took particular interest in the supernatural. She often spoke of having encountered deceased people in broad daylight on the main street of the village, and there was hardly a ghost story so wild that she was not prepared to believe it. Charlotte, who was of a different disposition, had previously merely laughed at her visions, but that day she went to see her in order to sound her out about the mysteries that were puzzling her.

After the unpleasant scene in front of the church, young Miss Löwensköld had again become aware of her own adversity. Once again she felt as she had in Örebro, when Schagerström told her about the banns, as if she had been captured and spirited away by powers unknown to her. She was bewitched. She felt as if some dark, evil creature was persecuting her, had separated her from Karl-Artur, and was continually sending new misfortunes down upon her.

Miss Löwensköld, who had been feeling nothing but faint and weighed down by inexplicable exhaustion for several days, was walking very slowly in the direction of the village, eyes lowered. The people who saw her probably thought she was stricken with remorse and did not dare to meet their gazes.

So it was with great effort that she reached the main street of the village, and she was just dragging herself past the high hedge that surrounded the organist's little garden when the gate to the property opened. She heard someone turn out into the street, in her direction.

She had no choice but to look up. It was Karl-Artur, and she was so upset at meeting him there, with no witnesses, that she stopped short. However, before he reached her, a voice from the garden was heard calling him back.

The weather was no longer as balmy as it had been earlier in the summer. Rain showers, brief but heavy, broke out at all hours and Mrs. Sundler had noticed a cloud gathering behind the ridge over by the woods. A few drops were just beginning to fall as she ran through the garden with her husband's long coat over her arm, to offer it to Karl-Artur.

As Charlotte slipped past the gate, Thea Sundler was helping Karl-Artur on with the coat. The two of them were only a couple of steps away from the young woman, and she could not help but look at them. Mrs. Sundler buttoned the coat around Karl-Artur, and he gave her one of his boyish laughs for being overprotective.

Thea Sundler, too, looked happy and at ease; there wasn't a trace of anything improper about it. And yet Charlotte felt as if she had had a revelation, watching Thea Sundler looking after Karl-Artur, for all the world like his mother or his wife.

'She is in love with him,' the young woman thought.

She hurried on past so as not to have to see any more. But time and again she repeated to herself:

'Of course, she is in love with him. How could I not have recognized it sooner? That explains everything. It accounts for why she separated us from each other.'

She was also instantly aware that Karl-Artur had no idea. He was probably still going along dreaming of his beautiful peddler girl from Dalarna. Although he was admittedly spending every evening at the organist's nowadays, what drew him there was probably all the lovely music they performed for him. And no doubt he needed someone to talk to, and after all Thea Sundler was a very old friend of his family's.

Actually, one might have expected the young woman to feel frightened or dismayed by her discovery, but that was definitely not the case. Instead, she raised her head, straightened her bent back, and regained her former upright, energetic posture.

'Thea Sundler's to blame for all these troubles,' she thought. 'But I do believe I can handle her.'

She felt like a person who has long been unwell, has finally been able to put a name to her illness, and is convinced that it is curable. She was filled with new hope, new self-confidence.

'I can't believe I could have imagined it was that accursed ring that was causing trouble again!' she muttered to herself.

She recalled that she had once heard her father talk about a promise the Löwensköds were said to have made to Malvina Spaak, Thea Sundler's mother. They had then failed to keep it, and a terrible curse had therefore been laid upon them. She had been going to see her sister to find out what she knew about it. Until that very moment everything that had happened to her in the last few weeks had seemed to her to be inevitable, decreed by destiny, and beyond her power to halt or avert. But if it was just Thea being in love with Karl-Artur that had caused all her adversity, then she would be able to find a way out of it herself.

Quite suddenly she abandoned her intention of visiting her sister, turned around and went home. No, the whole idea contradicted her way of thinking. She had no desire to believe there was some ancient curse that had to be beaten down. She wanted to believe in her own common sense, her own power, and her own creativity, without having to take account of any old, inexplicable witchcraft.

That evening, when she was undressing in her room, she stood looking for a long time at a little china figurine of Cupid on her desk.

'So she's the one you've been protecting all this time,' she said to Cupid. 'You've been looking after her best interests rather than mine. It was for her sake, because she was in love with Karl-Artur, that Schagerström had to propose to me, and that all these other things had to happen.

'It was for her sake Karl-Artur and I had to quarrel, for her sake that Karl-Artur had to propose to that peddler from Dalarna, for her sake Schagerström had to send me that bouquet, throwing all chances of reconciliation out the window.

'Oh, Cupid, why are you defending her love? Because it is forbidden? Is it true, then, that you take most mercy upon such love as must not be?

'My dear Cupid, you should be ashamed. Here you have stood, I put you here as the guardian of my love, and what did you do? You helped that other woman.

'Because Thea Sundler loves Karl-Artur you made me endure the slander, the satirical ballad and the whistle serenade without defending me.

'Because Thea Sundler loves Karl-Artur you had me accept Schagerström's proposal, you had the banns read for us, and perhaps you also intend to unite us in marriage.

'Because Thea Sundler loves Karl-Artur, you have made us all live in misery and terror. You spared no one, neither the old pastor and his wife here nor the old couple in Karlstad; they all had to suffer merely because you are protecting that fat little fish-eyed wife of the organist.

'Because Thea Sundler loves Karl-Artur you have robbed me of my happiness. I believed a horrid troll was guiding me to the edge of the abyss, but it was only you, Cupid, no one but you.'

She had begun in a playful tone but, overwhelmed by all the cruel fates she was calling to mind, she went on, trembling with emotion:

'Oh, god of love, have I not proven myself capable of love? Is her love more pleasing to you than mine? Am I not every bit as faithful, does a stronger, purer flame burn in her heart than in mine? Why, god of love, are you protecting her love and not mine?

'What can I do to placate you? Cupid, oh Cupid, consider that you are taking him, the man I love, in the direction of ruin and misery! Do you intend to give her the gift of his love? That is the only thing you have thus far denied her. Cupid, Cupid, do you intend to give her the gift of his love?'

She asked no more questions either of Cupid or of herself. Weeping, she retired to her bed.

THE FUNERAL OF THE WIFE OF THE CATHEDRAL DEAN

A few days after Beate Ekenstedt returned to Karlstad after her visit to the parsonage in Korskyrka, an extremely beautiful peddler girl from Dalarna had arrived, a peddler with the usual big leather rucksack on her back. But within the town limits, because the town had its permanent merchants, she was prohibited from pursuing her ordinary livelihood. So she left her rucksack at her quarters and went out into the streets with a little basket on her arm, containing bracelets of human hair and watch chains, all made with her own two hands.

The young peddler woman went from house to house seeking purchasers for these items, and so she eventually found herself at the Ekenstedt manor. The colonel's wife took a great liking to her lovely handicrafts, and invited her to stay with them for a couple of days to make some remembrances from a few long fair locks of her son's hair, which she had been saving since Karl-Artur was a child. The beautiful wanderer seemed to welcome this offer. She accepted it without hesitating, and got down to the task first thing the next morning.

Mademoiselle Jaquette Ekenstedt, who was quite good at handicrafts herself, spent quite a lot of time in the little room out in the yard where the hair craftswoman was working, to watch and learn. In this way there arose between the two of them a close acquaintance, you might even call it friendship. The young city girl was drawn to the poor peddler with her attractive appearance, further enhanced by her neat and tidy parish costume. She truly admired her purposeful diligence, her skilled hands and her good head, which showed itself very clearly in her ability to converse and answer questions quickly and to the point.

She was all the more astonished when she found that this keen intelligence belonged to someone who could neither read nor write, and she was more than a little taken aback when she came into the room unannounced once or twice and found her smoking a little metal pipe, but generally the relationship between them was a good one.

Another amusing thing was that the peddler girl used a whole lot of words and expressions mademoiselle Ekenstedt was unable to comprehend. And so it happened once, when she had invited her new friend into their home to show her all the beautiful things they had, that the only way the country lass could find to express her admiration was by saying: 'It's sure tough.' Mademoiselle Ekenstedt had actually been quite offended, until with a laugh she realized that the word 'tough' pronounced by a peddler from Dalarna was her way of expressing her admiration.

The colonel's wife did not seek out the hard-working hair craftswoman personally. She seemed to have decided to get to know her character, talents and habits through her daughter and thus to determine whether she might be a suitable match for her son. Because, from the very first glimpse of her, and being the insightful woman she was, the colonel's wife had surmised that the young woman was precisely that, her son's new fiancée.

Soon, though, a sad event brought the stay of the peddler from Dalarna in their home to an abrupt end. The colonel's sister, Mrs. Elise Sjöborg, widow of Cathedral Dean Sjöborg, who had lived with her brother and his family since her husband's demise, had a stroke, and it took her life after only a couple of hours. Preparations for a suitable funeral had to be made; every square inch of space was needed for seamstresses, bakers and upholsterers, who would cover all the furniture in black cloth. The peddler woman from Dalarna was shown the door.

She was called in to the colonel's office to be paid, and the domestic staff noted that this office conversation was an unusually long one and that when she left her eyes were red-rimmed from weeping. The kindhearted housekeeper believed she was sorry to be leaving so soon the household where she had been shown so much kindness, and as a kind of compensation invited her to drop in to the kitchen on the day of the funeral and share in the remains of the good meal that was sure to be served.

The funeral date was set for Thursday the thirteenth of August. The son of the house, Karl-Artur Ekenstedt, had been called home of course, and he arrived on the Wednesday evening. He was welcomed with open arms and his parents and sister devoted the evening until bedtime to hearing his own account of the love he was now being shown by all his parishioners. It was anything but easy to encourage the modest young man to speak about his triumphs, but because the colonel's wife had been kept somewhat abreast of developments thanks to letters from Charlotte Löwensköld, she knew what questions to ask to entice and compel him to describe all the tokens of gratitude and love he had received, and there is every reason to believe that her maternal heart beat with pure pride at what she heard.

It was perfectly natural that evening for no one to mention the poor toiler who had recently spent a couple of days in the house. The next morning was entirely devoted to preparing for the funeral, so Karl-Artur heard nothing about the visit of the beautiful peddler woman from Dalarna then, either.

Colonel Ekenstedt very much wanted his sister to be buried with due pomp and circumstance. They had invited the bishop and the county governor and every one of the best families in the city who had had any contact with the wife of the cathedral dean to attend. Schagerström, the foundry owner from Stora Sjötorp, was also one of the guests. He had been invited because his late wife had been related to the dean, and he accepted out of gratitude for this respect being shown him by a family who had every reason to resent him.

Once old Mrs. Sjöborg had been borne from the house to the singing of hymns and, after a long procession, buried in her grave, the guests returned to the house of mourning, where a large funeral dinner awaited them. It goes without saying that the meal was both long and elegant, and it is also practically superfluous to mention that the sense of solemnity and gravity befitting a funeral was duly observed.

As a member of the family of the deceased, Schagerström was seated close to the hostess at dinner, which gave him the opportunity to observe and speak with this remarkable woman, whom he had never before met. She made a powerful impression that day, lyrically beautiful in her mourning garb, and although it was not an occasion for the lively wit or playful merriment for which she was so well known, he found her conversation particularly uplifting and entertaining. He did not for a moment hesitate to allow himself to be harnessed to this charming woman's triumphal chariot, and was pleased to be able to offer her a little pleasure in return with his description of her son's sermon the Sunday before last, and its effects on the listeners.

After the meal, young Ekenstedt rose from his seat and held a eulogy to the deceased woman that was received by all present with great admiration. They were astonished at his simple yet captivating and intelligent eloquence and at how fine an overview he gave of the life of the woman whose funeral they had just attended, who seemed to have been very devoted to him. However, undoubtedly like many of the other guests, Schagerström was occasionally distracted by his mother, who sat there beaming with admiration and reverence for her son. One of the people sitting next to him at the table had mentioned that she was fifty-six or fifty-seven years old, and although her face hardly belied her age, he could not really imagine that there could be any young belle with such expressive eyes or such a fascinating smile.

So all went as well as could have been imagined until the guests had left the tables and were going into the next room for coffee, when a little incident took place in the kitchen. The serving maid whose task it was to carry in the heavy tray of cups, happened to break a glass and cut herself on a fragment, and the cut began to bleed. No one in the kitchen staff managed to stem the flow right away, and although it was only a small injury, she could not possibly carry in the tray because blood was dripping from her hand.

All the other housemaids refused to carry the heavy tray. So in desperation, the housekeeper turned to the peddler girl, who was strong and sturdy and who, as planned, had returned to share the leftovers with them, asking her to step in. Without a moment's hesitation she lifted the tray, after which the housemaid, a napkin over her hand, accompanied her into the drawing room to be sure the coffee was served around in the correct order.

Normally a housemaid with a tray would not attract any particular attention. But the very moment the handsome country lass in her colorful parish costume walked in among the funeral guests, all eyes went her way.

Karl-Artur Ekenstedt turned to her like all the others. For a moment he stared uncomprehendingly at her, after which he rushed over to her and seized the tray.

'Anna Svärd, there will be no tray carrying in this house for you,' he said. 'You are my fiancée.'

The beautiful young woman looked at him, half in fear, half in delight.

'No, no, let me finish!' she said with a deprecating gesture.

By then all the guests had entered the main drawing room. The bishop and his wife, the county governor and his wife, and everyone else present saw the son of the house take the tray from the country lass and set it on a nearby table.

'I repeat,' he said, raising his voice, 'there will be no carrying of trays for you in this house, because you are my fiancée.'

At once a loud, piercing voice was raised:

'Karl-Artur, remember why we are here today!'

The voice was that of the colonel's wife. She was sitting at the far end of the room on a large couch, as befits one of the main mourners. In front of her was a low, heavy coffee table, and on either side of her sat dignified, corpulent elderly ladies. She began to extricate herself and cross the room, which took some time, because her neighbors were so engrossed with

215

what was going on at the other end of the room.

Karl-Artur had taken the country lass by the hand and was drawing her toward the center of the room. She was embarrassed, and covered her eyes with one hand like child, but at the same time she looked pleased. After a few moments Karl-Artur stopped in front of the bishop.

'Until this very moment I had no idea that my fiancée was present in my home,' he said, 'but now that I have discovered her, I would like to begin by introducing her to you, your Grace, the guide of my soul and my bishop. I request, your Grace, your approval of, and your blessing on, my union with this young woman, who has promised to accompany me on the path of trials and tribulations it is fitting for a servant of Christ to walk.'

There is no denying that, although it was inappropriate in many ways, this conduct on the part of the young minister won him general sympathy. This bold acknowledgement of the simple woman he had chosen to be his bride and his eloquent words made many of those present inclined to take his side. His pale, handsome face was marked on this occasion by an unusual virility and force, and many of the men in the room had to admit to themselves that he was now taking a road they would have hesitated to travel.

Karl-Artur had probably wanted to say a great deal more, but there was a sudden shriek from behind him. The colonel's wife had risen from the couch and was coming across the floor to the group surrounding the bishop. But in her astonishment and haste she happened to catch the heel of her shoe in the hem of her long black dress, and she stumbled and fell. In falling, she hit her head on the sharp corner of a side table, causing a nasty cut on her forehead.

A cry of concern and perhaps a sigh of relief from the bishop, who was thereby rescued from an undeniably awkward situation. Karl-Artur released the hand of his fiancée and hurried over to his mother to help her to her feet. But that was more easily said than done. Although the colonel's wife had not fainted, as many other women in her situation might have done, it had clearly been a serious fall, and she was unable to get back up. In due course Colonel Ekenstedt, his son, the house physician and her son-in-law Lieutenant Arcker managed to get her seated in an easy chair and carry her in it up to the master bedroom, where her daughters and the excellent housekeeper took charge of getting her undressed and into bed.

It is easy to imagine what a frenzy this accident caused. The funeral guests remained in the drawing room in alarm, reluctant to leave without a report on the state of their hostess. They watched as Colonel Ekenstedt, his daughters and the domestics scurried to and fro with worried expressions on their faces, trying to find linen for bandages, liniment and wooden slats to use as splints for the broken arm the colonel's wife seemed to have sustained.

At last the servants informed them that the cut on her forehead, which had looked so worrisome from the outset, was not at all deep, but that, although the break was only small, her left arm would have to be held in a sling. The most serious problem seemed to be that one of her kneecaps was fractured. The colonel's wife would undoubtedly make a full recovery, but would be bedridden in the meantime, and have to lie completely still for no one could say how long.

When the guests had been thus informed, it was clear that their hosts had their hands full even without company, and they began to head home. While the gentlemen were in the vestibule gathering up hats and coats, however, Colonel Ekenstedt came rushing out. Looking around eagerly, he finally located foundry owner Schagerström, who was just buttoning his gloves.

'Mr. Schagerström, Sir,' he said, 'if it is not too much trouble I would be very grateful if you could stay for a few more minutes.'

With a look of some surprise, Schagerström took his coat and hat right off again and accompanied the colonel back into the now nearly empty drawing room.

'I'd much appreciate a word with you, Sir,' said Colonel Ekenstedt. 'If you can spare the time, do have a seat until the storm subsides a bit!'

Schagerström did have to wait for quite a while for the colonel to return. Eva Ekenstedt's husband Lieutenant Arcker kept him company, however, and very distressed by the situation, told him the whole story of how the young peddler woman had come to Karlstad and ended up spending a few days in the Ekenstedt home. The poor housekeeper, terribly upset at having been the one to ask the young woman to carry in the coffee tray, was more than happy to tell anyone who would listen how she had happened to invite her back for the day of the funeral, which was how the foundry owner was able to piece the whole episode together.

At last the colonel returned.

'The bandages are on, thank heaven. Beate is now resting peacefully in bed. I hope the worst is over.'

Wiping his eyes with a large silk handkerchief, he sat down. Colonel Ekenstedt was a tall, stately gentleman with a round head, red cheeks and an enormous moustache. He gave the appearance of a bold and lively soldier, and Schagerström was surprised to see him display so much emotion.

'You must find me a sorry sight, Sir, but that woman has been all the joy of my life, and the day anything happens to her it will be the end of me.'

Schagerström's thoughts, however, were none of the kind. He, who had been walking around alone at Stora Sjötorp for the better part of two weeks, fighting down his unrequited love for Charlotte Löwensköld, was precisely in the right frame of mind to understand him. He was delighted at the innocence with which this decent old gentleman spoke of his love for his wife. Instantly he felt sympathy for, and confidence in, the colonel, more so than he had ever felt for the colonel's son, although he would be the last person to deny that the young man was extremely gifted.

It eventually transpired that Colonel Ekenstedt had asked him to stay in order to talk with him about Charlotte.

'I beg you to forgive an old man,' he said, 'for meddling in your affairs, Sir! But I have, of course, heard of your proposal to Charlotte, and I just want you to know that we here in

Karlstad…'

He stopped abruptly. One of his daughters was in the doorway, looking in anxiously.

'What's the matter, Jaquette? Has she taken a turn for the worse?'

'No, no, Father dear, not at all. But dearest Mother has been asking for Karl-Artur.'

'Goodness, I thought he was still with her,' Colonel Ekenstedt replied.

'He hasn't been with her for a long while, Father. He helped carry dear Mother into the bedroom. Since then we haven't seen him.'

'Go look in his room!' the colonel instructed her. 'I imagine he went up to change out of his best suit.'

'At once, Father dear.'

She tripped away, and the colonel turned to Schagerström.

'Where was I then, Sir?'

'You were saying, Colonel, that you here in Karlstad…'

'Oh yes, of course. I was saying that we here in Karlstad were convinced from the very outset that Karl-Artur had made a mistake. My wife traveled to Korskyrka to investigate, and found that the entire matter had to have been…'

He stopped once more. Mrs. Arcker, his married daughter, had appeared in the doorway.

'Father dear, you haven't seen Karl-Artur by any chance, have you? Dear Mother has been asking for him and is ever so agitated.'

'Please ask my soldier-servant Modig to come in,' the colonel said brusquely.

His daughter left the room, but Colonel Ekenstedt found himself unable to concentrate on Schagerström. He paced the floor without speaking the entire time until the soldier-servant entered.

'Do you know whether that peddler lass is still in the kitchen?'

'God forbid, Colonel! She came rushing back into the kitchen sobbing and didn't stay for a single moment. She left at once.'

'And my boy? I mean young Doctor Ekenstedt?'

219

'He turned up in the kitchen asking after 'er a while later. When he heard she'd gone he headed out into the streets as well.'

'Well then, Modig, I want you to go right into town and try to find him. Tell him Mrs. Ekenstedt is desperately ill and wants to see him.'

'At your service, Colonel.'

At that, the servant left the room and Colonel Ekenstedt resumed his conversation with Schagerström.

'As soon as we realized the state of affairs,' he said, 'we began thinking in terms of achieving a reconciliation between them, but to accomplish that we had, first and foremost, to ensure that the peddler woman was out of the picture and then ...'

He interrupted himself, afraid he had been tactless.

'Ah, Sir, I am not putting this very well. My wife was the one who was meant to have this conversation with you. She would have known better what to say.'

Schagerström hastened to calm his nerves.

'I assure you, Colonel, that you are putting the matter quite sufficiently well. As regards my person, I can tell you that I am already entirely out of the picture. Miss Löwensköld has my permission to have the banns revoked whenever she pleases.'

The colonel stood up, took Schagerström's hand, shook it warmly and spoke with heartfelt gratitude.

'That will make Beate very happy,' he said. 'It's the best news I could have for her.'

There was no time for Schagerström to respond, because at that moment Eva Arcker entered the room again.

'Father dear, I'm at my wits' end. Karl-Artur has been back, but without going in to see Mother.'

She explained that she had been standing at the bedroom window when she saw Karl-Artur coming down the street.

'I see Karl-Artur,' she had cried to her mother. 'He must be very worried about you, Mother dear. He's rushing along.'

For a few minutes she expected her brother to appear in the sickroom, until suddenly Jaquette, still standing at the window, cried out:

'Dear God above! There goes Karl-Artur rushing back toward town again. He only came home to change his clothes.'

The colonel's wife sat bolt upright in bed.

'No, no Mother dear! Lie stock still as the doctor instructed!' Jaquette's sister Eva warned her. 'I'll see to it that Karl-Artur returns.'

She rushed to the window to unlatch it and shout to her brother to come back inside. But the top latch was stuck, giving their mother time to prohibit her from opening.

'You mustn't. Let it be,' she said.

Mrs. Arcker defiantly threw the window wide and leaned out to call her brother.

At that point, in her very strictest voice, the colonel's wife prohibited her from going on, and instructed her to latch the window. Then she said in no uncertain terms to her daughters that neither they nor anyone else was to call Karl-Artur back home. And now, she said, she would like the colonel to be brought into the bedroom, probably in order to give him the same instructions.

The colonel stood up to go and see his wife, and Schagerström took the opportunity to ask how Mrs. Ekenstedt was faring.

'Mother's quite uncomfortable,' said Eva, 'but none of that will matter if Karl-Artur just comes back. If only I could run into town and try to find him!'

'I understand that Mrs. Ekenstedt must be extremely attached to her son,' said Schagerström.

'Indeed, Sir, indeed! Mother is asking for no one but him. And now, of course, she is lying there pondering the fact that although he knows she was badly hurt he is not by her side, but running after that peddler woman instead. It's extremely difficult for our dear mother. And she won't even let us go and find him for her.'

'Under the circumstances I can understand Mrs. Ekenstedt's feelings,' said Schagerström. 'However, as she hasn't forbidden me to look for her son, I shall now go out and do my utmost to locate him.'

He was already half way out the door when the colonel

returned.

'My wife requests a word with you, Sir,' he said. 'She wishes to express her gratitude personally.'

Taking Schagerström by the hand, he led him quite solemnly into the sickroom.

Schagerström, who had not long ago been full of admiration for the charming, vivacious woman of the world, was deeply moved to now see her as a sorrowful patient, with a bandage around her head and a sickly pale face, looking diminished. Although the colonel's wife did not seem to be in pain, there was something extraordinarily stern about her countenance, almost threatening. Something else, far worse than the fall and the terrible bodily harm was afflicting her, awakening in her a proud, contemptuous wrath. Those around her, who knew what had aroused it, said to themselves that she might never be able to forgive her son the want of love he had displayed toward her that day.

When Schagerström approached the bed, she opened her eyes and scrutinized him, long and penetratingly.

'You love Charlotte, Sir, do you not?'

Schagerström found it difficult to bare his heart to this lady, a stranger to him, whom he had never met until that day. Nor did he find himself able to be dishonest to this injured, unfortunate creature. He said nothing.

The colonel's wife did not appear to require an answer. She already knew what she needed to know.

'Sir, is it your belief that Charlotte still loves Karl-Artur?'

This time Schagerström was able without the least hesitation to answer her that Charlotte loved her son with unshaken tenderness.

She gazed at him again with eyes veiled in tears.

'It is difficult, Sir,' she said very softly, 'when the person you love has no love to give you in return.'

Schagerström could tell that she was speaking to him as she was, because he knew what it was like to be rejected. And at once she ceased to be a stranger to him. Their pain united them. She felt with him and he with her. For this solitary man, her compassion was a comfort and a solace.

He moved slowly closer, raised her hand gently from the cover, and kissed it.

She then gave him a third long stare. It was not veiled in tears, and it penetrated him to the core, where it considered and searched, after which she said to him, almost tenderly:

'I wish, Sir, that you had been my son.'

Schagerström felt himself tremble. How could the colonel's wife have known to say these particular words? Could this woman, whom he had never met until today, be aware of how often he had stood weeping outside his own mother's door, longing for love? Did she know the anguish with which he had approached his parents, afraid to subject himself to their disapproving gazes? Did she know that he would have been proud to hear even the simplest peasant woman say that she would have liked to have a son like him? Did she know there could be no greater honor, no greater exaltation for him than these words?

Overwhelmed with gratitude, he fell prostrate to the floor by the bed. He wept, and tried to express his feelings in a few incoherent phrases.

The others present surely found him terribly easily moved, but who among them could have understood what these words meant to him? He felt as if all his ugliness, all his awkwardness, all his stupidity were falling away. He had felt nothing like it since the day his deceased wife had told him she loved him.

But the colonel's wife understood everything that was going on inside him. She said once more, as if to be certain he really believed her:

'It is true that I wish, Sir, that you had been my son.'

And he suddenly knew the only way by which he could repay the happiness she had given him, and that was to reunite her with her own son. So he hurried out to search for him.

The first person Schagerström met on the street was Lieutenant Arcker, who was out for the same reason. They then encountered Colonel Ekenstedt's soldier-servant, and together the three of them did what needed to be done. They soon knew where the peddler woman was staying, but neither she nor Karl-Artur was there. They checked all the other places where travellers from Dalarna were known to spend time, and asked the night watchman to keep an eye out for them, but it was all in vain.

Quite soon darkness fell over the city, and there did not seem to be anything more they could do. In this town, with its narrow, dark streets crowded with houses and hovels of every possible description, every single courtyard offering a multitude of hiding places, the prospect of finding anyone was minimal.

Still, Schagerström continued to walk the streets for hours. He had agreed with mademoiselle Jaquette that if Karl-Artur happened to come home she would light a candle in the attic window to indicate that there was no need to go on searching, but no such sign appeared.

It was already long past midnight when Schagerström heard rapid footsteps approaching. He had an idea who it might be. Soon the figure passed a streetlamp, and in the russet light he was able to recognize the thin form of Karl-Artur; and since he was going in the right direction Schagerström did not bother to address him, but merely followed him along the street until they arrived at the Ekenstedt manor.

He saw him enter and, although he could offer no further assistance, he was extremely curious as to what the encounter between mother and son would be like, and this curiosity propelled him forward. He opened the door just a moment after Karl-Artur entered the vestibule.

The entire family already surrounded the son of the house. Apparently none of them had had the peace of mind to go to bed. The colonel arrived with a candle in his hand, which he shone at his son as if to ask 'Is it you or someone else?' Both sisters came rushing down the stairs, hair in curlers but otherwise fully dressed. The housekeeper and Colonel Ekenstedt's soldier-servant hurried in from the kitchen.

Surely Karl-Artur had intended to creep silently up to his

room without waking anyone. He had made it half way up the stairs before being halted by the household deluge.

When Schagerström entered he saw that each of the sisters had taken Karl-Artur by one hand, as if to pull him along.

'Do come in and see poor Mother! You have no idea how she has waited.'

'What kind of behavior was that? Gallivanting around town without inquiring into your mother's health?' the colonel shouted.

Karl-Artur had halted on the stairs. His face was as rigid as cut stone. He demonstrated neither embarrassment nor contrition.

'Father, do you wish me to go in and see Mother right away? Would it not be better to wait until morning?'

'Yes, hang it, you must go in to see her. She is all in a fever with waiting for you.'

'Excuse me, Father, but it is no fault of mine.'

The son of the house glared in a most hostile manner. The colonel clearly did not wish to provoke an outbreak of his wrath. He said in a kind, persuasive tone:

'Just show her that you have come home! Go in and give her a kiss, and everything will be all right in the morning.'

'I cannot kiss her,' said his son.

'Damnation, son!' he began, only to check himself a moment later. 'Speak out! No, wait! Come along in to my study.'

He pulled him along in to his office, shutting the door in the face of all the curious listeners.

Very shortly, he came back out, approaching Schagerström.

'I would very much appreciate it, Sir, if you would attend our discussion,' he said.

Schagerström immediately accompanied him in, and the door shut once again. The colonel sat down on a chair behind his desk.

'Say right away now, what's got into you?'

'Father, as you say Mother has taken a fever, I shall have to explain myself to you, although I know very well that she was the real instigator.'

'Will you please make yourself clear?'

'What I mean to say is this, that after this day I shall never darken the doorstep of my parental home again.'

'My, my,' said the colonel. 'And for what reason?'

'The reason, my Father, is this.'

He pulled a roll of bills from his pocket, set it on the desk before the colonel, and pounded his fist upon it.

'I see,' said the colonel. 'She couldn't keep her mouth shut.'

'Oh yes she could,' said Karl-Artur. 'She kept it shut for as long as she possibly could. We have been sitting in the churchyard for hours, and yet she said no more than that she had to go her way and was never going to see me again. Not until I accused her of having found a new lover here in Karlstad did she tell me that my parents had bribed her in cash, to purchase my freedom. My father had also threatened to disown me if I married her. What choice did she have? She accepted the two hundred kronor she had been offered. It amused me to hear that my parents attached such a high price to my person.'

'In fact,' said the colonel, 'we promised her five times as much again when she married another.'

'She told me that as well,' Karl-Artur barked. He then became more vehement. 'I cannot believe my own father and mother would treat me this way! Two weeks ago Mama came to see me in Korskyrka. I spoke with her about my upcoming marriage. I told her that this young woman had been sent my way by Providence, that I was counting on her in order to be able to live my life according to the will of Our Lord. She was my hope, my happiness in life depended on making her mine. Mama listened to all of this. She appeared to be moved by it; she agreed with me. And now, only two weeks later, I find that she has done her best to keep us apart. What am I to think about her want of compassion, her duplicity? Can I but shudder to call that person Mother?'

The colonel shrugged a second time. He looked neither guilty nor remorseful.

'Ah, well,' he said. 'Beate was feeling sorry for you because she thought Charlotte had played such a foul trick on you, so she did not wish to quibble with you about your new engagement. But of course both she and I knew at once that you were making a terrible mistake. We thought it would all work out on its own in due course, but then the woman sent to you by heaven happened to come here, right into the sinners' den. Beate took her on in order to see what she was like. And there's no denying that she is a fine woman in many ways, but she can neither read nor write, in addition to which she smokes a pipe, and when it comes to cleanliness… Oh, my lad, we tried to arrange things for the best, and you would have been pleased with it all if only you had had some time to come to your senses. What ruined the entire business was that that cursed woman happened to carry in that coffee tray.'

'Do you not see, Father, what that was?'

'All I can see is that it was damned bad luck.'

'I see the hand of God in it. This woman has been appointed by God to be my wife, and so he put her once again in my path. And more than that. I see his just punishment. When I requested that the bishop bless our union, Mother hurried forward to prevent it. She said to herself that if she pretended to trip, to fall, that would provide the best disruption. But her maneuver was all too successful. God intervened.'

Now the colonel was abandoned by his previous cold-bloodedness.

'Have you no sense of shame, my boy? How dare you accuse your mother of such underhanded behavior?'

'Pardon me, Father dear, but I have had other opportunities as well recently to observe feminine wiles. My mother and Charlotte, well the two of them have taught my heart a lesson it will not be quick to forget.'

The colonel sat for a moment drumming his fingers on the desktop.

'I'm glad you mentioned Charlotte's duplicity. I was just going to bring it up myself. You will never make me believe that Charlotte abandoned you to make a wealthy marriage. She cares more about you than all the riches in the world. I believe the whole thing is your fault, but that she has borne the burden of guilt so that we, your parents, would not be angry with you and so that you would not be the object of censure in the eyes of others. What do you think of that?'

'She allowed the banns to be read.'

'Think about it, Karl-Artur,' said the colonel. 'Erase from your mind all the things you have been imagining about what a bad person Charlotte is. Can you not imagine that she allowed herself to bear the accusations in order to help you? She allowed the entire world to believe that your engagement was broken at her instigation, but think about it now, examine your conscience! Were you not the one who broke it off?'

Karl-Artur stood there silent for a few moments. He truly appeared to be doing what his father said, scouring his memories. Suddenly he turned to Schagerström.

'How can you, Sir, explain having sent that bouquet? Had you heard anything from Charlotte that Monday evening? Why did the pastor come to see you?'

'I sent the bouquet as a token of my admiration, 'Schagerström replied. 'I heard nothing at all from Miss Löwensköld that Monday. The pastor had no other reason to come to see me than to reciprocate my visit to him the day before.'

Karl-Artur sank back into his ruminations.

'In that case,' he said eventually, 'it is not inconceivable, Father, that you are correct.'

Both his listeners drew deep sighs of relief. This was true acknowledgement of an error made. Only a person of some stature would be prepared to make such an admission.

'And if that is so…' said the colonel, 'you must know at once that Schagerström has promised to renounce his claims…'

Karl-Artur interrupted him.

'There is no need whatsoever for Mr. Schagerström to sacrifice anything for my sake. Father, I beg you to see that I will never go back to Charlotte. I love another.'

The colonel pounded the desktop with his fist.

'It's no use trying to talk sense with you. Can you not see that such fidelity, such self-sacrifice, is of any value at all?'

'I consider it a dispensation of Providence that the ties between myself and Charlotte were broken.'

'I see,' said the colonel with great bitterness in his voice. 'Similarly, you must thank God for the fact that the bonds between you and your parents have now also been broken.'

The young man stood silent.

'Mark my words, you are on the road to perdition,' the colonel said. 'Basically, it is our fault. Beate spoiled you, making you believe you were a demigod, and I let her have her way because I have never been able to deny her anything. And now you reward her as I knew you would. Personally, I have always known that things would end badly, but that does not make it any easier now that my suspicions have been proven true.'

He stopped here, inhaling deeply and moaning.

'But tell me, son,' he finally said softly. 'Now that you have spoiled our nasty little plot will you not go in and kiss your mother, so she can be at peace?'

'Even, Father, if I have, as you say, spoiled your nasty little plot, how do you think I can ignore the deranged state of mind of my closest relatives? Wherever I turn, all I see is the love of worldly things and its consequences, vanity and deception.'

'Pay it no mind, Karl-Artur! We are people of tradition. We have our devoutness, as you have yours.'

'Father, I cannot.'

'For my part, I have now told you what I think of you,' the colonel went on, 'but her, her … oh you know she just has to believe that you love her. I plead with you on her behalf, Karl-Artur, for her sake and hers alone.'

'The greatest kindness I can show my mother is to go my own way without telling her how much pain she has caused my heart through her deception.'

The colonel rose.

'You. You have no idea what love is.'

'I serve the truth. I cannot kiss my mother.'

'Go to bed now,' said the old man. 'Sleep on the matter!'

'I've ordered a coach for four o'clock. That's fifteen minutes from now.'

'Your coach,' said the colonel, 'can come back at ten. Do as I say. Sleep on the matter!'

For the first time, Karl-Artur showed a slight sign of hesitation.

'If you, my father and my mother, would just alter your worldly way of life, if you would be prepared to live as people of low rank, if my sisters were prepared to serve the poor and the sick …'

'Do not abuse us!'

'What you call abuse is the word of God!'

'Nonsense!'

Karl-Artur raised his arms to the heavens like a minister at the pulpit.

'Then forgive me, my God, for rejecting my own parents! Let nothing that is theirs, not their attention nor their love nor their property nor their money ever touch me again! Help me to part ways with these sinners and learn to live in Your freedom!'

The colonel had listened without moving a muscle.

'The God in whom you believe is a merciless God, and I am sure he will answer your prayers. And always remember that the day you stand outside my door, begging and praying I, too, will remember them.'

These were the last words exchanged between father and son. Karl-Artur walked out of the room quite calmly, leaving Colonel Ekenstedt alone with Schagerström.

The old man sat for a moment with his head in his hands. Then he turned to Schagerström, requesting him to report to Charlotte on everything that had taken place.

'I cannot bring myself to write about it,' he said. 'Tell Charlotte everything, Sir, everything! I want her to know that we tried to help her, but that we failed deplorably. And please also tell her there is no one else in the world but her, not a single soul, who can now come to the aid of my poor wife and my poor son!'

SATURDAY:
EARLY AND LATE MORNING

I.

It was on a Monday, two weeks to the day from when Schagerström had proposed, when Charlotte realized that Thea Sundler was in love with Karl-Artur. The peculiar feeling this gave her, of now having the means to regain her lost happiness, remained with her for the next few days. In addition, on Tuesday the postman delivered a note from the colonel's wife, informing her that things were going even better than one might have hoped and that all misunderstandings would soon be resolved. All this encouraged her, a feeling she dearly needed.

On the Wednesday she heard that Karl-Artur would be going to Karlstad to attend the funeral service for Dean Sjöborg's wife. It was easy to see that Karl-Artur's mother would avail herself of the opportunity to talk to him about Charlotte. Perhaps, at last, her innocence would be revealed. Perhaps Karl-Artur would come back to her, touched by her self-sacrificing nature. She had no idea how the colonel's wife planned to accomplish this miracle, but she did know that Beate Ekenstedt was a person who could find solutions to problems that sank others into gloom and despair.

In spite of her great confidence in her prospective mother-in-law, the days when Karl-Artur was away in Karlstad felt intolerably long to Charlotte. She vacillated between fear and hope. She asked herself what the colonel's wife could possibly do when she, who saw Karl-Artur on a daily basis, had been unable to deny to herself that his love for her had been extinguished. They sat at the same table but he looked right past her. He had no idea she was even there. This was no misunderstanding, it could not be explained away. It was over for him. His love was like a sawn-off branch, there was no power in the world that could attach it back to the tree and make it grow.

Karl-Artur was expected home on the Friday, and of course that was the most difficult day for Charlotte, who sat from early morning at that dining room window with a view of the side building where he had his rooms, waiting. For the thousandth time she thought through everything that had happened, examining and scrutinizing, and felt just as unsure as ever. She expected to endure a long day of waiting, but Karl-Artur was back as early as four in the afternoon. He went right to his rooms, but came out again directly, obviously in haste and without even looking up at the main house. He walked through the yard-gate and turned toward the village. The person he wanted to see was Thea Sundler, not Charlotte.

So this was the result of the efforts of the colonel's wife. Charlotte was now certain they had been in vain.

She felt all her hope perish. She told herself that now she would never, never again let anyone make her imagine that there was help or aid to be had.

And yet hope still lived on inside her. At about six on the Saturday morning the housemaid came into Charlotte's room with a message from Mr. Ekenstedt, asking to speak with her. Right away Charlotte interpreted his wanting to see her at the first, early breakfast, as a sign of love. It was as if he were telling her he wanted to return to their old intimacy, their old habits.

She was certain at once that the colonel's wife had kept her promise and that the great miracle had been accomplished. She hurried down the stairs and into the dining room at such speed that her curls bounced.

But the moment she saw Karl-Artur she knew she was wrong.

He stood up from the table when she entered, but clearly not to receive her with open arms and kisses and outbursts of gratitude for having wished to protect him. He stood there silent for a moment or two, as if she had come to him so fast he had not been able to organize his thoughts, but after an instant of reflection he began:

'It seems, Charlotte, that out of pure kindness you took on the blame for the breaking off of our engagement. In fact you went so far as to accept Schagerström's proposal and to allow the banns to be read to make your deception more credible. I am sure you meant well, Charlotte, and believed you were doing me a great service. For my sake you have had to suffer the sneers of many, and I realize that I owe you a debt of gratitude.'

Charlotte had put on a cold face, and was standing more erectly than she had in weeks. She did not deign to respond.

He went on:

'Your behavior, Charlotte, appears to have been primarily intended to protect me from the wrath of my parents. I therefore feel obliged to inform you, assuming that was your aim, that you did not succeed. While I was in Karlstad, my parents and I argued about my impending marriage, and it led to a total breach in our relations. I am no longer their son and they are no longer my parents.'

'But Karl-Artur,' the young woman burst out, now full of renewed energy, 'what are you saying? Your mother, have you broken with your mother?'

'I must tell you, Charlotte, that Mama undertook to bribe Anna Svärd to make her marry a man in the village she comes from. She treacherously tried to destroy my life's happiness. She has no idea about the only important thing in my life. Mama wanted me to go back to you, Charlotte. She was even thoughtful enough to invite Schagerström to the funeral to have an opportunity to request that he give you up. But presumably I need not repeat all this. Of course, Charlotte, you know all my parents' doings. You looked so happy when you came in I assume you were expecting their little plan to have succeeded.'

233

'I know nothing of your mama's plans, Karl-Artur, nothing at all. The only thing she said to me was that she did not believe those lies Thea Sundler had been circulating about me. Because I knew you had been in Karlstad I thought she might have told you the truth. I was convinced she had when you sent for me. But Karl-Artur, let us not talk about me! Tell me you're not angry with your mother. Don't you want to go right back and make it up to her? Don't you, Karl-Artur?'

'How could I? It's Sunday tomorrow, and I have a sermon to preach.'

'Well, then write a few lines and send me with them! You must remember that she is an old woman! Until now she has retained her vitality, thanks to the pleasure she took in you. You have been her youth, her health. The very moment you abandon her she will become an old woman. All her jokes, her amusing nature will dry up. She will become more careworn and bitter than everyone else put together. Oh, Karl-Artur, I fear it will be the death of her! You, Karl-Artur, you have been her god; you can decree both life and death for her. Let me go to her, Karl-Artur, with a word from you!'

'I know all of that, Charlotte, but I do not wish to write. My mother was already ill when I left Karlstad. My father begged me to be reconciled with her, but I refused. She has been a hypocrite and a liar.'

'But, Karl-Artur, if she has been a hypocrite and a liar it was in your best interest. I do not know how they offended you when you were in Karlstad, but whatever they did, they did it in your best interest. You must forgive things like that. Can you not recall your mother from the days of your childhood? What would your home have been without her? When you came in from school with your high grades, would there have been any satisfaction if it had not given your mother such pleasure? When you came home from Uppsala every autumn and spring, would that have been a pleasure if your mother had not been there waiting for you? When the family sat at Christmas dinner, would anyone have enjoyed themselves if your mother had not been full of surprises and rhymes, if she had not decorated the straw Yule Goat? Think about all that, Karl-Artur!'

'Ah, Charlotte, I was alone on the road all day yesterday, thinking about my mother. Seen in the eyes of the world, she has been an excellent mother. I allow you this, Charlotte – seen through your eyes and those of the world, she has been. But can I give her the same testimonial seeing her with the eyes of the Lord and with my own eyes? I have wondered, Charlotte, what Christ would have said about a mother like her.'

'Christ,' said Charlotte, at once so moved that she could hardly pronounce the words, 'Karl-Artur, Christ would have overlooked the coincidental and superficial. He would have seen that a mother like her was prepared to follow Him all the way to the foot of the cross, that she would even have let herself be crucified in His place, and He would have judged her accordingly.'

'You may be right, Charlotte. Perhaps my mother would die for me, but she would never allow me to live my life. My mother, Charlotte, would never allow me to serve God. She would always demand that I serve her and the world. That is why we had to part.'

'It is not Christ who is commanding you to break with your mother,' Charlotte cried vehemently. 'It is Thea Sundler who has put those thoughts into your head, and that she and I …'

Karl-Artur interrupted her with a wave of his arm.

'I knew this was going to be an unpleasant conversation and I would have preferred to avoid it, but it was the very person you just mentioned, Charlotte, and whom you please to despise, who enjoined me to tell you, Charlotte, about the results of my parents' efforts.'

'Indeed!' Charlotte exclaimed. 'That doesn't surprise me in the least. She knew it would make me so miserable I could weep blood.'

'You are free, Charlotte, to interpret her motivation however you please, but it was she who pointed out to me that I had to thank you for all you tried to do for me.'

Charlotte, who realized there was no use being accusative and angry, tried to calm down and change the subject.

'I beg your pardon for my hot-headedness,' she said. 'Of course I did not wish to insult you, but as you know I have always loved your mother, and I find it terrible to think of her lying there ill, expecting a word from you she will not receive. Are you certain you will not send me? It would not at all have to mean that you wanted to be reconciled with me as well.'

'Of course you are free to go, Charlotte.'

'But not without a word from you.'

'Do not ask me again, Charlotte. There is no point.'

Something gray and threatening came into Charlotte's lovely face. She looked sharply at Karl-Artur.

'How dare you refuse?' she asked.

'Dare? What do you mean, Charlotte?'

'You just mentioned your sermon coming up on Sunday.'

'That's true, Charlotte.'

'Don't you remember that time in Uppsala when you were unable to take your exam because you had been rude to your mother?'

'I shall never forget it.'

'Yet you have forgotten it now. So let me tell you, and I can, that you will never again preach as you have the last two Sundays until you are reconciled with your mother.'

He laughed.

'No, Charlotte, do not try to intimidate me.'

'I am not intimidating you. I am just telling you what is going to happen. Every time you step up to the pulpit you will think about the fact that you refused to be reconciled with your mother, and it will sap all your strength.'

'Honestly, Charlotte, there is no use trying to frighten me as one frightens a child.'

'Mark my words!' the young woman cried. 'Consider them while you still have time! Tomorrow or the next day may be too late!'

She walked toward the door as she proclaimed this threat, and left without awaiting his reply.

II.

After breakfast the pastor asked Charlotte to come into his study, where he informed her that Schagerström, who must have passed by the parsonage late the previous evening, had sent his servant into the kitchen with a large envelope addressed to the pastor himself. However, the actual content of the envelope was a long letter to Charlotte. To the pastor he had only written a few words requesting him to prepare Charlotte for the fact that his letter contained sad and distressing news.

'I am not unprepared, Uncle,' said Charlotte. 'I spoke with Karl-Artur this morning and I already know that he broke with his parents and that the colonel's wife is ill.'

'What? What are you saying, my beloved child?'

Charlotte stroked the old man's arm.

'I cannot bear to speak of it now, Uncle. But please, may I have my letter?'

She took it from the pastor's hands, went up to her room and read it.

Schagerström's letter contained quite a detailed description of all the events of late, particularly the day of the funeral, at the Ekenstedts'. Although the letter had been written in great haste, it gave Charlotte quite a good idea of everything from the appearance of the peddler woman in Karlstad to her unexpected reappearance on the day of the funeral, of the unfortunate fall the colonel's wife had had, of her longing for her son, of Schagerström's visit to her sickbed, of the search and finally of the heated exchange of words between father and son in the colonel's office.

In conclusion, the author of the letter wrote that Colonel Ekenstedt had asked him to inform Charlotte of all this, quoting verbatim the old man's statement that Charlotte was the only person in the world who could now come to the aid of his poor wife and his poor son.

He concluded his letter as follows:

'I promised Colonel Ekenstedt to fulfill his requests, but as soon as I returned to my accommodation I realized, my dear Miss Löwensköld, that I ought not to trouble you with my presence. I therefore decided, rather than going to bed, to use the remainder of the night to write these lines. I beg your forgiveness for having written at such length. I suppose it is the knowledge that these words were going to be read by you that made my pen run on so.

'It is now late morning. My carriage has been waiting for several hours, but I am not quite finished.

'On a number of occasions I have observed young Ekenstedt, and at times I have noted in him a brilliant, noble spirit, which promises future greatness. But at other times I have found him harsh, almost cruel, gullible, touchy, and lacking common sense. I submit to you, Miss Löwensköld, my impression that the young man has been subjected to a bad influence, which is having a harmful effect on his character.

'You, Miss Löwensköld, have now been restored in the eyes of your fiancé, cleared of all suspicion. Since you and he see one another daily, it seems impossible that he could remain insensitive to your charm. The good relationship between you will surely soon be restored. In any case, it is the lively aspiration of your humble servant that your happiness, which I have disrupted, will be rekindled. However, please allow a man who loves you, and wishes you the greatest happiness, to warn you against the influence I mentioned above and advise you, if possible, to remove it.

'Will you permit me one more word?

'Needless to say, Colonel Ekenstedt's entreaty to you is mine as well. I feel boundless affection for Madame Ekenstedt, and should you require my assistance to come to her rescue, you can count on my being prepared, even for the greatest sacrifice.

Your devoted and humble servant
Gust. Henr. Schagerström'

Charlotte read the letter through more than once. When she had absorbed its contents fully, she sat completely still for a long time, wondering what these two men, the Colonel and the foundry owner, were expecting her to do.

What did the Colonel mean by his request to her, and why had Schagerström taken the trouble to write her this long letter in such haste?

The thought came to her that the banns would be read for the last time the next day. Did Schagerström expect, now that she had been told all this, to let the banns be read for them one more time, and thus become legally binding?

No, she absolved him instantly of any such intentions. He had not been thinking about himself. If he had, he would have written more guardedly. His words about Karl-Artur had been so very frank and openhearted. He had unhesitatingly exposed himself to the risk that she would take the letter as having been written out of a desire to bring injury upon a rival.

In that case, what *did* he think, what did he and the Colonel think she could do?

What they were asking of her she thought she understood. They wanted her to return a son to his mother. But how was she to do it?

Did they imagine that she had some kind of power over Karl-Artur? She had already attempted to persuade him, exercised all her eloquence, and nothing had come of it.

She shut her eyes. In her mind she saw the colonel's wife, lying there with her bandaged head and sallow face, somehow diminished. She saw the proud, contemptuous wrath that marked her features. She heard her say to a man she hardly knew but who suffered as she did from unrequited love: 'It is difficult, Sir, when the person you love has no love to give you in return.'

Charlotte stood up suddenly, folded the letter and put it in the pocket of her frock as if it were a talisman that might help and protect her. A few minutes later she was on her way to the village.

When she arrived at the hedge around the organist's garden,

she stopped for a moment, praying silently. Her intention was to persuade Thea Sundler to send Karl-Artur back to his mother. She alone was capable of it. Charlotte prayed to God to fill her proud heart with patience, enabling her to win over and move this woman, who detested her.

She had the good fortune to find Mrs. Sundler at home alone. Charlotte asked whether Thea could give her a few minutes of her time, and soon they were seated in chairs opposite each other in Mrs. Sundler's little parlor.

Charlotte felt she ought to open the conversation by apologizing for having chopped off those tresses of Thea's.

'I was dreadfully upset that day,' she said, 'but I realize it was a terrible thing to do.'

Mrs. Sundler gave an extremely obliging impression. She said she understood Charlotte's feelings perfectly, adding that she, in turn, certainly owed Charlotte an apology. She had believed Charlotte was guilty, and she could not deny that she had been extremely harsh in her judgment. But from that day on she would do everything, everything in her power to ensure that Charlotte's honor was restored.

Charlotte responded equally politely, expressing her gratitude for this promise, but adding that at the moment there was another thing she found more pressing than her own vindication.

She went on to tell Thea Sundler about the terrible accident that had befallen the colonel's wife, interjecting that Karl-Artur probably did not know how serious his mother's condition was. Had he known, he would surely have been incapable of leaving Karlstad without a kind word to her.

When she heard this, however, Thea became extremely guarded.

She said she had decided Karl-Artur was being guided in all his important decisions by what could only be divine inspiration. Whatever he did, he was walking the path of Our Lord.

Charlotte's pale cheeks colored a bit at these words, but she finished putting forward her petition without a bitter or offensive word. She merely explained how firmly convinced she was that the colonel's wife could never recover as long as she and Karl-Artur remained estranged. She asked whether Thea did not think it would be a terrible thing for him to have his mother's death on his conscience.

Mrs. Sundler replied in the kindest, most affable tone of voice that she had complete confidence in God to hold a protective hand over both mother and son. She said perhaps it was the intention of Destiny to move dear Mrs. Ekenstedt toward greater devotion.

Charlotte imagined the sallow face with its threatening expression, fearing that this was hardly the way to make the colonel's wife more God-fearing. But she refrained from any indiscretion, saying only that the reason she had come was to appeal to Thea to exercise her influence over Karl-Artur to achieve reconciliation between him and his mother.

Mrs. Sundler's voice dropped a register, her lisp became more pronounced, her tone more unctuously humble than ever. Yes, she might have some influence over Karl-Artur, but when it came to something as significant as this she did not dare exercise it. The decision would have to be his and his alone.

'She doesn't want to help,' Charlotte thought. 'It was as I thought. There's no use appealing to her compassion. She will do nothing without getting something in return.'

She rose with the same self-possession she had shown throughout the visit, said an extremely polite farewell, and turned to the door. Mrs. Sundler accompanied her, discoursing all the while on what a great responsibility it was to be the confidante of Karl-Artur.

Charlotte, standing with one hand on the doorknob, turned around and glanced at the room.

'Your parlor is extremely pleasant,' she said. 'No wonder Karl-Artur enjoys being here so much.'

Thea Sundler said nothing. She could not see what Charlotte was getting at.

'I can imagine what your evenings are like here,' said

Charlotte. 'Your husband sitting at the piano, you standing beside him singing, and Karl-Artur relaxing in one of those lovely easy chairs, listening to the music.'

'Yes,' said Mrs. Sundler hesitantly, still uncertain where all this was leading. 'That's right, we do have very pleasant evenings, as you say, Charlotte.'

'Sometimes perhaps Karl-Artur also contributes to the entertainment,' Charlotte added. 'I can picture him reciting a poem, or describing that little gray parsonage he hopes to have.'

'Yes,' Mrs. Sundler repeated. 'Both my husband and I consider it a great pleasure when Karl-Artur honors our humble abode with his presence.'

'If nothing disrupts it, that pleasure may last for years and years,' Charlotte went on. 'I don't suppose Karl-Artur will rush into marriage with his peddler woman. Life will be very lonely for him at the parsonage. He will certainly need a nice place like this to retreat to.'

Mrs. Sundler stood silent. Her ears were perked, her attention focused. She knew Charlotte was planning her words to some end, but could still not imagine what it was.

'If I had stayed at the parsonage,' said Charlotte with a chuckle, 'I might have been able to distract him from time to time when he was free. I know, of course, that he no longer loves me, but surely we still do not need to be like cat and dog? I would have been able to help him with the orphanage, for instance. When you see someone on a daily basis as we do, you develop a great many shared interests.'

'Naturally. But, Charlotte, are you really intent on leaving the parsonage?'

'I can't really say. You know, of course, that I was considering marrying Schagerström.'

With those words she nodded an amiable farewell and opened the door, really on her way out this time.

When she was in the vestibule, however, she must have noticed that one of her shoes was untied. She bent down and retied it. Just to be on the safe side, she retied the other one as well. 'I need to give her some time to deliberate on the matter,' she said to herself. 'If it's true that she loves him, she won't let me go. But if she loves him not…'

While she was bent over her shoe, Mrs. Sundler came out into the vestibule.

'My dear Charlotte,' she said, 'won't you come back inside? I was just thinking, you have never been to visit me before. Won't you taste a drop of my raspberry cordial? I don't want you to leave before I've offered you something. One must always treat a guest to a little something, you know.'

Charlotte, who had finally managed to retie her shoes properly, straightened up and accepted in an affable enough tone of voice. She wouldn't at all mind sitting in the nice little parlor for a few more minutes while Mrs. Sundler ran down to the food cellar to get the cordial and prepare their glasses.

'Well, at least Thea's not stupid,' she thought to herself. 'There's some comfort in that.'

Mrs. Sundler was gone for quite some time, but Charlotte did not take this as a bad omen. She waited calmly and patiently. Her eyes had the same look a fisherman has when he watches the fish swimming around his baited hook.

In due course her hostess returned with a pitcher of cordial and some cookies. Charlotte poured herself a glass of the dark red liquid and helped herself to a gingerbread cookie, taking little bites and listening to Mrs. Sundler's apologies for having taken so long.

'What delicious cookies!' said Charlotte. 'I suppose you use your mother's recipe. They say she was a kitchen genius. Aren't you lucky to be such a good cook yourself! Karl-Artur must find the food here better than at the parsonage.'

'I really doubt that, Charlotte. Don't forget, we are people of little means. But, Charlotte, let us not speak of such trivialities, let us remember poor Beate Ekenstedt! May I speak openly, Charlotte?'

'That was why I came to see you, Thea dear,' said Charlotte in her gentlest voice.

Neither of them raised her voice, in fact if anything they

spoke more softly. They sat perfectly still, sipping raspberry cordial and eating cookies. But both women's hands trembled, like those of eager chess players as the end of a long game approaches.

'I'd like to be perfectly honest with you, so I'll tell you I believe Karl-Artur is slightly overpowered by his mother. Perhaps not so much by her person, since she is in Karlstad and doesn't often have the opportunity to influence him, but he has noticed that she is making every effort to bring the two of you back together. And if you'll excuse me for saying it, this is what he fears more than anything.'

Charlotte smiled gently. 'Aha,' she thought. 'So that's her angle of attack. She is most certainly not a fool.'

'Are you saying, Thea, that you would be able to persuade Karl-Artur to travel to Karlstad and be reconciled with his mother if you could convince him that it would have no consequences in relation to me?'

Mrs. Sundler shrugged.

'I am merely expressing an assumption,' she said. 'He may also find his own weaknesses a bit overpowering. There is something very attractive to him about you, Charlotte. I can hardly imagine how any young man would be able to resist anyone as beautiful as you.'

'And so you think...'

'Oh, Charlotte, it's so difficult to say. But I believe that if Karl-Artur had some certainty to cling to...'

'So you're saying that if the banns were read for Schagerström and me for the third time tomorrow he would feel secure.'

'Which would be a good thing, of course... But Charlotte, the banns can also be revoked. And the wedding might not take place for a long time. You might go on living at the parsonage for years and years.'

Charlotte set her glass back down on the tray somewhat hastily. When she had left home that morning, she had known that there would be a high price to be paid for ensuring that Thea would allow Karl-Artur to see his mother again. But she had thought the banns would suffice.

'I see it like this, Charlotte,' said Mrs. Sundler, now almost in a whisper, 'that if you went right home and wrote a few lines to Schagerström, inviting him to the parsonage tomorrow so that you and he could be married shortly after the Sunday service, then …'

'It cannot be!'

Charlotte's words burst forth like a plea for mercy. It was the only thing in the entire conversation that revealed the young woman's suffering.

Mrs. Sundler continued without the least attention to the lament of the other party to the conversation.

'I don't know, Charlotte, what it seems to you cannot be. All I am saying is that if you wrote that letter and if it were expedited safely to Stora Sjötorp, the answer might arrive five or six hours from now. If the reply were favorable, I would do everything in my power to persuade Karl-Artur to go.'

'And if it failed?'

'Charlotte, I care deeply about Mrs. Ekenstedt. I am truly unhappy on her behalf. If I could only settle Karl-Artur's fears in that one respect, I do not believe I would fail. I am convinced that Karl-Artur would set off tomorrow, as soon as he has done his clerical duties. Before the marriage ceremony begins, Charlotte, you would be informed that he had departed.'

This was an explicit, thoroughly thought-through plan with no shortcomings or snags. Charlotte looked down. Could she do it? It would mean living her whole life with a man she could not love. Could she?

Yes, of course she could. Her hand fumbled at the letter in her frock pocket. Of course she could.

She downed the rest of her cordial in one gulp to clear her throat:

'I will advise you of Schagerström's reply as soon as I possibly can,' she said, rising to leave.

SATURDAY: AFTERNOON AND EVENING

I.

When one has something difficult ahead, it is a good thing to be able to say to oneself: 'It must be done. I know why I am doing it. There is no other way.'

Deep anxiety is relieved by feeling firmly convinced that the only thing to do is to submit. It is really true as people say that everything is easier to bear once a decision has been made and cannot be altered.

When Charlotte returned to the parsonage she immediately wrote to Schagerström. It was just a short note, but she found it quite difficult to formulate. Look what she finally managed to produce!

'With reference to the final lines of your letter, Sir, I request that you come to the parsonage at two o'clock tomorrow so the honorable pastor can unite us as man and wife.

Be so good as to send a brief reply with the messenger.

Your humble servant, Sir
Charlotte Löwensköld'

Once the letter was folded and sealed, Charlotte requested the permission of the pastor to send it with his coachman to Stora Sjötorp. Then she began to account to her two old friends everything that had happened, and to prepare them for what the next day would probably bring in its wake.

The pastor's wife interrupted her.

'Charlotte, listen to me now! You'll have to finish telling us all this later. Go up to your room and rest for a while. You look like death warmed over.'

She accompanied Charlotte up to her room, forced her to lie down on a couch, and covered her with a shawl.

'Let go of your anxiety now and sleep,' she said. 'Sleep as long as you can. I'll wake you as dinner time approaches.'

For a while Charlotte's thoughts continued milling around in her head faster and more painfully than ever, but gradually they settled down, finally seeming to have realized that there was no sense in fussing any longer, that the decision had been made and was irrevocable. And after some time the poor young woman fell asleep, and left it all behind her.

She slept for hours. The pastor's wife looked in on her as she had promised, when dinner was announced, but finding her sleeping she did not disturb her. No one woke Charlotte until the coachman returned from Stora Sjötorp with Schagerström's reply.

Charlotte opened it to find that he had answered with a single line:

'Your humble servant will be honored to appear.'

She sent the short note directly on to Mrs. Sundler, and for the second time Charlotte began to tell the pastor and his wife of her adventures, but once again she was interrupted. There was a letter from her sister, the wife of Doctor Romelius, asking Charlotte to come. She had had a severe lung hemorrhage that very morning.

'Good gracious, it never rains but it pours,' said the pastor's wife. 'I suppose she's developed consumption. I've thought for quite some time she was looking poorly. Of course you must go and see her, dear heart. I do hope it won't be too much for you!'

'I'll be just fine, just fine,' Charlotte reassured her, hurrying to ready herself for her second walk to the village that day.

She found her sister sitting in her drawing room in a high-backed armchair, surrounded by all her children. Two stood by her, two sat on a stool at her feet, and the two little ones were crawling about on the floor. These two were too small to know much of illness and danger, while the four bigger ones were sensible enough to be frightened and agitated. They seemed to be forming a ring around their mother to protect her from a renewed attack.

No one moved when Charlotte came in. The eldest boy made a warning gesture.

'Mama is not allowed to move or speak,' he whispered.

There was no risk that Charlotte would tempt her ill sister to speak. Something tightened in her own throat at the very moment she entered the room. She struggled to breathe and to hold back her tears.

The drawing room was small and sparsely furnished, containing only a set of furniture her sister had inherited after the deaths of their parents. This was a sofa, a coffee table, two armchairs, two side tables and six straight-backed chairs. They were handsome, old-fashioned pieces made of birch, but because they were the only things in the room, which had not even a scrap of carpeting on the floor or a potted plant on the windowsill, the room had always appeared very dull to Charlotte. When she had visited her sister she had found it distressing to sit in there, although that had not made any difference. Her sister had never invited her into any of the other rooms. Charlotte suspected that Marie-Louise lived in genteel poverty with her family, which explained why she had never seen the rest of their home.

Although doctors were usually quite well to do, Romelius spent all his time at the inn with a glass in his hand, so presumably he brought home next to nothing and left his wife and children to live in poverty and privation. It was easy to see that his wife, who loved him and did not want her sister finding fault with him, had kept her at a distance and not allowed her closer insight into how they lived.

So today, when her sister was extremely ill and wretched, Charlotte was very touched at having been invited into the parlor. She was protecting her husband even now.

Charlotte went up to her sister, kissing her on the brow.

'Oh, Marie-Louise, Marie-Louise!' she whispered.

Her sister looked up at her, smiling softly. Then she nodded toward her children, who were grouped around her, radiating concern, and back at Charlotte.

'Of course, of course,' said Charlotte, knowing full well what she meant.

'Come now, children,' she said in her firmest, most commanding tone, hardly knowing how she managed to muster it, 'Mrs. Forsius sent along some lovely pastries for you. They're in my bag out in the vestibule. Come along and see!'

She enticed them out of the room, gave them their pastries, and sent them out into the garden to play.

When she returned to her sister, Charlotte sat on the stool at her feet, taking her rough, work-worn hands in her own and holding them to her cheek.

'All right, my dear, while they're outside for a bit, tell me what is on your mind.'

'If I should die ...' the ill woman said, but stopped herself for fear of starting to cough.

'Heavens, I forgot you mustn't talk,' said Charlotte. 'But you are asking me to take care of the children if you should pass on. And I promise you I will, Marie-Louise.'

Her sister nodded. She smiled her thanks gently, as a tear dropped from the corner of her eye.

'I knew you'd help me,' she whispered.

'She's not even wondering how I could cope with such a tribe,' Charlotte thought to herself. In the face of this new tribulation, she had forgotten all about the events of the morning. Suddenly it struck her: 'Of course I'll be able to take care of the children. I'm going to be a wealthy woman. I'm marrying Schagerström.'

A moment later a new thought crossed her mind: 'Perhaps this is the explanation for everything that's happened: was it all so I would be able to help Marie-Louise?'

This was the first time she was able to contemplate marrying

Schagerström with anything approaching satisfaction. Until that moment she had only accepted the inevitability with patient subjugation.

She offered to help her sister into bed, but she shook her head. There was something more she wanted to say.

'Don't let the children live here with Richard,' she told her sister.

Charlotte nodded eagerly. And yet she was astonished. So Marie-Louise did not admire her husband unreservedly, as she had believed. She realized he was a drinker, and that the children would have to be removed from his sphere of influence.

It seemed her sister wished to confide yet another thought:

'I fear love,' she said. 'I knew about Richard's problem, but love compelled me to take him. I despise love.'

Charlotte knew that she was saying this as a kind of solace. She was trying to tell her that even the most powerful love could move a person in the wrong direction, could push a person into fateful mistakes. It was better to let common sense be one's guide.

She would have liked to reply that she, personally, intended to go on loving love with her dying breath and never be angry with love for having tormented her, but at that moment the doctor's wife was beset by her life-threatening cough, and so no answer was ever forthcoming. When it subsided Charlotte hastened to make her bed and bundle her into it.

That evening Charlotte did all the duties of the woman of the house in this little home. She made the children a meal, kept them company while they ate, and put them to bed.

But touching the clothing and bedding of this home for the first time, the pots and the china, she was appalled. How worn and cracked and badly cared for it all was! Even the most essential household items were lacking! How slovenly and incompetent their housemaid was! How patched the children's clothes were! How much the worse for wear were the table and chairs. One chair was missing its back, another had lost a leg.

Charlotte walked around, her eyes brimming with stinging

tears, not allowing them to fall. She felt a poignant sense of sympathy for her sister, who had endured all this poverty without complaint, without requesting help.

While doing these chores she looked in on Marie-Louise regularly. She was lying in her bed, apparently not in pain, and seeming pleased to be looked after.

'Shall I tell you a piece of good news?' asked Charlotte. 'Never again are you going to have to sink to such depths of exhaustion. I will be sending you a capable serving maid in the morning. You will be able to stay abed and rest until you are completely recovered.'

The sick woman smiled doubtfully. This was clearly a pleasing prospect, but Charlotte thought she could see in her face that something else was bothering her, something unresolved that was making her uneasy.

'It's too late for all this,' Charlotte worried to herself. 'She knows she's not long for this world. Nothing can comfort her.'

A few minutes later she was at her sister's bedside once more. She spoke to her sister about sending her to take the waters somewhere, where she would be well cared for.

'You know I am going to have plenty of money. You can depend on me.'

She was reluctant to talk about the Schagerström fortune in that way, but her sister appreciated it. The thought that Charlotte was going to be wealthy was the best cure for what was plaguing her.

She pulled Charlotte's hands close and stroked them in thanks, and yet she still did not look entirely calm.

'What can be troubling her?' Charlotte wondered to herself. She had a suspicion, but was not prepared to be receptive to it. Could it be that Marie-Louise also wanted to ask her to plead her husband's case? Not when she was lying there in her state of destitution, exhausted and sick unto death, surely? No, it had to be something else.

When Charlotte had put all the children to bed, she went in to say good night to her sister.

'I'll be leaving now, but shall go and ask the woman who is

251

on night alert for the village to sit by you tonight. And I'll be back in the morning.'

Once again her sister stroked her hand most lovingly.

'I won't be needing you tomorrow, but come back on Monday!'

Charlotte realized that she was expecting her husband, who was out attending to someone who was ill that night, to stay home on Sunday. And she preferred her sister not to encounter him.

The invalid continued to hold her hand. Charlotte knew she wanted to say something else to her.

She bent over the bed, smoothing a lock of hair out of her patient's face. She had the sensation of touching someone who was dying, and in a powerful insight that this might be the last time she saw her valiant, loyal sister, she did her best once more to meet her needs.

'I promise you Schagerström and I will look after Romelius.'

Oh, what an expression of joy passed over the face of the sick woman! She pulled Charlotte's hand to her lips.

Then she fell back on the pillows, at rest. Her eyes closed and in a few minutes she was peaceful and sound asleep.

'I knew it!' thought Charlotte. 'He was the one she was worried about. I knew she couldn't really despise love.'

II.

It was after ten that evening when Charlotte returned from her sister's. As she was about to open the yard-gate, the housemaid and the kitchen maid, who were also returning home, caught up with her.

They were quick to relate to her that they were coming from the foundry at Holma where they had attended an evangelical meeting in the old forge. Pastor Ekenstedt had spoken, and the place had been full to bursting. People had come from all over, not only from the foundry and the village.

Charlotte was about to ask whether Karl-Artur had been as eloquent as ever, but the two domestics were so eager to describe what they had heard, she couldn't get a word in edgewise.

'And Pastor Ekenstedt talked about you, Miss Charlotte, almost the entire time. He said that he and everyone else had judged you unfairly. There had been nothing underhanded or false in your behavior, and he wanted everyone in the congregation to know it.'

'He told us what you said, Miss, and what he said when you quarreled,' said the kitchen maid. 'He wanted us to know exactly what'd happened betwixt you. Though I didn't think it was quite right of him. There were a couple of young lads sitting right in front of me, and they were doubled over with laughter.'

'Right, and they weren't the only ones to laugh,' said the housemaid, 'though a´course the ones who laughed were the ones with no sense in their heads. Sure everybody else thought he was being wise. And in the end he asked us to join forces and pray for you, Miss Charlotte. Because you was now embarkin' on a hazardous path, he said, becuz you was marryin' a rich gentleman. And he reminded us of Jesus' words 'bout how difficult it is for the wealthy to be admitted to heaven… But, Miss, wherever are ya goin'?'

Charlotte rushed off without a word. She ran in the direction of the house as if pursued, through the vestibule and up the stairs to her room. Throwing off her garments without so much as lighting a lamp, she lay immobile, staring into the darkness.

'He's done it now,' she mumbled. 'Karl-Artur has murdered my love.'

He had previously failed. He had injured it, held it in contempt, slandered it, but it had not died. Without so much as a kind glance to nurture it, it had remained alive.

Now that this had happened it had to die.

She asked herself why what he had done now was more

difficult to endure than anything else. She was unable to explain it to herself, and yet she knew it was true.

Karl-Artur had surely had her best interests at heart. He had wanted to restore her honor. He had spoken, guided by his conscience. But it had nevertheless dealt the deathblow to her love.

She felt so bereft. Imagine having nothing to dream of, no one to long for! When she read something beautiful, the hero would not automatically have his features. When she listened to music full of longing, she would no longer be able to identify with it, because it would not resonate in her.

Would she see anything lovely in the flowers or the birds or in children now that she had lost her love?

The new marriage she was about to enter into stretched before her like a huge, barren desert. If she had had her love, there would have been something to fill her soul. Now she would sit there on that unfamiliar estate filled with emptiness and surrounded by emptiness.

The colonel's wife came into her mind. Now Charlotte understood what had made her so angry, why she had looked so stern and threatening. She, too, had been lying there thinking that Karl-Artur had murdered her love.

Charlotte's thoughts also went to Schagerström. She wondered what the colonel's wife had seen in him that had made her wish he had been her son. She had not uttered those words as an empty phrase, no, she had meant something by them.

Charlotte did not have to ponder long before she knew what the colonel's wife had seen. She had discovered that Schagerström was able to love, as Karl-Artur was not. He could not truly love.

Charlotte smiled incredulously to herself. Was Schagerström more capable of love than Karl-Artur? He had certainly been quite thoughtless both the first time he proposed and when he arranged to have the banns read. But the colonel's wife was the most perceptive person she knew. She realized that Schagerström would never murder the love of anyone who loved him.

'Indeed, it is a terrible sin to murder love,' Charlotte whispered to herself, lying there.

A moment later she found herself wondering whether Karl-Artur had acted out of malicious intent. He, who had been her fiancé for five years, ought to have known that nothing would hurt her as deeply as his talking openly to a crowd about her and her love, making her the object of ridicule or intrusive sympathy. Or had Thea Sundler urged him on, so as to finally be rid of Charlotte? Had she not been satisfied with having got her married and out of Karl-Artur's life, had she also found it necessary for him to deal her this mortal affront?

It made little difference whose fault it was. At that moment Charlotte felt the same loathing for them both.

She lay there for some time, in impotent fury. Now and then a tear dropped from her eye, dampening her pillow.

But in Charlotte's veins flowed ancient, noble Swedish blood, and in her soul resided true Swedish willpower, that high-minded, proud willpower that never countenances defeat, but rises to new battles with unbroken strength.

Suddenly she sat up in bed, banging her fists.

'There is one thing I do know,' she said. 'I shall not give them the pleasure of seeing me miserable in my marriage.'

And when that good intention had taken root in her soul, she lay down and slept. She did not wake up until eight, when the pastor's wife brought a breakfast tray in, with a bouquet of flowers to make a proper start to the great day that was about to begin.

THE WEDDING DAY

I.

Schagerström arrived at the parsonage at two o'clock Sunday afternoon, as Charlotte had requested. The wealthy foundry owner came in his great landau. The horses and harnesses were gleaming, the footman and coachman were in full livery, with flowers in their vest pockets and the carriage apron removed to display gleaming, knee-high leather boots set off nicely against white leather trousers. Although their master was not nearly as formally garbed as they, he arrived dressed for the occasion, with a fine collar and cuffs, a white vest and well-tailored gray dress suit, and a rose in his buttonhole. In short, anyone who saw him and his equipage would be sure to think: 'Good heavens! Is wealthy Schagerström off to be married?'

Upon entering the parsonage he was touched by the generous reception he received. To tell the truth, during these recent worrisome times the parsonage had had something closed and inhospitable about it. It is difficult to explain how this made itself evident, but a sensitive person noticed the difference immediately.

That day the white yard-gate was open, as was the front door. All the blinds on the upstairs windows, which had been drawn for weeks, were up, and the sun was allowed in to bleach the carpets and furniture covers as much as it pleased. But this wasn't the only change. There was a special glow to the flowers, the birds were singing in a particularly cheery way.

Not only the dainty young housemaid but also the pastor and his wife were waiting on the front steps to receive him. The old couple embraced Schagerström, kissed him on the cheek, patted his back and called him by his given name, all very informally. They treated him like a son. Schagerström, who had spent a sleepless night full of anxious struggling with himself to find the right way forward, felt his spirits rise as distinctly as if a painful toothache had gone.

They took him into the pastor's inner sanctum, where Charlotte was waiting for him. She was dressed in a light silk dress shot through with different colors, and she looked enchanting, in spite of the fact that her attire seemed a bit out of fashion. One might have imagined that, having no suitable dress herself, she had borrowed this one from the pastor's wife, who had dug it up out of one of the huge chests in the parsonage attic. It was short, very low cut, and sewn as if to suit a person whose waist was up near her armpits, but it looked perfect on Charlotte. No one had gone out of their way to make a garland for her hair or to borrow a wedding diadem, but the pastor's wife had helped her put up her curls with a tall tortoiseshell comb, and the hairstyle was well suited to the dress. Around her neck she wore a double row of wax pearls with a lovely clasp, and she had matching bracelets around her wrists. None of these things was of any particular value, but they became their wearer. She looked like an old-fashioned portrait.

When Schagerström bent down to place a kiss on her hand she said, with a slightly tremulous smile:

'Not long ago, Karl-Artur left for Karlstad to be reconciled with his mother.'

'No one but you, my gracious lady, would have been able to achieve such a miracle,' said Schagerström.

He understood that Charlotte had managed to persuade young Ekenstedt to make the trip by agreeing to marry him, Schagerström. Exactly how these matters coincided was beyond his ken, however, and to tell the truth he was quite displeased with the whole affair. You will understand: he admired the self-sacrificing nature of this young woman, he was glad to think that the colonel's wife and her son would be reconciled and yet … to put it briefly: he would quite simply have preferred the young woman to be marrying him for his own sake, and not because of young Ekenstedt.

'It was *"the bad influence"* you wrote of,' Charlotte went on. '*The bad influence* would not be content with any less than my marrying and leaving the parsonage. And it all had to happen without delay. There was no mercy.'

Schagerström particularly noticed the word mercy. He thought it must imply that Charlotte was now indescribably tormented at having to give him her hand in marriage.

'Gracious lady, I am devastated…'

Charlotte interrupted him.

'My name is Charlotte,' she said with a little curtsey. 'And I intend to call you Henrik.'

Schagerström bowed in acknowledgement of this piece of information.

'I intend to call you Henrik,' Charlotte repeated with a little quiver in her voice. 'I understand that your late wife called you Gustav. I want her to have that name to herself. One must not deprive the dead of that which is their own.'

Schagerström found himself astonished once again. He thought this must mean that Charlotte no longer harbored the same distaste for him that she had shown in Örebro the last time they met. He felt his spirits change course once more. Had suspicion and humility not been second nature to him, he might have felt entirely happy.

Charlotte asked him if he would be content for the ceremony to take place in the pastor's outer chamber, where so many other couples had been united in holy matrimony over the years.

'I believe the pastor's wife would have liked to see us married in the upstairs drawing room,' said Charlotte, 'but it seems more solemn to me down here.'

Actually, the situation was thus. Charlotte, wanting to spend that morning in heart-to-heart conversation with her old friends and protectors, had not allowed the pastor's wife to waste the time dusting and cleaning the drawing room, which had not been used for so long. She hadn't so much as allowed the pastor's wife to be involved in preparation of the meal to which she was going to treat the newlyweds.

The young foundry owner had no objections to the office, and the marriage ceremony was held forthwith. The coachman and footman from Stora Sjötorp, the tenant farmer and his wife, and all the help from the parsonage were called in to witness the ceremony. The old pastor read out the vows, with the chaffinches and the sparrows chirping so eagerly and cheerfully outside the window one might have thought they knew what was going on and wanted to raise their finest wedding hymns in celebration.

When it was all over, Schagerström stood there slightly at a loss, not quite knowing what to do, but Charlotte turned to him and raised her lips for a light kiss.

She really was bewildering. He thought he had prepared himself for all eventualities: tears, hard-heartedness, haughty arrogance, everything but this cheerful submissiveness.

'I'm quite sure anyone who sees us thinks I must be the one who was forced into this marriage, rather than her,' he thought to himself.

He could find no other explanation than that Charlotte considered it most consistent with her pride to look pleased.

'But she's certainly putting a good face on it!' he mused, slightly vexed and at the same time full of admiration.

Later, when the four of them were at the table having a late lunch which, according to the pastor's wife, had been pulled together from what they had by the grace of God, but which was plentiful in any case, Schagerström really made an effort to cast off his gloom. The pastor and his wife, who were of course not the least bit surprised to see him feeling a bit awkward about his position, did all they could to liven him up, and after some time they appeared to have succeeded.

At least they managed to get him chatting. He began to

describe his travels to foreign parts and his efforts to improve the Swedish iron ore industry on the basis of what he had learned abroad, in England and Germany.

While he was speaking he noticed Charlotte listening to him with undivided attention. She craned her neck, eyes wide, hanging on his every word. He assumed this was merely performance. 'She's putting it on for the sake of the old pastor and his wife,' he thought. 'She couldn't possibly be interested in matters about which she knows nothing. She wants the old couple to believe she is in love with me. That's all it is.'

Actually, this explanation appealed to him more than the previous one. It did him good to see how attached his wife was to these splendid elderly people.

Toward the end of the meal, however, the atmosphere grew more muted. It was impossible for the old couple at the parsonage to avoid the realization that Charlotte would very shortly be leaving them. Charlotte, that brilliant creature with her silly pranks, her wild nature, her sharp tongue, her hot temper. Charlotte, of whom they had so often had to disapprove. Charlotte who, because she was so loving, they had had to forgive so much, would no longer be living in their house. How empty and dull life was going to be!

'Well, at least you'll be coming back tomorrow to pack your belongings. That's one good thing,' said the pastor's wife.

Schagerström knew they were trying to comfort themselves with the thought that Charlotte was not moving far away, that they would be seeing her often, and yet he also felt he could see them shrinking, their backs bending, their faces becoming furrowed. Starting today there would be no one who could keep old age from overtaking them.

'We are so pleased, Charlotte, dear heart,' said the pastor, 'that you are going to have a fine home and a good husband, but you know, you know... We will miss you. We will miss you more than I can say.'

There were tears in his voice, but his wife rescued the situation by telling Schagerström about the time her husband told her what he would have done if he had been fifty years younger and a bachelor. Everyone just had to laugh, and all their morose thoughts were swept away.

When the landau drove up to the door and Charlotte moved toward the pastor's wife to bid her farewell, the older woman pulled her into the next room and whispered:

'Keep an eye on your husband, my dear, for the rest of the day. There's something troubling him. Keep a good eye on him!'

Charlotte promised to do her best.

'Incidentally, he looks quite handsome today. Have you noticed? His finery suits him.'

Charlotte took her by surprise with her answer:

'I have never thought he did not look handsome. There is something powerful about him. He reminds me of Napoleon.'

'Good heavens!' said the pastor's wife. 'I've never thought about that. But I am pleased to hear that you think so.'

When Charlotte came out onto the front steps, ready to leave, Schagerström noticed that she was wearing the same hat and mantilla she had had on in church exactly four Sundays before, which he had found simple and unbecoming at the time.

Now he found them utterly charming, and in spite of everything he was overcome by a wave of pleasure at the fact that this young creature was now his, and would be accompanying him to his home. As Charlotte was saying a seemingly endless round of goodbyes, he approached her, took her in his strong arms, and lifted her into the carriage.

'That's it, that's it, keep it up, keep it up!' the pastor and his wife shouted after him, as the carriage drove once around the yard, decorated with flowers, and out through the gate.

II.

It more or less goes without saying that the young foundry owner had second thoughts almost immediately. It was unkind of him to frighten Charlotte. If he went on like that, she might think he considered the whole event something more than a performance, and that he might make a true husband's claims on her.

Charlotte really did look a bit anxious. He noticed how she withdrew toward the corner of the carriage, as far from him as she could possibly move. But this did not last long. Before they reached the village, Charlotte was sitting close beside him once again, smiling and chatting.

Ah, well, it was easy to understand that she would want things to look good as they rode down the village street. It would be different, of course, once they were alone on the country road.

But Charlotte continued as she had begun. She spoke in a lively, cheerful way throughout the journey. And the subjects she chose were largely intended to show him that she took her marriage entirely seriously.

She began by speaking of his horses. First she wanted to know a little about the team of four that were pulling the landau. Where were they bought, how old were they, what were their names, what kind of lineage did they have, were they easily frightened, had they ever bolted? She went on to ask about all the other horses at Stora Sjötorp. Might there even be regular riding horses -- proper, trained riding horses? And saddles? Oh, was there really an English lady's saddle?

She spent a moment feeling sorry for the horses at the parsonage. They would fare badly now, as she would no longer be there to exercise them.

At that, Schagerström was unable to resist a comment.

'The other day in the mail coach, a woman I do not know was saying,' he commented, 'that a certain lady had severely abused her benefactor's poor, innocent creatures.'

'Pardon me?' Charlotte exclaimed, but then she realized what he was referring to and burst out laughing.

There is something quite remarkable about a good laugh. All at once the newlyweds felt like close friends. All the solemnity and formality between them vanished.

Charlotte went on asking questions. What kind of workshops and equipment did they have at Stora Sjötorp? How many hearths did the forge have, and what were the names of the smiths, their wives and children? She recalled there also being a sawmill there, was there not? Aha, and a flour mill as well? How many millstones did they have? What was the miller's name?

It was quite an interrogation. Schagerström felt dizzy from all the questions. Sometimes he was not able to answer fully. He could not account for how many sheep he had, nor was he sure how many milk cows there were in the barn, or how much milk they gave.

'You'll have to ask the supervisor,' he said with a laugh.

'I must say you don't seem to keep track of things very well,' Charlotte replied. 'I suspect things are in a terrible state at Stora Sjötorp. I shall have my hands full getting them back in order.'

She seemed less than displeased at this prospect, and Schagerström gladly allowed that he had long been wishing for a real house tyrant, one of those forbidding women of the house like Mrs. Forsius.

When he mentioned the supervisor, Charlotte became curious as to how many gentlemen were usually present at dinner at the manor. She asked in detail about the household arrangements, the number of housemaids and servants. Did he have a housekeeper? Was she capable?

Nor did she forget the garden. When he informed her that there was both a hothouse and a greenhouse for grapes she was more than a little astonished, and as happy as when she had heard that there were riding horses.

It is easy to see that Schagerström was anything but bored on this journey. When the carriage turned onto the little road that led through the woods to his home, he had to admit to himself that the twenty kilometers between Stora Sjötorp and Korskyrka had been wondrously short that day.

Otherwise, he was careful not to get his hopes up. 'I understand her perfectly,' he said to himself. 'She is striving to accept the inevitable. And chattering to keep her thoughts at bay.'

Upon arrival, it was clear that everyone at Stora Sjötorp had outdone themselves that day.

No one could really understand what had possessed their master. Although he had received the letter from the parsonage at three o'clock on the Saturday afternoon he hadn't said a word to anyone about what was imminent until quite late that evening, when he suddenly realized he was going to have to get hold of a wedding ring. One of the estate supervisors had been ordered to the nearest town and instructed, if necessary, to wake the goldsmith from his best hours of sleep to sell him a plain gold band with their names engraved in it.

Fortunately, the supervisor had not kept the matter a secret, but informed as many of the staff as he could that a new mistress would be arriving the very next day. At least they were lucky in that respect. How in the world would the housekeeper otherwise have had time to air out the best rooms, remove the furniture covers and dust everything? How would the gardener have had time to get all the gravel paths raked and all the flowerbeds weeded? And how would there have been time to clean up and polish all the uniforms, boots and harnesses, not to mention the landau itself? Their master had walked around the place as if in a trance, and had not been fit to arrange anything himself. Johansson, his valet, had been forced to pick out what he considered a seemly wedding suit, using his own judgment.

Luckily, though, there were people on the staff who knew what needed to be done when a young mistress was about to arrive. Both the housekeeper and the gardener had been there in the years when the widow of Chief Justice Oldencrona had been mistress of Stora Sjötorp, so they knew very well how to prepare an appropriate reflection of the status of the estate.

More or less because it was the thing to do, the housekeeper had asked her master for orders concerning his return on the Sunday before he departed, and the gardener had taken the same precaution. Schagerström, of course, had not really planned for a reception at all but, he said, if Mrs. Sällberg would be so kind as to prepare a little welcoming dinner and if the gardener thought he had time to raise a flowered arch, he would be most grateful.

Once they had secured his *carte blanche*, these excellent people had simply waited for Schagerström to leave so that they could begin their preparations for a virtually royal welcome.

'We must bear in mind, Mrs. Sällberg,' said the gardener to the housekeeper, 'that she is of noble blood, and surely knows how things are done at a place of this size.'

'No, coming from a parsonage I truly doubt that she has any idea,' the housekeeper countered, 'but that doesn't prevent me from wanting to show her I know what I'm about.'

'I wouldn't be so sure,' the gardener replied. 'I've seen her in church, and she certainly doesn't look like your run-of-the-mill companion to an elderly pastor's wife. You should see her bearing. She reminds me of the lady who was our mistress here at Stora Sjötorp in the olden days. Looking at her warmed the cockles of my heart.'

'However highborn or not she may be,' the housekeeper went on, 'I'll be pleased to have a young mistress in the house. There'll be balls and parties. I'll have a chance to prove my worth. That will be very different from cooking, day in and day out, for a few gentlemen who come in to the dining room, gobble their meals and leave.'

'I just hope it won't be too much of a good thing,' the gardener chuckled. 'Anyone who's been under the wing of Mrs. Forsius for years surely knows how to run a household.'

He hurried back out; it was high time to get down to work. If he was going to have time to raise four flowered arches and prepare decorations with their names intertwined in flowers he couldn't talk the day away.

Still, the gardener would never have finished the task if he hadn't had so many eager assistants. But every single person who lived or worked on the estate was quite carried away. There was going to be a mistress up in the manor again, someone they could turn to with their worries, with their aches and pains. A mistress was far superior in this respect to a master. A mistress stayed at home, was willing to listen to whatever a person had on their mind, whether it was about one of the children or one of the cows. It was almost too good to be true to think that she would be coming this very day.

A couple of the young boys spread the news to all the tenants on the estate, and in every croft and dwelling everyone's best clothes were taken out and put on, in order to go up to the manor and catch a glimpse of the newlyweds. But every person who turned up was immediately put to work. The arches were raised, all the old flags and banners from the days of the previous owners were located and hung along the lane. They even found a couple of small cannons so they could fire a salute. There was more hustle and bustle than we can really imagine.

But by six, when the newlyweds drove up the lane to Stora Sjötorp, everything was done and everyone was ready.

The first arch stood on the forest road, and every smith from the forge was there, each raising his sledgehammer over his shoulder, greeting them. At the second, at the edge of the woods, all the farmers were gathered, their shovels raised in greeting, while at the third arch, which marked the beginning of the lane, all the workers from the flour mill and the sawmill stood shouting hurrah, and at the fourth, at the entry to the manor yard, they found the gardener, surrounded by his assistants, proffering a lovely bouquet. Up at the house, finally, the estate manager, the accountants, the supervisors, the housekeeper and all the serving maids were assembled, bowing and curtseying.

In fact, things were not in such perfect order as portrayed here. Still, everyone was in the best possible frame of mind, they shouted their hurrahs until they were hoarse, even once the carriage had passed the arch they were assigned to stand by. The children ran alongside the carriage in a most unceremonious manner, the cannon salute rang out at highly unexpected moments, and the entire arrangement was so pretty and so festive that the late chief justice's equally late wife would have been pleased if she had been looking down from her heaven, and thought that Stora Sjötorp and her old gardener were doing her proud.

Schagerström, who had not at all planned on such a grand reception, began to feel a little annoyed that his subordinates had taken such liberties, but fortunately before he could vent his dissatisfaction he looked Charlotte's way.

She sat there with a huge smile on her face, at the same time as there was a tear at the corner of her eye, and her hands were clasped.

'Oh it's lovely, it's lovely,' she whispered, 'just lovely!'

All of it: the arches, the flowers, the flags, the shouts of hurrah, the kind smiles, the shots from those little old cannons; it was all for her, it was to wish her welcome to the estate. And she, who had become accustomed over the last several weeks to the feeling that everyone despised and was avoiding her, she who had felt suspicion and censure follow her every movement, she who had hardly dared leave her home out of fear of being insulted, she was grateful, touched, and honored beyond her worth or her rank.

There were no satirical ballads, no prickly bouquets, no scornful laughter; what greeted her were joy and rapture.

She extended her arms to the people. She loved this place and its inhabitants from the first moment she saw them. She felt she was entering a new, happy world. She wanted to live and die here.

III.

What a pleasure for a man to bring his young bride into a fine home! To walk her from room to room and hear her exclamations of pleasure, to hurry a step or two ahead of her, open the door to the next room and say: 'I suppose this one's not too bad.' To see her flutter like a butterfly, playing a chord on the grand piano, rushing over to a work of art, glancing into a mirror to check whether the looking glass gave a favorable reflection of her, scurrying to the window to see the wonderful view!

But what anxiety must it not give rise to when in the midst of all this she bursts into tears, what haste one must make to inquire as to the problem, what honest vows one must make to do one's utmost to eradicate any concerns she might have!

What joy it must bring to hear that nothing was the matter except that she has a sister who is ill, and living in bare, ugly rooms while she is quite undeservedly able to enjoy all this amazing magnificence! What pride one must feel in being able to promise her that she may render unto this sister every form of help she requires, in fact if she wishes on this very evening…

Oh, no, not this evening. Tomorrow will be quite soon enough.

And so that sorrow is dispensed with. She puts it entirely out of her mind, and returns to the tour of the manor.

'This chair,' she says, 'is extraordinarily comfortable, and over there by the window would be a most suitable spot for a needlework table.'

Yes, it is clear that she will look utterly charming at her needlework table, but at the very same moment one is reminded of something one was in the process of forgetting. This is no proper marriage. It is merely pro forma. The whole thing is just a sham. Now and then she looks as if she were taking it seriously, but one knows, of course, what she really thinks.

Yet there is one thing that can be enjoyed: going along with her until it is absolutely necessary to acknowledge the truth, letting the game continue for a few more hours, taking pleasure in it as she is taking pleasure, hiding one's anxiety deep in one's heart and seizing the moment.

Yes, in that way it is possible to continue the tour of the manor with the same sense of happiness for the entire time until the butler comes to announce that dinner is served.

And is it not wonderful to offer her one's arm and escort her into a dining room with a magnificently laid table, with fine china and gleaming crystal and polished silver, to be able to take a seat with her and be served a dinner befitting royalty, eight courses, with wine gleaming in the bottles and food that melts in one's mouth, food one barely notices one is eating?

And then to relax into the pleasure of sitting beside a young woman who is everything one loves, who is intelligent and unpretentious, who knows her etiquette, who is extremely mischievous, who can laugh and cry at once, and who displays a new quality of character with almost every minute that passes!

Perhaps it is also a great pleasure to be drawn away from all this, just as one was beginning to lose one's senses, when the gardener, who is playing master of ceremonies of Stora Sjötorp for the evening, comes to announce that everything is ready for the barn dance, but that the dancing cannot begin until the master and mistress are there. They are the bridegroom and bride, and must dance first at the wedding ball.

What a wonderful way to celebrate one's marriage! Not among one's equals, who might be envious or critical, but among admiring subjects who more or less look up to one as if to a god and goddess. To begin by following custom and leading one's bride once around the smooth barn floor, and then to abandon the dance to watch her dancing, watch her take a turn with the smiths and the millers, with the old men and the lads, and dance with each of them with the same good cheer. It was wonderful to sit there thinking of fairy tales and poems about elves that joined in people's dancing and enticed handsome young men with them to the woods! For when one sees her floating over the dance floor among the crowd of hardworking men and women, she seems to be made of something other than earthly stuff, of something higher and better.

Yes, sitting like that begrudging each minute that passes until, at last, one notes that the time has come, that the wedding day is over, that the empty, earnest life must recommence!

IV.

As regards Charlotte, she constantly had the pastor's wife's warning ringing in her ear: 'Keep an eye on your husband, my dear, for the rest of the day. There's something troubling him. Keep a close eye on him!'

She, too, had noticed how quickly his moods shifted from joy to dejection, and she never started a dance without checking that he was still in the barn, and the moment her partner left her, she went over to her husband and sat down at his side.

Because she was one of those people who has an eye for everything, she had observed when they walked past the stable on their way to the barn that the little coach Schagerström used for longer journeys had been pulled out of the carriage shed. That had made her even more concerned and watchful.

When dancing with the coachman, she tried to pry a little information out of him:

'You're not losing track of the time, are you? What time had your master planned on leaving?'

'I don't believe the time's been quite set, my lady. But I've taken out the coach and harnessed the horses. I can be ready lickety-split.'

Well, at least she now knew what she was up against! But her husband was still sitting there, talking calmly with his subjects, and so she thought it prudent to pretend ignorance. 'I suppose he had planned to go off this very evening,' she thought, 'but he may have changed his plans now that he sees I am not as great a danger as he had imagined.'

But a few minutes later, just at the end of quite a long reel, she noticed that he was gone. It was darkest night out now, and the only light in the barn came from a couple of lanterns, but she was suddenly quite sure he was nowhere inside. She looked around for the coachman and her husband's valet, her worries growing. They, too, seemed to have gone.

Throwing her shawl around her shoulders, she moved toward a small group of young people who were standing in the wide doorway to the barn to cool down after the dance, said a few words to them and then slid silently out into the night, without anyone noticing.

She was such a stranger to the estate she hardly had any idea which way the manor house was. But she noted a faint light in the distance, and hurried that way. As she approached, she saw that it was a lantern on the ground outside the stable. Indeed, the coachman was readying the conveyance, and had just brought out the horses.

Stealthily, Charlotte moved in the direction of the carriage, unseen. She had an urge to wait for a moment when the coachman had his back turned and sneak inside. When the coach drove up to the house and Schagerström came to take his seat, she would let him know exactly what she thought of that kind of attempted escape.

'Why doesn't he discuss whatever is bothering him with me?' she wondered. 'He's like a timid schoolboy.'

However, before she had a chance to act on her intention, the coachman had finished. He hung the reins over the rail and put on his coat, which had been lying across his seat. He was just about to hop up onto the coachbox, when he apparently remembered the lantern. He calmed the horses with 'Steady,

271

boys!', walked over and picked up the lantern, put it out, and carried it back into the stable.

Of course he did all this as fast as he could, but just nearby someone was waiting who was even quicker. As he closed the stable door, a whip cracked. An eager shout set the horses off through the gate, which the coachman had already opened, and down the lane. The carriage vanished into the dark of night. All that could be heard was the rolling of the wheels and the tramping of hooves.

If ever a coachman has run faster than his own horses to get to the manor and report to his master that some accursed rascal had made bold to jump up on his box and driven off with his coach right in front of his nose, it was Lundman, the coachman at Stora Sjötorp, that night.

In the vestibule he encountered Schagerström talking with the housekeeper, who was just reporting to him that the new young mistress was nowhere to be found.

'You asked me, Sir, to tell Madame that you no longer had time to sit in the barn, but that Madame was free to dance as long as she wished, and I was about to tell her when …'

The coachman didn't have the patience to let her finish her sentence. He had something more important to impart:

'Sir!' he began.

Schagerström turned to him.

'What on earth has gotten into you?' he inquired of the coachman. 'You look as if someone had stolen your horses.'

'That's exactly what's happened, Sir!'

He told his story.

'It's not the horses' faults, Sir. They'd never of gone off and left me if somebody hadn't jumped up on my box. I only wish I knew who…'

He halted in mid-sentence. Schagerström was doing something quite incredible. In the presence of his coachman, his valet and his housekeeper, he had dropped into a chair and was roaring with laughter at their consternation.

'Aha, so you don't know who would dare to steal my horses,' he chortled.

The three servants just gaped.

'We've got to catch the thief,' he managed to say once his laughter had subsided. 'Lundman, get three riding horses saddled just as fast as you can. Johansson, go along and help him. And, Mrs. Sällberg, you had better go up to our rooms just to be sure, and check that your mistress is not there.'

The housekeeper mounted the stairs, but returned immediately to report that Madame was most definitely not up there.

'Dear God, Sir, surely there hasn't been an accident?' she asked.

'It all depends on how you see it, Mrs. Sällberg, mark my words! Until now we have been our own masters here at Stora Sjötorp, but now we have one who will rule us all!'

'Well, that's something to be glad for, certainly, Sir.'

At that, Schagerström, wealthy Schagerström, took the old woman by her sturdy shoulder, and waltzed her once around, shouting:

'Oh, Mrs. Sällberg, you face your fate with appropriate submissiveness. I do hope I will be able to do so as well!'

At that he rushed out to search for the runaway, in the company of his coachman and his valet.

Just a short while later all was resolved. The escapee was being held captive in one corner of the carriage with Schagerström by her side. Lundman was on the box, driving quite sedately home to the estate, while Johansson, the servant, led the riding horses.

Charlotte had driven the carriage quite fast, covering at least five kilometers before she reached a series of steep hills. No matter how hard she cracked the whip, she was unable to make the horses move faster than a walk after that, which resulted in her ignominious defeat.

For a couple of minutes there was silence in the carriage. Then Charlotte asked:

'So how did it feel?'

'It was overwhelming,' said Schagerström. 'I understand how

a wife must feel when her husband runs away from her.'

'That was my intention,' said Charlotte.

The next moment Schagerström felt a hard grip on his shoulder.

'You're feigning. And laughing. You never really thought I meant to run off.'

'My dearest,' said Schagerström, 'the only truly happy moment I have had today was when Lundman came to inform me that you had stolen my horses.'

'Why was that?' asked Charlotte in monosyllables.

'My sweet, I realized you didn't want to let me leave.'

'That isn't it at all,' Charlotte objected. 'But the whole village had been talking about me already for three weeks, and if you had gone off…'

'I know,' said Schagerström. 'I realize it would have been too much for you to bear.'

He laughed out of love and pleasure, only a moment later to speak once more in a deadly serious tone:

'My dearest, let us talk this through once and for all! Tell me, did you know why I wanted to leave this very evening?'

'Yes,' the young woman said firmly. 'Yes, I knew.'

'So why did you prevent me?'

Charlotte said nothing. He waited a long time for her answer, but she did not break the silence.

'When we get home,' her husband told her, 'you will find a letter from me in the bedroom. In that letter I tell you that I have no intention of taking advantage of the circumstances that tossed you into my arms. I want you to be completely free. You need not consider our marriage anything more than pro forma.'

He was quiet again, in anticipation of her answer, but none came.

'In the letter I also tell you that, as a token of my love and in order to make up for all the suffering I have brought upon you, I intend to bestow Stora Sjötorp upon you as your very own. Once a legal divorce has been decreed between us, it will give me great pleasure to know that you will go on living here, where every person on the estate already adores you.'

Another long silence, with no response from Charlotte.

'This little adventure in no way affects the content of the letter,' Schagerström went on. 'Initially I misinterpreted it. Now I realize it was nothing but a prank you were playing on me so as not to be disgraced in the village again.'

Charlotte moved somewhat closer, after which he felt her warm breath on his cheek, and heard her whisper in his ear:

'The greatest imbecile on God's green earth.'

'Pardon me?'

'Shall I repeat myself?'

In haste, he put his arm around her and pulled her to him.

'Charlotte,' he said, 'you must speak out. I need to know what I am up against.'

'All right,' she said somewhat tetchily. 'It's not a very pretty piece of news, but you may be pleased to hear that yesterday, around this time, Karl-Artur murdered my love.'

'He did?'

'He murdered it. I suppose he was tired of it. I nearly think he did it intentionally.'

'My dearest,' he said, 'leave Karl-Artur out of this. Speak of me! If your love for Karl-Artur is dead, that does not naturally mean…'

'No, of course not. Oh, how I wish you did not require such long explanations!'

'No one knows better than you what a fool I am.'

'You see,' said Charlotte, slowly and thoughtfully, 'it's quite remarkable. I do not love you but I enjoy your company, I am safe with you. I can talk to you about anything, I can ask you for anything, I can jest with you. I find it so calm and pleasant, it's as if we had been married for thirty years.'

'Kind of like the pastor and his wife,' Schagerström interjected, not without a little bitterness.

'Kind of like that,' Charlotte went on in the same musing tone. 'Perhaps that does not suffice for you, but I think it's quite a fine result after just one day. I like having you next to me in the coach, and the way your eyes follow me when I dance. I like sitting down to a meal with you, and living in your home. I am grateful to you for having taken me away from all that misery. Stora Sjötorp is charming, but I would not want to live here for a single day if you were not here. I couldn't bear the idea that you were going to run away from me. And yet ... if what I felt for Karl-Artur was love, this is not love.'

'But it may turn into love,' Schagerström said softly, and it was clear from his voice that he was moved.

'Perhaps it may,' Charlotte answered. 'And do you know what? I don't believe I would object if you kissed me.'

Schagerström's traveling carriage was an excellent vehicle. It carried them along the road without bouncing or bumping. The young foundry owner was able to exercise the permission granted.

TRANSLATOR'S AFTERWORD

Remarkable as ever in her final trilogy of fiction, leave it to Selma Lagerlöf to entitle the middle volume *Charlotte Löwensköld*, and then to fail to present anyone by that name until after a long first chapter, on page 37 in this edition! Nor had the reader made Charlotte Löwensköld's acquaintance in the slim first volume of the trilogy, *Löwensköldska ringen* (1925, in English *The Löwensköld Ring*, 1991 and 2011).

As *Charlotte Löwensköld* (published in 1925) is the middle volume of a trilogy, this Afterword is relatively brief, with the promise of a longer one at the end of volume 3, *Anna Svärd* (1928), to be published by Norvik Press in this series in 2015.

The surname of Löwensköld does appear in the second sentence of *Charlotte Löwensköld*, but only to distract the reader, since the protagonist of this chapter is Beate Ekenstedt, née Löwensköld. She is indirectly related to Charlotte, being the sister of the Baron Adrian of *The Löwensköld Ring,* who nearly dies as an effect of the cursed ring of the title of that volume.

The novella *The Löwensköld Ring* is a story of revenge. Although this second volume of the trilogy refers in passing to the above-mentioned curse, it does not return with full force until *Anna Svärd*. In *Charlotte Löwensköld* it rests heavily, albeit unspokenly, on Beate Ekenstedt and her son, Karl-Artur. In her Lagerlöf biography *Livets vågspel* (2002), Vivi Edström refers to *Charlotte Löwensköld* as the 'great mother-son drama' of Swedish literature (p. 493). I can only agree.

Karl-Artur is Charlotte Löwensköld's fiancé and the male protagonist in both *Charlotte Löwensköld* and *Anna Svärd*. His

278

mother is described in almost excruciating detail in the first chapter, and the reader soon comes to see that she is tyrannical in her love for her son, and has such high expectations of him that they cannot but be foiled. Toward the end of the novel, in one of his more insightful moments, Karl-Artur says to Charlotte: 'Perhaps my mother would die for me, but she would never allow me to live my life.' (p. 235, 'Saturday: Early and Late Morning'). There precisely, is the rub.

Charlotte Löwensköld and Thea Sundler, the two other women central to this novel, stand as representatives of this mother's love, at opposite ends of the spectrum. Charlotte is good, kind, lovely and lively, while Thea represents the serpent in Karl-Artur's paradise, the demonic side of overbearing love. Karl-Artur shifts, in the course of the novel, from being a student his mother hopes will become a professor, to a curate his mother and Charlotte imagine as dean or bishop one day, only to escape the sphere of influence of his mother by turning to fanatical Pietism, with encouragement from Thea Sundler. Henrik Wivel writes insightfully of this change that when Karl-Artur 'believes that by breaking off his engagement with Charlotte he has first and foremost released himself from the authority of his mother, he is, with the paradoxical irony of the novel, more than ever subjected to maternal power – in its diabolic version.' (Wivel, 1990, p. 305).

Ulla Torpe writes of the 'Sundler strategy that is the driving force of the story from beginning to end. To ensure that happiness in love will not be: to prevent the union of people who love one another except for during very brief periods, to complicate every conceivable idyll' (Torpe, 1983, p. 64). And indeed it is Thea Sundler who becomes the bearer of the curse.

In a letter to Elisabeth Grundtvig, her Danish translator, dated February 9, 1925, Selma Lagerlöf wrote: 'The material I am working on now is a true story, but it has a remarkable amount in common with other books I have written' (quoted in Ulvenstam, 1955, p. 58). In 1920, Lagerlöf had been given a collection of letters written by a clergyman by the name of Estenberg and containing, as Lagerlöf wrote to Grundtvig, the story of 'a young pastor who, after an argument with his fiancée, proposed to a young peddler woman from Dalarna, the first woman whose path crossed his, and married her. This caused a separation between him and his parents, who disowned him, and after some time he took to drink, fell into the hands of an ingratiating flatterer, and eventually died in poverty with his wife, the woman from Dalarna' (letter dated November 12, 1925, quoted in Ulvenstam, 1955, p. 55).

According to Lagerlöf scholar Lars Ulvenstam, the cornerstone of the universe of Selma Lagerlöf's imagination was 'a firm belief in a moral order based on the responsibility of human beings for everything they do: good or evil' (Ulvenstam, 1955, p. 52). That belief is the key to *Charlotte Löwensköld*. The main characters in this novel, so skillfully drawn by Lagerlöf in terms of their social setting, their personal psychology and their gender, lead the reader to follow a story in which the pages virtually turn themselves. And the hub of this moral universe is the wealthy Schagerström, whose upbringing is portrayed so sensitively and with such irony in the chapter 'Child of Good Fortune'.

Ambiguity is always one of Lagerlöf's most interesting stylistic features, and in *Charlotte Löwensköld* it comes to the fore not, as Sarah Death writes in her 'Translator's Afterword' to *Lord Arne's Silver*, as to the 'question of who knows what, and when' (2011, p. 93), but more the question of whether we can ever dare to imagine that we know what another person is thinking and feeling (as opposed to what he or she has said or done, or failed to say or do), however well we may believe we know that person. This question was raised toward the end of *The Löwensköld Ring* when Malvina Spaak believes the young Baron Adrian Löwensköld to be in love with her, and acts accordingly. In *Charlotte Löwensköld* the question arises on nearly every page, and the plot thickens as a result. Lagerlöf not only masters ambiguity in *Charlotte Löwensköld*, but the novel also virtually drips with irony.

I have seldom taken such pleasure in translating a novel. It has been a great privilege to put my hand to a text so perfect and so complete, and with a happy ending to boot. Little does the reader sense what is in store for these wonderful characters in the third and final volume of the trilogy. Many of them endure a great deal of pain in *Anna Svärd* as the curse rears its ugly head, and human frailty takes its toll as well. There are a few hints in *Charlotte Löwensköld*, but they are gentle. Fortunately the reader can also look forward to wondrous laughter in *Anna Svärd* with, I hope, as much enjoyment as I am having while translating it.

The only previous translation of *Charlotte Löwensköld* was made in 1927 by ubiquitous Lagerlöf translator Velma Swanston Howard. It has long been out of print but is available as a reference volume at the National Library of Sweden, and I had it brought up from the stacks once when I was at the library, but have not examined it in any detail.

My sincere thanks to Sarah Death and Helena Forsås-Scott for their generous and patient readings of the manuscript and to Elettra Carbone at Norvik Press for all her assistance, as well as to my husband Robert for his eagle eye and generous heart.

Linda Schenck

References

All translations from Swedish reference literature are my own.

Death, Sarah, 'Translator's Afterword', in Selma Lagerlöf, *Lord Arne's Silver*, tr. Sarah Death. London: Norvik Press, 2011, pp. 89-98.

Edström, Vivi, *Selma Lagerlöf. Livets vågspel*. Stockholm: Bokförlaget Natur och Kultur, 2002.

Torpe, Ulla, 'Den vedervärdiga kvinnan från Korskyrka', in Ingrid Holmquist and Ebba Witt-Brattström, eds., *Kvinnornas litteraturhistoria*, Vol. 2: *Nittonhundratalet*. Stockholm: Författarförlaget, 1983, pp. 57-72.

Ulvenstam, Lars, *Den åldrade Selma Lagerlöf. En studie i hennes Löwensköldscykel.* Stockholm: Albert Bonniers förlag, 1955.

Wivel, Henrik, *Snödrottningen. En bok om Selma Lagerlöf och kärleken*, tr. Birgit Edlund. Stockholm: Albert Bonniers förlag, 1990.

SELMA LAGERLÖF

Nils Holgersson's Wonderful Journey through Sweden
(translated by Peter Graves)
Volume 1: ISBN 9781870041966
Volume 2: ISBN 9781870041973
UK £12.95 per volume
(Paperback, 348 and 372 pages)

Lord Arne's Silver
(translated by Sarah Death)
ISBN 9781870041904
UK £9.95
(Paperback, 102 pages)

The Phantom Carriage
(translated by Peter Graves)
ISBN 9781870041911
UK £11.95
(Paperback, 126 pages)

The Löwensköld Ring
(translated by Linda Schenk)
ISBN 9781870041928
UK £9.95
(Paperback, 120 pages)

Selma Lagerlöf (1858-1940) quickly established herself as a major
author of novels and short stories, and her work has been translated
into close to 50 languages. Most of the translations into English were
made soon after the publication of the original Swedish texts and
have long been out of date. 'Lagerlöf in English' provides English-
language readers with high-quality new translations of a selection of
the Nobel Laureate's most important texts.

AUGUST STRINDBERG

Strindberg's One-Act Plays: A Selection

Simoom, Facing Death, The Outlaw, The Bond

(translated by Agnes Broomé, Anna Holmwood,
John K Mitchinson, Mathelinda Nabugodi,
Anna Tebelius and Nichola Smalley)

To most English-language readers and theatre-goers, Strindberg is mainly known for naturalistic plays such as *Miss Julie* and *The Father*, but the dramatic production of Sweden's national playwright is infinitely richer and more extensive than these would suggest. This volume presents four of Strindberg's lesser known one-act plays, *The Bond*, *Facing Death*, *The Outlaw* and *Simoom*, written between 1871 and 1892, which showcase Strindberg's remarkable range. *The Bond* and *Facing Death*, which fall at the end of the time span, are familiarly naturalistic plays set in contemporary European settings which demonstrate Strindberg's provocative engagement with contentious issues of his day. The early experiment *The Outlaw*, however, takes place in the frigid landscapes of the Viking north, drawing heavily on the style of Icelandic sagas. In *Simoom*, written in 1889, a practically gothic narrative transports us to the scorching deserts of French-colonised Algeria, allowing us to observe the beginnings of Strindberg's experimental, mystical phase which culminated in *A Dream Play*. Different as the four plays are, however, when read together they form a thematic unity, revealing the beating heart of Strindberg's creativity, the issue at the core of his writing: love as a war eternally waged between man and woman, husband and wife, children and parents and individuals and society.

ISBN 9781870041935
UK £9.95
(Paperback, 128 pages)

HENRY PARLAND

To Pieces

(translated by Dinah Cannell)

To Pieces is Henry Parland's (1908-1930) only novel, published posthumously after his death from scarlet fever. Ostensibly the story of an unhappy love affair, the book is an evocative reflection upon the Jazz Age in Prohibition Helsinki. Parland was profoundly influenced by Proust's *À la recherche du temps perdu*, and reveals his narrative through fragments of memory, drawing on his fascination with photography, cinema, jazz, fashion and advertisements. Parland was the product of a cosmopolitan age: his German-speaking Russian parents left St Petersburg to escape political turmoil, only to become caught up in Finland's own civil war – Parland first learned Swedish at the age of fourteen. To remove Parland from a bohemian and financially ruinous life in Helsinki, his parents sent him to Kaunas in Lithuania, where he absorbed the theories of the Russian Formalists. *To Pieces* became the focus of renewed interest following the publication of a definitive critical edition in 2005, and has since been published to great acclaim in German, French and Russian translation.

ISBN 9781870041874
UK £9.95
(Paperback, 120 pages)

Lightning Source UK Ltd.
Milton Keynes UK
UKOW07f0810130115

244398UK00009B/125/P